Wellesley Wives

By

Suzy Duffy

The Writer's Coffee Shop
Publishing House

First published by The Writer's Coffee Shop, 2012

The Writer's Coffee Shop
(Australia)   PO Box 447 Cherrybrook NSW 2126
(USA)   PO Box 2116 Waxahachie TX 75168

Paperback ISBN- 978-1-61213-109-2
E-book ISBN- 978-1-61213-110-8

A CIP catalogue record for this book is available from the US Congress Library.

Cover image and design by: © QuartSoft, Tatyana Shevchenko

www.thewriterscoffeeshop.com/sduffy

About the Author

Suzy Duffy is an international and #1 bestselling author. She is Irish but moved her five kids, one dog, and current husband to Boston, USA in 2009 because of the downturn in the Irish economy. Since arriving in the States, the U.S. economy has nosedived, too. She's now considering a time share in Fiji!

She stays (arguably) sane by writing and loves learning about America and the American way of doing things. She has started a New England series of novels. The first is called Wellesley Wives and now she's working on Newton Neighbors. Her genre is romantic comedy because that's how she sees life.

Other than this, Suzanne was a national radio DJ and television presenter in Ireland before she started writing. She has also been an interpreter in the United Nations, Geneva, a water ski instructor in Crete, and a corn cutter in the south of France.

Her ambition is to keep all her children healthy and happy while staying married (to current husband), and to produce a book a year for the next forty years. Then she'll have a rethink.

Acknowledgments

I want to thank my literary agent, David Forrer at InkWell Management for all his support and encouragement with Wellesley Wives. Dave, you're the best.

At TWCS, thanks to Amanda Hayward, Caryn Stevens, Kathie Spitz, Jenn McGuire, Janine Savage, Jenny Pedroza, Annelies Ivens and the rest of the wonderful team. I want to say a very special thank you to my amazing editor, Shay Donovan, who has been my friend, my teacher, my confidante and a real blessing in my life. Shay, you are a treasure!

In Swellesley Wellesley, thanks to Elise Adler, Wendy Bedrosian, Dira Cannistraro, Melissa Clancy, Becky Connors, Linda Duffy, Bernadette Dore, Jessica Dormitzer, Bettina Eikeboom, Josephine Emmert, Lucia Epstein, Cory Floyd, Terri Godley, Diana Goober, Beth Harrington, Susan Hartigan, Katie Healey, Laura Heffernan, Gemma Hogan, Kathy Copeland, Gail Kraft, Toni Jolley, Jessica Mead, Pamela McMahon, Johanna Murray, Carol Mosley, Gail Musikavanhu, Patty Nolan, Deirdre O Kelly-Lynch, Ellen Oh, Sheila Olson, Anabela Perozek, Amy Raftery, Meg Reilly, Laurie Roberts, Michelle Specht, Phyllis Spinale, Kate Staehly, Olivia Swan, Evelina Taber, Humaira Tariq, Barbara Thomas, Connie Walsh, Shelley Why, Beverly Yee & Tiffany Zides. You are all fabulous.

I have saved the best till last. Thanks to Michael, Alannah, Saskia, Lily, Zola, Hugo, all the Duffys and Higgins for letting me do what I do. I love you.

Dedication

For the wonderful wives I've met in Wellesley, MA.
You are fabulous.

Definition of Wellesley Wives: Genre—female. Usually with 25% lower BMI than the average American wife and 1275% greater net worth. They tend to be more capable than they realize and more envied than they wish. The average Wellesley Wife is smart, beautiful, and confident. There are two sub species of Wellesley Wives. The older variety migrate to Florida, the Caribbean, or South America for the winter, while the younger ones stay at home to nurture, educate, and raise the next generation of Wellesley Wives.

Part 1

New England

Chapter 1

Popsy Power

Lady Gaga poured through powerful stereo speakers and a pounding bass beat pulsed through Popsy. She had no idea where the car's sound system was located. Nor did she care. All she knew was that the weather was absolutely perfect to test-drive a shiny new red Ferrari. The car dealer had already put the roof down and volume up, so all she had to do was turn the key in the ignition, put her sunglasses on, and roar off the dealer's forecourt.

Driving through the leafy suburbs of Wellesley made Popsy smile. What could be lovelier than this, she wondered, except perhaps owning this spanking new Ferrari?

She fell in love with the car right away. The power under her was palpable. Normally she wasn't aggressive on the road, but the urge to put her foot to the floor was immense. She adored the sound of the engine's growl. It was like a wild animal—harnessed.

Even slowing down at traffic signals was fun. Because when Popsy stopped at the lights outside Whole Foods with the music blaring, she saw the jealous glances she was receiving. Some people were surreptitious, but most openly gawked. It was really quite gratifying.

She witnessed a very pretty blonde thumping her boyfriend when she caught him overtly ogling Popsy. She laughed. Yes, she definitely felt sexier in this car than in her own slightly more conservative Mercedes.

Popsy would never have considered herself a red sports car kind of gal, but that was before she had actually tried it.

"What the heck," she said as she caught sight of her reflection in the wing mirror. "After all, it is my birthday."

An hour later, when she got back to the showroom, her husband Peter was waiting for her. He'd insisted she test-drive it on the actual day of her birthday. But even Peter, with his contacts, couldn't have organized the incredible weather. He was also the one who said she must test-drive it alone.

"You won't get the same sort of thrill with somebody else in the car. You need to be by yourself, with the wind in your hair and the music loud," he'd said, and as usual, he'd been right.

Popsy had come to realize a long time ago that Peter was right about most things. He was a formidable man, still very handsome and thankfully a very wealthy one, too, because she was fairly sure that this year's birthday present wasn't going to come cheap.

"Well?" he asked, his expression saying he already knew the answer.

"I love it!"

Peter grinned. "Didn't I tell you, doll?"

"Don't you think we're going to look a bit ridiculous, you know, with both of us driving Ferraris?" She reluctantly cut the engine, but Peter shook his head.

"I'm planning to change mine soon."

"Oh?"

"Yeah," he said. "Ferraris are becoming way too ordinary. Everybody's driving them these days." He smirked at the car rep who tried to look like he wasn't listening. But of course he was.

Popsy got out of the car, handed the dealer the keys, and came over to her husband. She snaked her arms in under his jacket and pulled him close. "You know, you really spoil me. And I love you for it. Now tell me," she kissed his earlobe, "how expensive is this particular love token?"

"You don't want to know," he said, his voice getting deeper. Popsy knew she could still work her magic on him anytime, anywhere. He pushed her back a little to avoid getting too aroused.

"$200,000? $300,000?" She took his hands.

"Split the difference," he said and Popsy let go of him in shock.

She'd been picking random figures out of the air for fun. Her real estimate was closer to $80,000. "Two-hundred-fifty grand? For a car?"

Peter smiled winningly. "Yep, now double it."

"For yours and mine?"

"No. For yours and yours. That little baby," he said, openly admiring the Ferrari as it was gently maneuvered right up to the window of the showroom, "is $500,000. It's a special edition, doll. But then again, so are you."

"Yes, but Peter, that's too much money to spend on a car."

He ran his finger along her lips. "Hey, hey, hey . . . you're worth every cent."

"I'm glad you think so," she said without much conviction.

"You know, it's less expensive than your hair bills." He laughed at her sudden self-doubt.

"Now just wait a minute. I've spent nowhere near half a million on my hair." She put her hand to her head protectively. He used to tell her she looked like Goldie Hawn, but recently her best friend, Sandra, said she was more Kim Cattrall. Popsy was blessed with large dark brown eyes, fair hair, and a curvy, sassy figure. It took a lot of maintenance to keep it as blond as she did, but she wasn't going to revert to boring light brown at this stage in her life.

"I'm not complaining." He laughed. "You know I love your look." He winked at her and stroked her hair. "In fact, I think it's perfect for a Ferrari driving girl, but yes, the bills I've seen coming through have been pretty impressive. $2,000 to get your hair done?"

"Oh, that. Um, Ricardo was trying out a new state of the art treatment. It was rather expensive."

"What was he doing? Putting actual liquid gold through your hair?"

"Yes. It's a new product that claims to have tiny nuggets of real gold." She swung her head around to give him the full view of her recently done hair.

"More like nuggets of bullshit if you ask me."

"Peter . . ." She pretended to look horrified, but this was typical of him.

He was a ruthless businessman and liked to win. He didn't like the feeling that somebody was overcharging him. But for the benefit of her beautiful hair, and her happiness, he pretended to look sheepish—which of course he wasn't—and replied, "Sorry, doll. You look great. Honest."

"But the car . . . It really does seem so expensive. What if I crash it?"

"It's insured," he said, putting his hands on her shoulders. "Now I have to go and sort out some paperwork. Nothing for you to worry your pretty little golden head about. What are your plans for today?

"I have a ladies' charity lunch. It will probably take up most of the afternoon, and then you and I are going out this evening. Is that still good for you?"

"Absolutely, I can think of nowhere I'd rather be tonight." He looked at her warmly.

After all these years, they still had a terrific relationship. Popsy kissed him again. "Thank you for the most amazing birthday present I think I have ever had."

"You're worth every last cent and the same again," he said. "Go and enjoy your ladies' lunch."

"What are you doing for the rest of the day?"

"I have a meeting at the bank." He pretended to yawn. "Boring but necessary."

"Why don't you tell them to get lost and we can spend the day together?"

"Believe me, doll, there's nothing I would like more, but I have to keep them sweet."

Popsy thought she caught an edge in his voice, and she was all too aware how tough the economy had been for the last few years. Thankfully, Peter's business group had not been hurt too much by the global downturn.

"Everything okay? Nothing to worry about, I mean?"

"No chance." He laughed. "They love me. I'm the only guy in the city still capable of paying them what I owe."

"Yes, but they would never call in their loans suddenly or anything?"

Peter looked completely self-assured. "Absolutely not. That would be suicide for them. They could never do that. Relax. This is just a regular meeting. It's only lunch."

Half an hour later, Popsy Power was in her favorite flower shop. The sweet smell of the tiger lilies hit her first, and then as she meandered around admiring the colors and foliage, she picked up the richer smell of roses and the subtler scent of the freesias.

"Well, hello there, Mrs. Power," Karen said from behind the counter.

She smiled when the woman's face brightened. "It's a ladies' lunch today, Karen," Popsy said. "What with Halloween just around the corner, I'd like to bring the hostess something with a lot of orange in it. Could you do me up a center table arrangement, please?"

"You got it," Karen said. "I have some great Chinese lanterns." She pulled out the incredibly delicate stems with large bulbous orange seed heads. "If I pair them up with orange daisies and black grass, you'll have a real Halloween theme going. I also have these," she said as she pulled out a miniature witch on a stick and added it to the foliage.

"Perfect."

On her way home, Popsy mentally ticked off her to-do list. Her birthday was shaping up to be very nice. Already, she'd had her hair and nails done, taken her new car for a test-drive, and picked up the dry cleaning. All she needed to do now was remind Matilda to do the silver and perhaps get a start on setting the table.

Today's lunch would be fun, but her dinner party on Saturday night was what occupied most of her thoughts. Peter's business partner, Jack Hoffman, would be there with his wife, Sandra. They were easy to entertain, being Popsy and Peter's best friends, but she was also having some European investors and their wives whom she'd never met before.

She was used to corporate lunches and black-tie dos because Peter kept a high profile in the business world. And while she didn't particularly like the public lifestyle, she loved the lavish clothing budget and the jewelry he'd bought her over the last twenty-nine years. Peter reasoned that she had to look magnificent all the time if he was to look successful, and she wasn't going to argue with that. But she did find the whole public image thing a little wearing after all these years.

Even on vacations, Peter worked. She had often, at his request, thrown big parties in their Florida home—but that was the life of a successful businessman and it was hardly going to change now.

Almost thirty years married, she thought. Wow. That was another big date looming on her calendar.

She and Peter would be celebrating their anniversary on December twenty-sixth. How fast those years had gone by. She'd only been twenty when they'd tied the knot. She'd felt so grown-up back then, but looking back, she realized that they'd been little more than babies. She remembered her parents expressing concern about their ages at the time, but she wouldn't listen.

Popsy's parents had been wealthy, and she'd received a private education just outside Wicklow in Ireland, where she grew up. Her friends teased her that she still had the accent. She didn't believe it, but her daughters did sometimes come out with an Irish expression or hint of an accent, having lived with her influence for so long. As it happened, that wasn't a problem since the Bostonians loved the Irish more than the Irish liked themselves.

She'd met Peter while doing a sabbatical year at Boston College, and he'd pursued her hard. While he hadn't been very rich when they got married, it was pretty clear that he was on his way, and she'd never looked back.

She was fifty today with two terrific daughters to show for it and still so happy. How lucky was she?

She turned the car into the driveway of her house on Cliff Road and saw the front door open. The jet-black paint of the door momentarily shined in the sunlight as it swung closed again. Popsy watched her firstborn come down the steps. In Rosie's arms was her own firstborn, five-year-old Natasha.

Popsy left the shopping and her purse in her car and quickly ran over to hug them. "Rosie, I wasn't expecting you! If I'd known, I would have been here."

"I just popped in for a minute." Her daughter smiled. "We wanted to wish you a happy birthday."

"Oh, thank you." Popsy beamed. "And how's my favorite granddaughter?" Her smile brightened as she turned her attention to the youngster.

"Mom, what are you going to do when Lily has a kid? She might have a girl."

Popsy raised a perfectly sculpted eyebrow. "Oh, is there something I don't know?"

Rosie laughed. "No, no, it's just that the chances are—at some point in the future—you're going to have another granddaughter and Natasha, here," she hugged her daughter tight, "will wonder why you've stopped calling her your favorite."

Popsy waved her hand in a sweeping gesture. "They will all be my favorites. It's a grandmother's privilege."

"The most glamorous grandmother in New England, I think, and happy birthday. So tell me, are you going somewhere special today? You look terrific."

Popsy smiled gratefully. "Thank you, pet. Today is a ladies' lunch out in Marlborough, nothing too serious. Just a friendly natter. What about you? Any plans?"

"No. Today it's just me and Natasha. I think we might go to Boston to see if we can find a nice winter coat for her—or me." She smirked with a hint of devilment in her eyes.

The expression reminded Popsy of Peter. Rosie took after her father, and

Lily looked like her. Popsy knew that Rosie thought her sister was the beauty in the family, but it wasn't true. Rosie was very pretty, too, just in a different way. She had Peter's square face and hazel eyes. It was more a handsome look, but nonetheless striking. Rosie's figure was a little fuller, too, but she'd had a baby and she certainly wasn't fat. It was just that Lily and her mother were particularly slight. Lily also had her mother's platinum hair, but she'd told Rosie a million times that it was more to do with good hairdressers than good genes.

"You're still good for lunch on Sunday? That will be my family birthday party."

Rosie nodded. "But we brought your present today. I left it inside with Matilda."

"Oh, you shouldn't have, honey. And Marcus?" Popsy asked about Rosie's husband. She wasn't certain whether it was her imagination or not, but she thought she saw Rosie hesitate for a split-second. "Everything okay?" Popsy instinctively reached out and rubbed her daughter's arm, but soon Rosie was in full control of her emotions again.

She pasted a broad smile on her face. "Yes, he's fine. We're fine. We'll all be here on Sunday." Rosie buried her nose into her daughter's neck and inhaled her little girl smell like perfume.

Popsy knew that her daughter and son-in-law had a tumultuous and passionate relationship. In fact, the fights they'd had when they were still in the dating stage convinced Popsy that they would never last. But then Natasha came into their lives and changed everything. Popsy assured both of them, but especially her daughter, that she didn't have to get married, but by then they were starry-eyed with each other and their beautiful daughter. Who could blame them? Popsy thought Natasha had settled them down somewhat, but judging from Rosie's behavior, there must be some new trouble at home.

"Look, would you like to come in for a cup of coffee and a chat, just while I'm getting changed?"

"No, really. It's all good. Like I told you, we're heading into town to spend Daddy's money." She took a few steps back. "We'll see you Sunday, but everything is fine—honest." Another slightly forced smile.

Popsy was fairly certain her daughter was lying, but she didn't have time to push the issue. The truth was, Rosie was regularly in need of her mother's attention, but she decided tough love would have to suffice this time around. "All right, pet. Well, come over a little earlier than your sister on Sunday so we can have some one-on-one." She winked.

Rosie nodded and half-grinned. "Perfect. Enjoy your party in Marlborough."

"It's only lunch." Popsy shrugged. That was the phrase Peter had used with her only a couple of hours before. Funny how it came to mind, she thought. "I don't expect anything too wild to happen," she said as she mounted the steps to her perfect New England house and her perfect suburban life.

Chapter 2

Rosie Power

As Popsy prepared for her ladies' lunch, Rosie started to cry. She was stuck in appalling Boston traffic on her way into town to buy a coat that she didn't really need, with a daughter who didn't really care, and when she got home, she would attempt to model it for a husband who wouldn't really notice. Yes, this was a *really* bad day.

All she'd actually needed was an excuse to get away from her mother as soon as she began to probe. She was very good at that. Popsy had a way of reading her daughters quickly and getting under their skin, and Rosie wasn't ready to deal with her problems on the doorstep of her parents' palatial Wellesley home.

Now that she'd managed to get away, it occurred to Rosie that she could just exit the Mass Pike at the next junction and go home. But she didn't even have the emotional energy to do that. She'd told her mother she was going to town to look for coats, and that is exactly what they would do, even if it wasn't necessary. Frustratingly, the four lanes of traffic on the highway were gridlocked, and that meant they were trapped. She couldn't move forward, and even if she wanted to, she couldn't turn back. Little Natasha was happy in a world of her own thanks to the iPad which churned out Barney and all of his friends ad nauseam for the child's amusement.

As she inched along going nowhere fast, Rosie felt more tears start to fall. She was miserable, and other than her mom, she didn't know who to turn to. Her younger sister, Lily, had certainly been no help. There was less than a year between them, but to Rosie it felt like a lifetime.

Friends and family called them "Irish twins" because they were born in the same year. Rosie arrived in January and Lily the following December. It had certainly been fast work on her mother's part, but that was just about all the sisters had in common. Rosie was the passionate, melodramatic sister. Nobody had to tell her that. It was quite clear from a young age.

She always got into trouble in school. During her years at Newton County Day School, Rosie could claim three suspensions and an expulsion while Lily, her perfect little sister, was an honor student in her senior year. Rosie used to tease her that she was a goody-two-shoes, but she was jealous of her younger sister's perfect academic records and her first-class economics degree from Princeton.

Even Lily's figure was better. Rosie wasn't large, but Lily was prettier and smaller, more petite. She tried to convince herself she was better off because she was the one with the husband and family. Now that she'd given up work, she lived a life of leisure.

Lily didn't have any men in her life. It sure was a little strange but was probably because her sister worked so darn hard. Too hard by Rosie's standards but then again, Rosie didn't like work at all.

She'd become a stewardess because she liked the idea of seeing the world for free, and despite what her parents told her, she'd thought it would be a glamorous and desirable occupation. But now she knew a stewardess was just a glorified waitress. Back in the old days, the training involved how to make the perfect martini. In Rosie's case, it was how to restrain a passenger at thirty-five thousand feet. Still, on the plus side, it was how she came to meet her husband Marcus. He was a pilot. Such a cliché, but one that resulted in adorable little Natasha and a wedding the year after that.

Rosie tried to convince herself she *did* have it better than Lily, but it wasn't easy to do, especially after the argument they'd had the day before.

She'd asked her little sister out for lunch. That wasn't so unusual but this time Rosie did have an agenda.

They'd arranged to meet at Boston's trendy Boylston Street because there was a fabulous new bistro there and it wasn't far from Lily's work. Ironic that even though Rosie had traveled fifteen miles to get there while her sister only had a quick walk from her office, Lily was still the one who was tardy. She'd been running behind since the day she was born. Thinking back, Rosie decided Lily had been in a bad mood from the moment she arrived at the restaurant.

"Hi, Sis. Jeez, I'm sorry I'm late," she'd said as she approached the table. But Rosie shook her head.

"Not a problem. As you can see I don't have Natasha with me, so I'm really savoring the quiet."

Lily plonked down, visibly relieved that she wasn't in the doghouse with her big sister. "Thanks, but no Nat? That's a shame."

Rosie laughed. "You can borrow her any time you want, Lil. Just say the word."

They glanced up as the waitress arrived at their table. She granted them a big smile, handed them their menus, and began to recite the specials. Lily, who loved food, listened intently.

Annoying that she was the skinny one . . .

Once their orders were placed, Lily focused on her sister. "So how've you been? Is Natasha well?"

It irked Rosie how her daughter's health and wellbeing seemed to have superseded her own. She was no longer Rosie Power, lively Boston socialite. Now she was just a mom and a wife.

"Natasha is fine and so is Marcus. He's in London today and tomorrow, but he'll be back in time for Mom's birthday lunch. What about you? Any news? What have you been up to?"

"Oh, you know, same ol' same ol'." Then her face lit with pride. "Hey, I got a promotion."

"That's fantastic!" Rosie was genuinely happy for her.

Lily was very smart but she didn't sell herself hard enough. Rosie had always told her sister that she needed to promote herself more.

She worked for one of Boston's larger banks and that was just about all Rosie knew of her career. Okay, she always seemed to have plenty of money and she drove a very nice convertible Merc, but that could have been a present from Mom and Dad for all Rosie knew. Rosie had received an apartment in Beacon Hill when she gave birth to Natasha and then a fabulous red sports BMW from her parents as a wedding present. The property was rented out now, but her parents had told her that each grandchild would be given an apartment as a birth present.

"So, what are you working on now?" Rosie asked, briefly wondering what it actually was that her sister did on a day-to-day basis. Okay, so she knew it involved moving money but that was about it.

"Oh, it's more of the same," Lily said. "Only now it's with bigger funds, so they pay me more."

"Well, I should say in that case lunch is on you." Rosie laughed. "But it's not. I asked you, so I'm paying. Would you like a glass of wine?"

Lily smiled. "Sister, if I drank now, I'd never make it back to the office. And if I did, I'd lose that promotion pretty fast. Why don't you have one, though? You should be celebrating the fact that you're out without your little girl."

It was all the convincing Rosie needed. "You know, I think I will. The French won't even eat without the benefit of a glass of something to wash it down. I'll just have a small glass of white with my Waldorf salad."

They chatted easily for most of the meal, and eventually Rosie got up the nerve to raise the subject she really wanted to discuss.

"So, um, Lily, you know how you once said you'd be happy to watch Natasha for me if I ever wanted to get away?"

It was clearly a loaded question, so Lily's reply was guarded. "Yes . . ."

"Well, I was wondering if I could take you up on that offer."

Lily looked a little nonplused. Rosie knew that normally her sister was out of the house from six in the morning to nine at night most every day, but Lily had made the offer to watch Natasha and Rosie really needed the help.

Lily had a slightly trapped expression on her face as she looked around the restaurant. Finally, she glanced back at her sister. "When did you have in mind?"

"Oh, I haven't booked anything yet. Marcus just asked me if there was any chance of getting away and my first concern was who I would trust with my little girl. She's too precious to have a nanny. I would need to be sure that she's with somebody I know and trust."

"Where is she now?"

"She's on a play date. Don't forget she has preschool Monday through Friday, so that will help."

Lily swallowed hard. "It's just that I've never actually babysat before. I'm not sure that I know what to do."

Rosie sensed that her sister would agree with just a little more pushing. "Oh there's nothing to it." She reached over and covered her sister's hand with hers. "And Natasha is such an easy little girl to look after. You could move into our house if you wanted, so you'd have all the kid stuff. You know, plastic bottles, sippy cups—all of her things."

"Ohmygod, she still has sippy cups and plastic plates?" Lily pulled her hand back. "Do I need to sterilize them?"

Rosie burst out laughing. "Hello, Lily, I was joking. Natasha is five. Actually, she still does use a special plastic plate but only because she likes it. Other than that, she's just like you and me."

Lily wavered.

"Don't worry, Sis. She's easy to care for. I can write everything down, and she'll even tell you things herself at this stage. Because, God knows, she talks nonstop.

"No. Really?" Lily pretended to look shocked. "I wonder who she inherited that from?" she asked, teasing her older sister who was equally chatty.

"Cheers." Rosie raised her glass. "There's so much to say and so little time." She smiled at Lily.

"What does she eat?"

Rosie laughed and rolled her eyes. "She eats what's offered—usually what I'm eating. She *is* human."

Lily frowned. "Rosie, really, I'm not sure if I'm up to this. I mean, I might be able to get the time off work, but it's taking care of someone so little that worries me."

Rosie wouldn't take no for an answer. "You'll be fine, and don't forget, Mom will be able to help you anytime. You're the only one I'd trust with her, Lil,"

"Hey, what about Mom? Have you asked her?"

"I'd prefer you," Rosie said, ignoring the fact that her mother was an option. She was just nervous that Popsy would want to know everything about the resort and that wasn't a good idea. Rosie kept the pressure up. "And it would just be for a week. The time will fly. Natasha sleeps through the night now, so you'll even get a full night's sleep."

"Jeez, that hadn't even occurred to me." Reluctantly, she gave a slight nod. "But if you say I'm really the only person you trust, I suppose I could step up. It's just that I'm a little nervous. But heck, how hard can it be?"

Rosie was thrilled and ordered a second glass of wine to celebrate. "So, tell me your news," she said, pushing her plate away. "Any interesting men in your life?"

Lily didn't even look up as she shrugged, sighed, and finished off her chicken salad. "You know all the good men are taken." She half-smiled.

"This is crazy, Lil. You're the best looking woman I know. I'm sure you could have any man you wanted. What about that guy you met last year? Matt. He was really into you. Why did he get the boot?"

"He didn't get the boot because we never actually dated." Lily was clearly uncomfortable with the conversation.

"What? Why not? I saw the way he was flirting with you when we were having lunch that day in town."

Lily shook her head. "Rosie, he was younger than me by three years—a kid. Very sweet but nonetheless a child. Yeah, we flirted a bit but then one day he just stopped."

Rosie laughed. "Well, he may be a kid, but he's a kid with a six pack that belongs in a men's Calvin Klein ad."

"Selling what?"

"Who cares. The guys are always practically naked."

"How do you know what Matt's body was like anyway?"

"Am I wrong?" Rosie asked. "It was abundantly clear just by looking at him."

"No, you're right. He is in great shape. He works out a lot, I think."

"He's sounding better and better. I still remember what he was wearing. Those tight-fitting blue jeans and that white T-shirt . . . It was obvious that underneath that all-American cotton he had an all-American body made for all-American sin!" She winked at her sister. "And he was clearly into you. If I had an offer like that, I would have made a run for it—toward him, not away."

Lily smiled. "Yeah, he's hot, but come on, Rosie, you wouldn't seriously go for a guy that much younger than you, would you?"

"In a heartbeat." Rosie smirked. "You shouldn't have let him get away. Is he still available?"

"I have no idea, and anyway, he's too young and immature. Besides, I don't think he's even into me anymore."

Rosie finished off her second glass with a flourish. "Lil, first, he didn't look any younger than you. So what's three years between friends—or even lovers? It's not exactly a huge chasm. And second, if there's anything I've come to understand about men, it's that they are all permanently immature, even when they're older. Look at Dad. Mom still does everything for him because he's like a little boy. And third, men have been dating younger women for centuries. Why should they have all the fun?"

"What about Marcus?"

"What about him? He's just as bad. You know, they're all machismo and bravado while we're dating them, but believe me, that wanes very quickly and in no time you're left with the little boy who needs mothering." She snapped her fingers in the air as if to express the speed of the change.

"Wow, I'm sensing some issues here, Sis," Lily said softly with a little laughter in her voice but also a thread of sincerity.

Rosie thought it was a good time to open up. If this didn't convince her little sister to babysit, nothing would.

"Yeah, I guess you are. That's why we need to get away. We haven't been alone in years. I don't know if you remember, but even on our honeymoon, Natasha came with us!"

"Oh dear." Lily looked sympathetic. "If I can get the time off work, I'll be able to take care of Natasha. Let's compare schedules when you have dates in mind because I'll need to run them by the HR department."

Rosie nearly knocked over her glass and the empty plates as she tried to stretch over their small table to hug her sister.

"Oh, you're the best. I'll repay you, some time, some way, for this."

Lily smiled. "If you can just try to have a good time with Marcus and maybe find the inner man inside the boy struggling to get out, that would be a great achievement."

Rosie heaved a sigh. "Yes, it's a nice idea, but things have a way of settling down once you're married. I suppose it was silly to think we could keep that passion going indefinitely."

Lily reached across the table to touch her sister's hand. "Come on, Rosie. That's what vacations are all about. You can focus on each other completely, drink lots of champagne, and rediscover why you originally fell in love."

Rosie gave her a skeptical smile. "To be honest, what I think men, and perhaps all of us, really need is a little variety."

Lily pulled her hand back. "What do you mean?"

"Don't be too shocked. It's pretty common. I'm just saying that I think this is what Marcus—that is to say what both of us—needs." It was difficult to articulate. "Well, it's a little excitement—something different. Have you heard of these swingers' vacations where it's, um, sort of like the 60s? That would certainly put the fizz back into our marriage."

The waitress reappeared to clear away their plates and Rosie's wine glass, which saved Lily from having to answer.

"Would either of you like a coffee?" the waitress asked.

"Oh yes." Rosie smiled at her. "I'll have mine large and black, please." She looked at Lily and winked.

Reflecting back, she knew it was stupid to bring the matter up with her little sister. Lily was too straight, too understated. She should have kept it to herself, but for once, she'd really thought she and Lily were communicating on a level beyond pleasantries. How wrong she'd been. She should have kept the nature of the vacation to herself because the conversation had gone downhill from there. She remembered how upset her sister became at the lunch.

"Are you seriously thinking of going on one of *those* types of vacations? They're for middle-aged adulterers—sad souls who can't keep their lives on track. They hide behind alcohol and sex with strangers. What you and Marcus have is so much more. You have love, intimacy. God, Rosie, you have Natasha!"

"Don't you dare drag her into this. It has nothing to do with her."

"It has everything to do with her." Lily wrung her hands. "Is it because she arrived before the engagement ring did?"

"No!" Rosie said hotly.

"Well then, you're her parents. You owe it to her to stay together, to cherish each other—not to go out banging half of a tropical island." In her excitement she'd raised her voice a little, and they'd gotten more than one interested onlooker.

"Can you keep it down?" Rosie hissed. "She'll be at home and perfectly cared for. You know being a full-time mom isn't quite all it's cracked up to be. You can only take about a thousand episodes of Barney before going slightly nuts." Rosie was on a roll. "You have no idea what it's like to get dressed and cleaned up in the morning, only to have banana flavored yogurt poured down your cashmere sweater. If you go to the hair salon and get to look good for once, your kid gets near you and there's half a jar of jelly in your roots. It's been a fairly exhausting half-decade. You have no idea, Lily. None.

"Marcus and me, we both need to be reckless again. We need to remember what it's like to be young and wild—to *live*." Full of conviction, Rosie was ranting, desperate to defend her actions. "You might like to try it sometime. When did you last let yourself go? Really let go? You take life far too seriously. Get yourself laid. That would be a start."

Rosie suddenly stopped. Had she gone too far?

"Well, if you think sleeping around is living," Lily put her fingers up as if to put quotation marks around the word *living*, "I feel very sorry for you. That makes you no better than the dogs in the street. I would have thought your level of engagement with your husband was slightly more advanced than that. Then again, I suppose dogs don't have pre-nups," Lily added angrily.

Both women fell silent. That had been a low-blow on Lily's part and it hurt Rosie. Her father had insisted Marcus sign a prenuptial agreement to protect her wealth. It always made Rosie feel guilty to think about it. She thought it had demeaned Marcus in some way, and she knew that he felt it, too.

Lily was the first to apologize. "Sorry, I shouldn't have mentioned the pre-nup."

"No, you shouldn't have," Rosie snarled. "Look, just forget it. What Marcus and I do in our spare time is our business."

Lily raised her hand. "Actually, you're right about one thing, it is your business, and only your business. And to be honest, I want no part in it. I cannot express to you what a mistake I think you're making. And to show how much I object, I'm withdrawing my offer to watch Natasha."

"What?" Rosie looked at her sister open-mouthed. "You can't be serious!"

The girls locked eyes. Lily was fiercer than Rosie had ever seen her. "I'm deadly serious. You and Marcus are obviously having a bit of a rough patch, but if you go down this road, you'll do untold damage to your apparently already fragile marriage. I am in no way helping you to self-destruct. I'm sorry, but as far as I'm concerned, wherever you go on vacation, Natasha is going with you."

Rosie was speechless as Lily rose from the table, rummaged in her purse, and threw down a twenty-dollar bill. "I'd also rather pay for my own lunch, thanks," she said and swept out of the restaurant.

As she exited, the waitress arrived. "Here you are, ma'am. Your large black."

Rosie's mood plummeted as she realized it really was her job to phone her little sister and apologize. It was pretty clear that Lily had said nothing to their mom about the fight, but even so, Rosie was going to have to make peace between them. Worse than that, by fighting with Lily, she'd lost her babysitter. As a last resort, she'd hoped to ask her mother, but Popsy had been in a rush this morning and it wasn't the time to ask for such a big favor.

One thing Rosie was certain of, she had to get away with Marcus soon. And it would have to be to one of those swinging clubs because he more or less told her that she could come if she wanted, but he was definitely going. If she didn't tag along, she was going to lose him after only four years of marriage. The idea of that was worse than any wild getaway could be.

Naturally, Rosie was worried about going on a vacation where it was just a big orgy, but other people swore by them. She'd watched some late-night shows on what they called "the lifestyle," and all the couples seemed perfectly happy with the arrangement. She would just have to ignore Lily's conservative attitude and embrace this new experience with her husband.

Chapter 3

Sandra, the Friend

"Happy birthday, gorgeous," Sandra gushed as she climbed into the passenger seat of Popsy's car. "You know, I really should be driving. It's your birthday. You should be able to have a drink or three."

"Relax." Popsy smiled at her old friend. "It's going to be a long day, and I'm going out later with Peter. Besides, I'll allow myself a glass or two to celebrate."

"So," Sandra squeezed her friend's leg, "how does it feel to be fifty?"

Popsy groaned as she pulled her car out into traffic. "You know I can't believe I am. I mean, I actually feel the same as I ever did. To be honest, I think I'm still in my late thirties or even my early forties, but fifty? God, where did the time go?"

"I know. It's unbelievable, right? I'm forty-five. I mean, *forty-five*!"

Popsy made a grunting sound. "Sandra, where I'm standing, forty-five looks real attractive. Just keep doing those tummy crunches and running those marathons."

"You know it. Actually, I think I need to up my game," Sandra added, sounding gloomy for a moment.

Popsy noticed and changed the subject. "How's Jack? Working twenty-four-seven, I assume?" Jack was Sandra's husband and Peter's business partner.

"Yep. Don't they always?" Sandra had slipped back into her happy mode.

"How do they keep going? I mean, when is it ever enough?"

Popsy smiled surreptitiously. She remembered having the very same conversation with Jack's first wife some twenty years earlier. Peter may have been a workaholic, but Jack worked even harder.

Jack's first wife, Olga, couldn't stand it. She'd given up competing with his business empire and had walked out with their three little girls almost two decades earlier. Jack managed to find the time to acquire another wife, but he didn't want any more kids and Sandra had bent to his will.

Sandra was a decade younger than Jack, and as a newcomer to their social circle, she'd been star struck by their lavish lifestyle, wealth, and general comfort. She would have agreed to anything just to become the second Mrs. Hoffman. Though Popsy reckoned that she'd paid a very high price for her level of wealth.

Sure, she got the title of being wife, but without the kids. Life was very lonely because Popsy knew how much Jack was away. During the first years of their marriage, Sandra had tried to travel with him, but she was always left behind in a strange hotel room for the duration of their visit. The novelty of travel soon wore off.

So Sandra took up running. She ran and ran and then ran some more.

Jack and Sandra had been married for about thirteen years now, and Popsy considered them as settled as her and Peter.

"Tell me about today's party. Who is Jenny having, and what are we supporting again?" Sandra asked.

Popsy laughed. Sandra was always upbeat and a powerhouse of energy, but she was definitely a little scatterbrained.

"It's for The Children's Hospital in Boston. Remember? Tell me you've brought your checkbook."

"Naturally." She tapped her Chanel handbag. "I knew it was a fundraiser, I just couldn't remember which fund we were raising."

"I know that feeling. Isn't it getting a little crazy? There seems to be so many of these lunches at the moment."

"Well, we don't have to go to all of them, girl," Sandra said.

Both ladies fell into companionable silence and let the New England countryside unfold around them. Already fifteen miles outside Boston, Wellesley was not too thickly settled. Well-kept clapboard houses lined the perfectly tended streets in a nice, tidy, spacious order. But moving out toward Marlborough, using the back roads as Popsy did, the countryside became less populated, and there were even fields with cattle and orchards.

The New England fall never failed to impress. With literally millions of deciduous trees, the color explosion was like nowhere else on the planet. Locals called it the "crimson tide." The green leaves of summer gave way to deeper shades of red, and the wave of change slowly swept over the land from north to south. Every year it was different because the depth and range of colors depended on how many inches of rain the trees got in the spring, how much sun in the summer, and how cold it was in autumn.

Whatever the combination of factors, there was simply nowhere as beautiful as the Northeast in the fall. Fiery oranges clashed with brighter yellows, while mad magentas fought with the deepest burgundy. The combination was invigorating and was almost always set off against a clear and astonishing azure sky. The result pulled in the tourists, or "leaf peepers" as they were known, by the millions.

Sandra, it seemed was also drinking in the autumn colors. She sighed in contentment. "I love this country."

Popsy said, "I hope the winter's not too cold."

"Why? It's a great excuse to pull out the furs, darling," Sandra said. "Maybe it's even time to buy a new mink." She looked at Popsy. "And we all know how ladies get minks . . ."

Popsy and Sandra chorused the answer together. "The same way minks get minks!"

They laughed at the old joke, and Popsy glanced sideways at her friend. "Sandra, you are wicked."

"Me?" She pretended to look affronted. "I think you mean *us*, dear. And, yes, we are wicked." There was a house decorated for Halloween with a life-size witch sitting on its front doorstep. "We are the wicked wives of Wellesley," she said with a witch's cackle.

"Wicked but wonderful," Popsy replied in a more refined tone.

"Perhaps." Sandra looked pensive for a moment, but equally quick, she snapped back to reality. "We are due a visit to the fur vault in Bloomingdales. I love that place, and anyway, I assume you'll spend a lot of time in Florida when the snow arrives."

Popsy nodded. "I like to get away from the cold. I love autumn—the crispness, the colors, the cycle of life and all that. I wouldn't even mind the winter if it snowed less."

Sandra shook her head. "Oh no. The snow isn't the problem. It's cleared away so fast. It's the dark nights I hate. The clocks go back next week, and it'll be getting dark by lunchtime. It's terrible."

"It's not that bad." Popsy laughed. "It gets dark at tea time, perhaps five or six o'clock but no earlier. Think of those lovely log fires and romantic candlelit dinners you can have with Jack."

"Yeah, right." She examined her new French manicure. "The last time I had a log fire evening with my husband was . . . was . . . I don't remember."

"I don't believe it." Popsy reached over and nudged her friend's knee. "Don't tell me the wild flames of passion are subsiding after all these years."

It was an ongoing joke that Sandra and Jack appeared to have the most passionate marriage that either woman knew, so Popsy was surprised.

"Snuffed out, more like. Poôf." She clapped her hands together.

Popsy now understood the seriousness of this conversation. "Sandra, what are you saying? You and Jack aren't in trouble, are you? God, you're the best thing that ever happened to him."

Sandra gave a watery smile. "Maybe I'm getting too old for him," she whispered.

"Old?" Popsy shrieked. "How could you be too old? First, you're five years younger than I am, so what does that say about Peter and me? And second, what makes you think Jack would even want someone younger? He wouldn't have the energy."

Sandra wasn't convinced. "We had a bit of a fight last night. He said I was like an old woman," she admitted while studying her Manolos.

"I'll kill him," Popsy said through gritted teeth as she redirected her attention to the road. "Why did he say something so stupid? You have the figure of an eighteen-year-old, you're gorgeous and, anyway, he's never there."

"I was a little weepy. I don't know if you remember my friend Katie Meyers? I think I told you about her IVF treatment. Anyway, she just gave birth to beautiful twin girls. I saw them last week, and I guess something inside me just melted. Oh, Popsy, Katie is forty-five and she managed to squeeze two babies out. I felt like this was my last chance, so I brought it up with Jack."

Popsy pulled the car over to the side of the road. Some things were more important than lunch. She undid her seatbelt and hugged her friend. Words weren't necessary.

After a while, Sandra continued. "I know I said I wouldn't push him for children. I know I agreed that his days of babies were over, but I didn't understand what I was agreeing to." Sandra wept into her friend's hair. "Is it so awful to want a baby? Is it so terrible to need what nature intended? It's not like we don't have the money. I could get all the help we'd need, so it wouldn't affect Jack's life too much. Besides, he's out of the house so much maybe it wouldn't impact him at all."

Popsy didn't agree. A child would turn their world upside down, but she wasn't going to argue now. What Sandra needed was a shoulder to cry on and someone to listen.

"I've tried to ignore my feelings. I've tried to suppress them and tell myself that I'm being selfish. Jack's daughters are grown, and he doesn't want any more. That's his prerogative. He told me that from the word go. I didn't mean to do a U-turn, but it just happened. What am I going to do?"

Popsy looked at her miserable friend. This time she really was looking for advice. What possible options could she offer that would solve this conundrum? She shrugged. "What are your choices? I mean, if Jack doesn't want kids, how can you bring one into his life?"

"I could leave him," she whispered, studying her hands.

"What?" Popsy thought she was hearing things. She stared incredulously at her old friend. "You would consider taking it that far?"

This time it was Sandra's turn to shrug. "Well, he's never home. It's not like I have a full and loving life with him, and he won't give me the only thing I really want—no, I really *need*. That's not a good place to stay, is it?"

Popsy's mind was whirling. In this short conversation, Sandra had gone from contented society wife to dejected, disillusioned, possible divorcee.

"That was fast." She didn't mean to say what she was thinking. It just slipped out.

"What?" Sandra gave Popsy a sharp look.

"Sorry, Sandy. It's just that a few minutes ago you were talking about upping your game. I thought you wanted to get into even better shape—if that's possible—for Jack's sake."

"I never said it was for him." Sandra gave her a naughty grin. It looked like she was cheering up. "Getting into better shape is for me, if I'm going to get pregnant."

"So, you're going ahead with getting pregnant, even against his wishes."

Perhaps she was uncomfortable with Popsy's interrogation because Sandra pulled the sun visor down to examine her reflection in the little mirror.

"Popsy, I don't know what I'm going to do. All I know is that this life isn't a dress rehearsal, and I'm not going to sit around like some idiot and live a life I may look back on and regret."

"Now that I get." Popsy put her hands back on the steering wheel.

"So I'm going to do whatever's right for me—um, as soon as I figure out what that is." Sandra glanced at Popsy and half-smirked again. Then they laughed the relieved kind of laughter that follows a teary session.

"Well, good for you, Sandy, and I'll support you whatever you decide to do."

"Will you start by driving me to a hotel in Marlborough before we get to Jenny's? I have some major makeup repair work to do before I meet those girls." She snapped the sun visor back up. "Come on, let's get going."

Popsy started the car up. "Sir, yes sir." She gave a mock-military salute.

"I didn't plan to dump all of that on you, Popsy. I'm sorry."

"No problem. That's what friends are for. In fact, do you want to skip Jenny's thing and go for a long lunch in that gorgeous little coffee shop in Marlborough? We can find a quiet table and you can tell me everything."

Sandra shook her head. "What? And miss the unveiling of the new Renoir? No way. My marriage will still be in trouble after Jenny's lunch. Much more sensible to go and enjoy ourselves first."

Popsy didn't know what to make of their conversation. In all the years she'd known Sandra, she'd never heard her speak like this. Perhaps she was exaggerating. She and Jack may have simply had a fight or something.

She decided she couldn't do much else until her friend wanted help, so she patted Sandra's hand and agreed. "How very sensible you are. We can talk any time you feel like it, but for now, tell me all about the new Renoir."

~*~

Jenny Lennox was a consummate hostess. Because she'd chosen to live farther out of town, she had more land. In Wellesley, where Popsy lived, real estate was at its priciest. To have a pool at the end of the garden, which of course she had, was considered an achievement. But living just fifteen miles west meant tennis courts and swimming pools were the norm. The paddocks and the helipad were the new "must haves," and now Jenny had a Renoir to top it all off.

Popsy couldn't help but be a little envious as she glided up the perfectly landscaped, one-mile driveway. She watched a chopper take off just as they arrived at the front of the house.

Sandra, it seemed, felt likewise. "Who would be so tacky as to arrive in a chopper?"

"We would, if we could," Popsy said, thinking about the Ferrari she'd test-driven only a few hours earlier.

The Victorian-style house looked exquisite in its country setting, and at this time of year, it was festooned in a blaze of deep crimson Virginia creeper. Enormous oaks flanked the house, magnificent in their autumn color. It was impossible to look at it and not long to live in the country. As the thud-thud-thud of the chopper faded into the distance, a flock of crows cawed overhead, reclaiming their territory in the large and ancient trees along the front driveway. The house had perfect symmetry with three windows on the right and three on the left of the grandiose front door. Steps swept up to the door, which for today's event was left open. Popsy took a moment to admire the huge urns on either side.

Pyracanthas had been clipped to look like a giant ball and were in full bloom; they were covered in bright orange berries. These were under-planted with variegated ivy, which spilled out of the urns and down to the ground. It gave a feeling of understated opulence with a Halloween twist. Popsy made a mental note to do something similar in twelve months' time.

Once inside, they were greeted by beaming caterers offering a choice of sparkling water or even more sparkling champagne. Both women went for the champagne.

Jenny Lennox descended upon them in a flurry of air kisses and exclamations of how good everybody looked. Popsy gave her the flower arrangement she'd brought, and Sandra presented her with a jar of limited-edition caviar. As usual, Jenny insisted that they "shouldn't have" but took the gifts with grace.

Checks were deposited into an aquamarine objet d'art that was stationed just inside the front door. It was, doubtless, a terrifyingly expensive piece of glasswork, but Jenny was blasé.

"Just toss the donations into the vase there and come in to where all the fun is."

Stripped of their checks and armed with a champagne flute each, they were ushered into the drawing room. Popsy got the distinct impression that they were being herded like cows.

"Cheers, to your health and future decisions." She winked and clinked glasses with Sandra, and they headed into the fray.

Popsy and Sandra had a way of working a party. They would arrive together, then drift apart to mingle, but then they would drift back together again at regular intervals when either one of them needed moral support. This way they got to meet interesting new people but had each other as backup if they were a little lost. This method had worked well for them over the last thirteen years.

It didn't take long before Popsy was standing in front of the much-discussed Renoir. It was larger than she expected, almost two feet by two feet, and the frame made it look even bigger. It was hardly surprising then that it took pride of place over the mantelpiece in Jenny Lennox's enormous drawing room.

"Exquisite, isn't it?" the lady beside Popsy inquired.

"It is beautiful. Isn't she lucky? A genuine Renoir."

"It better be genuine. Eddie paid a cool $100 million for it."

It was enough to make Popsy snap around to face the lady she was talking to as opposed to admiring the painting. "I'm sure it can't have been that much. $100 million? That's too expensive, isn't it?"

"Cheap at the price." The lady sniffed.

Popsy wondered if perhaps her companion had drunk a little too much champagne. "How do you work that out?"

"That's what Jenny told him it would cost to stay in the marriage." The redhead moved closer to whisper. "I understand that poor Eddie was caught being a naughty boy, and when Jenny discovered it, she threw him out. He begged her to take him back, which of course she did, but for a price. This little token of affection."

Popsy was incredulous. "That's a lot of affection," she said and looked back at the painting.

"Yes, I hear it is a really good painting—*La Petite Fille*. Jenny tells me it's a charming and irreverent portrayal of the hedonistic life and subtlety of lust in the late 1800s."

"Ah." Popsy felt the need for more champagne. "Good to know." As far as she was concerned, it was just a really pretty painting done by a very famous artist. But wasn't art full of hyperbole like that?

Before she had to expand on her views, mercifully her art critic companion took her leave, which gave Popsy a few moments to admire the painting by herself. It was a true gem, beautiful, but how in tarnation did anything get to a value of $100 million? She understood how it could happen with diamonds and precious stones, but art? Wasn't that subjective?

"So what do you think?" Sandra asked as she came up beside her.

"I think it's gorgeous, and did you know that it was a 'charming and irreverent portrayal of the hedonistic life and subtlety of lust in the late 1800s'?"

Sandra looked at Popsy, arching her eyebrows. "I never would have guessed."

Popsy nodded. "I also heard that Eddie Lennox paid $100 million for it."

"In fact, I had heard a rumor, but I wasn't sure that it was true. Nice round figure. You know, in all likelihood it'll be worth double that in twelve months. Do you get taxed on fine art appreciation?"

Popsy pulled her friend closer and glanced around to ensure that nobody was within earshot. "Yes, but did you hear why he bought it? I heard Jenny discovered he was having an affair. This is the peace offering, his 'get out of jail free card,' if you will. A frigging Renoir."

Sandra said nothing and studied the painting.

"Did you hear me, Sandy? Did you know about this? Was Eddie Lennox offside? Evidently he had a mistress. Well, I assume it's *had* and not *has* if he's bought the painting and the Lennoxs are all happy family again.

At last, Sandra tore herself away from the painting and looked at her friend. "Who told you this?"

"That woman over there. The tall, striking strawberry-blonde." Popsy gestured discreetly.

"Figures." Sandra sighed.

"Why?"

"Because she's the mistress."

Chapter 4

Sisters with Secrets

It was late Saturday afternoon before Rosie got up the nerve to visit her sister. She'd accepted the fact that there was no way Lily would babysit for her at this stage, but of bigger concern now was the consideration that her sister might try to get their mother involved. The last thing Rosie wanted was Popsy getting wind of her vacation plans.

This time she had the good sense to bring her daughter with her. Lily adored little Natasha and spent a fortune on pretty dresses for her. Rosie again wondered why her sister didn't make a bigger effort to find a man and have a few kids.

Lily lived in one of Boston's most exclusive waterfront developments in the heart of the city. There were humungous gates and a security guard at the entrance, but Rosie knew the code number, as well as most of the security guys. Tonight the guard on duty seemed to recognize her, or perhaps her red BMW, because he gave her a cursory nod and opened the gate. This was a relief because the weather had turned bad as the day progressed and the rain was now relentless.

Some weeks earlier, Lily had given Natasha a beautiful little canary-yellow rain coat. The hood was in the shape of a duck's head, and the rim at the top jutted out like its bill. There were little brown boots to match, the tops of which were the same bright yellow, and they were painted to look like webbed feet. Natasha loved the ensemble, and at the first sign of rain, she would put it on and wear it all day, even indoors. When Rosie suggested they go visit Aunt Lily to show her how pretty she looked in it, Natasha didn't have to be asked twice.

Again and again, Rosie went over what she might say. The truth was she knew she would have to do a complete U-turn with her sister. Somehow she would have to convince Lily that she'd seen the error of her ways. She would say that Lily was right, and she and Marcus were going away alone to focus on each other. She might even say that it was a direct result of their fight, but that might be going a bit too far.

All of this, of course, was complete nonsense. The truth was Marcus was determined to have an "alternative" getaway. He was dying to try something new and a little risky, but Rosie had been having serious second thoughts. It was correct to say that Lily's attitude had swayed her, and she was back to being unsure about what to do.

Of course, it would've been wonderful if she and Marcus could work things out alone, but he was adamant that everybody was "doing it," and at least they were being open and honest. Marcus talked about all the guys he knew that were having affairs behind their wives' backs.

"And what about the women?" he'd asked. "My pals aren't having affairs by themselves."

He was insistent that there were as many women out there being unfaithful as there were men. Rosie tried to argue that a lot of married men ended up with young, single girls, but he laughed and said those days were gone. Just as many married women were getting with younger single guys.

It was much better for a couple of intelligent, mature people in a stable marriage to jump in together and have some fun in a crazy resort that facilitated this sort of thing. Then they come home and are contented. When he said it like that, it did seem to make sense, but the truth was that Rosie still wasn't convinced.

In fact, she knew she didn't want to have sex with another guy. She would hate to be with a stranger. But it seemed Marcus wanted a little variety, so she may as well go into it with her eyes wide open as opposed to turning a blind eye as so many wives did.

"One crisis at a time," she said to herself, and Natasha looked up at her, so she smiled. "Isn't that right, honey? One thing at a time."

Natasha nodded but didn't look too interested.

Under normal circumstances, she would've had to buzz the front door to get into Lily's building, but there was a couple coming out as she arrived and they held the door open for Rosie and Natasha. As she walked through the lobby, she tried to come up with the right words to use on her sister.

Being five, Natasha loved elevators. She liked to push the buttons, and the distraction made Rosie happy. She still didn't have her little speech thought out. She'd only gotten as far as "I'm sorry," but she decided that it was a good start.

The elevator chimed all too soon.

"Bing!" Little Natasha mimicked the sound as she skipped out.

There were only two penthouses on the top floor, one to the left and another to the right, and the hall area was small. Natasha saw her Aunt Lily standing at the already-open door, and she lunged toward her. Rosie followed a pace behind.

"I'm sorry," Rosie blurted as she noticed her sister in a tiny bathrobe and quite obviously nothing else on underneath. Natasha was clinging to her auntie's bare knee with great affection. The man who must have had his arms wrapped somewhere very different took a hasty step back. He, at least, was dressed. It was quite clear that he'd been leaving but was lingering with his good-byes.

"Oh!" Lily gave a guilty gasp. In that same moment Rosie felt a surge of relief as she realized she wasn't the only girl in the family with dirty little secrets.

"Hello, Uncle Jack." She took a step forward and kissed Jack Hoffman on his very flushed cheek.

"Uh, sorry I came unannounced, Lily," he muttered. "I should have called to see if it was a good time." It was a pathetic attempt to cover his guilty tracks. Jack had sandy blond hair with just a scattering of silver through it. He was a fit and good looking man, but he was old!

"Me, too, Lily," Rosie said. "Sorry I didn't buzz before I came up. You know, to give you some time. There was a couple at the door downstairs and they let us in." She smiled wickedly, looking between her sister and Jack Hoffman.

After her little sister's nauseating high moral stance just a few days earlier, it was good to see her squirm. Everybody knew that Jack wasn't their *real* uncle, but he did feel like family. Evidently more so to her than to Lily.

They'd practically grown up with Jack in their lives. Rosie even remembered his first wife. She'd been in her teens when they broke up. She and Lily were at his wedding to Sandra, and here was her sister in a very compromising position with the man that was like a second father to them. How weird was that?

As quickly as possible, Jack backed away and escaped down the emergency stairs, incapable of waiting the seconds it would've taken for the elevator doors to reopen.

Rosie looked at her little sister. She smirked and gave a quizzical look. "Lily?"

Lily didn't even bother to pretend or lie. It would've been futile. Instead, she scooped up her niece and walked back into her apartment. Rosie followed them and closed the door behind her.

"Can I make us some coffee? I think we need to talk." Rosie walked into the kitchen as Lily focused all her attention on the duck coat and boots.

Natasha danced in a little circle so her aunt could fully appreciate the outfit.

"I was looking in the fridge for some low fat milk when, lo and behold, I found this bad boy open and looking forlorn," she explained when Lily glanced up.

Her sister looked riddled with guilt, and Rosie was enjoying the sudden turn of events.

"Well, it would be flat in a matter of hours. Seems a bit of a waste not to drink it, right?"

Lily shrugged and wrapped her arms around her body like she was cold, and Rosie came to sit beside her.

"It's not what it looks like," Lily said, taking the glass of champagne she was offered.

"Oh, you're not screwing Uncle Jack?" Rosie whispered, but her words were still brutal.

Lily gestured to Natasha as if to say: not in front of the child. But Rosie wasn't going to let her daughter stop her from getting to the bottom of this.

"Natasha, if you watch *Sponge Bob* on Aunt Lily's bedroom TV, I'll buy you fries on the way home. Deal?"

"Yay!" She squealed and took off at top speed for her aunt's room. Lily jumped just as fast. "Jeez, my room is a bit of a mess."

Rosie sank back onto the deep, soft sofa, enjoying the moment.

How quickly things can change. She'd been so dreading facing her sister's moral high ground when all the time she was the one with the morals of a pirate.

Lily returned a few moments later, only this time she was wearing a cashmere sweater and leggings. She pulled the sleeves down over her hands —her guilty "tell."

"Come on," Rosie said. "Spill the beans." She patted the sofa next to her.

Lily did as she was ordered, but she sat on the edge of the cushion nervously. "I love him."

"So do I—but in an uncle way, Lil."

"No, I love him more than that," she said with stronger conviction this time.

"So how long have you *loved* him?"

"Oh, you wouldn't understand." She flopped back onto the sofa.

"Try me." Rosie took a swig of champagne.

"It's been almost a year now. He and Sandra haven't been getting along, and we go to the same gym."

"And?"

"Oh come on, Rosie. Do you need to have every lurid detail?"

"That would be good." She grinned, but then continued a little more seriously, "For God's sake, Lily. All the guys in the world and you pick Dad's partner to have an affair with. Jeez, he could be your father. He's old enough."

"Age doesn't matter."

"Not now, but it will in another twenty years. And what about kids? His daughters are the same age as we are. This is so wrong, little sis."

Rosie felt anger beginning to rise. Here was her sister utterly remorseless, yet condemning her for doing something she hadn't even done yet. "You know what, you're some hypocrite. You're having an affair with a man who's already on his second wife. He happens to be a *very* close family friend, and you have the nerve to give me grief about—oh, I don't know—experimenting. But at least it's within the confines and honesty of my own marriage."

Lily rose to her feet again. "See, this is why I didn't tell you. I knew you wouldn't understand. I figured you'd judge me like this just because I'm the other woman. You, of all people, Rosie. You claim to be open minded. You've known me longer than anybody else. I'm sure you know I don't go out looking for trouble. I didn't want this. I don't want to hurt Sandra. To be honest, I even like her." Then she sat down again. "The problem is, I like her husband even more."

Rosie softened a little and began to rub her sister's back the way she used to when they were little girls. "What are you going to do?"

"I don't know."

"Well, do you think it's a long-term affair or just something you're doing at the moment?"

Lily swung around with a look of great intensity in her eyes. "I adore him. I want to be with him forever."

Rosie shook her head gently. "You know, I envy you. I haven't felt passion like that for years."

This made Lily smile. "Yes, it's really amazing." She took her big sister's free hand in hers. "It's all-consuming. I really love him."

Rosie drained her glass and stood. "The problem is, passion always fades, honey. It can't last. It's like fire. In its prime nothing is as intoxicating or as beautiful, but then it passes. And if you're lucky, you're left with the warm glow, and that's if you're lucky. If you're unlucky, even that goes out, but I promise you one thing: the flames—the heat you feel now—that just doesn't last."

She put her glass on the mantelpiece and noticed the fire had died down. Poetic, she thought as she walked to the bedroom. Then she tried to use a happy voice for the sake of her daughter. "Come on, Natasha, it's fries time."

"You won't tell anybody, will you?" Lily was staring at the floor.

"No, I'll keep this quiet if you keep our conversation about my vacation plans to yourself."

"I'll even watch Natasha for you."

"Leave that with me." Rosie sighed. She didn't want to blackmail Lily into babysitting. That didn't feel right.

Lily walked them to the door. "See you at Mom's tomorrow?"

"Yep, Marcus is coming. You won't say anything to him, will you?" Rosie looked nervous. "I don't want him to know I've told you."

"No way. We're both sworn to secrecy." Lily tried to smile but couldn't quite manage it.

The sisters parted with polite, uncomfortable good-byes. Thankfully, Natasha seemed unaware of any undercurrents.

"I wanna press the button," Natasha squealed, wriggling to get her hand free from her mother's grasp. She got into the elevator and pressed *G* for the ground floor.

The doors glided closed smoothly, and Natasha looked at her mother.

"Bing," she echoed the noise.

Rosie smiled down at the best thing in her life and nodded. "Bing."

Chapter 5

Dinner

Popsy threw open her front door to welcome her friends into the house. "Jack, Sandra, come in." A large gust of wind and a few fall leaves made it in the door with her guests.

"It's turning into a bit of a wild one, I'm afraid," Jack announced as he handed Popsy a bottle of champagne and planted a kiss on her cheek.

"Jack, you know better than to bring a gift."

"And you know better than to think I wouldn't." He laughed and removed his coat. "Big change in the weather. Have you heard? They say we're going to get the tail-end of some hurricane that hit the south last week."

"You know the weather people always get it wrong," Sandra said as she slid out of her full-length mink.

Popsy wasn't sure, but it sounded like they were already bickering. She tried to lighten the mood.

"Storm or no storm, I'm so relieved you're the first here. We can have a drink and talk about the visitors before they arrive." She smiled conspiratorially. As they walked past the doors to the dining room, Sandra commented, "You've pulled out the big guns tonight, I see."

"Popsy always was the best hostess," Jack agreed, but Sandra glared at him.

"What? Better than me? You don't think I'm a good hostess anymore?"

Both Popsy and Jack looked at her in surprise. Sandra was very sensitive tonight, and Jack was having no part of it. Jack rolled his eyes but said nothing. Popsy realized with a little concern that there was definitely something in the air between the Hoffmans, and it certainly wasn't chemistry. She also knew that it was up to her to lighten the mood because she was damned if her dinner party was going to be ruined by their arguing.

"Oh, he's just charming me, Sandy." Popsy forced a laugh. "You know that Jack only wants me to give him the biggest plate of my home cooking."

"You cooked? Or Matilda?" he asked, poking fun at her and ignoring his wife.

Popsy's maid was famous for her cooking, and since she'd moved in some twenty-nine years earlier, the kitchen had become her domain. The irony was that Popsy was actually a good cook, but Matilda was very territorial so Popsy left her to it. The only time that she got a chance to sneak back into the kitchen now was when the housekeeper had a day off.

Popsy gently elbowed Jack. "You know what I mean, mister. It's my cooking if I paid for it. I have to admit that I do have caterers in. Even Matilda deserves some time off."

He winked at her. "Just teasing. Where's Peter?"

"He's in the study poring over spread sheets again." Popsy sighed. "I'd much rather he was pouring the champagne, but I suppose I'll have to do that myself."

Jack straightened. "I'm sure he would, too, Pops. Today was rough."

She'd already heard this from her husband. "I'm sorry it didn't go as planned."

Jack shrugged as if it was nobody's fault in particular, then excused himself.

The men had been trying to put together a particularly complex financial arrangement with their new European business associates. To the best of her knowledge, all five men had been locked away in a Boston hotel room all day and this evening's meal, when it was booked some weeks back, was meant to be the bonding session—post the deal's closure.

The problem was that Peter came home early saying that everything had fallen through. There was just too big a gap between how far the European team was willing to go and where Peter and Jack were able to meet them. There would have to be further discussions. That also meant that tonight was going to be strained, as opposed to celebratory.

Not exactly a good way to start a night. She sighed. For this reason she was delighted that Sandra and Jack had arrived first.

While the men talked tactics in the study, the women headed for the kitchen. Popsy needed to check on the caterers, and Sandra needed a drink.

"This isn't good, is it?" Sandra asked.

Popsy didn't understand. "Wild Alaskan salmon en croute? I thought of doing a clam chowder to start, but that's a bit predictable, don't you think?"

Sandra waved her hand. "I don't mean the food. I mean the deal."

"You mean for C&J Industries?" Popsy handed her guest a glass of champagne and took one for herself.

"Yes."

Popsy relaxed a little. C&J industries was the name given to the network of businesses their husbands ran together. It was originally called "Cap & Jet Industries," but it had been abbreviated years before. She and Sandra headed for the comfort of the drawing room.

"Don't panic about the boys. They're always complaining about these deals, but they do come off at the last minute. Wait till you see. By lunchtime tomorrow, it will all be settled."

Sandra didn't look convinced, but she seemed glad to hear such optimism. Then Popsy pulled her closer. "Now on to more important matters. How are you and . . ." She didn't say Jack's name but gestured with her head toward the study.

Sandra sighed. "I don't know. In all honesty, he's driving me crazy. I think he knows I'm up to something because he actually turned me down for action before we came out this evening."

Popsy was just about to take a sip but pulled the glass away from her mouth. "What? *Action* action?"

"Yes," Sandra whispered urgently. "Sex—action." She took a large gulp of her bubbles. "You don't think he knows I've had the coil taken out, do you?"

"You had it taken out? When? Why didn't you tell me? Popsy took Sandra by the arm and guided her friend to the oversized antique sofa.

"I didn't tell anybody," Sandra said. "I'm telling you now though, aren't I? Look, you don't suppose he can, you know, feel a difference?" Sandra glanced at her groin and back at Popsy with a meaningful look.

Popsy tilted her head. "I doubt it. You could ask him."

"But then he'd know I've had it taken out."

"So he doesn't know you're skydiving without a parachute, so to speak."

Sandra gave Popsy a blank look. "*Skydiving?*" Popsy always came up with the weirdest pseudonyms for sex.

"You know what I mean," Popsy whispered. "I don't want to say 'having sex' in case the help hears."

Sandra shrugged. "I don't think Jack knows anything, but as I said, we're not doing a lot of skydiving, as you put it, right now. How can I get pregnant if I can't convince him to skydive in the first place?" she whispered.

Popsy's mind raced. This was all happening so fast. Sandra could be making the biggest mistake of her life, but then again, it was her life.

"Are you sure, really sure you want to take this step alone, without discussing it with your husband?"

"I can't talk to him," she replied. "It's this way or no way. Besides, there's a darn good chance nothing will happen at all. As we discussed the other day, I'm forty-five. Maybe I'm too old."

Popsy disagreed. "If you haven't hit menopause, you're not too old. I remember my doctor saying that. In fact, they call it the 'sting of the dying bee.' "

Just then, one of the caterers entered the room to freshen their glasses, so the ladies fell silent for a moment, but as soon as he was gone, Sandra spoke. "Tell me about the dying bee thingy."

"Well, I heard that when a bee knows it is going die, it will often sting just for the heck of it—just to go out in a blaze of glory, if you know what I mean. You need to watch out for bees in the fall. Nasty bunch." Popsy shook her head and studied her glass as she thought about the bees.

"What? You're saying this is me going down in a blaze of glory? Popsy, I don't plan on dropping dead this winter." She sounded annoyed.

"No, no, that's not what I meant. It's just that, as you—or rather any woman—stops producing eggs, her body sometimes goes into overdrive and she'll produce a load in say the last six months before menopause. She'll also have very strong, um, urges to produce babies."

Popsy knew she should choose her words carefully. "Your urges, that is to say, what you feel at the moment about wanting a baby—that could be real. And if it is, chances are you could be fully loaded with eggs." It didn't quite come out as she planned because she felt a little loaded herself with the champagne, but Sandra looked delighted.

"So what you're actually saying is what I'm feeling is perfectly natural and there's a good chance I'll get pregnant because I'm loaded with eggs as well as hormones."

"Did I say that?" Popsy tilted her head. "It's just that I haven't had time to eat at all today, and a glass is enough to give me a buzz."

"You sure you're not just a dying bee?" Sandra nudged her and smiled. It appeared that she was in much better form all of a sudden. "This is great news. I'll be preggers in no time."

"Now just hold on a second there, honey," Popsy said, trying to stem her friend's enthusiasm just as the doorbell rang.

"Honey? Ha, that's a good one! Now come on, get up." She rose to her feet and headed for the door. "That will be the others."

"Sandy," Popsy stayed sitting, "the caterers will answer the door. Listen, a word of advice. Go easy on Jack."

"What?"

"It's just that, well, you seemed quite frosty with him, even angry, when you came in."

"No, I wasn't—"

"You did kind of go for him there, when you arrived. I mean, he was only giving me a compliment. It wasn't an indirect shot at you, but you took it that way. Sandra, trust me, you need to lighten up a little."

Sandra looked genuinely surprised. "Funny, I thought he was just trying to annoy me."

Popsy shook her head and stood. The sound of strangers' voices filled the hall. "Maybe you need to get away together. Spend a little time remembering all the reasons you fell in love in the first place."

Sandra put her arm around her friend's waist and gave her an affectionate squeeze. "Good idea. Plus, it will give me lots of chances to seduce him." Then she became more serious. "Because, to be frank, if I don't have a baby with him within the next few months, I'm going to leave him and find myself a younger man who really does want a family."

Such strong words worried Popsy. She looked at her friend of so many years. These conversations were similar to the ones she'd had with Olga twenty years ago. He'd stopped having sex with her, too, and that was the first sign their marriage was in trouble.

Was she witnessing another Jack Hoffman breakup? Popsy decided to talk with Jack later in the evening, if she could.

The Europeans were very reserved and their wives were perfect guests, but as Popsy expected, everybody's guard was up. These nights were very different from having a shower of friends in for supper in the kitchen. Even though it masqueraded itself as a dinner party, everybody knew that this was work. After having two glasses of champagne earlier, Popsy nursed the same glass of wine all night.

She discussed culture and fine art with her guests without referencing the business connection. They all talked about favorite ski resorts in both Europe and the U.S., and they sparred in a polite manner over the best sun spots in the world. Everybody commented on the storm brewing outside and said they hoped that it would not affect the next day's flight schedules.

The truth was, working dinners were quite wearing. In other circumstances, she may have ended up being friends with women like these, but this was business, or "war" as Peter sometimes called it, and her job was to entertain in a cordial manner. The one plus was that everybody knew the rules, so before midnight, the guests politely took their leave.

Popsy was happy enough to see them go. It would have been a much better night if the business deal had gone through, but the five men were meeting again in the morning at seven. Nobody was interested in staying up late, not to mention partying.

"Thank God that's over." Peter sighed as he headed to the liquor cabinet to fix himself a large whiskey. Just like his wife, he didn't drink much while in the company of prospective business partners, but now that they were gone, he was free to imbibe. "Ladies? Jack? What will you have?"

"Mine's a brandy," Popsy requested. "And Peter, in the future, please don't arrange these dinners until the deal is done."

"Here here," Sandra agreed. "And I'll have a brandy, too."

Jack was more pensive. He clasped his hands together as if in prayer.

"Jack?" Sandra looked at her husband. "You okay?"

"What? Oh yeah, I'll have a whiskey. You know, if they don't go for this deal tomorrow—"

"They will. They have to."

Popsy heard the tension in his voice, a certain urgency she hadn't noticed before. "Oh come on, guys. If it doesn't get done, there'll be other deals. No need to worry."

She took the glass Peter was handing her but didn't miss the look he gave his business partner. "Peter?" She glanced from one man to the other. "What's going on? What's up?"

But her husband just winked at her. "Nothing you need to concern yourself with, doll. Have I ever let you down before? We're just stressed because it's a big deal. But don't worry, I'll get it over the line. I always do."

Jack headed out, and Popsy assumed he was going to the bathroom. She decided this was her chance to catch up with him, so she waited about three minutes, and then followed him.

From the dining room there was a long hall to the bathroom and kitchen, so she was able to wander down in the pretense of getting more ice. But Jack wasn't in the bathroom. He was on his phone and glanced up when Popsy walked up to him.

"Everything okay?" She knew her voice was too perky, but what the heck was he doing out in the hall making phone calls? "Are you calling the driver, already? Stay for a little while longer."

"No, no, just checking my messages. I'm driving this evening."

Now was her chance, for sure. She touched his arm. "Jack, is everything okay? It's just, well, I've known you for a long time, and I like to think I know you pretty well. You seem a little . . . distracted," she said, trying to find the right words.

He looked straight into her eyes like he might find some answer there, then he heaved an enormous sigh. "Life is complicated, Popsy." He managed a smile. "That's all there is to it. Life is really complicated."

"Can I help?" She cupped his face in her hands. "I mean, you and I, there's very little we don't know about each other at this stage. You're like a brother to me and Peter, and of course, the girls. They think of you like the uncle they never had."

He pulled away. Had she touched on something? It was the reference to children. Sandra was right.

"Is it Sandra? I mean, she's a friend of mine, but if you need somebody to listen . . ." She tried to reach him, but the moment was gone. "How about lunch?"

"What?" He looked confused.

"Why don't I treat you to lunch?" She smiled at him, but he looked even more tortured.

"Popsy, haven't you learned by now? When somebody says 'it's only lunch,' it's never only lunch."

"Jack," Peter said as he came down the hall, "your whiskey's getting warm. Do I have to drink it for you, too?"

He looked glad for the interruption. Jack regarded her with a smile now fixed firmly in place. "Thanks for the offer, Popsy, but really, I can handle my own life. You just take care of yourself." He squeezed her shoulder in a paternal manner.

"Excuse me?" She was a little surprised by the turn in the conversation.

"Just watch your back," he added in a low voice.

"Me? Jack, what are you talking about?"

But he was walking away from her. Then he glanced back over his shoulder and put his finger to his mouth as if to say that it was a secret.

"I'm absolutely fine," Popsy protested. "My life has never been better."

But Jack was gone.

"Why would I need to watch my back?" she whispered, quite put out by her old friend. "I'm not the one whose partner is thinking of leaving them."

Chapter 6

The Morning After

Popsy was still half-asleep when she felt the empty space where Peter should have been.

"Honey?" she called, assuming he was in his en suite bathroom, but he didn't reply. "Peter, where are you?"

She pulled the eiderdown comforter over her in an effort to get cozy again and felt the soft sheets slide along her limbs. Popsy realized she was naked and then she remembered the night she'd had with her husband after their guests left. Peter still knew how to make a woman feel loved, even after all these years. She smiled smugly as she tried to slip back to sleep.

An elegant, arched bay window with double bay sashes ensured their bedroom was flooded with natural light by day but the hand-woven, ice-blue, silk curtains were still drawn shut. Peter had obviously left early enough this morning to leave them closed so she could sleep. A thick winter-white carpet covered the expanse of the room and absorbed any noise that there might have been—not that there was any this Sunday morning. All was quiet.

The room may have been dim, but Popsy's mind was clearing. Despite her best efforts, it looked like she was not going back to sleep.

The last thing she'd said to him before they'd fallen asleep the night before was to be home in time for lunch. "The girls are coming. I want my birthday lunch to be perfect."

"Yes, dear," he'd mumbled and almost instantly started to snore.

"Darn whiskey," Popsy grumbled as she pulled herself up into a sitting position and switched on her antique bedside lamp. To be fair, over the years she'd become accustomed to her husband's snoring, and now she was able to sleep right through it, but it would be nice if he was a quiet sleeper.

Like the rest of the house, Popsy had decorated their bedroom with antiques. Her parents had given her a lump sum when she married, and all of it went into their home. Early in their marriage, they'd taken a vacation to New Orleans where they found the most amazing antique shops and art galleries. As a result, Popsy had furnished her entire house with Victorian, Georgian, and Edwardian treasures.

Of course these days it was so out of vogue, but she didn't care. She loved their bedroom. It was warm and welcoming, and the old pieces gave her a feeling of security and permanence.

The bed was the only exception she'd made to her "everything should be antique" rule. It looked like it was from the mid-1800s, but was, in fact, a modern reproduction. Peter had insisted.

"I don't want a bed that hundreds of people have slept, screwed, and quite possibly died in," he'd argued persuasively umpteen years ago. "I want a brand-new bed, and what's more, I want the biggest bed money can buy— one that I can chase you around for the next fifty years. I guess I want a bed that I can sleep, screw, and maybe even die in myself! But at least I'll die happy."

Popsy had it custom made to look old but with every modern comfort and back-saving piece of technology she could get. The result was a four-poster bed that could have slept six if they felt the urge, which of course they never did. It was maybe her favorite place. Her comfort zone she would call it. Their "play zone" Peter had nicknamed it.

Popsy thought it was worth every penny of the tens of thousands she'd spent. The four posters did not hold up a canopy over the bed but rather stood proud. Over the years, Peter had been very inventive with all of them. And while current trends were more Feng Shui than Louis XIV, Popsy was certain that romance would never go out of fashion. Oceans of brilliant white cotton on a bed of deep mahogany had worked for her and her man for almost thirty years now, and she wasn't going to change the winning formula.

Sitting in a cloud of white pillows with her knees drawn up to her chest and her comforter pulled under her chin, Popsy let her mind rest on the events of the evening before. The dinner party certainly wouldn't go down in history as the best she'd ever thrown, but it wasn't all bad. The business friends of Peter seemed quite nice, but she wished the deal wasn't taking so long.

What gave her the most concern this morning were Sandra and Jack. His warning came back to her again. Why did she have to watch her back?

Peter had made it abundantly clear how much he was still in love with her. Okay, so they didn't have sex every night, but she rarely turned him down. Given a second glass of champagne she could, on occasion, even initiate things. So Popsy was pretty sure that Jack wasn't trying to warn her about her husband's possible philandering.

What else was there?

Work? It couldn't be. The boys were good businessmen, and she knew her financial position was secure. It always had been.

So what had Jack been talking about?

The girls? Popsy always worried about her daughters. Was Rosie happy? Why hadn't Lily found the right man yet? Then again, what mother didn't worry about her children? She'd once heard an old saying that "a mother was only as happy as her saddest child." It was so true. Well, the girls were coming over for lunch, so she could talk to Rosie then and find out what was on her mind.

Popsy slipped out of bed and headed to the bathroom.

She caught sight of herself unclothed in her full-length mirror as she walked the floor. It made her stop and have a look. She didn't usually parade around the room with no clothes on because Matilda could walk in at anytime, and Lord knew if Peter walked in and saw her naked, he would get ideas for sure. It just wasn't something she did too often. But it was Sunday morning, so Matilda was off, and she knew that Peter was at the office. She looked at her body—the body of a now fifty-year-old woman.

"Wow." She sighed. "Where did all those years go?"

The bedside lamp didn't give off much light, so she threw open her enormous blue silk curtains to let the daylight in. There was an elderly man walking a dog along the street, and he glanced up as if some telepathic male messaging system had told him that there was a naked woman opening her curtains.

Why in heck had he looked up just then? Popsy hid behind the swathe of silk.

Then she returned to the mirror, well away from the window.

She groaned. "I think I preferred the soft light."

There was no doubt that time was taking its toll. She was still skinny.

Popsy had always been slight, but her boobs had drooped—seriously drooped. They were like a couple of balloons that had deflated over time, and now they just hung on her chest. How depressing. She lifted them up, one in each hand, in the hope that they would somehow look a little re-inflated, but they still looked like deflated balloons, only now they were sitting on a shelf of sorts.

Popsy let them flop down again. Maybe Sandra was right. A little boob job might not be a bad thing. Then she looked at her stomach. She turned sideways to look at it from another angle, and she inhaled as much air as she could. The chest looked better with her lungs full of air, and the tummy in a little, but she still looked pretty old and leathery. She breathed in-out, in-out a few times to watch the result. It was slightly comical and mildly amusing.

"Better than getting depressed about it," she muttered. "Come on, Popsy. It's not that bad. Your pins were always your best part."

She studied her legs, making them look as good as she could by standing on her toes. It helped. While they still had reasonable tone, she could see that varicose veins were protruding from her calves and inside her thighs.

"Those are new." She groaned.

She was definitely going to get them done. That wasn't even considered plastic surgery anymore. It was just "maintenance."

Even with reasonable calf muscles, her legs had lost a lot of their definition and firmness, so they were pretty scrawny-looking. She tried to do the lunge thing that her gym instructor once made her do. It was kind of like a genuflection, only frozen in the halfway position. Popsy thought it might give her leg muscles more tone, which it did until she fell over.

Undeterred, she got up and turned around to study her backside by looking over her shoulder. Using the tippy toes technique again, she saw that it looked better. In fact, she thought it didn't look too bad.

"Okay, I still have one asset in good condition." She sighed, somewhat relieved. "There's no doubt. Aging is nasty." She gave up on the navel gazing and headed into the bathroom to have a soak.

She continued talking to herself. "Well, at least I'm still alive. Looking young isn't everything. Being happy is." Popsy thought about her lovely family coming over later for lunch to help her celebrate her fiftieth birthday. "That's really what it's all about."

Unlike the rest of the house, Peter and Popsy chose modern for the bathroom. The bath was not on four claws as one might expect in a house full of antiques. They had opted for a sunken, built-in Jacuzzi. The shower had been changed for the rain forest type only a few months earlier, but Peter insisted on all the side sprayers, too.

The Jacuzzi was Popsy's favorite. The only disadvantage was that it took a long time to fill. She turned both faucets to full-blast while she brushed her teeth. Then, just as she had with her body, she examined her teeth and gums. Were they aging, too? Probably.

She was used to seeing her face on a regular basis, but what with the birthday and the rest of the assessment, Popsy had a real hard look at herself now. "Oh dear," she mumbled as she saw the lines under her eyes. In fairness, there weren't many.

She was holding her own pretty well, but still she thought Sandra had a point. Perhaps it was time to up her game. She worked out with Sandra now and again, but Popsy usually went along for the chat and never particularly exerted herself, while her friend pushed it as hard as she could.

Yes, she decided, it was definitely time for her to spend more energy on looking good. Not so many long, slow walks and more importantly, not so many long, slow lunches.

Popsy added a bath bomb to the water and sat on the side, waiting for it to fill some more and for the fizzing to stop. She thought about Sandra. That girl really was in a bit of a place at the moment. One minute she was talking about walking out on the marriage and the next she was considering getting pregnant. There was quite a chasm there. Popsy felt pretty sure that the road to happiness was somewhere in between the two, but Sandra didn't appear to be in any mood to take advice just yet.

She dearly hoped she wouldn't do something she was going to spend a lifetime regretting. Jack would have a fit if he thought Sandra was trying to get pregnant. How long had she been trying? Maybe she was pregnant already. It would certainly explain the tears on the way to the ladies' lunch and the irritability with Jack the previous night.

She tested the water and was satisfied that it was full enough and just the right temperature. She slipped in. It was heaven. She let her head slide under the surface and massaged her scalp. Then she pushed with her feet until her head came back up and her hair was slicked back.

"There are very few things in life better than a good soak," she announced to the room. Then she let her mind wander back to the night before.

When the Hoffmans had gone home, Popsy had snuggled up to her husband who was sitting on the sofa. "Have a good night, Peter?" she asked, gently trying to get his attention.

"Mmm." He seemed to be miles away.

"They were a rather reserved lot, I thought. Your prospective investors."

The talk relating to his business dealings did the trick, and he tuned in. "Huh? Don't let their manner fool you. They would eat you for breakfast," he said, seeming to notice for the first time that she was sitting right next to him.

She stroked his leg absentmindedly. "Funny, I found them quiet—not anywhere near as dynamic as you are, darling."

Peter yawned and stretched his arms high above his head. "I have a feeling that their guard was up because we didn't manage to make a deal. You might have seen another side of them if our negotiations had gone well." He wrapped his arm around her shoulders and played with a loose tendril of her hair.

She smiled as she thought about it now. She'd had her hair done in an up-style for the previous night, but by the end of the evening, after all the "playing" with her husband, it looked like a haystack. She poured a golf-ball-size dollop of shampoo into her hand and lathered her hair.

She would be back in the hair salon in a few days, but she was happy to blow dry it herself today. The long, shaggy look was a bit too casual for every day, but it would be perfect for a Sunday lunch with family. The up-style of the previous night had been for Peter's benefit. He once told her that the back of her neck was one of the sexiest parts of her body, so she used it often as a weapon of seduction.

Last night, just like most others, it worked like a charm. Within minutes Peter's mind was very much off business and on Popsy. She found she could seduce him as easily today as she could thirty years ago.

"Watch your back indeed," she fumed, thinking about Jack Hoffman as she rinsed out the shampoo and lashed in an extra load of conditioner for good measure. Popsy could still attract her husband's eye with just the slightest manipulation, but she usually made it seem like it was his idea. He sometimes liked it when she took the lead, but he was a "Type A" man. He liked to think he was in control at all times, so she let him believe it, even when it wasn't the case. The previous evening was no exception.

Gently stroking his leg and most importantly, pretending to not even notice what she was doing, was sufficient to haul her husband's brain back from his business empire. Pretty soon he was a lot more focused on his assets in hand, so to speak. He'd started with her hair but made it clear that he had other places in mind. Peter didn't play games. As soon as he wanted sex, he wanted it instantly. He was aroused fast and had to be satisfied just as fast.

Popsy had read romance novels that talked of men who spent hours pleasuring their women. That wasn't Peter. But what he lacked in technique, he certainly made up for in enthusiasm. He was so passionate and hungry for her that it turned her on, too.

It had been every bit her intention to seduce him after what Jack said. She had no idea what he was talking about, but she planned to find out. The first objective was to reassure herself that she still had all of her husband's undivided love and attention. The Renoir story had shocked her more than a little.

Lying on the plush Afghan carpet of her drawing room floor the night before, it seemed pretty clear from her perspective that she still had his affection.

"God, you're so gorgeous," he'd mumbled into her disheveled hair as he made love to her.

"So are you, Peter. I love you and only you," she'd whispered, lying under him, welcoming him into her body.

"Me, too," he agreed, sounding even more muffled. "Only you. God, you're the best thing that ever happened to me, doll."

Thinking back on their romantic interlude now, Popsy was certain there was nothing to worry about in the romance department, so what in the heck was Jack talking about? Why did she need to watch her back if her husband was still so happy pinning it into the ground?

Chapter 7

Sandra's Surprise

Sandra Hoffman's life was similar to her best friend Popsy's in so many ways. Both women had charmed lives. Their days consisted of shopping for new clothes and accessories, maintaining their highly polished style, and running the oh-so-smooth lives of their husbands.

Of course Popsy had the children who—although grown up, and in theory, on their own at this stage—still took up quite a bit of her time. Of this, perhaps Sandra was a little jealous. She tried not to be, but it was so darn difficult.

Popsy and Sandra sometimes met in the gym and after that they might go for lunch together or to a charity do. They often went into town to see what was new in the shops, but all too often, Popsy was rushing off to meet a daughter or spend time with her exquisite granddaughter.

Sandra longed for a little of that family life. A long time ago she'd tried to forge links with Jack's children from his first marriage. He had three beautiful daughters, but the girls had a strong loyalty to their mother. Their home was in New Jersey, and they had no real interest in acquiring a second mom.

Sandra had a brother who was married with two teenage sons, so in theory she did have family to fuss over. The problem was that she and her sister-in-law didn't get along, so they'd sort of drifted apart. A few years earlier Ben, her brother, moved from New York out to California, and she hadn't been to visit them. Ben was a few years older than her, and he kept asking her to visit but she didn't. It was just unfortunate but Sandra was quite sure that the reason for their estrangement had every bit as much to do with Laura pulling Ben away from her, as with her own reluctance. This was tough because she really did love her big brother. It was just too difficult to stay in touch.

The flipside was they'd never visited Sandra either. She didn't have enough room to accommodate four guests, but then again, maybe they could have managed somehow.

Her home was the ultimate luxury apartment, but it only had a couple of bedrooms. She had made a strong argument for three when they were designing the internal layout, but Jack had insisted on only two. He bought it just after they'd gotten married. It was the penthouse in Wellesley's most desirable apartment block.

Since the apartment was connected to Wellesley's only six-star hotel, The Celtic Crowne Plaza, they had full hotel facilities twenty-four hours a day. This meant that the apartment was cleaned thoroughly daily with sheets changed and laundry collected—exactly as if they were staying in the hotel. Naturally, she had full use of the hotel's gym, swimming pool, and hair salon, but she could also have the beautician come to her apartment and dinner could be sent up from the restaurant. They could even order a drink from the bar if they didn't feel like making it themselves. She also had a state-of-the-art kitchen, but it didn't get much use.

"Far easier to order from the hotel's kitchen," Jack had said. And he was right, of course, but Sandra felt he was wrong about the apartment layout.

Three bedrooms would have been more welcoming to his three daughters and her brother's family. It wasn't as if it wasn't big enough, because they had the space. The apartment stretched over five thousand square feet. The truth was, Sandra had a deep suspicion that Jack had railroaded the two bedroom design through so it would be quite clear that there were no babies coming into their life.

"As if," she harrumphed this morning while getting out of bed.

Her head hurt. She'd drunk too much the night before, but her conversation with Popsy had upset her, and the business dinner had been a crashing bore. Jack gave her nasty looks all night, so she'd taken to the wine with a vengeance. She hadn't gotten drunk or anything, but three glasses were enough to give her a hangover. Nothing the gym wouldn't get rid of she decided—only she'd go later.

Sandra fixed herself a slice of toast, a glass of orange juice, and a mug of black coffee. Jack had told her that he would be up and out very early in a last-ditch effort to salvage the deal with the Europeans. But he had been kind enough to drop *The Boston Globe*—essential Sunday reading—onto the kitchen table before he left.

Newspapers were brought to the front door of her apartment every day and left on the mat. He must have seen it on his way out and brought it in for her. That was thoughtful.

With her breakfast tray carefully settled on her bed and the paper on her nightstand, she returned to bed, content. It was a glorious way to start a Sunday. Sandra pushed the button next to her light switch and the curtains rolled back to reveal a very pleasant morning. Whatever storm was in the air the night before had blown itself out. She took a bite of blackened toast smothered in coarse-cut marmalade—just the way she liked it.

The Sunday paper continued to dwell on the state of the U.S. economy, which really was depressing. Could they not find something happy to write about? she wondered as she searched for the fashion and lifestyle supplements.

In the travel section, an article on Ireland and Dublin caught her eye. She'd never visited, which was odd because the shopping was supposed to be terrific and, of course, Popsy was originally from the area and often mentioned it with fondness. Surely that alone was reason enough to go.

She took a drink of coffee and settled down to learn all about Popsy's hometown. By the time she got to the end of the article, Sandra decided it was definitely worth a visit. It had all the big stores that London and New York had, but in a more compact city.

The photographs of the area in autumn were breathtaking. Old cobbled streets were flanked by impressive Victorian houses, still in perfect condition and being used as homes and offices. Alongside this enviable old world, the Irish had built a magnificent new financial district similar to Boston's glass monoliths. Dublin had the best of the old world and the new. It was a beautiful city.

Of course, there was also the famous Irish hospitality. The people were quite literally like no others. The article said researchers had found the Irish to be the happiest people on earth and most likely to laugh.

Why was that? she wondered.

She envied them. Why had she never managed to visit?

She was sold. But then she thought about Jack. He wouldn't be happy to drop everything and go on a shopping trip.

Was it her imagination or was he becoming more grouchy? More difficult to please? She'd only broached the subject of babies with him once, and he almost hit the roof. He'd been furious with her—really angry.

"We had a deal!" he'd shouted as he stormed around the room. "You knew full well coming into this marriage that I didn't want any more children. I can barely keep up with the three I have."

Thinking back on it now, Sandra felt sad. She did know that was how he felt, but she'd changed her mind. It wasn't supposed to happen, but life had a funny way of changing people, and now all Sandra really wanted was to start a family before it was too late. If it wasn't already too late.

She felt that old familiar panic rising again. If she didn't have a baby, what was life all about? There had to be more to it than shopping and running. It was all right for Jack. He had three kids already, but those girls didn't want anything to do with Sandra, so that left her out in the cold with no children to care for.

Surely Jack was the one being unreasonable. If he truly loved her, he would give her this one precious gift. She wouldn't expect him to do anything. She would do it all. In fact, they wouldn't even have to move.

A million times in her mind, Sandra had renovated the second bedroom into a nursery. In her imagination, it was always yellow because she didn't know whether she wanted a boy or a girl. She just wanted a baby—one for herself. Was that so awful?

Her mood plummeted and she tried to focus on the paper again. Dublin. How had Dublin set her off on her baby fantasy? Sandra took another bite of her toast, but it had gone cold now. The sugar-hit from the marmalade hadn't helped her headache, so she decided she needed something stronger and headed out to the medicine cabinet in the kitchen for some painkillers. She kept them in the press under the cutlery drawer.

I'll have to move them, she decided, thinking about how easily a toddler could get to the colorful bottles of medication.

"Stop!" she yelled. She didn't need to childproof the apartment because there were no children in it, or any coming anytime soon.

After tossing two large pills into her mouth, she took a large gulp of water to wash them down then went back into her bedroom. There was no point in putting it off. She really needed to get to the gym. Running was the only way she knew to rid herself of a hangover. Plus, it might get babies out of her head.

Catching a glimpse of herself in the hall mirror, she realized she looked a bit green, too. She definitely wasn't able to drink as much as she once could. Popsy may have thought Sandra was still young, but she didn't feel it. At forty-five, she couldn't party as hard as she used to. She'd felt a big change between twenty-five and thirty-five. It never occurred to her that she would drop another gear from thirty-five to forty-five. What would fifty-five bring?

The fact that her skin had an olive tone made her look even greener. Sandra had Italian blood, so her complexion was usually enviable, but not this morning. With long, dark, poker-straight hair and her tanned skin, Sandra knew she was attractive. And she'd managed to keep her figure so fit that she would pass for a woman ten years her junior.

She put it all down to the gym and weight training, but women in their social circle were a lot less forgiving. Sandra had heard the rumors flying around. People wondering how much work she'd had done, but everything was achieved in the gym with the small exception of her bust. That she had bought from a particularly good plastic surgeon in Boston. As she'd worked the weight off the rest of her body, it had come off her breasts, too. She didn't even tell Jack until after the fact, but he was suitably impressed with the result and not upset by her secrecy.

The biggest advantage of Sandra's running addiction was her rock-hard figure. Even at forty-five, she had a body that a twenty-something would be proud of. When people asked her how she kept such a perfect figure, she would simply smile and say: I run. But that never seemed to be a good enough answer. They would often ask her if she had a special diet. Any allergies? Perhaps she was a non-drinker.

It always amused her that people wouldn't accept the genuine reason and would go looking for other magic solutions. She would shake her head, losing patience. "No, I eat everything, and I like my wine, too, but I do run —every day."

Inevitably, they would look at her in bewilderment as if they were missing something. Only once had she gotten confrontational about it. Sandra had been at a lunch in the city with a few other ladies when a young, precocious girl came up to her. She was wearing the same dress, only a few sizes bigger.

"Where do you get off wearing that dress?" she'd asked.

In her defense, it was a pretty daring dress—a black mini. It was figure-hugging with a deep V-neck that flashed a lot of cleavage at the front and an even deeper one at the back. But what the heck? She could carry it off.

"What did you say?" Sandra asked without a smile.

"Look, we have the same dress only you're so . . . so—*skinny*." She spat the word out like it was an insult. "I mean, you're probably older than my mom and still you're wearing dresses like that. Did you have your tummy stapled or something?"

Sandra laughed because the poor kid was just looking for advice, but she'd wrapped it up in a boxing glove. She stood and pulled the girl over to a private corner while Popsy and their friends talked amongst themselves.

"Look, honey, I'm not sure I'm old enough to be your mom. But leaving that aside for the minute, if you're asking me how I look like this, I run. That's all you need to do. Just take up running."

"Oh, I'm not built for running," the girl explained. "My legs go everywhere. I'm good at walking, but it's never made me look like that." She gave Sandra the up-down stare.

"You ask me how I do it. I tell you how. Then you don't believe me, so I can't help you." Sandra went to sit down.

"I've jogged a bit," the younger girl said.

But this is the point where Sandra snapped. She turned. "That's bull," she said, making the girl blink in surprise.

"Huh?"

"I said bull. You don't have the body of a jogger. You have the body of a walker. I have the body of a woman who runs ten miles a day, six to seven days a week. You want to look like me? Do what I do. There's no silver bullet, no magic answer. Just get off your ass and run, and as for your legs going everywhere, that happens to most people. Get on a treadmill and they can't go too far astray. Now, if you don't mind, I'd like to get back to my friends."

The young girl just walked away. When Sandra returned, the ladies at the table gave Sandra a discreet round of applause.

"You sure put that kid back in her place," one of them said.

"Yes, well, they think they can have it all. I swear I'm sick of it. They think they can eat and drink like sailors and look like super models. If you want something, no matter what it is, you have to work for it." She tried to calm herself down. "Why can't they see that?"

Sandra realized she should take her own advice. If she wanted a baby, she would have to work harder to get it—only not in the gym, but in the bedroom. It was a lot more difficult than it sounded. She was desperately trying to figure out the best time of the month and had even started using the over-the-counter ovulation kits. They didn't seem to be working, and on top of that, she'd have to engineer a way to seduce her husband. That was not as easy as it once had been.

Jack often worked late, and she was asleep before he even got home.

Sometimes he would even turn her down for sex. This was new and it shocked her. He'd always been game for a bit of romance, but in the last few months, he didn't seem too interested.

Was it because he was getting old? Or was he losing interest in her? Sandra didn't know, but it did seem that forces were conspiring against her.

Getting Jack to—what was it Popsy had called it the night before? *Skydive*. Getting Jack to skydive her—or should that be skydive *with* her? —either way it wouldn't be as easy as it had been a decade ago. Most importantly, every month counted at this stage. She wasn't even sure if she was still ovulating regularly.

Popsy's story about the sting of the dying bee had given her solace. Maybe she would produce twins. Who knew what the future could hold?

As she picked up the paper from her bed, she saw the photograph of Dublin on the cover of the travel section and decided that what she needed was a weekend away—a girls' weekend—and nobody was better to get away with than Popsy.

She was always fun and such a terrific listener. Popsy might even have some suggestions on how to put the pep back into Jack's step. She and Peter seemed to be very much in love after all these years. They had two amazing daughters, too. Now Rosie was happily married with a beautiful little girl, and it was probably only a matter of time before their daughter Lily fell into the arms of some lucky guy.

She decided to book flights and accommodations in some plush hotel and give it to her best friend as a belated birthday present. What a nice surprise that would be. It would also give Jack a little time to miss her. When she returned, he would be eager to welcome her home and into their bed.

Delighted with her new plan, Sandra left their penthouse apartment and headed to the hotel's gym. She smiled at her reflection in the elevator mirror and whispered, "Absence makes the heart grow fonder."

Chapter 8

Lunch

"Out of sight, out of mind." Popsy sighed, thinking about her hometown.

By mid-morning she, too, had seen the Sunday papers, and the feature on Dublin caught her eye. She hadn't thought about Dublin in so long.

Originally from Ireland, Popsy had come to Boston College for a sabbatical year. That's when she'd met Peter and that's when she fell in love. Peter was a force of nature. He'd swept her along with him in his adventure through life, and she had loved every minute of it. Thirty years married this Christmas. Maybe a vacation back home would be a nice way to celebrate. Naturally, early in her marriage, she'd gone back often, but because she was an only child and both her parents had passed away, she hadn't returned. There was always so much to do in the U.S., so many places to see. Of course, she also had their winter residence in Palm Beach.

According to the piece, her old neighborhood was now ranked as one of the top ten cities in the world to visit. There was amazing history, scenery, and shopping—the new religion.

Having finished the article and her mid-morning coffee, Popsy set about getting sorted for her family lunch. There was no time to dawdle over the Sunday paper, she decided. She had her family coming to visit.

Popsy knew that today's lunch was meant to mark her birthday, but Wednesday was Halloween, so she decided to give it a seasonal theme, too. She had pumpkins for outside the door and a friendly looking scarecrow for the center of the garden. She tried to convince herself she'd bought all these decorations for Natasha, but the truth was that she loved tinkering around in the yard, and any excuse was good enough to get out and decorate.

Popsy had bought bales of hay for the front steps to give it a sort of harvest festival feel. On top of these, she placed a second scarecrow, this time a girlie one in a pink checked shirt and blue denim dungarees. Beside her she placed a very realistic-looking toy crow. Standing back a few yards, she was delighted with the result. It looked like a stage setting for *Fiddler on The Roof*. She giggled. It was all very country, very fall, a little over-the-top, and definitely not anywhere near as stylish as Jenny Lennox's exquisite pyracantha urns.

"Oh, what the heck," she said. She dressed the entire yard with her darling granddaughter in mind. It would make a perfect Halloween play area for her, Popsy decided, utterly contented.

Lunch was an ambitious affair: beef wellington, roast potatoes, red cabbage in a sweet balsamic vinegar reduction, and pumpkin pie with whipped cream for dessert. Her family wouldn't like that she'd gone to so much trouble, but her excuse was that she had all the time in the world. Unlike Rosie, she didn't have to run after little people anymore and, of course, Lily worked so hard.

No, Popsy's life was much easier and a good deal more pleasant, yet Jack's words still haunted her. While she'd been perplexed the previous night, now she was just plain annoyed.

"Why the hell do I need to watch my back?" she asked their black cat, Tiger. "My life is fine." Tiger purred in agreement.

The cat always agreed with her. It was gratifying. She'd wanted to call the little black cat Jade, but Peter pushed for Tiger, even though the cat had no stripes and was female. Peter said he'd made his money in tiger markets and that a cat called Tiger would bring them luck. So far, so good.

She looked great in the center of the Halloween decorations at the front door, but she point-blank refused to stay there. Popsy forced Jack's comments out of her head again, gritted her teeth, and focused on setting the lunch table.

Rosie and her little family were the first to arrive. As hoped, the bales of hay and scarecrows were a big hit with her granddaughter. Natasha insisted on staying outside and playing with everything.

Rosie tried to argue. "She'll ruin your display."

"I made it for her. If she ruins it, so what," Popsy said, walking from the front door and back into the kitchen with her daughter and son-in-law. "So, tell me, what's new with you guys?"

She looked from Rosie to Marcus. He was a fine-looking man even though he was getting a little light on top. He stood about six-foot-four, and it was pretty clear why her daughter had fallen for him. Doubtless he was still popular among the flight crew, but now he was a married man. Before they had a chance to talk, Natasha was back and pulling her father by the hand.

"Daddy, come with me," she insisted.

"We can catch up later." Popsy smiled and shoved a bottle of beer in his hand. Then he went out to chaperone his little girl in the front garden.

"Don't let her run out onto Cliff Road," Popsy chanted out of habit.

"Mom, do you really think he would let her do that?" Rosie asked.

"Sorry, it's a mother's job to worry, and you know grandmothers worry even more. They've seen more things go wrong."

"Oh?" Rosie sounded intrigued as she poured herself a glass of wine. "Is something wrong?"

Popsy stopped short. "I don't know."

She was pretty certain there was trouble with Jack and Sandra, but perhaps it was normal. Every couple went through difficult phases. That was only natural, and as for Peter's business deals, well, the downturn was hurting everybody. No business was immune. If the road got a little bumpy, they could ride it out together. They'd come this far.

Popsy noticed that Rosie was looking at her with a slightly worried expression, so she snapped out of her daydream and smiled. "No, nothing to worry about, darling." She focused on her firstborn. "What about you?" she asked. "I know there was something on your mind the last time you were here, and I couldn't really stop. Sorry about that. Will you tell me now?"

Rosie sighed and moved from leaning against the table to leaning against the counter.

"Mom, I wouldn't ask you if I had any other choice, but Marcus and I really need to get away. We need some time to ourselves without Natasha."

Popsy nodded.

"The problem is, there's nobody I really trust to watch her—other than you."

Popsy smiled, understanding what was being asked of her. "I'm more than happy to do it."

"But she's an inordinate amount of work, Mom."

"Nothing I haven't done before." Popsy laughed and crossed the room to hug her daughter. "I can think of nothing I'd like more, pet. I've been waiting five years to be asked. I love the idea of having Natasha all to myself for a whole week. Oh my! Matilda will love the addition to the family. You know it must be dull just cleaning up after Dad and me all the time. She would grab the chance to play with a little girl for a week or so. I can't imagine why we didn't think of this sooner. When do you want to go?"

"Oh, Mom, really? You're sure it's not too much?"

"Too much? Rosie, I swear to you, one of the thrills of becoming a grandmother is the chance to mind babies again, but the best part is that I get to give them back before it becomes monotonous."

They laughed as they hugged. "Thanks so much, Mom. You have no idea what this means to me."

"Where do you think you'll go?" Popsy's question was innocent enough. But it seemed to catch Rosie off guard.

"Um, somewhere in the Caribbean. We want to be guaranteed good weather, and it's always sunny down there."

"Of course," Popsy agreed, but she saw her daughter's face and she knew the girl was hiding something. Why ever would Rosie look so guilty over a silly old vacation?

Popsy shook herself. She decided she was definitely getting paranoid, seeing things where there was nothing to be seen. First Jack and now Rosie. Pity, because her intuition used to be razor-sharp, and now she was losing her edge. Must be something to do with getting old, she decided as she set about whipping the cream.

"Here comes Auntie Lily." Natasha rushed into the kitchen, pink-cheeked and runny-nosed from the chilly October air. She must have been jumping on the bales of hay, because twigs of straw were shoved in her coat pocket like a not-so-secret stash. Marcus walked behind his little daughter with his arm draped around his sister-in-law's shoulder.

"Hello, honey." Popsy came over and kissed Lily. "Now that I have my two babies with me, I'm happy." She sighed with maternal contentment. "I simply couldn't ask for a better birthday present."

Rosie glanced at her sister and raised a glass as if to say hi. Lily gave a slight nod back.

"Come see Grandma's scarecrows, Mommy," Natasha demanded.

Marcus and Rosie were dragged out to admire the Halloween decor by their very determined little girl, which left her alone with Lily.

"So how've you been?" Popsy started as she always did with her youngest. She worried that Lily worked too hard and didn't have a serious man in her life. It was time she thought about settling down and providing her with a few grandchildren.

Lily gave her a bright smile. "I'm great. Happy Birthday, Mom." She handed Popsy a birthday card with a small bag attached that was clearly a Macy's gift card. "I hope you don't think it's too impersonal. It's just I don't know what to get the woman who has everything."

"That was most thoughtful of you, honey," Popsy said. "I will have great fun with it. Perhaps we can have lunch together there and you could help me spend it. Now pour yourself a glass of wine and fill me in on all your news."

As usual, Lily's life was all about the office and her job. Popsy knew that her daughter had stopped telling her about the friends that were getting married and having babies. It worried her. She checked the beef wellington and stirred the red cabbage, re-basted the roast potatoes, and listened to her beautiful, clever daughter tell her about Boston's financial world. Two o'clock came and went with her daughters, granddaughter, and son-in-law all filling her in on their lives, but there was still no sign of Peter.

"What the heck is taking your dad so long?"

"I'll call him and get him moving," Lily said and headed out.

Rosie had returned and hovered around the stove, nursing her second glass of wine and picking at the red cabbage.

Natasha came running into the kitchen again. "Grandma, Auntie Lily has a new boyfriend!"

Rosie dropped a piece of red cabbage onto her cream silk sweater as she jerked her head around.

"Nat," she squealed. "No. Oh shit—my top."

"Rosie, what have you done?" Popsy laughed anxiously. "Red cabbage? That will never come out." She shook her head and looked back at her granddaughter. "Why do you think Lily has a new boyfriend, darling?"

"Natasha!" Rosie tried again. "Come here and help Mommy. Get a towel, quick."

Natasha skipped over to her mother, obviously delighted to be asked to help with a real emergency.

" 'Cause I saw her kissing Uncle Jack. He's her new boyfriend," Natasha explained as she ran over to Popsy. "Can I have a towel please?"

Popsy laughed. "Of course, pet." She wet a towel and handed it to her. "Children, they have such wonderful imaginations, don't they?" she asked. "Honey, I'm afraid red cabbage stains just don't come out. I think your top is ruined."

Rosie was panicking loudly now. "I loved this top," she whined as she dabbed it with the cloth Natasha had given her.

Lily walked back in. "Dad's on his way." She smiled. Then she saw Rosie's anguished face and stained sweater. "What happened?"

"I got red cabbage on myself." Rosie moaned. "Look at it, Mom. Help."

Popsy ignored her eldest's overreaction and focused instead on Lily. It was too funny. "I was just hearing about your torrid affair with Uncle Jack, but then Rosie spilled red cabbage on herself."

Lily looked at her older sister incredulously and shook her head, bewildered. "You told her? Why the hell would you do that? What possible benefit could it bring to you? Honestly, Rosie, just because your life is going down the toilet, there's no point in dragging me down with you." Then she flashed her mother a furious look. "Yes, well, did she tell you that she and Marcus are going to a swingers' resort in the Caribbean?"

Rosie screeched, "Lily. Stop."

Popsy wasn't following. "Oh, the Caribbean? I know about that, but what are the swingers?" She looked at Rosie. "Are you taking up golf, love?"

Rosie slapped her forehead just as Marcus walked into the kitchen. "Peter's home and Jack's with him. Are the Hoffmans coming for lunch, too?"

Now it was Lily's turn to squeal, and she ran out of the room.

"We're in here," Popsy called from the kitchen, still confused about Lily's outburst. Surely her daughter knew she was only joking about Jack. Still, it wasn't like her to be so hysterical without reason.

"Lily, don't go far," she shouted after her. "I'll serve up straight away." Peter and Jack walked into the kitchen.

"Jack." Popsy smiled. "You wouldn't believe what I just heard. It's so funny." She laughed but stopped when she saw the grave expression on his face.

"I think you better sit down, Popsy," he said. "In fact, everybody better sit down. We have some very bad news."

Marcus brought Natasha to the drawing room where he switched on the Disney Channel and promised her she could stay up late if she could give the grownups a few minutes to talk while Rosie went out to get her sister.

Popsy came over to her husband and saw his ashen face. "Darling, are you feeling all right? You look ill."

He didn't meet her eyes but shook his head. Gently she guided him to the large antique pine table that dominated the center of the kitchen, and he sat down. It was their first purchase as a married couple. Big enough to seat eight, it had been far too big for their first house, but Popsy had insisted. It was at this table she'd told Peter she was pregnant with Rosie and less than twelve months later that she was pregnant with Lily. Rosie and Marcus announced their engagement sitting at this table. To Popsy, it embodied the heart of the family. If her husband had some bad news for her, this was the place to hear it. The table was so heavy and solid that Popsy felt its support when she needed it. She was on one side of her husband and Jack, their lifelong friend and business partner, was on the other. Popsy knew that sitting there, she could weather whatever they were going to say.

"What's the matter, Peter?" she asked again without waiting for her daughters to return. This time he managed to look her in the eyes, but he looked lost, disconnected. Was this the same man who'd made love to her on the dining room floor just the night before? She was getting scared to see him so beaten. In all their years together, she'd never seen him like this.

Marcus hovered until the girls got back, and then they all sat down, too.

"Has there been an accident? Peter? Jack? Talk to me. You're really scaring me."

"It's all gone," Peter whispered.

"What's all gone?" Popsy asked.

"Our business. It's all gone down the tube. A lifetime's worth of work, wiped out by a few belligerent investors."

Popsy looked at Jack. "What is he saying? Is it the deal? Did it not go through?" She felt her own panic rising. "But it's not the end of the world, is it? There'll be other deals."

But Jack shook his head. "That was our last hope. We've bet the farm once too often. We're finished. Broke. Over."

Lily frowned. "What deal was this?"

"We'd been trying to sell a majority share of C&J Holdings. It was the only way to save the company, and these guys from the UK—they were our last chance. They turned us down. We were offering them a sweet deal, but they just don't trust the global property markets anymore. They know it's at an all-time low, and think it will take decades to get a good return. They're off to Canada instead."

"Is C&J Holdings insolvent?" Lily asked.

Her father laughed. "Insolvent, in the doghouse, in the brown stuff. Call it what you want. It's gone. We'll have to file for Chapter 11 tomorrow."

Rosie touched Peter's hand. "Dad, I'm really sorry to hear that, but you still have this fabulous house and the one in Florida. You have stocks and shares and loads of money in the bank."

He shook his head. "I'm not so sure about that. I've used the equity in this house. The bank owns it now."

"But this is your home. Surely it could never be taken away from you."

Again, he shook his head. "This building is in the loop. I used it to cross-guarantee things a few years ago. Back then it seemed like perfect business sense. Jack thought so, too."

"Jeez, your penthouse in The Celtic Crowne? You're going to lose that?" Marcus asked, articulating what the others were thinking anyway. Jack looked like his business partner—shell shocked—almost immune to what was being discussed.

"My home?" Popsy whispered. "This house? It's not ours?' She said the words, but the meaning wouldn't compute. This was just too big to comprehend. "I'm going to lose everything? But this is my home. These are my things. I bought everything you see here, even the paint on the walls. It's all mine." She was holding the table so hard that her knuckles were white with the effort.

Rosie's eyes filled with tears. "Oh dear God."

Lily focused on her father. "What were you saying about the banks, Dad? Have they threatened to do anything? Wouldn't that take weeks, even months?"

Popsy watched Peter cover his face with his hands. Had he started to cry? It was looking like this had been coming down the track for some time. Jack glanced at Lily with a look of anguish. It was like she was living in a dream and everything was happening in a fog.

She heard a hiss from behind her and realized with little interest that she was burning the cabbage. She went and took the pan off the heat, but it was futile. The red cabbage had become a hard lump of purple charcoal. In a slight haze, she remembered Rosie's cream sweater and looked over to see if the stain was still there. If it wasn't, then this was all a nightmare and not real at all. But the red mark was still there. She looked from her eldest daughter to her youngest daughter and then from Peter to his business partner—or was that *ex*-partner?

"Jack?" she asked. "Are you having an affair with Lily?"

Lily jumped to her feet and squealed again, much like she had a little earlier. "Mom!"

Jack said nothing but his eyes flashed toward Lily. The shock and sadness he had shown about the business vaporized with that one simple question. Suddenly he looked even more serious, and guilty as sin. He glanced at

Popsy and then at Peter. His jaw stiffened as he clenched his teeth together like he was preparing to fight. Popsy recognized the look, and so did Peter, apparently.

"What the hell?" he asked, swinging around. "Jesus, Jack. I had an idea that you were playing offside, but with my daughter?" He jumped to his feet and kicked the heavy kitchen chair back violently. "I trusted you! Damn it, you're like a father to these girls. Of all the fu—"

He lunged for Jack and tried to grab him by the collar but instead Peter fell, full force and at an awkward angle on top of him. Jack pulled away and Peter fell to the floor—hard and lifeless.

Popsy shouted, "Peter, what are you doing?"

Marcus, who had moved toward the men instinctively, now rushed to Peter's limp body on the kitchen floor. "Oh God, he's collapsed."

"Somebody call 911," Lily screamed, but Marcus already had his cell phone out.

"Daddy!" Rosie cried. "Hurry, Marcus."

Chapter 9

Hospital

Popsy sat in a daze outside the ICU with Rosie. All they knew was that Peter had suffered a mild heart attack, he would be kept in ICU for observation overnight, and they'd been told to wait outside Intensive Care until he was settled.

"For a day that started out with such promise, I must say, this is a bit of a letdown," she said, her voice dripping with misery and sarcasm.

"Oh, Mom." Rosie bent down so she could hug her mother yet again. "It's been crazy. Let's just get Dad straightened out this evening and then we'll worry about everything else."

Popsy let her eyes close and her head loll back against the back of the chair. "Did you know?"

"About what?"

"The other things." Popsy opened her eyes again and looked at her eldest.

"Well, obviously I had no idea about Dad's bombshell. I didn't even know his business was in trouble. I thought he was weathering the recession pretty well." She avoided mentioning Lily as she plonked down onto the seat beside her mom's.

"I'm not talking about the business problems," Popsy said impatiently. "I'm talking about your sister. Did you know about Lily and Jack? God, I can't believe I'm even saying this."

Rosie felt enormous guilt. "I only found out yesterday—last night, to be exact. Believe me, it came as a hell of a shock to me, too. Natasha and I went to visit Lily, and we bumped into Jack."

"Even Natasha knew about it?" Popsy groaned.

"Mom, I don't really think Natasha has any idea what she does or doesn't know. She did see the two of them arm-in-arm, but I'm pretty sure I could have explained to her that they were just kissing goodbye if Lily hadn't gone off the deep end this evening."

Popsy spun around. "Gone off the deep end? You think she should have kept it all as her sordid little secret? Are you condoning this behavior?"

"What? No." Now Rosie was defending herself. "How do you figure that? I'm just trying to rationalize the evening. I don't think anything. I'm as stunned as you." She saw her mother cool a little, so she tentatively added, "But I don't think Lily would have wanted it to come out like this."

"And just how the heck do you think it should have come out? Lily is sleeping with your father's best friend. Damn it, Sandra is *my* best friend. Jack is her godfather for Christ's sake."

"Um, no, he's my godfather."

"You know what I darn well mean. He's *a* godfather in our house. Lily's done so much damage. She may even kill her father before she's finished. The shock is what pushed him over the edge tonight."

"Now hold on there a minute. Dad is a tough old boot. I know he was trying to go after Uncle Jack, but it's pretty fair to say that the business had his heart under a lot of strain, too. You don't blame Lily for Dad's heart attack, do you?"

Popsy stayed silent for a moment. Rosie knew that she was maybe thinking about blaming her younger daughter.

"Lily is miserable about what happened tonight. I know she is. She's called me seven times already."

"Good. Stupid, stupid girl. Of all the men on the planet, why Jack? Why so close to home?"

Rosie shrugged. "Damned if I know."

They fell into a strained silence. They could talk all night, but there was no rationalizing Lily's behavior. Who knew where it would all lead.

"This might not be the best time to take up golf," Popsy said at last.

"What?" For a moment Rosie was confused.

"Golf. Isn't that what Natasha, or was it Lily, was talking about? Isn't that why you're going off to the Caribbean?"

"Oh that? Um, yes, wouldn't it be fun to take up golf, Mom? Marcus thinks he's a great golfer. A lot of the pilots play on their days off, and if he's doing it, then so am I. Why do you think it's not such a good idea?"

"Well, it's a very time-consuming sport, and if you have a child, it's difficult to be away for a full day. Even harder if you had two children, I'd guess." She looked at her daughter with a sideways glance and Rosie understood.

She laughed at her mother. "Not an issue, Mom. We're not even trying. Natasha is a full-time job for me." As she said it, she realized that her mother looked like she was going to cry.

"Well, you're going to have to get to it and give me a few more grandchildren because Lily certainly won't anytime soon. Jack is dead-set against having more kids. What is Lily doing with an old rat like him, anyway?"

Rosie took her mother's hand. "Don't go there, Mom. We have bigger things to worry about right now. Lily is being stupid, but it's not the end of her life. We'll talk sense into her—you and I—over the next few weeks." She forced a smile and squeezed her mother's fingers reassuringly.

Popsy nodded and pursed her lips together.

"But, you have to try to stay calm. Your job is to stay strong and healthy. We need to get Dad well and then figure out just how bad his business situation is, and then we'll think about Lily. Okay?"

Popsy gave her a weak smile. "Where would I be without you, darling?" She stroked Rosie's hair like she used to when she was little. "Thank you for being so strong and focused. You're right. We'll worry about all of that later."

As the young, and not unattractive, doctor approached them, Popsy jumped to her feet. "What news?"

He smiled sympathetically at both women then focused on Popsy. "As you were told, Mrs. Power, your husband has had a mild heart attack. What I can tell you is that he's now stable and all of his vitals are good. The best thing you can do for him is to go home and get some rest. He'll sleep all night, and you'll be able to visit him in the morning." He glanced back at the ICU doors.

"Can't I see him now?" Popsy pleaded.

Rosie flanked her mother. "We just want to say goodnight," she said. "We won't try to wake him or anything."

"Please, doctor," Popsy asked with tears in her eyes.

The doctor seemed to weigh the situation. "You're his wife so you can go in alone. But only a minute. It's late, and there are other patients in there. Don't attempt to talk to him or even touch him. Don't do anything to disturb him. Just have a quick look to appease yourself and come back out."

She nodded.

Then he looked at Rosie. "You'll have to wait till tomorrow. This is Intensive Care. If he's moved to a private room then, which I hope he will be, you'll be able to see him a lot more."

Rosie had no fight left as she watched her mother head out with the doctor.

She fell back into her armchair. There was just so much to take in. She couldn't quite comprehend what the failure of her father's business would mean to her. Was it really going to include the house? Would it impact her life? God forbid.

Would her parents need to stay with her? That really would be a disaster. Small chance of them shacking up in Lily's apartment after tonight's debacle. Rosie phoned her husband. It was late, but she figured he was waiting for an update.

He answered on the first ring. "Hey, how are you? Thanks for the text. Any more news?"

His concern made her feel better. "Hi, honey. Nothing new, just a lot of waiting. Dad's stable. He's in the ICU and Mom just went in to see him."

"Oh God, is he going to be okay?"

Rosie thought she might cry, so she tried to be strong. "Yes, he's stable now. If all goes well, he should move into a private room tomorrow. That's one step down the danger zone from ICU, I guess. They have to run a battery of tests before he's let out, but he seems to be okay. What about you? What happened after we left? Where are you now?"

Rosie heard Marcus heave an enormous sigh. "Jeez, what a day. I guess you saw Lily in tears before you left. She was crying and saying this was all her fault and then Jack started to comfort her. Gotta tell you, honey, it was really weird seeing them together. I'm so used to thinking of him as your uncle."

"What do you mean?" she whispered. "Are you saying they're openly affectionate now?"

"Well, he was hugging her, and yeah, I guess he was holding her in a fairly non-uncle kind of way. He just kept telling her that it would be okay, and he would take care of her. Rosie, he's way too old for her, and what about Sandra?"

"I don't think she knows yet, but I agree with you that he's too old. Lily will be twenty-eight in December. What is he? Mid-fifties? You do the math, but it's not pretty."

"No, it's not. They left together but not before she left about a hundred messages on your cell. Did you call her yet?

"No, I wanted to talk to you first."

"Thanks, babe. Nat and I are fine. She fell asleep in the drawing room."

"You're still at Mom and Dad's?"

"I didn't want to leave because I figured your mom would be coming home at some stage and I didn't think it was a good idea for her to return to an empty house."

Rosie's heart skipped a beat. "You're my hero. Thanks, and you're so right. I hope I can convince her to come home soon because it's been a day and the doctor says there's nothing we can do here. We might be there in about an hour, if I'm lucky."

"We could all stay with your mom tonight if you'd like," Marcus offered. "I don't fly again until Tuesday. It might be nice to stay here with her—just so she has people around."

"Marcus, have I told you lately that I love you?"

"I love you, too, even if it turns out that you're broke."

"I know. Scary, isn't it? Who knows how that will all unravel."

"Time will tell, babe. By the way, Matilda got back here about an hour ago, so I had to tell her. I guess she was going to help with the cleanup. I hope that's okay."

"I guess so. How did she take it?"

"She kinda lost it. Crying and banging her head with her fists. It was a bit awkward, so I gave her a glass of sherry and she calmed down a little. I told her Peter was going to be fine and that seemed to do the trick. Now she's done a total blitz on this place. It's spotless. I wonder if she would come and live with us."

"I know, she's amazing, isn't she? But she's very comfortable with them. I don't think you'd ever get her to move. I never thought of telling her. Glad she's okay, though. Look, I gotta go. I think I should call Lily before Mom gets back."

"Brave woman. Good luck with that. See you soon." She hung up feeling better about her own marriage than she had in months. Ironic that a good old-fashioned crisis would bring them closer together, she thought as she dialed her sister.

"Is he okay?" Lily asked, sounding half-crazed.

"Shhh, he's fine. Calm down, Lily. Look, I'll have to hang up when Mom comes back. She would be furious if she knew I was talking to you."

"I know. I'm so sorry. You see, I thought you told her."

"I guessed that, but we had a deal," Rosie said, relieved at last to talk to her sister and explain what actually happened.

"I know. I was just so freaked out I wasn't thinking straight, and when I heard Mom, well, I just assumed—stupidly. Sorry."

"Chill. How would you know? Damn it, how could either of us have known Natasha would understand what was going on? I'm sorry she blew your cover."

"For once I'm regretting how sharp my niece is."

"I was trying to distract everybody with my stupid red cabbage fiasco."

"What happened?"

"I spilled the juice on myself when I heard Nat start to talk about you and, um, Jack. And then when you walked in. I tried to distract you, but I couldn't get you to listen to me."

"I should have known better. I was just so darn nervous. Now, tell me about Dad."

"He's okay. He's out of danger. Mom is with him in ICU."

"ICU?" There was renewed panic in Lily's voice.

"It's just a precaution. He'll be moved to his own room tomorrow. He's going to be fine. Talk to me. Is Jack going to tell Sandra?"

"He says he has to. Now that Mom and Dad know, the cat is well and truly out of the bag. He's going over there now to tell her, and he's going to leave her."

"Oh God, Lily, what have you done?"

"What have I done? We love each other. We want to be together."

"Yes, but at what cost? You're breaking up his marriage. Have you thought about that? Are you sure you want to go this way. Can you live with the guilt?"

"It's simpler than that. I just can't live without him. Whatever pain I cause along the way, I can't help."

"How convenient for you." Her sister was disclaiming all responsibility for a situation that was of her own making. "I suppose you can't help the fact that Mom will lose her best friend, and Dad, too, at a time when they're going to really need them."

"Rosie, you don't understand."

"Oh, I think I do. I understand perfectly. Now if you'll excuse me, Mom is coming back and I don't want to get caught talking to you." She ended the call without giving her sister a chance to respond, even though her mother was nowhere in sight.

Popsy was standing at the foot of Peter's bed. Her husband had never looked so frail or old. He was only fifty-two, but he looked eighty-two. What a toll life had taken on him. It shocked and terrified her how much humans relied on, yet took for granted, their hearts.

Peter's attack wasn't even that big, yet you'd think he'd gone through twelve rounds with Mike Tyson. He looked like half the man he was just the day before. Of course, being in a bed surrounded by life support equipment didn't help. She was relieved to see that he wasn't using most of the machines around him. There was one that looked like it might breathe for the patient and another that just looked like a computer to her, but the machines that made sense were those wired up to his heart—his dear and ever-so-precious heart.

Popsy vowed that if they got out of this mess, she was going to take him away from all the pressure and stress of his executive life and find the simpler pleasures. It couldn't be that hard to find a small bar on a beach somewhere. They'd run away to some idyllic tropical island and work in a bar together.

The girls were old enough to fend for themselves. Well, she wasn't sure about Lily anymore, but at least she had a good job. Besides, it was time she stood on her own two feet. She desperately wanted to touch him—just to stroke his face to let him know she was there, that she loved him, and that she didn't care about the money, but the doctor was hovering at the nurses' station and keeping a very close eye on her. She would have to wait until tomorrow.

Popsy had no idea what she was going to do about her younger daughter and the fallout from that the situation. It was going to kill her friendship with Sandra. Of that there was little doubt, and that saddened Popsy enormously. They'd become firm friends, but she didn't think any friendship would survive this level of betrayal. It wasn't even Popsy who'd betrayed her, but it would be guilt by association. The future really didn't look bright, but one thing she was absolutely certain about was that Sandra had to be told.

Chapter 10
Jack and Sandra and Sven

Sandra's day had turned out much better than she'd expected. She felt energized and upbeat by the time she was leaving the hotel fitness center some hours later. As usual, going to the gym had cleared her mind.

Her ego boost was even better than her endorphin rush because a certain German resident of the hotel had proved to be a very pleasant distraction while she worked out. She'd noticed him as soon as she walked into the gym.

There was often a scattering of good looking men in the place because it was the fit guys who worked out. The unhealthy men were in the bar. Sandra never did anything about it, of course, but still, it didn't hurt to look, and the gym always had plenty of eye candy.

That morning, as luck would have it, the only treadmill available was the one next to a very attractive, tall, well-built blond gentleman. He was running, and she could see that he had a long, even stride. His breathing was steady, so he had to be in good shape, but she didn't want to get caught staring, so she looked away.

In front of each machine was a small television monitor with about a hundred channels. And in front of that, a floor to ceiling mirror. This was helpful if you were on the weight machines because the trainers had taught her to watch her form to ensure she was working out properly. To a lesser extent, the wall of mirrors was handy on the treadmills, too, because it gave

Sandra ample opportunity to scope out the guy beside her.

She started with a fast walk just to warm up, but soon she was running and matching his pace. It felt good to run in rhythm. While they'd made no eye contact, nor had they spoken, running with the same stride was a sort of communication—a bonding. It felt nice, like they were partners.

Sandra decided to have some fun. She upped her speed a little, moving faster, and then they were out of rhythmic beat. As she'd hoped, he glanced in her direction and then he moved his pace up to hers. They ran in harmony for another few minutes but for her own amusement, Sandra did it again. It was tough physically, but a pleasant distraction. He rose to her challenge again.

By the third time she'd increased her speed, Sandra knew she wouldn't last long. At a flat-out run of nine miles an hour, she was sprinting hard and he had the advantage of longer legs. Chances were this was a game he would win. He matched her fastest speed, but then something happened and he hit the emergency stop button. He didn't quite fall, but he jumped off the treadmill and stood back as it slowed down. It was a vigorous enough move for her to hit her stop button, too.

"Are you okay?" she asked as her machine slowed.

He had his hands on his knees and was hyperventilating as he tried to catch his breath. Then he looked up at her and smiled. It was a nice smile. His face was square and strong with searing blue eyes, and he had a good tan even in October.

"I'm fine thanks. I thought I was going to fall, so I hit the stop button." He laughed. "The truth is I was trying to keep up with you, and I couldn't. I'm not that good." He had a rich German accent—warm and deep—but he seemed fluent in English. That was good because she didn't know German. He shrugged and stood.

Now, given the chance to see him face-to-face, Sandra reckoned he was athletic enough for her—if she was looking, which of course she wasn't. But oh, what beautiful babies he would make.

Only twenty minutes into her run, she had a soft sheen of sweat on her skin. She wiped her face dry. "I'm sorry if I distracted you," she said, flirting. "But if you're not hurt, I'd better get back to my run before I cool down again."

He waved her on. "Oh yes, you go on. You're hot."

She did a double-take to see if it was a German-English translation thing or if he was flirting. He gave her a mischievous grin. She decided he knew exactly what he was saying.

Sandra plugged her headphones back into her ears, powered up the music on her iPod, and got back to running at full speed. She could see from the mirrors that he hadn't gone too far. He was over at the free weights. She figured their paths might cross again.

Sandra didn't think that she was doing anything wrong. A mild flirt was good for a woman. She wouldn't do anything about it, and he was probably married anyway. He looked about forty. Yep, too handsome to be single. Or maybe he was gay. It seemed like all the best-looking guys were these days. Either way, he kept himself in really good shape.

While the running kept her thin, it was the weights that gave Sandra her toned figure. She was a pro on the resistance training machines. Most women stayed away from them for fear of bulking up, but Sandra knew that was stupid. She just kept the resistance low and the reps high, and now she had the biceps of a twenty-year-old. Even her bottom was still tight and high thanks to thousands of lunges. They were painful but effective and "better than Botox in the buttocks," she'd often say to Popsy, who didn't like to break a sweat.

Mr. Atlas from Germany was on one of the machines she wanted, but Sandra didn't want to hover while he worked, so she decided to use the machine beside him which exercised almost the same set of muscles anyway. Looking at her reflection as she worked out, Sandra couldn't help but be happy with her boob job, which was shown off to particularly good effect as she worked her biceps, triceps, deltoids, and pecs.

"Are you staying in the hotel?" he asked when he'd finished with his weights.

She was still working out and was a little out of breath. She shook her head. "I live here. You?"

"I arrived today. I'm here for a week on business."

"What line of business are you in?" She disengaged from the machine, unable to flirt properly while working so hard.

"I'm a doctor. It's a medical conference connected to the Leahy Clinic."

"Ah, nice. Does that mean the hotel will be overrun with doctors for the week? I guess all their wives will be in here, too."

He smiled and gave her a look that Sandra recognized—game on. "No wives on this trip."

"She'll miss you at home, I'm sure. Where is home?"

He laughed and threw his head back, clearly enjoying her full-on flirt. "I'm German, but my home is now in Ireland."

"Oh, I was just reading about Dublin this morning."

He nodded. "I saw it, too. In *The Boston Globe*. It's a great city. You should come to visit some time."

Sandra laughed. "Doesn't your wife mind you inviting strange women to your adopted home?"

"She might." He looked like he was thinking about it. "If she existed." Then he smiled. "I'm not married."

She couldn't believe it. How in heaven did a doctor this good-looking get away without being snatched up?

"Seeing as I am all alone in your beautiful town, perhaps you could show me some of the sights. I understand Wellesley has many charms."

Sandra thought of Jack and laughed. "I would love to show you around, but I'm afraid my husband might not be too impressed if I went off with a rather attractive German doctor whose name I don't even know."

He stretched out his hand, gracious in defeat. "My name is Sven Richter." His German accent was even more pronounced when he said his name— deeper, sexier. "My regards to your husband. He is a very lucky man. And your name?"

She took his hand and gave him a firm shake. "I'm Sandra Hoffman. Lovely to meet you, Sven, and I have a feeling you'll have a very nice time here. The locals will be very welcoming to you, I think." She risked a wink.

He was so handsome and built like a Marine—utterly gorgeous. If she were single, what a different story this would be.

Innocent flirting was underrated as a sport, she decided as she got back to her penthouse. First thing, Sandra checked her cell for messages because everybody knew she didn't take her phone to the gym. The evening before Jack had said he would probably be back from the office by lunchtime. The meeting was supposed to finish around then.

There was a message from him saying that the morning hadn't been great, and he wouldn't be home until mid-afternoon. She should have lunch without him.

"Oh, Jack. On a Sunday? Seriously?" She spoke into her phone even though he wasn't there.

He sounded strained and tired. If only he went to the gym more and the office less, then just maybe he could have some of Sven's vitality and rather attractive brand of energy. Her husband told her he'd started using a trendy new gym in Boston, but she didn't think he went too often.

Sandra had a long, luxuriant shower, and she took the time to use a deep conditioning treatment on her hair. The warm color shone with a healthy gleam when she did this, and she liked the pampering. With all the time in the world, she didn't rush drying her hair straight and then she clipped it up in soft rings so she could cover herself in vanilla and elderberry body moisturizer. Even though the weather was clear outside, the temperature had taken a dip, so Sandra chose a pair of black lamb's wool loose pants to slip into. She paired this with a fitted black cashmere turtleneck sweater and charcoal Uggs.

She felt totally snug and satisfied as she hit the switch for the gas fireplace. It flared to life, throwing tongues of blue and white flames six inches up behind its glass wall casing. She found the remote control to the built-in sound system where she'd left it the night before and switched that on, too.

The air was filled with U2's "Beautiful." Sandra sang along and it made her think about her plans to visit Dublin. She got on the computer and chose the best package she could find for herself and Popsy. It would be better to present it as a bought and paid for gift, but she did take the precaution of being able to change the dates just in case Popsy had other plans. Sandra decided that February would be a good time to visit Ireland, and with luck the weather would be better than Boston's by then.

She wanted to tell her best friend right away so she could clear her calendar, but she didn't want to phone in the middle of Popsy's birthday lunch. She decided to hold off until later in the day, and instead headed to the kitchen to think about lunch for one.

Sandra opened the fridge door looking for inspiration but found none. She just wasn't the cooking type. She thought about her and Popsy and how they often laughed about this. For two such good buddies, they really didn't have much in common.

Popsy loved to cook, Sandra didn't. Popsy was reserved and graceful; Sandra was a little wild and unashamedly outgoing. Popsy was devoted to her husband. Sandra was on the fence about her future with hers. She felt herself get a little emotional and decided to have a glass of champagne for lunch.

"Stop thinking like this," she said as Bono sang about going to another place. Then she remembered her plan to surprise Jack with a baby. Women had been doing it for centuries. That's what she would do.

Champagne in one hand and the Sunday paper in the other, she sat in front of her beautiful gas fire with the music for company and wondered if she would be able to seduce her husband when he got back from work later.

"You look like hell. It must have been a tough fight." Sandra laughed lightly when Jack walked into their home a little while later.

"Sandra, we need to talk."

"That sounds ominous," she said trying to cheer his apparently somber mood.

"Look. There's no easy way to say this, and I'm very sorry it's happened, but I've fallen in love with someone else."

Sandra didn't believe what she was hearing. It was a practical joke. She was the pretty, younger woman with the older man. If anyone was going to have an affair, it was supposed to be her. "What are you saying, Jack Boy?" She used her pet name for him while she grasped the soft wool upholstery on her criminally expensive sofa.

"I'm telling you the truth. I've fallen in love with another woman," he repeated. "I'm afraid it's out. What I mean is, it's been made public, so I wanted to tell you as soon as possible. I'm going to move out now and take some things with me. I'll come back in a couple of days to take the rest."

"What? That's it? You're just walking out? Just like that? Don't you think we should at least try to—oh, I don't know—talk? Do you even love me a little bit? Jack?"

"I do love you, Sandra, but this was just so overwhelming. I—we couldn't fight it."

"One question, Jack." Her voice was dangerously calm. "Just one question. How old is she?"

He shook his head by way of an answer.

"That young? Really? I'm guessing early thirties?" Sandra's voice was cold and angry now.

Jack didn't respond.

"What? Even younger? Jeez, not in her twenties? Is that even legal? You know, my brother said you'd do this. Fourteen years ago when we got engaged, he told me to be careful. If you did it once, you might do it again. And he was right." She stood and walked over to him. "You bastard. You fucking bastard."

She slapped him across the face with all her strength. He took it and stood his ground.

"All these years and you wouldn't let me have kids, and now, just as I begin to get a little old myself, what do you do? You trade me in for a kid? You bastard! I'm going to take you for everything you've got, and let's see if she still likes you when you're broke."

Jack met her glare. "I'm afraid there's more, Sandra. Please sit down."

"No, I fucking well won't. What in hell could you add to that crap that could make it any worse? No, wait a minute. Let me guess. Your new lover is a guy."

Jack rubbed his brow and looked tired. "Sandy, don't be silly."

"Silly? Me, silly?" She was shouting now. "I'm not the one screwing a teenager!"

"She's not a teenager."

"Oh, excuse me. Am I splitting hairs? Well, okay then. I'm not the one who feels the need to dip my wick into every post-pubescent bitch in heat that comes onto my horizon. Don't call me silly. You're the absolute asshole. You—"

"We've been wiped out!" he shouted.

She stopped her rant for a moment, not quite understanding this new development.

He brought his voice back down to a normal level. "Financially, I mean. Last Friday the banks told us they were calling in our loans. We got them to give us the weekend to come up with a rescue plan, and those Euro investors were our last hope, but it didn't work out. That's it. I'm ruined. I'll start again and I'll try to support you, but as of today, we're ruined." He looked like he might cry.

"Please, spare me the histrionics. If you think I'm going to believe that crap, you must really think I came down in the last shower of rain. But I'm the old one, remember? I know bullshit when I hear it, and I'm hearing a hell of a lot of it right now. Jack, I know you have funds off every shore in this country and quite a few in the Caribbean, too, and if you think you can tell me you're out of here with all our money—make that *my* money— you're sadly mistaken."

He raised his hands as if to say he was beaten. "Okay, okay, but at least I've told you the truth." He sighed. "But there's something else I need to tell you."

"Jesus, Mary, and sweet Saint Joseph! What more can you add to this?" Sandra desperately craved the cigarette she'd been denying herself for the fourteen years since Jack first told her he didn't like them.

"Peter Power had a heart attack a little while ago. Now, he's going to be all right. It was just a small turn. But the thing is—well, he was trying to hit me at the time because he'd just discovered that the woman I'm in love with is his daughter, Lily."

Sandra looked at him for a moment without blinking or moving. "Even Ben's mind didn't go that low." She wasn't sure if she was more angry or repulsed at her husband's words. "I don't know whether to hate you or pity you. Jesus! What incredible stupidity, what vanity, what utter immaturity . . ." She looked around her as if looking for help. "But I do know one thing, Jack Boy, my heart is a little stronger than Peter Power's," she said as she turned and picked up the immense Waterford glass vase that was resting on the table beside her.

It was full of water and late-blooming irises, making it a heavy weight. But with the supernatural strength she had at that moment, it felt feather-light as she threw it at her husband's head with enormous force.

He raised his arms to protect his skull, and it bounced off his forearm before hitting the ground. There, the prohibitively expensive jade glass lay smashed into several not-so-expensive pieces.

"You wanted a break?" She sneered at him as she wiped her forehead. "You got a break. Now get out of *my* house, you bastard!"

Chapter 11

Lily

Lily threw open her front door to welcome Jack home. "Come in, darling. How did it go?"

Things were happening so fast, probably too fast, but all she could really do was hang on and let the cards fall where they would. She'd had an appalling evening. In truth, a terrible twenty-four hours, and now she was totally wrung out. Ever since Rosie found out about Jack, Lily figured it was only a matter of time before the whole thing blew up.

Jack was a lot more sanguine. Of course, he had a lot more experience with this kind of thing. He'd already been through one divorce and knew what was involved. But this time it should be a good deal easier. There were no children involved. Sandra was incredibly strong, and Jack had insisted that he and his wife had been growing apart for years. The relationship was breaking up even if Lily hadn't been in the picture. This didn't help Lily right now, though. She'd seen the look of disapproval on Rosie's face the night before. She knew deep down that she was now "the other woman"—something Lily never thought she would be. Before it happened to her, she'd been very intolerant of such women. Now life had taught her to be less judgmental.

But by far the worst of all was her father's heart attack. Why now, of all times? If it was a week earlier or later, that would have been bad enough, but just at that moment? Was God punishing her already?

She'd never done anything bad in her entire life, and now her only sin was falling in love with a man in a bad marriage. The problem was that Jack was so connected to her family. Everybody thought they had a claim on him. Her father considered him his best friend and business partner. Her mother thought of him as her best friend's husband. Even her sister claimed Jack as her godfather. If people would just leave them alone to live in peace, things would be okay. But what about her father? When he did get better, which by all accounts he would, would he ever forgive her? Would he cut her out of his life? That would be a dreadful price to pay.

Lily and Jack had talked a great deal about how their relationship could move forward. The plan had been for Jack and Sandra to break up first and then slowly, he and Lily would bring their relationship out into the open. It would have been a whole lot smoother than what had actually happened, but there was no going back now.

That said, Lily had been getting impatient. They'd just celebrated what she called their "first anniversary." It was twelve months since they'd started their affair, and still Jack had made no moves toward leaving Sandra. He'd stopped sleeping with her, this much she knew, but Lily was getting just a little annoyed. Time was ticking by, and she was beginning to think about marriage and babies. She wasn't getting any younger. She'd decided that twenty-nine was a good age to get married, and that meant an engagement soon. Which would be a little difficult with Jack still married to someone else.

Last year had been the fastest of her life. A new gym had opened in Boston's financial district, and she'd gotten an invitation to try it out through her work. Naturally, she didn't know anybody at first, so it was quite a pleasant surprise to bump into Jack the second time she visited. She was surprised to see him at first because she knew there was an amazing gym in The Celtic Crowne Plaza, but Jack said he always preferred the newest game in town.

Lily had always loved Jack—in an uncle kind of way—but somehow in this new environment, their dynamic shifted slightly. She'd never thought of him as a man, but watching him exercise altered her perception.

Many months later, he explained that for him it was the same. At first he was appalled that he could think of her like that. He remembered her birth. He couldn't believe how one minute she was little Lily with platinum pigtails and dolls, and now all of a sudden she was this fully developed, drop-dead-gorgeous hedge fund manager.

In the beginning, as soon as they each privately realized how they felt, they both tried to ignore it. But it was as if fate was conspiring to get them together. They kept bumping into each other at the gym. Out of politeness, they would stop for a short chat, but with firm resolve, they both walked away.

Lily was the first to crack. She went to the gym at times when he was more likely to be there. If he didn't show, she hung around and did even longer stretches on the treadmill until he arrived.

He said he'd tried to avoid her after he realized he was developing strong feelings for her, but she'd wind up being there whenever he went.

Then one night, when the gym was almost empty, Lily told him that her muscles were sore and she was going to grab her swimsuit and sit in the hot tub for a while. She had earned it. She asked Jack to join her.

By the time they were in the hot tub, they had reached the point of no return. She made the first move. Jack was sitting on the plastic bench beside her. They were up to their chests in frothy bubbles, and Lily simply reached over and kissed him. She had been kissing him all her life but this time she kissed him like a woman—not a niece.

He wrapped his arms around her and kissed her with passion. Within minutes, it was clear they needed some privacy. Either that or they were going to get kicked out of the gym.

"Come back to my place," Lily had whispered.

"I can't. This is nuts," Jack said, but his conviction was feeble.

"Yes, it's nuts, but come back anyway." She jumped out of the water and ran for the locker room.

"Wait, come back, Lily. We have to talk."

She ignored him and left. At the time, Lily couldn't believe it was happening, but she was also thrilled that it was. She'd thrown her clothes on over her swimsuit and rushed out to her car. As she did, it occurred to her that Jack didn't know where she lived, so she scribbled her address down on a piece of paper and stuck it on his windshield. Then she went home and waited.

A half hour passed and then another. Lily began to panic. What if he didn't come? She was so fired up for him. The old Uncle Jack of her youth was gone.

Her parents had great taste in friends. He was an exciting, dynamic, good-looking man—okay, a few years older than her, but so what? He was a ten out of ten, and she wanted him.

In the time she was home, she managed to light the fire, throw a bottle of champagne in the fridge, and take a shower, but she was running out of steam. What could be taking him so long?

She thought about calling him but decided it was too desperate, so she paced the floor instead. At last her buzzer sounded, and she let him up. There was no way it would be anybody else at almost midnight. She also knew that the next door neighbors were away, so she felt perfectly safe opening the door to him, naked.

"Lily, we need to talk—" He looked up and saw her with nothing on but an inviting smile. "Oh dear Lord," he whispered as she took him by the hand and closed the door behind him. He really didn't have a chance.

She led him into the drawing room and slowly undressed him in front of the fire. They made long, slow love. He was patient with her and treated her like a china doll. He stroked and held her. He was gentle, watching her all the time to be sure he was doing what she wanted. She loved being cherished. Men her age were too fast and furious. Jack had years of experience.

And so their affair began. It was very physical for the first few months. The secrecy added an excitement that Lily loved, too. Dinner at her parents' house was always thrilling for her. She could see Jack's heightened sense of worry, and it gave her a feeling of power over the man that liked to dominate.

In the gym or anywhere else their paths crossed, Jack was very serious about keeping a distance between them, but she liked pinching his bottom when nobody was looking. It scared him, which excited her. He would try to chastise her when they were alone in her apartment, but she would seduce him and bring him close to tears with what he called her "perfect body."

She got everything she needed from Jack. She wanted a man with whom she felt safe and protected. He took care of her in a paternal way, but he also satisfied her in bed—and on the drawing room floor . . . and on the kitchen counter. Everywhere in her apartment, actually.

They'd even managed to get a couple of weekends away, which was bliss.

Jack had surprised her for her birthday the previous year with a weekend in New York. It was just before Christmas and the affair was still very new. He'd booked a suite in the Pierre Hotel. The luxury was at a level even Lily hadn't experienced before, though she'd led quite a charmed life in the Power home.

Jack spared no expense. He flew her in on a private leer jet and they were met by their personal driver who drove them to their hotel in a large black limo. She felt like a rock star or foreign dignitary. All they were missing were the little diplomatic flags on the front of the car. The hotel suite was exquisite, too. Overlooking a snow covered Central Park, it was much too big for two people who were going to spend their entire weekend in bed, anyway.

But, of course, they hadn't spent all their time in bed. The Turkish marble bathroom proved very pleasant, too, but New York was just too exciting and beautiful a city to ignore—especially at Christmas. Jack took Lily ice skating at the Rockefeller Center. Then they visited the observation deck and looked out over the entire city from seventy floors up.

He took her shopping in Tiffany's. It had only been a little awkward when the young assistant had asked them if they were buying a ring, which they weren't. Lily had settled on an ornate key made of platinum and set with brilliant teardrop diamonds. Jack also bought her the matching twenty-four inch platinum chain, studded with diamonds. That way she could wear it always but slip it under her clothes if Popsy or Sandra were near.

"The key to my heart," she'd told him.

"I like to think of it as the key to *my* heart, darling."

Their second secret weekend away hadn't been quite so perfect. Jack had business in the Czech Republic. It was a massive shopping plaza development just outside Prague that he and her father were investing in. Originally, Jack was supposed to go alone, so she'd been more than happy to tag along, but twenty-four hours into their weekend away, her father called and said he'd decided to come, after all.

This was a disaster. She had to hide in the bedroom for the rest of the weekend. Jack's mood plummeted because he was very stressed about the possibility of them bumping into each other in the hotel lobby. Meeting in the city so far from home would be impossible to explain. There was nothing they could do. Lily had to stay prisoner in their hotel room.

On the second night, her dad had suggested going with Jack to his room to discuss some business. Jack had panicked and said it was not a good idea because his room was a mess. Her dad had backed down without making a fuss, but Jack said it felt awkward. He must have suspected Jack had a woman with him, but he said nothing about it. Chances were that he wanted to remain clueless since their wives were so close.

Little did he know that it was his own flesh-and-blood hiding up in the room of a pretty basic hotel in Prague. Looking back on it now, Lily thought it was funny, but at the time, it had been a low point. The worst part was that she and Jack had flown there first class, but her dad expected to fly home with Jack, so this meant she had to stay an extra day and fly home alone.

She figured it was all part of being "the other woman."

At least it was all out in the open now, and she and Jack could walk the streets together and not live their entire lives in secret. Of course, there was still all the fallout to deal with, but she'd always known that was coming. It was just such a damn shame it got out the way it did. Still, it was a relief that her parents knew.

Jack was back from his soon to be ex-wife's house, looking pretty shaken, so now Sandra knew, too.

Lily had toyed with the notion of greeting him naked, just as she had done on that very first night, since this was a bit of a first, too. But somehow it seemed like a bad idea. Her father was in ICU, and Jack was probably feeling battle-weary after the showdown with Sandra. Perhaps a stiff drink was a better idea.

"You look shattered." She put an arm around his waist and walked him into the drawing room. A fire was blazing and the television was on.

"Jesus, that was tough." He sighed as he fell onto the sofa and gazed into space.

"She didn't take it well?"

"You could say that. I was half-thinking that we'd need to get you a bodyguard for the next few weeks, but then I remembered I can't afford it. Wow, Lily, she was angry. She really went for me." He showed her the big bruise beginning to form on the inside of his forearm.

"Jack, that's assault," Lily said, heading to the fridge for some crushed ice.

"Not really. She was in shock. She just lashed out, but I didn't have time to get any clothes."

"That doesn't matter. You have a mountain of stuff here." Lily came back with a clump of crushed ice wrapped up in a hand towel. She sat on the sofa next to him and gently pressed it onto his arm. Then she looked at his face. "You know, you've got a nick on your eyebrow, too. Was that from Sandra as well?"

"Yep. It's not too bad though, is it?"

She shook her head. "You're strong." She smiled at him and kissed the hurt eyebrow. "Are we going to be okay, Jack? It's just that Dad's in the hospital, there's this thing with Sandra, and now Rosie isn't really talking to me. I haven't dared to even try to talk to Mom. She might take Sandra's side over mine in this."

"No, she won't. You're her daughter."

"She might."

"Take it from me, as the father of three girls. Daughters always side with their mothers and vice-versa. It might be a little rough for a while, but you and your mom will survive this. Me and your father? Now that's a different story. Christ, I can't believe he's in ICU. What's the prognosis?"

Lily filled him in on what she knew, and he in turn gave her a blow-by-blow account of his visit with Sandra. It was an exhausting day and very late when they realized that neither of them had eaten since breakfast.

Lily fussed over Jack and his wounds much more than they needed, but the truth was that even though her relationship with her parents and sister was probably at an all-time low, in secret she was really happy. At last—at long last—she had Jack all to herself. He was living with her in her apartment. Yes, even though it was the darkest day in her family's life, it was the best possible day for her and Jack.

She made them both a mushroom and tomato omelet while Jack watched the late night news. Already Lily's mind had latched on to the idea of seducing him as soon as they'd eaten. He was always in a better mood after sex. It would soothe him and help him sleep better.

She chose one of his favorite bottles of red wine, a Bordeaux that was particularly full-bodied and heavy. Personally, she found it a little too robust, but tonight was about getting Jack back to happy. Armed with the food and the wine, she returned to the love of her life and soon-to-be, she hoped, husband.

He was reading an e-mail on his phone. "Oh crap. Olga knows." Jack groaned and pushed away the food.

"Your ex-wife knows about us?"

"I'm not talking about us." He sounded impatient. "C&J. How the hell did she get wind of it so fast? Sandra must have told her, that bitch."

She put the two untouched plates down and sat next to him. It was clear that while his love life was a little complicated, C&J Industries was his primary focus. Lily loved Jack, but she needed to remind herself that, just like her father, business came first and family second. C&J Industries was the great love of his life, and now it looked like it was dying.

Chapter 12

Rosie & Marcus

"It's good to see you guys." Marcus kissed Rosie and Popsy on their cheeks and shut the door behind them. He'd thought Matilda was sleeping, but she reappeared when she heard the front door.

"Oh, Mrs. Power, Mrs. Power. *Dios mio*. How is Mr. Power? He such a good man. He cannot die." She cupped Popsy's tired face in her well-worn hands.

There wasn't much of an age difference between the two women, but Matilda had looked and acted like a grandmother in all the time the Marcus had known her. His wife said she was a godsend, having come as an au pair from Colombia almost thirty years earlier. She arrived a week after Rosie did, and she'd just never left.

Matilda moved from being a nanny to housekeeper as the girls grew, but the only thing she absolutely refused to do was drive. Over time, Popsy and Peter had tried to convince her to get lessons at their expense, but she wasn't interested. She walked or taxied anywhere she wanted to go, and the train at the bottom of Cliff Road took her straight in to Boston. Matilda was a regular mass-goer and had a few friends in the Colombian community in Boston, but other than that, she stayed in the house.

The Powers had converted their guesthouse into Matilda's living quarters when Lily turned fifteen, and the housekeeper had lived there ever since. It had every comfort and convenience. Was it any wonder Matilda was so happy with them?

Popsy, on the other hand, considered herself the lucky one to have Matilda. Both women were happy with the arrangement.

To celebrate her tenth anniversary with the family, Peter had bought her a small house in Wellesley. He figured it was due after ten years of faithful service, but Matilda made it clear she had no intention of leaving them, then or ever. Peter said the house was a form of pension plan for her. This kind of generosity was typical of the Powers. Matilda had had it decorated and furnished to her liking, but she never rented it out. Popsy knew that young Colombian girls stayed there sometimes when they needed a little help. Matilda might sleep there on the weekends, but often as not she remained at Cliff Road.

Peter tried to talk to her about renting it out or taking out a mortgage on it so she could buy a second and maybe a third property, but she wasn't interested. It was her little piece of independence.

She didn't look very independent tonight, however, with her tear-stained face.

Even in her exhausted and depressed state, Popsy found the strength to soothe her. "It's okay, Matilda. It was a heart attack."

Matilda gasped and covered her face.

"Shhh, he's going to be okay. You know Peter. It would take more than one little heart attack to take him down." Popsy and Matilda walked back to the kitchen.

"Where did you put Natasha?" Rosie asked.

Marcus shrugged. "Matilda showed us to a room upstairs. I think it was yellow. She was sound asleep when we moved her, so she might be scared in the morning."

"That's my old room." Rosie smiled. "I bet Tilly did that on purpose," she said. He knew it was her old pet name for the nanny. Matilda was like a second mother to Lily and Rosie. "Oh, Marcus, what a horrible day."

"Let's try to get your mom to bed and then we can talk."

Popsy and Matilda were in the kitchen settled at the same table that Peter had been sitting at only a few hours earlier when he collapsed. Matilda was amazing. The only sign of the earlier party was the untouched pumpkin pie with a candle in it. Popsy tried to convince Matilda to have a slice.

In the end, all four of them sat down and had a cup of strong decaf tea and a large slice of pie.

"Natasha will be furious she missed the birthday pie," Rosie said as she chomped.

"She can have some for breakfast," Popsy said. "It's my birthday and these are extraneous circumstances."

"I think that's a great idea," Marcus said and smiled.

"Hey, Matilda, these guys are going to let us watch Natasha for a week. How about that?"

Matilda gasped and covered her face with her hands, only this time it was out of joy. "I am so happy."

Even after all this time, her English was pretty poor, but she was sharp as a pin and extremely astute.

"When you go?" Matilda asked.

Rosie turned to her husband for some guidance, but he smiled and shrugged. "Whenever she likes," he offered. "Flying isn't a problem for us because I get free flights every year. All we have to do is decide on a date and book it."

"Where will you go?"

Again, Marcus answered, "Wherever she likes."

Rosie watched Popsy and Matilda nod at each other. Her husband was saying all the right things. Even Rosie was touched. Maybe her father's heart attack had impacted her husband. He was clearly as shaken as the rest of them, and between that and the inevitable public scandal of C&J, he might shelve all his crazy party notions and start to cherish the woman he had at home. Rosie's mind flashed to a scene where he was sweeping her away for a romantic vacation—just the two of them—alone. That's what she really needed.

Full of birthday pie and sweet tea, Popsy and Matilda headed off to their beds. Rosie tried to get her mother to take a tablet of some sort to help her sleep, but she insisted she was okay.

"It's not serious," Popsy kept saying as if the repetition would make it a reality. "He's going to be fine."

Popsy confirmed that Rosie and Marcus were to sleep in the guest bedroom and Natasha was in her mother's old room. Then she put the cat out and set the alarm before heading for bed. "Making everything run as usual helps me stay sane during this madness," she said when Rosie tried to help with Tiger.

Marcus wiped down the kitchen table while Rosie cleared away the pie and the cups.

"Your mom seems pretty together for a woman who just saw her husband have a heart attack," Marcus said and threw the cloth into the sink.

"I don't think it's hit her yet to be honest," Rosie said. "I mean she's barely had time to think and as for Lily—Jeez."

"Yeah, I think that might be an even bigger issue in the long run. How will your father be able to work with Jack Hoffman from now on?"

"I'm not sure that there is any going forward. I think the business is really gone. I suppose their professional relationship of thirty years will dissolve along with the company. Damn Lily. He was my godfather. Now I don't want to see him again—ever. What the hell was he thinking?"

Marcus came over to where Rosie was leaning against the counter. She was pulling a hand towel through her hands over and over. He took it from her and gathered her into his embrace. "This will all sort itself out in time, honey. Take a leaf out of your mother's book. Don't think about it all so much."

Rosie rested her head against his broad, warm chest. She knew he was right.

"Remember the Ostrich Plan?"

She smiled softly. Of course she remembered the Ostrich Plan. How could she forget? But she let him talk. It was soothing to listen to his deep, warm voice.

He laughed. "You were so uptight before our wedding. I thought you were going to have a nervous breakdown. All those stupid little details driving you nuts."

"They were important to me." Rosie didn't meet his eyes but focused instead on removing imaginary bits of fluff from his shirt. "At least, they *felt* important back then."

"I know, but to the rest of the sane world, they were crazy. Anyway, I remember trying to talk sense into you but it was impossible, and then I don't know where I was—Hong Kong, I think—and I saw this cute little ostrich stuffed animal."

"I still have it, you know."

"Do you? That's great. Maybe you need to pull it out again. Anyway, you wouldn't listen to me, but somehow that little stuffed animal got through your stubborn head, and I was able to convince you to be like an ostrich and bury your head when a problem came up. Nine times out of ten, the problem dissolved."

Rosie pulled back slightly and looked at him. "You were very wise," she agreed. "And I'll grant you that the Ostrich Plan works for most problems, but there is that one time when you just can't ignore something. You have to face it head on."

"Give me an example from our wedding of a problem you ignored that came back to haunt you."

"The candy-coated almonds didn't arrive until two weeks after the wedding."

"Okay, but you managed to send them back and get a refund. Right?"

She was reluctant to lose the argument, so she didn't answer.

"And did anybody gasp and comment on the appalling lack of candy-covered almonds on the tables? Did anybody even notice—you included? You had forgotten that you even ordered them until they showed up late."

She gave a guilty grin. He was right—again.

"So, all I'm saying is over the next few weeks, unless it's really pressing, adopt the Ostrich Plan. Bury your head in the sand and let whatever problem is looming just wash over you."

Rosie stared at the floor like a reluctant child, and Marcus lifted her chin as he might with Natasha. "Pwomise?" he asked, using his Natasha voice.

"Pwomise," she agreed.

The house was warm and quiet as they headed up the stairs to the guestroom.

"Thanks for everything today," she said as she slipped into a nightgown that Tilly had thoughtfully left for her on the bed. "Thanks for staying here and taking care of Matilda and Natasha and waiting up for us to come home."

"Hey, it's the least I could do. I like your old man. He really is a good guy, and I'm sorry to hear the business is going under. I thought he was set up for life—you know, just working for the hell of it. Do you think he really meant it about losing this place?" he asked as he looked around at the abundant luxury.

Like the rest of the house, Popsy had decorated the visitor's bedroom in antique furniture. An enormous bed dominated the room and the deep chestnut color of the headboard was the same as the two bedside tables. The carpet, curtains, and bedding were all shades of cream and white so the room felt bright even against the dark wood.

"It'll be morning before I manage to get into the bed," he grumbled as he flung all the decorative pillows on the floor.

"Shhh, Marcus. Mom might hear you." Rosie climbed in on her side.

He checked to make sure the door was closed. "Didn't she take a sleeping pill?"

"I tried but she refused, and her bedroom is just next door," she said and switched off her bedside lamp.

But Marcus wasn't easily scared.

"Guess we'll have to be very quiet in that case.

It had been a trying day, and it was bliss to lose herself in the arms of her husband. Tonight she needed life-affirming love. Nightclothes and worries were soon discarded as they found each other. He was her strength, her rock. The one she could cling to as her old pillars of strength crumbled. With C&J Industries gone, she'd lost all her old security and now that her father was lying in the ICU, she wondered if she was she going to lose a parent, too. All she could rely on going forward was Marcus and Natasha.

He kissed her and then pulled back. "Are you crying?"

"Just a little," she whispered. "Don't worry. Even ostriches cry sometimes."

Ever so gently, he rubbed the tears away and put kisses in their place. Even in the darkness, Rosie could feel the weight of his stare just as much as she could feel the weight of his body. "I love you," he whispered as he moved with her.

"I love you, too."

But just a few moments later he said, "This isn't working, is it?"

"I'm sorry. I must have too much on my mind. I thought that this was just what I wanted, but now that we're here, I can't."

"Where's my little ostrich?"

"I tried that. There's just too much to ignore tonight."

Marcus took the hint and rolled over, giving her the space she needed, but he put his arm around her shoulders and kissed her again. "I really do understand. And to be honest, I feel a little weird doing it in your parents' house anyway. I mean, imagine if your mom heard us. How gross would that be?"

"Pretty gross. And what about Matilda?"

"She's in the guesthouse, isn't she? It would have to be a hell of a performance for her to hear us."

"True, but we have our days," she whispered.

"We do, babe, and today just isn't one of them. You okay? No more crying?"

Rosie nodded against his chest.

"I really need to take you away from all of this," Marcus said.

"That sounds good. Somewhere warm and sunny with long golden beaches and aquamarine water."

"For sure. Now that your mom and Matilda have agreed to babysit Nat, I'll start looking for somewhere good to go."

"We'll have to wait for Dad to get out of the hospital first, though."

"Sure. He'll be out in a matter of days. We'll figure out the dates tomorrow, but let's say sometime around the end of November, early December. Sound good?"

"Oh, Marcus, that sounds perfect," Rosie said, feeling better already.

"They have a new club in Bogota, very discreet. It has a strict twenty-five to forty-years-old rule, so there would be no dirty old men there for you. Only cool, young, open-minded guys and gals, of course. You're going to love it."

She couldn't believe her ears. He still wanted to try out a swinging vacation. How could she have been so naive to think he would change?

Be an ostrich, she thought. Be an ostrich.

Chapter 13
Popsy and Sandra

Popsy had never had a panic attack, but if she did, she was pretty sure it would feel something like what she was experiencing right now. Breakfast was out of the question. Already she felt like she could be ill any second, and that was with nothing inside her.

She now understood she'd been in shock the day before. The doctor at the hospital had told her as much, but this morning she was clearly waking up to the reality of her situation. Not surprisingly, she'd had a pretty appalling night's sleep, but she forced herself to stay in bed until 6 a.m. After that, it was no use. She was up and dressed by 6:30, so to try to pass the time, she went for one of her powerwalks. Anything was better than sitting at home and waiting for the hospital visiting hours to begin.

When she phoned, they were very understanding. They told her Peter had slept well, but she knew it was a drug-induced sedation, and they couldn't tell her anything else until the resident had done his rounds and made a decision on where he was going. Therefore, she walked.

Without intending to, Popsy ended up at The Celtic Crowne where Sandra and Jack owned the penthouse apartment. It wasn't possible to see their windows from the road, because they had enormous balconies, but she glanced up anyway.

Was Jack there with Sandra? Had he come clean yet? Popsy was worried. Would Peter even be able to stay in the same room as Jack when he got better? Would the men become enemies? What about Sandra? Would she blame Popsy in some way? Would their friendship perish on the rocks of this romance? Thank God for Rosie. At least she seemed to be in a good place, heading off to the Caribbean with her husband, to play golf no less.

How was Lily? How could she have been so stupid? Had Popsy done something terribly wrong when raising her daughter for her to make such an error in judgment? Perhaps it was Peter. Could it be that he was so busy with his work that Lily had missed something fundamental when she was growing up?

Now the girl needed a father figure, because it was pretty clear that was the role Jack filled. Why else would she end up with him?

Yes, she decided, her daughter *thought* she loved Jack, but Popsy knew that that was foolish. Young girls were meant to fall in love with young boys. Then they got married, had babies, and grew old together. That was what little girls had been taught from a very young age.

What about her? Would she be able to grow old with Peter? How in the hell did he have a heart attack? There were no warning signs. No signs, period. Peter never got sick, never even caught a cold. He worked seven days a week and loved it. How her life had turned on a dime, she reflected as she walked past the front of the hotel.

Popsy resolved to visit Sandra straight after Peter. First, she would phone Jack to give him fair warning, and if he refused to come clean, she would do it for him—bastard. Stupid, selfish bastard.

By the time she got home, the house was awake and everybody was in the kitchen. Natasha was still an early riser and couldn't believe that she was allowed to have birthday pie for breakfast. Matilda was fussing over her like an old mother goose. It was a terrific distraction for her. Rosie looked pretty tired, too.

"Did you sleep well?" she asked her daughter, concerned.

"Not the best night ever. Same as yourself, I'd guess," Rosie said and kissed her.

"Marcus still asleep?" She poured herself a large glass of water. Rosie shook her head. "No, he went home to get a change of clothes for everyone. We were thinking of staying here for another night. How do you feel about that?"

Popsy shook her head. "You're very sweet to mind me, darling, but really, I'm okay. Of course, I'm horrified that Dad is in the hospital, but I've been on to them already. They're happy with the stable night he's had. I know he'll be home in a few days, and to be honest, I'm not even worried about the business collapsing. All that matters is we have each other and everybody is healthy. I just want to get your dad home. I'm thinking I might follow you and get him away to the Caribbean when he's strong enough."

Rosie busied herself with making the coffee.

"That's a great idea, Mom, but I have to tell you Mr. Crowley, the company lawyer, called this morning. He wanted to speak to Dad and said it was urgent, so I had to tell him—in strictest confidence, of course. It might be a good idea to keep Dad away from him for a few days—just so he doesn't get stressed again. What do you think?"

Popsy was pensive for a moment and didn't speak.

"We'll be okay," Rosie said.

"Oh, I know. I just wonder if we'll lose the house," Popsy said, sounding a little shaky.

"Not today's problem. Remember what we discussed about prioritizing. Do you want me to keep you company when you visit Dad?"

"No, honey, if it's all the same to you, I want to see Daddy alone this morning. I think we need to talk a little—you know, about the business and how he wants to handle it. What he wants me to do, if anything. I daresay he'll have a thing or two to say about your sister, too. Have you heard anything?"

"Actually, I called her last night. She was so worried about Dad. She feels so guilty."

"Good." Popsy was not in a forgiving mood. She scrubbed the glass she was holding and polished it with a towel.

"I think Jack might have talked to Sandra last night, you know, come clean."

"Is that what you'd call it?"

Rosie raised her hands. "Hey, don't shoot the messenger. I'm not even sure if he did, but Lily seemed to think so. Maybe he even moved out. I don't know what actually happened. I just thought you should know."

Popsy forced herself to calm down. "Thanks, pet. I'm sorry if I seem to be snapping at you, but I am glad to hear Sandra knows. It was on my to-do list for later."

"Jeez, quite a to-do list: visit ICU, inform best friend that your daughter is sleeping with her husband . . . It's going to be a long day," Rosie joked, and Popsy laughed.

"True, but what's a girl to do?" She put the now ridiculously clean glass away and placed her hands on her hips. "I suppose I need to talk to Mr. Crowley. I need to know what he's doing about filing for Chapter 11 and if he'll have to postpone it because of Peter being in the hospital. I wonder if I'll need to get commercial lawyers or an independent accountant. I have no idea what to do."

"Talk to Dad, but don't stress him."

"That's my plan."

The hospital looked very different on a Monday morning. Popsy and Rosie had come in with the paramedics via the emergency room the day before. While that was pretty busy, the rest of the place seemed somber and quiet. This morning it was bustling with activity and people were everywhere. Popsy found it reassuring.

Meeting the doctor on duty was heartening, too. He was confident about moving Peter later in the morning but also said that he would be in the hospital for at least a week. He was able to confirm, thanks to the elevated creatinine phosphokinase, that Peter had definitely had a heart attack. There were a number of further tests he needed. He called one an "electro angiogram," and Peter was scheduled for one later that day. There was a small blockage discovered during the earlier tests, and he said they might have to do an angioplasty to clear it out.

On the plus side, it would mean they'd found the cause of the heart attack, but on the minus, it did mean heart surgery, albeit a minor procedure. Decades ago it was a big deal, but nowadays it was pretty uncomplicated and he'd be right as rain quite soon. But until they found the cause of it, they said he shouldn't be under any stress.

"No stress," she repeated and nodded in earnest, but inside, she panicked. How was that possible?

"Thank you, Doctor," she said and forced a smile. Popsy reckoned that a company going bankrupt was something Peter could handle. It was his rogue *daughter*, and not rogue *trading*, that had induced his heart attack.

"Hello, doll," he said when she came into his room. His voice was frail, and he still looked poleaxed. It shook Popsy to see him so ill.

"Hey, you. What a fright you gave us all. How are you feeling?"

He gestured for her to come closer, and closer again, until her ear was right next to his lips. Then he kissed her. "Gotcha," he said and smiled weakly.

"You still have it, darling, but don't stress yourself." Popsy sat in the seat next to the bed and took his hand.

"I'm fine. They have me doped up so I can't chase any of these nice nurses."

"There'll be none of that for some time yet," she whispered but winked at him at the same time.

He made an "aw shucks" gesture but didn't try to talk.

"Everything's fine at home. Marcus and Rosie stayed with me last night. You know, just for some moral support."

He nodded and closed his eyes. She was surprised at how sedated he was.

"I think Matilda has fallen in love with Natasha. She adores having a child to fuss over, and Nat even managed birthday pie for breakfast."

"Maybe we should have another baby," Peter joked, keeping his eyes closed.

Popsy laughed. "Not out of this body, you won't. You'd need to trade me in to manage that trick." She'd said it before she realized how close it hit home. Peter opened his eyes.

"Where's Lily?"

Popsy shook her head and dropped her gaze to the bed. In her head she berated herself for inadvertently bringing up the one subject she was trying to avoid.

"You don't know where she is?"

She shook her head again. "I haven't seen or spoken to her. I assume she's at work, but I have no idea what happened last night."

Peter said nothing for a while, and Popsy was happy for the silence.

Then he said, "I'll kill him when I get out of here. I swear, I'll kill him."

"Stop talking nonsense. You almost killed yourself yesterday. I'm not letting you within a mile of Jack Hoffman. I'm serious. You're to stay calm and think nice thoughts." Even as she said it, she knew how ridiculous it was. "Your sole function at the moment is to get better. Then you and I are going away from all of this. We might not ever come back. If I find a nice beach bar in the Bahamas or Australia, who knows, I might just whisk you away forever."

He smiled as if the idea had appeal.

Then a nurse arrived. Couldn't she just leave them alone?

"Well, Mr. Power, perhaps that's enough excitement for now. I see your heart rate going up. What did we say to you about getting excited?" Her loud voice seemed a gross intrusion.

Peter flinched but didn't reply. He just closed his eyes again. The nurse addressed Popsy.

"I'd say that's enough visiting for this morning, dear."

"But I only just got here."

"This is ICU. There shouldn't be any visitors in here at all."

She studied the notes at the bottom of his bed.

"I gather we're losing Mr. Power later today." Popsy disliked her tone. The nurse made it sound like she was misplacing patients and nobody was going to misplace her husband while she was around. Then the nurse said in a softer voice, "You can spend more time with him there."

That's when Popsy realized that perhaps she did understand and was just trying to sound flippant to keep everybody calm. The ICU was a pretty stressful place. Either way, her hovering indicated that Popsy's time was well and truly up. She managed a quick kiss on her husband's cheek before the nurse escorted her to the door.

Popsy wasn't happy, but she couldn't do anything about it. She had to conclude that the hospital staff knew what they were doing and rest was what her husband needed more than anything else.

Just as much as Peter needed rest, Popsy decided, Sandra would need a friend. The worrying bit was whether or not she still qualified as one.

"Mrs. Hoffman, there's a Mrs. Power here to see you," the hotel receptionist said into the phone intercom.

Popsy couldn't hear Sandra's reply but she knew it was rude because the receptionist looked flustered and then hung up. "I'm afraid she's unavailable right now," the young girl improvised.

Popsy had visited Sandra's home thousands of times. She even recognized the receptionist. "Look, the truth is Sandra and I had a bit of an argument last night. I just want to go up to talk to her—to say sorry. Can you please try one more time?"

With visible reluctance, the receptionist phoned through again and when she hung up she said, "She really doesn't want to see you." The receptionist looked a little more shaken after receiving what was clearly a tongue-lashing from Sandra.

Popsy knew that she wasn't going to get past this kid. She was too wet behind the ears and obviously terrified. There was a certain folklore surrounding the permanent residents of the hotel. At the time the hotel was built, over a decade earlier, a six-story tower was added with what were then the most luxurious and secure residences in Wellesley.

There was also a major scandal surrounding them, because it was the tallest structure in the town and the building permits had been turned down several times. There was still some mystery surrounding the ultimate green light to its construction, but C&J Industries were not involved in the development. So Jack used to laugh it off, pleading innocence. There was no doubt the penthouse was the jewel in The Celtic Crowne Plaza Hotel.

Back then Jack Hoffman had been licking his wounds, having just concluded his divorce from Olga. His ex-wife took the three girls to live in New Jersey, by the sea, and he didn't fight it. Pretty soon after, he and Sandra agreed to move in together. His ego got the better of him, and he bought what was back then Boston's most expensive piece of real estate—the only penthouse in The Celtic Crowne Plaza Hotel.

To the young receptionist, the idea of even phoning the penthouse, let alone getting into trouble with the resident, must have been terrifying.

The hotel porters were another story. Popsy knew most of them from over the years. To her good fortune, Noel, the head porter, was walking toward the elevators.

"Noel," she called after him, and he stopped and smiled.

He was in his sixties and had been with the hotel since it opened. He was a gentleman and a veteran of the hotel industry. More importantly, like Popsy, he was Irish.

"Mrs. Power, it's yourself. Are you here for a function or are you on your way up to Mrs. Hoffman?" His soft, warm accent was still as thick as the day he'd left Ireland.

She filled him in on a story similar to the one she had given the receptionist, but Noel was a good deal more sympathetic and open-minded.

He tapped the side of his nose and escorted her to the residents-only executive elevator. There he used his security key to get the elevator to go straight up to the top floor. Only senior management or the head porter could do this. It meant that Popsy could at least get to Sandra's front door, if not quite into the penthouse.

He stepped out of the elevator just before the doors closed and winked at her.

"Twasn't me who let you up, girl."

"Bless you, Noel. I didn't even see you today," she said, her own accent reverting to its old patter, and winked back as the doors glided closed.

There was only one penthouse, so when Popsy reached the top floor, she wasn't worried that anybody else might overhear their conversation. When she got there, she knocked on the door gently. "It's me, Sandra. Please let me in. We need to talk."

There was no reply, so she knocked a little harder. "Sandra, it's Popsy."

"Go away."

"I'm not leaving until you at least speak to me," she said, sounding a lot more confident than she felt.

"You came, you heard my voice. Now go away."

"Sandra, I want to see you. Please open up."

Popsy waited for a moment or two. "I can stand here all day if you like, talking at you like this."

There was a moment of silence, and then she heard the double bolt sliding. Sandra swung open the door but walked away without saying anything or acknowledging her and flopped onto the sofa.

Popsy knew that Sandra was going to be upset, but it was shocking how fast her home had fallen into a state of chaos. The rooms looked utterly trashed—like there'd been a herd of teenagers through the place on a booze and cigarette binge. It smelled like a full ashtray and looked about as appealing. Very un-Sandra like.

Popsy ignored it all. "Thanks for letting me in. I wasn't sure if you were going to talk to me."

"I don't want to." Sandra took the TV remote and turned the volume up.

Not really sure what to do, Popsy watched the film with her. "What's this?" she eventually asked.

"*Something's Gotta Give.* It's a good movie, but I think it's too happy for me today." Sandra looked like she was going to change the channel.

"Oh, I don't know. There's a very good crying scene at the end if it's the movie I'm thinking of. Is Diane Keaton in it?"

Sandra nodded.

"Yes, I know this. You get to see Jack Nicholson's backside, too. I loved this movie."

Such positivity seemed to annoy Sandra. She switched the television off. "Look, I'm not sure that you should be here. I have a lot going on in my head, and I really think I need to be alone. You, of all people, should get that."

"Please don't hate me," Popsy said. "I can't believe what's going on. I just can't. I do feel guilty, but I don't want you to blame me. You're my best friend. Peter's in the hospital, and I'm not talking to my daughter. I can't even say her name. Please don't shut me out."

"Oh, Popsy. How do you end up being the victim here?" Sandra grabbed her packet of cigarettes. "You're the one with all the cards—the adoring husband, the beautiful daughters." Sandra let that comment hang for a moment. "Too beautiful, by all accounts. You even have the grandchild box ticked, and what the hell do I have?"

She paused to light up and inhaled deeply, making herself cough.

"I have nothing, that's what. I was the second wife. We're already a pretty despised bunch, and now I've been discarded. I have no kids, no grandkids, and if Jack's telling the truth, then I'm broke, too."

"You heard about C&J?"

"He told me last night, and I didn't believe him, but that didn't stop me from calling Olga to tell her." Sandra almost smiled.

"You didn't!" Popsy gasped.

"Hey, why the heck not? It gave me a certain satisfaction. I guess we're in the same boat now—the ex-wives club." Sandra looked at her. "What does Peter say about it?"

"He had a heart attack. He hasn't said much since he tried to thump Jack last night."

"He was trying to punch Jack when it happened?" There was a slight smile on her face, so Popsy smiled back and nodded.

"It all happened so fast. I asked Jack was he having an af—well, you know—with Lily, and Peter went crazy and lunged for him. That's when he fell over. The doctors say it was a small attack, but it still scares the hell out of me. You hear all the stories these days about middle-aged men just falling over dead. That could have been Peter." As she started to cry, Sandra handed her the box of tissues.

"I'm sorry, Popsy. Peter is a great guy. Please tell him I hope he's feeling better and thanks for trying to take Jack down, too. Don't worry too much about Peter. He's tough. Wait and see, he'll be up and around in no time."

Popsy blew her nose. "I know. It was just a warning call, but still. Yesterday was definitely the worst day of my life. First the business, then Lily's bombshell, and then Peter. Some birthday lunch. I never want to have another birthday."

"That reminds me, I got you a present." Sandra got up and headed into her study, taking her cigarette with her.

Popsy thought about opening the curtains and the windows while she was gone but decided not to risk annoying Sandra. She was picking up the newspaper when she saw the broken vase with flowers scattered all over, and the enormous water stain that had formed on the wood.

"Oh my God, Sandra," she whispered. "Your beautiful floor. I don't think that stain is going to come out now." She rushed into the kitchen, which also looked like a hurricane had hit it, and grabbed a dish cloth and the trash can.

"What are you doing?" Sandra walked back into the room. "Oh, don't worry about that. I tried to kill Jack last night."

Popsy gathered all the dead Irises. "It's not Jack I'm worried about. It's your famous flooring." She still remembered when Sandra had ordered the most expensive Calamander wood floor. The wood was very rare and grew only on the Indonesian island of Sulawesi. When Jack heard about it, he insisted they get it just *because* it was the most expensive. And now it was ruined—crazy.

"You have a serious water mark here, I'm afraid." She examined the stain. "If it had been wiped up straight away, it might have survived, but not now that the water has soaked in."

Sandra lit a new cigarette from her last one and Popsy, who was a passionate anti-smoking person at the best of times, said, "Don't do this to yourself. Not the cigarettes." It had been so tough for Sandra to give them up when she first began dating Jack. To start again seemed insane. "Come on, this isn't the answer. You're stronger and better than this. Just because your husband—"

"Ex-husband. No man does that to me and gets away with it."

"Sorry. Ex-husband. That's exactly what I'm talking about. You're the strongest person I know, and I'm sorry if I came across as the victim. You're the one who's going through hell here, and I just want you to know that you're amazing and brilliant—"

"Okay, okay, I get the message. I'm friggin' magnificent and he's the idiot. I get it. So tell me this: why am I the sad old fool sitting here all alone while he's off living the life?"

Popsy forgot about the floor and came to sit beside her friend on the sofa. She hugged her and rocked her gently, and Sandra started to cry.

Chapter 14

Happily Ever After?

By Monday evening, Lily wasn't even sure if her legs would carry her from the car to her apartment. Work had been horrible. The news about her father and Jack's business going into Chapter 11 had hit the financial circuits around town, and that included her employer.

There was a restaurant on the top floor of the bank. While staff often went out to local parks or pubs for lunch, it was easier and most days faster to dine on the bank's top floor. The food was even subsidized because the bank liked staff to socialize together. It also meant they were less inclined to be late getting back.

Lily went there most days because she was still flying high after her promotion, and it was good to network with senior management or sit with her own team. They often talked about work over lunch and pooled their knowledge on how certain world markets were moving. Over the last few months, it had been very difficult to make money with so many countries in dire financial straits, but Lily kept her risk spread wide and focused on the Far East markets, which were her area of expertise. Thankfully, they were still pretty stable compared to Europe and the U.S. She'd been enjoying quite a few pats on the back thanks to her business plan, and she'd assumed her promotion was because of this, but her boss, Mr. Jones, had given her a decidedly icy stare as she carried a tray past the top brass's lunch table.

"What's his problem?" she muttered to one of her coworkers as she sat down next to him.

"Who? Jones? Don't worry about him. He's just smarting over C&J."

"Damn it. That's not my fault. He knows I have no involvement in that business. We talked about it before."

Her coworker, Matt, looked intrigued. "When did you talk about it?"

She shrugged. "Loads of times actually. The most recent was about a month ago. He asked me how my father was and how the business was. I told him the usual. Both were great."

"Now you know why you're getting the cold shoulder." Matt took a bite of his sandwich. "You said that the business was . . . what did you say? Great? When obviously it was losing money hand over fist."

Lily looked at him. "You're not suggesting he was serious. He was just making small talk—asking me how my father was. He wasn't looking for inside information. That would be illegal."

Matt pretended to look shocked. "Mr. Jones, do some insider trading, sorry, chatting? Never!" Then his demeanor changed. "Come on, Lily. You're not that innocent. Or are you? Why do you think he's always so nice to you? Why do you think you got that generous promotion?"

She whipped her head around. "Don't tell me you think that I got the promotion because of my dad. Matt, I'm sorry, but that's just sour grapes. You know as well as I do I worked my ass off for that promotion. I earned it."

"Yeah? How much did you make the bank last year? What are your yields for the last four quarters? I'll see you and raise you on all of them. I worked just as hard as you did, and I'll bet I brought in more cash. But alas, I don't have a daddy who's in bed with us to the tune of—what is it now? $100 million? The bank wants to keep clients that valuable very happy. If that means keeping daddy's little girl moving steadily up the chain of command, so be it. Even if poor suckers like me get left out in the cold as a result."

Lily was incandescent with rage. "I've never heard such bull," she snarled to the man she thought was her friend.

"No, and you don't want to hear it now, Lily, but I'm only saying it because what comes 'round goes 'round. Your father was a big asset to this bank, and so you were, too. Now, he's a liability. Think about it."

"What?"

"You heard me. They won't fire you because you could sue them for unfair dismissal, but don't be surprised if you're offered another promotion that would involve you moving to the South Pole."

She wasn't able to finish her lunch. She couldn't sit there and take Matt's hyperbole.

"I have to go."

Her first instinct was to call her father, but that was impossible. The second person she thought of was Popsy, but that was another no-go. That left her with Jack. He didn't answer. He'd told her that he was going to have a manic day with lawyers and accountants, but he would take a call from her, wouldn't he? She left a panicky message with the request that he should call her right back. But no call came.

She refused to believe he hadn't checked his messages all day, yet that had to be the only solution because there was no way he would've left her hanging. He was head-over-heels in love with her. He had just left his wife for her. Jack had better love her with everything he had, she thought, because she had lost everything she loved by going to him.

The afternoon crawled by, and everything seemed to conspire against her. The computers crashed in the morning. She lost a valuable account in the afternoon. During the day some brave souls came into her office to say how sorry they were about C&J Industries, but she flicked her long blond hair and said it had nothing to do with her. The only person who got to her was Emily.

Emily was Lily's closest friend at work. They'd started together years ago, but Em wasn't half as ambitions. She'd been more of a social animal and now she was married to a lawyer.

They had twin three-year-old boys, and Emily's husband wanted her to be a stay-at-home-mom and produce a few more babies. She was toying with the idea. Her career wasn't nearly as impressive as Lily's, but that didn't bother Emily in the least. The friendship had been forged when they were both young and socializing on the Boston scene, and even though their lives were going in opposite directions, their friendship was solid.

Since the twins' arrival, Emily had job-shared and only worked three days a week now. She came in a few hours after lunch.

"Hey, how are you?"

Lily was so happy to see a friendly face. "Oh, Emily, thank God you're here. I need to talk with you. Can we go for a drink after work?"

Emily shook her head sadly. "Sorry, the au pair is off at six. That gives me thirty minutes to get home in rush-hour traffic. I know I'm going to be late as it is. You okay? This about your dad's company?"

Lily folded her arms on her desk then dropped her head onto them. "And the rest." She moaned.

"Is your dad okay?"

Lily looked up and nodded. "Yeah, if you call spending the night in the ICU of Newton Wellesley Hospital, good."

"What?"

Lily got up and closed the door. "Where do I start? Yesterday was my mother's birthday lunch, and it accidently got out there that I was—well, I've been having a relationship with my father's business partner."

Emily's face lit up, on hearing such fabulous scandal. She beamed at her old friend. "You bad girl," she whispered. "He's not married is he?"

"Well, um, technically speaking, he is, but he's separated now." She tried to paint it in a better light than it really was, but Emily was no fool.

"How long has he been separated?"

"Since lunch yesterday." Lily had the decency to look ashamed.

"Lily Power, you really are a naughty girl. Who'd have thought it?" Lily wasn't sure, but it seemed like the smile was weaker on Emily's face now.

"Whatever. Look, the problem is that when Dad heard, he blew a gasket and maybe a heart valve, too, because he had a heart attack. You won't tell anybody, will you?"

Emily pretended to zip her lips.

"And now Matt tells me the only reason I got my promotion is because the bank was playing political games with C&J. You don't think that could be true, do you?"

Emily shrugged and examined Lily's stapler.

"Emily?"

She looked up. "What the hell do I know about senior management policy? All I can say is it wouldn't be beyond them to play games like that. On the other hand, you know you worked for that promotion. You earned it on performance, so ignore Matt. He's just jealous."

"That's what I told him."

"Forget work. Tell me all about this man you're seeing. I had no idea."

"Neither did anybody. We kept it under wraps."

"Because he was married?"

Lily started to feel uncomfortable talking about Jack, and she was tired after her sleepless night.

"I'll tell you all about it over a drink sometime."

"Wednesday after work?"

She forced a smile. "It's a date." Now she regretted mentioning any of it. Emily would pump her for information, and she didn't really feel good talking about it. Funny, she thought she'd feel relieved when it was out in the open, but in fact she felt guiltier than ever.

Lily hoped that Jack would be home by the time she got through the bad tempered Monday night traffic, but there was still no sign of him, so she tried Rosie again. She needed to know about her dad. Had he been moved out of ICU? Did Rosie think Lily could call her mom yet? In other words, had their mother cooled down enough? Rosie's phone went straight to voice mail. At a loss for something to do, she did what she did best. She buried herself in work.

It was very late when she heard the key in her front door but it still managed to give her a little thrill. Lily had given Jack a key to her apartment months earlier, and he'd often let himself in, but this was different. He was letting himself into their home. The thought was exhilarating.

"Hello, darling." She jumped up from the sofa and went to hug him.

"Christ, what a day." He groaned and slipped out of his navy cashmere coat. Then he threw it on the sofa and wrapped his arms around her. "How are you, babe?"

"Well, not great," she started. "I haven't—"

He stopped her from continuing by putting his hand up to her mouth because his phone rang. He answered it fast and walked into their bedroom.

"Ronnie, thanks for getting back to me. Look, we need to meet." That was all Lily heard before he shut the door.

She'd been about to ask if he'd heard any news about her father. Surely Jack had made some sort of contact because of what was happening with the business.

She waited for his phone call to end—and waited and waited. After an hour, she decided enough was enough. This was their first official night together as a couple, and she was darned if Jack was going to spend all of it on the phone.

She quietly opened the bedroom door and peeked in. Lily wanted to get Jack's attention, but she didn't want the guy he was talking with to know she was there. Jack had his back turned to the door and didn't notice her coming in. She tiptoed over to where he would see her. He glanced up and smiled.

She still knew how to get his attention. All men were the same.

Had she come in with some food or an attitude, he would have waved her out, but Lily chose to walk in with nothing on, save an inviting smile.

"Look, Ronnie, I have to go. Uh, something's come up. We'll talk in the morning." Jack hung up without waiting for a reply.

"Wow, angel, what a way to be welcomed home," Jack enthused as he began to strip.

Lily thought he was in terrific shape for a man of fifty-five. Of course, recently he worked out as much as Lily did. All that work had paid off. He had a firm stomach and well-toned arms. He carried no extra weight, so his jawline was strong and square. His eyes, which admittedly had a few lines around them, were still bright blue.

But Jack's biggest attraction was his raw energy. He always looked pumped and excited about life. It pulled her in, and others, too.

She was proud to stand by him because he was a magnificent man. Okay, he was a little older, but it just didn't matter. He was nuts about her and she about him. Life would be perfect just as soon as her dad got better and the business stuff settled down.

Lily was small like her mother. At only five-foot-three, she'd longed to be taller, but she was petite, too. So overall she was well-proportioned. Jack was able to lift her up when she wrapped her legs around him. He was fit enough to carry her like that for as long as it took, and it didn't take too long this evening.

"Baby, I love you," he growled as he gave her his undivided attention. It turned her on, just as much as it did him. She pulled his short hair violently and screamed out, not giving a thought to their neighbors.

"That was a highly effective way to get me off the phone, gorgeous." He smiled at her. They were lying on top of their bed, naked and sated.

"I thought you might have been on all night if I didn't try something drastic."

"Sometimes drastic works," he said, but she could tell he wasn't talking about them anymore. His mind was back on business.

"How did today go?" she asked as she got up to find her bathrobe

"Where are you going?" He sounded hurt.

"I thought I might get us something to eat."

"Yeah, I don't think I ate today." He also got up and threw a towel around his waist before following her into the kitchen.

"So, tell me everything."

Jack ran his hands over his face as if to wash away the bad memories of the day. "We knew it was coming, but that didn't make it any easier. I need a drink. Can I get you something?"

Lily shook her head. She didn't like to drink on a Monday. It was too early in the week. She pulled a gourmet dinner for two out of the freezer and threw it in the microwave.

"The banks froze all our accounts today."

"What?" She sat down at the table.

"We knew it was coming. I was in the commercial court first thing this morning with your damn bank. They'd already appointed their own liquidator, and by noon, the accounts were frozen. The bastards were fast. They didn't even give me time to file for Chapter 11. This is the worst possible scenario."

He buried his head in his hands. "I wish your father was here for this." Jack looked beaten. "The press is going to have a field day. That's it. With the accounts frozen, Cap & Jet Industries has officially ceased trading. Jeez, what a mess. Lily, I have to tell you the next few months are going to be very rough. Your father and I have upset a lot of people. We didn't mean to, and you know they all loved us while we were making a profit. But now we owe quite a lot of people quite a lot of money and there simply isn't any. I'm afraid we're very deep in negative equity."

"What do you mean when you say you've upset a lot of people? How much have you upset them?"

"Ballpark? I'd chalk your dad down for about $100 million and me around the same. Everything we had was leveraged and cross guaranteed. That's why he doesn't hold much hope for that beautiful house of his."

"Do you think they'll lose it?"

"Yep."

"What about Sandra in The Celtic Crowne?"

He shook his head. "It'll have to go."

"Can't you fight? You and Dad?"

"What the hell do you think we've been doing for the last six months? Jesus, when things are good, the women are happy and ask no questions, but as soon as things go bad, it's 'what are you going to do about it?' Christ, I've tried everything I can think of."

He looked desperate, so she tried to be strong. She still had her job, her car, her apartment. "We're going to be fine, Jack. I can support us. There may not be any private jets for a while, but we can slum it on the commercial airlines."

"Lily, I don't want to upset you, but do you own this apartment or does your dad?"

"I do." She was glad for the distraction when the microwave pinged.

"Do you have a mortgage on it in your name? Or, if not, do you have the deeds?"

She didn't look at him because she was sliding the dinners out of their plastic casings and onto her Vera Wang dinner plates. Lily had wanted to have a romantic homemade dinner for their first meal together, but the day had just run away from her, and then there was the traffic and the trauma hanging over her at the moment. "I don't have a mortgage. This place was a gift from my parents when I graduated college. I assume Dad has the deeds somewhere."

"You'll need to check that out," Jack spoke softly.

"You don't think this place could be wrapped up in his portfolio, too, do you?"

Jack didn't answer, which told her all she needed to know.

Chapter 15

Sandra

Even seeing Sven's fine physique at the gym Tuesday morning didn't cheer Sandra up. When he tried to catch her eye, she looked away. She knew she could have him if she wanted. Attracting guys had never been a problem for her, but keeping them seemed to be quite another matter.

Usually she had earbuds in because fast-music thumping made her push herself. It also meant she was difficult to approach. But today, in her misery, she'd forgotten them and her bottle of water.

She avoided the treadmill near Sven, fearful he might try to strike up a conversation. When he moved on to the weights, she stayed on the stair stepper. Sandra climbed faster, farther, and for longer than usual. She thought if she worked herself harder, punished herself, maybe, just maybe she could be distracted for a moment—for even a second. Was it possible to forget she was alone again? She'd been dumped, like an old dishwasher. Replaced by the newer, younger model.

Of course, this happened all the time. Damn it, she'd even seen it done to Jack's last wife, but at least Olga got a big house in New Jersey. She got the art collection and the ponies, but best of all, she got the kids. Sandra was the one who'd lost most because she'd given Jack her best years.

And what did she have to show for it? A nice collection of diamonds, furs, and some now-bitter memories. Even the good experiences were tarnished because they were with the man who was having fun with another woman at the same time. She still couldn't quite fathom it. What really shocked her was the thought that if he crawled back now and apologized, she might take him back. She didn't know how to stand on her own two feet anymore.

It was odd how everybody thought she was so strong, but it was all show. She was fragile, she just knew how to hide it. Large cars, diamonds, and penthouses could cover a lot of insecurity.

"I think you're going to wear that machine out." Sven's voice was warm and friendly. Sandra hadn't seen him approach. She was too caught up in her own miserable world. She was a good eighteen inches over his head because she was up high on the stepping machine, so she looked down on him.

"Oh, you know, work hard, play hard. That's my motto."

"Well, you're certainly working that machine pretty hard. Did you have a good day on Sunday?" He smiled and put his hand on the machine. "That was when I last saw you."

A lifetime ago, she thought. Since then my husband has walked out on me. His business has gone under, and my best friend's daughter has shacked up with the only man I've ever loved.

"It's been busy," she said.

"Still no time to take me around some of your beautiful sights?"

Sandra couldn't believe it. Of all the days and all the gyms, this guy was hitting on her even though he knew she was married. The anger had to go somewhere. All her frustration needed a vent. This guy had picked the wrong woman to cross on the wrong day.

"Are you asking me out?" she asked, keeping her voice pleasant.

He shrugged and gave a not unattractive *guilty as charged* sort of grin.

"And you know I'm married?" She had to be sure that she had it right.

This time he winced a little but again kept grinning at her.

"There aren't enough single girls out there for you to prey upon?" She could feel her temper climbing. "You felt the need to come to Wellesley and destroy a perfectly happy marriage?" Sandra got off the machine. She was five-foot-eight, but he stood a good five inches over her. Her hair was up in a tight ponytail and today she was in a pair of aqua blue running shorts and a matching top. She wore no makeup. It hadn't been high on her priority list that morning, so she knew she didn't look her best, but that didn't matter.

"You know, it's guys like you that have the world in the mess it's in."

From the look on his face, Sandra could tell Sven was beginning to realize that this conversation was not going to be as pleasant as their previous one.

"Okay. Sorry." He tried to back off.

"No, actually, it's not okay. It's not okay at all. If your kind kept your nosy little peckers out of healthy marriages, I think a great deal more couples would survive. It's people like you—"

Sven turned and walked away. She guessed he wasn't going to stand there and listen to her berate him. Pity, she thought. It felt good to let him have it. Jerk.

How did Popsy get such a good guy? How did you know a good man from a bad one? Of course, Sandra had known from the beginning Jack had a pretty bad track record.

She tried to get back on the machine, but the flood of adrenaline had subsided. Plus, she'd lost the urge to climb a thousand steps and get nowhere. She went over to the weights and concentrated on her crunches. Looking at herself in the mirror, Sandra thought she looked good, even as the jilted wife. Of course, she didn't look twenty anymore, but still.

She would have to get back out into the world at some point, but how would she ever trust a man again? All the good guys were surely taken by the time they were fifty. She would either have to find another man on his second marriage or some total loser who hadn't been snatched up for some reason. She wondered which category Sven fit into when it hit her there was a third category: widowers. Women usually outlived their husbands, but there had to be a select few where this wasn't the case.

Maybe I'll check out the death notices, she thought miserably.

How low had she fallen and how fast, she realized, losing all desire to be in the gym.

If Sandra didn't get out and find some purpose for her day, it was possible she would hit the white wine by mid-afternoon. Worse than that, she might have a cigarette. It had been the toughest battle of her life—well, up until now. Sandra was furious with herself for starting again. No excuse was a good enough one to smoke, not even a breakup.

Mercifully, by lunchtime the weather was fabulous. It was pretty warm for the last week in October, which was unusual. The Halloween decorations the hotel had erected in the main foyer seemed incongruous with the blue skies and high temperatures outside. Sandra decided to walk into town to buy some magazines. The sunlight would do her good.

There were a number of ways to get to town, and she didn't consciously make the decision, but she wound up walking past Popsy's house just as a car was being delivered. Already some passersby had stopped to see the flashy fire-engine-red Ferrari get offloaded from the tow truck. Popsy was coming out of the house as Sandra approached.

"What's this?" she asked her old friend.

"Sandra, thank goodness you're here. Oh my God, I never thought this would arrive now. Not after, well, all that's happened."

"Birthday present?" Sandra whispered to which Popsy nodded, looking guilty.

"But not now. Well, I just assumed that it wouldn't arrive. Surely the car dealers know."

"Maybe Peter paid in cash?" Sandra said quietly, not wanting to be overheard by the onlookers.

This was possible because the men often "lost" cash profits by buying diamonds and going on vacations, but Sandra thought it was unlikely for a tangible asset like a car.

The guys worked fast unloading the Ferrari and polishing it up one more time. Then they got Popsy to sign a ream of forms and take possession of two sets of keys. Once they were gone, it was just her and Popsy with the onlookers and a half a million dollars' worth of metal.

Soon enough, the envious onlookers wandered off, but Sandra knew the last thing her friend felt was enviable.

"What are you going to do with the Merc?" she asked mischievously.

Popsy looked at her old friend and giggled. "Jeez, Sandra, life is just so crazy right now, but I have to tell you, it feels less so with you here."

Their relationship seemed to be fragile but alive, considering what it had been through in the last couple of days.

Popsy continued, "I have no idea what I'm going to do. Sell it, I guess. I'll wait till Peter is out of the hospital and ask him. I have no idea where the title is."

She took a walk around the Ferrari. "You don't think this is a bit too flashy, do you?"

Sandra laughed. "Darling, you know you can never be too rich or too thin. If you have it, flaunt it. That's what I say."

"Yes, but that's just the point. I don't think we have it anymore," Popsy whispered as she came back to Sandra.

"Don't worry about that now. Look," she said and gestured toward the car and then the sky, "it's a fantastic day, we're in the best of health, and we have a shiny new red Ferrari. Does it get better than this?"

"So, not too flashy?"

Sandra pretended to look frustrated. "Flashy is fabulous. Come on, sugar. Where are you taking me on our maiden journey?"

"What the heck, I'm celebrating." Popsy smiled. "Peter got the results back yesterday from his angiogram, and he's all clear. No blockages. That means no surgery."

Sandra bear-hugged her. "Oh, Popsy, that's the best news I've heard all week. Peter's going to be just fine. Didn't I tell you he would be?"

"You know, you're right. I'm going to nip inside to get my jacket and sunglasses." She headed for the house but then turned back suddenly. "Here, catch," Popsy said and threw the keys to her. "Why don't you start her up and put the roof down?"

It wasn't exactly how Sandra had seen her day panning out, but it was a lot of fun and even though she was nervous at first, Popsy insisted she was a great driver, and the car was insured. They drove down Route 9, enjoying the fall sunshine while they played with all the buttons and chatted about how complicated their lives had become.

Popsy filled Sandra in on how Peter wasn't allowed a phone, iPad, computer, or anything else he could use to do work, and she was nervous this was enough to induce another heart attack. She said she was going to see him later that day and get the test results regarding what caused the attack.

Popsy also talked about Lily and admitted that she hadn't spoken to her yet because she was furious with her. Sandra didn't say it, but she took enormous solace from that small piece of information. It meant that Popsy really was in her corner, which was a huge relief.

She rubbed Popsy's shoulder and filled her in on her adventures in the gym with Sven, and she added that she hadn't had any contact with Jack.

On their way home, they popped into The Cheesecake Factory in the Natick shopping mall to have a coffee and some cheesecake. They were able to linger, admiring all the home goods and kitchen accessories. There was a sports store that Sandra loved because she was always looking for nice new gym clothes, and Popsy was consumed with the Disney Store full of pink princess outfits and toys for Natasha.

She was already pretty well-known in the store because she spent so much money there. Today was no exception. She bought a new princess dress, a candy-pink nightgown with matching slippers, and a tiara, but she decided she couldn't leave the matching pink throne behind. Since she had her hands full, she forfeited the wand. This was plenty for one day.

Just as everything was getting gift-wrapped, Sandra appeared beside her. "How are you doing?" she asked.

"Great," Popsy said. It was nice to be out with her best friend again and not thinking about Peter or her daughter. Without even looking at the total, Popsy handed over her platinum piece of plastic. The sales assistant swiped it, frowned, then swiped it again. She glanced at Popsy. "I'm sorry your card has been declined."

"Oh," Popsy felt the panic rising, but having Sandra by her side calmed her.

"Your card was declined?" she asked.

"You don't think that this is—"

"No, no way, Popsy. Far too soon. That wouldn't be for weeks or months."

Popsy wanted to believe her but couldn't help wondering if this was the beginning of their personal credit crunch—the implosion of their lives. Peter had told her about friends who'd filed for Chapter 11, and she knew it was a very painful process. She thought it didn't affect things like private bank accounts for months, if ever. It all depended on how it played out, but it wouldn't hit her yet, right?

"Here I have cash," Sandra said and took three hundred dollar bills from her purse and handed them to the cashier.

Popsy was grateful but surprised. When they were walking back out to the car, laden down with all of her goodies, she quizzed Sandra. "Thanks a million for bailing me out in there. I don't carry that much cash on me. I didn't know you did, either. Is it safe?"

"Safer than leaving it in Jack's account. I don't usually carry this much money, but then Jack never walked out on me before. First thing Monday morning, I went into the bank and withdrew everything I could. I had no choice."

"Very shrewd, girl. Was it easy?"

"No, now that you mention it. They have a time lock on their safe, so I had to come back. It has to do with money trafficking. They put up a good fight, too. They asked what I wanted so much cash for since everything is done by plastic these days. I said that I was going to a cash-only charity event, and they believed me."

"I think you were very wise. May I ask how much you managed to get?"

Sandra looked at Popsy and smiled with satisfaction. "Would you believe

$100,000? Hey, what can I say, I'm a big giver, especially when I'm the charity."

Despite the laughter, Popsy felt sorry for Sandra. How had it come to this so fast? She didn't know if she would ever be able to forgive Lily for being so horrendously selfish and stupid.

Sandra stroked her arm. "You know, I hurt like hell and I'm really pissed at Jack, but I'm okay with you. Really."

Popsy felt anxious. "Are you sure? I feel so bad about all of this, even though I had no idea. I'm so sorry."

"You don't have to apologize. You won't believe this, but I feel a little sorry for Lily, too. She has no idea what she's getting into. Jack is an idiot, and a selfish one at that. Lily won't be able to have kids with him. That's my biggest regret after all these years."

Popsy shook her head. She couldn't see a solution, only broken homes and friendships. Well, at least she and Sandra had weathered the storm

Sandra handed the car keys back to Popsy. "Come on, your turn to drive this beauty. Where to?"

"Shall we go visit Rosie?" Popsy suggested. "Her gardens look fantastic at this time of year and the views are really spectacular. Have you been to her house in Weston?"

Sandra said she hadn't and would love the minor detour. It wasn't like she had anything else to do.

"Oh my God, that car!" Marcus said. The reaction was effusive and ecstatic, and Popsy found that very gratifying. It wasn't often he got fired up about something of hers. He studied the Ferrari like it was a piece of fine art or some sort of deity. In fact, it really did look like he was worshiping it as he got down on his knees to examine the finer points of its design.

"Big boys' toys." Rosie laughed and invited her and Sandra inside. "Mom, you shouldn't have." She chastised her mother yet again for her over-generosity, but Natasha was thrilled and insisted on getting into the princess costume right away.

"Where's the wand?" she asked crossly.

It was at this point that even Popsy thought it might be high time for Natasha to learn about "less is more," but then, she wondered, how could she, a Ferrari driving granny, preach about cutting back?

They turned down the offer of coffee and Halloween muffins, having just eaten in Natick, but were delighted to take a walk around Rosie's beautiful garden.

Built on a height just next to Weston's huge water reservoir, the views over the lake were supreme. Today the blue of the sky was reflected in the water, and it filled Popsy's heart. Every time she saw it, she wanted to move to Weston. Although her home on Cliff Road had almost everything she wished for, the one thing it didn't have was a view like this.

Water calmed Popsy's soul—well, that, and the large rambling garden.

Rosie had used an English landscape artist to design her yard when they first moved in, just after Natasha was born. The result was a garden more suited to England's Wimbledon than New England's Weston, but now it was well-established and looked like it had been there for decades. Tall trees were shipped in and mature shrubs planted, all to give the illusion that the garden was old. The most striking feature, and the most expensive according to Rosie, was the long verdant yew hedge. Rosie explained that yew was very slow growing, but she had them shipped in from Europe already ten years old.

"It's funny to think those saplings were growing before I'd even met Marcus." She gestured over to the perfectly clipped wall of green that surrounded the entire perimeter of the garden. The yew hedge stood at about twelve-feet high and gave the house an enclosed feeling. It was reassuring and offered a perfect backdrop for her late-flowering snow-white, mophead hydrangeas and the pink nerines which gave a very welcome blast of color just before winter shut down the garden.

"You're lucky the house is on a hill or that enormous hedge would've blocked out that incredible lake view," Sandra said.

"Yes. We have the best of both worlds." Rosie took them along the little paths that meandered through the larger garden shrubs. The rhododendrons had done their blooming for the year and already the buds were growing for next season. And even though the two ancient Elms at the back of the house had lost their leaves, the maples were a riot of furious red and burnt orange.

"I wanted to do something similar to what you did for Halloween," Rosie told her mother. "Of course, I need to hurry up or the trick-or-treating will be over before I've even hoisted my haystacks!"

Popsy looked at her daughter and raised an eyebrow. "Rosie, tomorrow is Halloween so you might want to think about it for next year."

"No, no. I'll do it this afternoon. It's all good," Rosie said and smiled.

Popsy was happy that her daughter seemed to be in a much better mood. At least she had one child whose life was heading in the right direction.

After about half an hour of enjoying Rosie's garden, she and Sandra took their leave. Marcus was the saddest to see them go. He liked the car very much.

Sandra was quiet as they headed home. "They really have it all, don't they?"

"Rosie and Marcus? It sure looks that way, but I guess we never really know."

"Yes, but he's a wonderful guy, and good-looking, too. They have a beautiful house with a spectacular garden and great views, but the best thing is that little grandchild of yours. I envy them. I guess I envy you."

"Sandra, you and I know better than to be jealous of others. The truth is, we never have a notion of what's going on in somebody else's house. I hope Rosie and Marcus are okay, and I think they are, but how do any of us have any idea of what the future holds? The trick is to enjoy today." She looked over to Sandra to gauge her mood. "What's that sign you have hanging in your bathroom?"

" 'Don't waste time waiting for the storm to pass. Love, laugh, and dance in the rain.' "

"That's it. You have to remember to keep dancing."

Sandra looked contemplative for a moment. "Okay, I may not be loving or laughing a lot, but I'm dancing. Believe me, I'm dancing as fast as I can."

Chapter 16

Rosie's Choice

Rosie had a decision to make. That's what it boiled down to now. Was she going to do what Marcus wanted or stand up for herself? If she bent to his wishes, she would demean herself and do something that might lead to the destruction of their relationship.

There were important things to consider. Would once be enough for him? Would he become addicted to "swingers' " vacations? He'd started calling it "The Lifestyle." More like "life wreckers," she thought.

What if she put her foot down? What if she told him this was not what she wanted to do because it would rob them of something sacred, something intimate that up till now only they had shared? She sighed and sat down at her computer. If she stood firm and refused to do this, he'd go without her. It was that simple. Either swing with him or be left swinging solo. As for the intimacy thing, it was no secret they'd both had partners before they got married. So, this thing about what "only they shared" was a kind of bogus. At least that's what Marcus had said to her when she'd tried to make that argument to him.

"What are we? Born again virgins?" Then he laughed at his own joke. It was true. The first time they'd had sex was before they'd even started dating. It was at their Christmas party. Rosie had thought he was very attractive, and one thing led to another pretty darn fast. Only after that first encounter did they start to date. Sex was just a physical thing for Marcus, and back then it had been the same for Rosie. But the years *had* changed her, and now for her it was intimate and private. How could she explain that in a way he would understand? Anytime she tried, she failed.

Reluctantly, Rosie switched on her computer. She put the words "Swingers" and "Caribbean" into the search engine, and to her surprise, there were one hundred and twenty-five thousand results. "In only twenty-five seconds," she said. Well, she must not be the only person who'd researched the subject.

There were luxury vacations in St. Lucia for couples only. She clicked on the first one she saw. It certainly looked classy enough. Very luxurious and five stars was about as good as it gets. Then to her dismay, or perhaps delight, she realized it wasn't a swingers' resort but just a couples one.

Next she came across Amor Travel on the Riviera Maya in Mexico. The waters were light turquoise blue and the sand snow white. It looked gorgeous. Then she read: Couples only. Clothing optional.

Ohmygod!

In a panic, she minimized the page and went to check on Natasha, fearful that her daughter might catch her. The little girl was glued to the television, which usually would've delighted Rosie because it gave her all the time she needed to e-mail friends and Facebook. But today she would have been happy if Natasha was demanding her attention.

"Everything okay, Nat?" Without looking away from the box, the little girl nodded.

Rosie had no more excuses. She went back to the computer and reopened the page.

"Secluded ambiance," she read quietly. "Well, it should be if they're serious about doing what they're doing—in public." She snorted.

She was somewhat relieved to see a "house rules" icon. Maybe there was some sanity in this place. There was something about dressing appropriately in all the restaurants and a strict no drugs policy. She hoped alcohol was the exception because there was no way she could do this without at least one bottle of wine inside her.

Another rule was no intimacy with staff members. She liked the sound of that.

The last rule was: Please respect all other guests and remember that no means NO.

This was too much to think about, so she shut down the website and went to watch *ScoobyDoo!*

Twenty minutes later she was back. She had to resolve this wretched matter or her husband would. This time she bounced into another resort altogether. The place looked even more upscale. It wasn't at all seedy like she'd been expecting. The couples in the photographs looked like honeymooners and not porn stars. The resort insisted it was only for the open-minded and those into "experimentation." It talked about feeling free to explore and discover new and exciting possibilities.

Puh-lease, she thought. Just call it what it is—an orgy.

She clicked on the "Lifestyle Hotels" option and saw they had places all over the world. Rosie had already decided if she was going anywhere, it would be the Caribbean. At least that way she could get a good suntan while she was turning down all those "open-minded" guys—if there were any. Ironic, she realized. If anybody approached her, she'd die but if they didn't, she'd be crushed. What did she want?

The chain was called Broader Horizons. Their slogan was: Where our horizons are as broad as yours. There was a nice-looking resort in Mexico, just south of Playa del Carmen. She'd never been there before. Perhaps she could leave the resort some days and go shopping while Marcus was doing . . . whatever. The idea had merit.

She looked through the hotel's highlights. There was a clothing-optional swimming pool. Oh joy, she thought. She could even wear a bikini. Maybe if she kept her glasses on and her book held high, everybody would leave her alone.

There was a clothing-optional Jacuzzi, too. Better to give that a wide berth. Who knew what was swimming around in that hot tub of desire? There was a sensuous playroom for couples only. No getting around that one. The only playrooms she'd ever been in were full of five-year-olds. The Barbies and balls in this would be of a very different variety.

Rosie clicked on the resort's home page. "Enjoy a vacation where your life is without boundaries. Redefine yourself," it promised, but this scared her. She'd worked hard to build her boundaries, and she'd happily defined herself as a loyal wife and mother. Now this vacation was threatening to take all of that away.

Public sex was not permitted.

Hallelujah, she thought. The resort seemed to have some standards.

Sex was permitted in the hotel lounge, on the beach and in the sea, in the Jacuzzi, in the playroom, and in the pools. That was more sex than she'd had on her honeymoon. Dammit, how much sex did people need these days? Whatever happened to quality and not quantity?

The resort also had tennis courts, and Rosie wondered if she would be allowed to wear a sports bra. Playing in the nude would be a challenge, for sure. It brought a whole new meaning to "eye on the balls," as her old tennis coach used to say.

There were special evenings of entertainment, too: Costume night. She could guess what it would be like. Tropical and monsoon night—the mind boggled. The Saturday slumber party—doubtless everybody slept together that night, for a change. The Monday night alternative party. She wondered if that was the night you actually went home with your partner, because he was probably the only person you hadn't seen all week.

There was another thing that put her off. All the people in the photographs were skinny. Would she be the only chubby tourist? If so, she'd surely be left behind. Had any of those girls had babies yet?

Either way, she would have to go on the biggest diet of her life. She didn't really plan to sleep with anybody other than her husband, but there was a good chance she was going to get her butt pinched, or at the very least, checked out. She would need to be able to hold her own in a bikini, or worse.

Should she get a full wax job down under? Would it be obvious she'd had a baby? Oh God, this was a bad idea. Her boobs would be droopy compared to the young women in the photos. Babies and breastfeeding did that to you. Before Natasha her body was fine, but a lot had changed.

If somebody had told her that within a few years she would be considering going on a swingers' vacation with her husband, Rosie would have laughed. She was a one-guy-gal and vice-versa. The problem was that it seemed he wanted a different "one-gal" every day. At least he'd had the decency to discuss it with her so they could do something about it together. This wasn't half as bad as Lily and Jack.

Lily had been so two-faced and Jack a total jerk—the lowest of the low. Compared to Jack, Marcus was a prince. Honorable and honest. He just had a voracious sexual appetite. She would have to learn how to live with it, or else she might find herself in the same position as poor Sandra. Yes, she decided, things could be a lot worse. A whole lot worse.

Marcus walked in. "Hey, there you are, babe. I wondered where you'd gone to." It was impossible to miss the photographs of frolicking and scantily clad couples on her computer screen.

"Whoa." He was on it in an instant. "This looks great, doesn't it? Broader Horizons," he said. "Mmm, I like the sound of that."

Rosie didn't answer. He knew she was reluctant. She'd made it clear enough.

"Come on, it'll be wild," he said. "We're in this together. The only reason you're not into it is because you're too repressed. You were the ultimate party girl when we first met. Where's the wild child gone?"

She wanted to say that the "wild child" had dilated to ten centimeters and breastfed for ten months and now she was a Yummy Mommy, but Marcus didn't want to hear that. He wanted a vixen. She smiled weakly.

"I'll help you find the old you," he said as he took over the keyboard and moved around the website with a lot more confidence than she had. Marcus was enthused and laughed out loud. "Playroom." Without much delay, he headed straight for the booking option. There was a discount rate available for mid-February.

"You're talking about Valentine's Day? That's supposed to be a time for us," Rosie said.

"This is for us," Marcus said.

She didn't argue.

"So, can I book this?"

"No. I have to check the dates out with Mom first. What if she's not free to take care of Natasha?"

"She said any time was good."

"Yes, but what about Dad? Marcus, we can't rush them. Let me ask her if the dates are okay, and then we can make a decision." This was only half-true. The other half was that she was still trying to come to terms with the notion they were really going to do this.

"Well, the dates are good for me and the price is great. So if she's okay to take care of Natasha for that week, we're all systems go. Right?"

Against her better judgment, Rosie agreed.

She was relieved to go into their normal playroom and watch the mind-numbing entertainment of *Scooby Doo!* There was something reassuring about that cowardly dog, and Natasha loved cuddling up to her on the sofa. She'd often told Rosie that she liked television, but she liked it much better when mommy watched it with her.

Her daughter gave her such pleasure. It was so fulfilling to be loved unconditionally. As far as Nat was concerned, Rosie was perfect. "You're the most beautiful Mommy in the world," Natasha had told her earlier. "I think you're a queen." With praise like that, how could she not feel wonderful?

Marcus, however, wasn't so happy. He was always trying to change her. "Where's the girl I married?" he would say. She laughed at him but knew he was right. She'd changed so much. Rosie had been a party girl when she was a flight attendant. She and Marcus had whooped it up all over the world. They were platinum members of the mile-high club. They'd even had sex in the cockpit of a jumbo jet halfway across the Atlantic while three-hundred unsuspecting passengers watched *Casino Royale* while eating chicken or beef.

The difference for Rosie was she'd "been there, done that," and she'd well and truly finished with that phase. Marcus still wanted to live that high life. There was no question they were on different flight paths. She was the one who'd changed, so it wasn't fair to blame him. He hadn't fallen in love with a homely, mommy type. Marcus had loved her because she was up for anything, anywhere, anytime. Thinking back, she knew they'd been good times. Very good.

Perhaps Rosie needed to rediscover her fun side. Surely at twenty-eight, it was a little early to be hanging up the stilettos in exchange for furry slippers. She was turning twenty-nine in January. Life was flying by. If ever she was going to do something as wild and crazy as this, it should be now. Maybe an alternative vacation wasn't such a bad idea. Nobody would know, and it would certainly put the spark back in their relationship—maybe even an inferno.

She smiled. What was she so scared of? It was terrific motivation to lose the couple of pounds she'd put on. Many women would jump at the chance to sleep with someone other than the one they were chained to in wedlock. If it all went south, well, they'd just come home and chalk it up to experience. Marcus was right. Life was for living. They'd been dead for long enough. She jumped off the sofa, upsetting Natasha's snuggle.

"Sorry, angel. Mommy just needs a quick word with Daddy. I'll be right back." She nodded begrudgingly.

Marcus was easy to find because he was still in the study checking out the various swinging resorts. He spun around when she entered the room.

"You know what? You're right. I don't know what I'm scared of. Let's just do it," she said.

"You're kidding."

She shook her head. "No, I'm not. Book it. Mom said she was happy to take Natasha any time, so let's just go. By the way, she thinks it's a golfing vacation, so let's keep it that way, all right?"

Marcus smiled like *Scooby Doo!* "Wild child is back in the house," he announced as he logged back into the vacation booking page. "And I'll pack my seven iron!"

"Marcus!" She laughed and went to stand over him. "I'm going for a run.

I'm going to run every day between now and then, so I'm in good enough shape."

Marcus looked up. "Babe, I think you're perfect just the way you are."

She headed out of the study. "Thanks, sweetheart, but you're not the one I'll be trying to impress."

Chapter 17
Popsy & Peter

By Wednesday, Popsy was hoping to see some real improvement in Peter. These were difficult times, what with the business being up in the air and the situation with Lily. She thought her younger daughter would've at least tried to make contact by now, but part of her was relieved she hadn't. Popsy was still furious with her. Bad enough she wanted to shack up with a much older man, but why did it have to be Jack? Of all the middle-aged, lonely old souls in America, she had to pick a married one—and Peter's business partner. She still couldn't fathom it and had no real desire to dwell on it, either.

Peter was always able to temper her moods. She needed him home. Thankfully, the doctors had seen nothing troubling in his tests the day before, so it looked as if his heart attack was due to the stress build up at work and compounded by Lily's little bombshell.

Popsy had resolved to get Peter away from everything. The idea of the castaway shack on a tropical island was still strong in her mind. She'd even picked up a CD in the supermarket the day before. It would be the soundtrack for her new car, and it was called "Tropical Island Rhythm." She'd expected the likes of Bob Marley and Shaggy. Instead it was instrumental, all pretty bland, but what else could she expect for three bucks? And it was still better than listening to the depressing newscasters talking about the economic downturn and double dips.

When she drove to the hospital, she switched it on to get that summer feeling. The sound of steel drums and calypso filled the car and helped transport her to another world. Living in some remote location that didn't have internet access sounded like bliss. She would go barefoot most of the time and get a deep tan. The only stress on Peter's heart would be when he was making love to her in their hammock bed.

The reggae music flowed as Popsy glided her Ferrari into the gas station. The young guy who came out was obviously delighted to be filling up such a beautiful car. She slid her window down.

"Premium, I'm guessing," he said, pointing to the most expensive gas available. She nodded and got out of the car. "Fill it up, please. I'll pay inside, I want to get some things in there, too."

Popsy wandered into the gas station and headed straight for the magazine stand. She'd decided to get a few for Peter to cheer him up, but then a travel magazine caught her eye. The cover was a picture of alabaster sand being lapped by exquisite aquamarine water. Her CD—bad though it was—had definitely put her in a calypso frame of mind. She picked it up. It put Rosie's holiday plans into her mind. Lucky girl! She had phoned the night before to confirm the dates. Mid-February was fine by Popsy, but she'd have been happy to do it sooner. She was dying to spoil her granddaughter rotten by letting her stay up late to watch Disney movies and taking her into Boston to buy her the most exquisite little outfits. It was like being the mom of a toddler again. They were the best years of motherhood, even with the sleepless nights and childhood illnesses. At the time, it had seemed so frantic with the constant need for new clothes as her daughters had grown so fast. Little children, little problems, big children, big problems, she thought, bringing it back to Lily.

Popsy forced the thought out of her head and focused on Natasha again. An entire week was just the right amount of time. Of course, if she had any pressing engagements, Matilda could take her for a few hours. She wondered if Peter would still be at home recuperating. Was there even a job for him to go back to? He wasn't going to work with Jack any time soon. Maybe he'd retire. Maybe she'd make him. Popsy noticed the attendant had finished filling her car. With her magazines in hand, she went to pay for everything. Popsy handed over her credit card and wondered which island in the Caribbean would suit them best. There were so many: Grand Cayman, St. Barts, St. Lucia.

"Your card's been declined," the young man said, interrupting her daydreams just as she got to the Dominican Republic.

"Oh!" Popsy grimaced. "So sorry. Damn thing's been giving me trouble. Here, try this." She handed him another card.

"Declined," he said a moment later, his smile gone. Rather sheepishly, Popsy pulled out another two cards. They were turned down, too.

"Look, I'm really sorry. I have no idea what's going on," she lied. "Do you have an ATM? How much do I owe you? Forget about the magazines for now. If I just pay for the gas, how much is it?"

"Sixty bucks. There's an ATM at the back, just past the coffeemaker."

She nodded. It's more than a coffee I need now, she thought as she tried to look calm and walked over to the ATM. How could she possibly have forgotten about the card? She was so distracted with Peter's turn and the girls' that it just skipped her mind. Very silly of her, she thought.

Could their accounts be in trouble already? Sandra had been certain that it would take weeks, or even months. Popsy believed her, but all of her cards had been declined, and the cash machine was just as uncooperative.

She wasn't sure what to do, so she loitered at the cash dispenser while the few people at the counter paid for their things and left. Then she walked up to the cashier. She'd been in here a million times and even half-recognized the guy.

"I'm afraid I have a bit of a problem," she started uncertainly.

He gave her a response that he'd doubtless trotted out a few times before. "Can you leave the car here and go home to get some cash?"

It was too far to walk, but Popsy wasn't even sure if she had any cash about the house. She kicked herself now. Why didn't she keep a small stash in case of emergencies? She used to keep a fifty under the cookie jar when the girls were younger, but now there didn't seem any need. There were always nearby cash machines and everybody, even taxi drivers, took plastic these days. "No," she replied. "You see, I'm on my way to the hospital. My husband's had a heart attack and now something's happened to our accounts. Can I leave you my name and address? You know I'm good for it." She tried to sound confident and was pretty sure he would know her from coming in since forever, not that they'd ever acknowledged such a fact.

"Problem is, I'm not the boss. I don't have the authority to tell you it's okay."

Popsy looked around. "Well, where is he?"

"At lunch."

"At ten thirty in the morning?" she said without thinking. Maybe not the smartest thing to say.

The guy glared at her. "He started at five."

Popsy felt beaten.

"I have an idea," he said with a grin. Instinct told Popsy that she wasn't going to like what he was about to say, but she was open to anything. "Hold on a second, honey." He winked at her as another customer paid for their gas and left. Popsy hated the way he called her "honey."

"Okay, how much cash to you actually have on you?" he asked her.

Popsy had no choice but to come clean. "Only a few bucks."

"I'll give you the cash," he said.

She looked at him through narrowed eyes. He was not to be trusted. She knew there was more to come. "Go on," she said.

"For a fee," he said.

"Keep talking."

It was clear that he was enjoying his power trip. She desperately wanted to just leave but knew that he could call the police if she did. Plus, it wouldn't be that easy to hide a red Ferrari, even in Wellesley where there were quite a few of them.

He took out his wallet. "Let's see now." He examined the contents. "Let's say I give you, oh, one hundred bucks. You can pay for your gas and maybe get yourself lunch, too. Then you come back here tomorrow and give it back to me. With a little interest, of course."

That was the sting.

"How much?" she asked, her voice flat. He was a little thug.

Again he took his time and rubbed his chin as if he was trying to find a mutually satisfactory figure. "Shall we say, two hundred?"

"Two hundred?" Popsy screeched.

"And fifty?"

"Are you out of your little mind?" Popsy shouted.

"And I'll need a little security," he said and eyed her rings.

"You little shit," she snarled. "They're my wedding and engagement rings."

"Not that one." He pointed to her right hand where she wore an enormous sapphire surrounded by diamonds. When she'd had it insured, it came in with a value of $90,000. That would be more than this guy made in a year —make that five years. "This is honest-to-God daylight robbery."

He put up his hands. "Hey, lady, I'm only trying to help. If you don't want it, that's cool by me." He played the hapless victim role well.

Popsy stood there mute while another customer came and went. She tried to phone Sandra and got her voice mail. She was probably in the gym again. Next, she tried Rosie. No reply there, either. For a moment, she thought about phoning Lily but dismissed that notion just as fast. She was on her own.

She hadn't ever been in a spot like this, but she knew a bully when she saw one and the only solution was to meet fire with fire. The store was empty again, so she placed her hands palms-down on the counter. He was a small guy, so they were looking at each other eye-to-eye, and he seemed to lose a little of his confidence.

"I'll give you two-hundred tomorrow for one hundred today, but you can forget the rings. You're not getting them," she said, her voice low and hard.

"No security, no deal."

"Two-hundred and fifty. That's my final offer. Take that or I'm off to the cops to report a case of blackmail."

His expression flashed uncertainty for a moment. "Gimme your phone, and I'll give you a hundred bucks. Then come back tomorrow with the two-fifty you owe me."

How did he make it sound like he was doing her the favor when she was getting absolutely robbed blind?

"I get my phone back tomorrow?"

He nodded and took the cash out of his wallet. Popsy didn't want to even handle it, he repulsed her so much. She took it anyway and handed over her beloved BlackBerry, as well as the sixty dollars for the gas.

"I'll be back here first thing tomorrow. What time do you start work?"

"Nine," he assured her.

"Good," she said and walked out, quietly wondering if she'd ever see her phone again.

Chapter 18

Breaking Out

"Hey, doll, happy Halloween. It's great to see you."

Popsy thought her husband looked stronger and healthier than he'd been all week. He'd been moved to a private room. This was all good.

"Boy, am I happy to see you looking better." Popsy crossed the room to kiss him and give him a hug.

"Did you bring my stuff?" He sounded much more like the old Peter she knew and loved.

"It's all here," she said and tapped the small suitcase. He'd told her to bring fresh clothes and toiletries. He wanted his phone, too, but she'd conveniently forgotten that. The doctors were still insistent on no excitement. She pulled the visitor's chair beside his bed and sat down. "How are you feeling?"

"Terrific. Never better. To be honest, if their machines didn't say otherwise, I would go so far as to say I don't think I had an attack at all. It was more of a fall than anything."

"Peter, you had a heart attack. You have to accept that or you'll end up having another one. There are going to be changes around here. Are you listening to me?" she asked but knew he wasn't. He was out of the bed and taking the small case into his en suite bathroom.

"Hey, don't worry, doll. It's over. I'm great. Look at me." This was so typical of him. On a normal day, Popsy loved his positivity and irrepressible nature, but not now. He left the door open so they could talk.

"You're going to have to slow down. That was your body warning you not to work so hard. If you don't listen, it might send you a stronger message next time."

She went to look out his window. The view was calming. She was six floors up and as far as the eye could see, it was treetops—a leafy canopy like little heads of broccoli, only now some had turned red or yellow.

Peter's electric razor started. He was getting cleaned up.

"I'm not in denial," he shouted. "But I'm not going to roll over and die either. You have to move on and get over setbacks."

Was he talking about his health or his business empire? She didn't want to ask.

"Have you heard from Lily?"

A plane high in the blue sky left a streak of white behind it as it moved across the horizon. She idly wondered where it was going and if things were easier there. "No," she called back. "Nor do I want to."

The razor stopped, and Peter came out of the bathroom. He'd taken off his pajama top. On his chest were the white stick-on patches the hospital used for monitoring him. They disturbed Popsy and reminded her how fragile he'd been only a few short days ago.

"What did you say?"

"I said I haven't heard from her. Peter, are you sure you're feeling okay? I mean, I know the tests came back clear and you have no blockages, but we still don't know why it happened."

"I certainly do. Jack Hoffman. Can you believe it? I swear I want to kill him. In the past few days, I've even thought about taking a contract out on him."

"You wouldn't."

"I would if I thought I could get away with it."

"You wouldn't!" Popsy said.

"Don't worry. I'm not going to do it. It was just a fantasy, and speaking of fantasies, I've really missed you for the last few nights. Come and give your man a hug."

She was so happy he sounded like himself again. The essence of Peter had returned. Only now did she realize how much she'd missed his strength and humor. She rushed into his arms and hugged him with all her strength.

"So, do you have your Halloween costume ready for me tonight?" he teased. It made Popsy laugh.

"I could dress as the grim reaper and go get Jack and Lily," she grumbled.

"That's not exactly what I had in mind," he said. "Listen, don't be too hard on Lily, doll. I've done a lot of thinking while I've been in here. Remember, she's just a kid. It's Jack who should know better."

"You're not angry with her?"

He shook his head. "Nah, he played her. It's what he does. I'm mad at myself for not protecting her better from his kind."

"Speaking of protecting, I should be minding you better," she said. "Can I get you anything?"

He nodded. "Where's the phone? I need to make a few calls."

Popsy tried not to look guilty. "Um, I forgot it."

"What?"

"Sorry, honey. I was in such a rush leaving the house."

"Okay, give me yours."

"I don't have it."

"Seriously? Your BlackBerry? You're never parted from that. What's up?"

"I have my new car," she said, trying to change the conversation.

Peter laughed. "It was delivered? Great. Do you like it?

"I love it," she enthused, relieved to be off the topic of phones. "Sandra and I took it for a spin yesterday. We went out Route 9 and then over to Rosie's house. Marcus was speechless with envy. We really had some fun."

Peter spoke as he headed back into the bathroom. "So you and Sandra are okay?"

"I think so. I mean, it's tough and awkward, and I know she's heartbroken, but she's strong, too. I think she'll survive."

The razor started up again. "He's some asshole," she heard him grumble more to himself than to her. Should she tell him about the bank accounts? She was terrified of putting too much stress on him if she did.

He came out of the bathroom with a towel wrapped around his waist.

"I'm going to take a shower and get all this crap off my chest, doll. Do you want to grab some lunch? I'll be done in about twenty minutes."

"Peter, they've frozen our bank accounts."

"What?"

"Our cards. I don't know what's going on. None of them work. Some little thug in the gas station has my phone. I had to give it to him as collateral to pay for the gas."

"Of all the low-down . . . Where is Jack in all of this? I have to talk to him."

"I haven't spoken to him yet. It started yesterday. One of my cards was rejected, and I didn't realize how bad it was until I tried all of them to pay for the gas today, and they were refused."

"You're right. It sounds like the accounts have been frozen. What is Jack up to?" Peter took her hands. "I will straighten this out, but don't forget we have about $20,000 in cash in the safe at home."

"Oh, I didn't know that."

"And that's not all. We have a bank account in your maiden name with $500,000 in it. Remember?"

"What? I didn't know that."

"No? Gee, I would have thought I told you." He shrugged and then continued, "It was done fifteen years ago, and I never go near the account. It was started in case of a rainy day. Well, honey, I think today might be a little wet."

"Monsoon, more like. Well, if you did tell me, I'd forgotten all about it."

"You see? When I say we're broke, I mean no more private jets, but we're not destitute yet."

"Oh Peter, I was so worried."

He hugged her again. "Shhh, it's not that bad. All the information on that account is in the files at home under the name 'Popsy Heffernan.' It was in New York. I do know it's an Irish Bank. You liked the romanticism of that."

"Okay, now I remember."

He pulled back from her and grinned. "So how much cash do you actually have on you right now?"

She shrugged. "I still have to pay for the parking. I have no idea what that will be. I have forty dollars on me right now."

"Oh, doll, I'm so sorry I've let this happen. You should never have been put in this position. Okay, we'll skip lunch. You can raid the safe when you get home, and I'll send a few of the boys from the office over to the gas station to get your phone back. Capiche?"

Popsy was so relieved to have Peter back in control.

"Sit down and watch some television or enjoy the view while I grab a quick shower."

She nodded and sat. As the water started up and her husband sang to himself, she marveled over how much he was able to take in stride. Okay, it was great that they had a small stash put away, but she knew they'd lost a good portion of their money. And they owed the banks, too, so that meant they were now in negative equity. How deep they were in debt, she didn't know.

There was so much she didn't understand. Well, at least she was getting her phone back. Popsy understood what Peter meant when he talked about sending the boys around. It was fair to say he had some shady guys in the building trade. The boys to whom Peter referred were big. They'd scare that little thug witless. Good.

He seemed so blasé—so together. What was he going to do now? Start again? Not if she had anything to do with it. Was half a million enough to live on? Perhaps they'd go to some tropical island and just sunbathe for the rest of their lives. No, that would never work for Peter. He was too impatient. He needed to be active. Maybe if his heart was up to it, he might like to take tourists on shark safaris.

"Okay, let's go," Peter said as he walked out of the bathroom a few minutes later. He was dressed and looking like he was ready for a day at the office.

"What are you doing?" she asked incredulously, jumping to her feet.

"I'm coming home with you."

"No, you are not! I'm sure they want to observe you for a few more days, maybe even another week. They don't know why you had your attack."

He waved away her concerns. "I know more than they do, and I can tell you, I'm fine." He tried to take her arm, but she wouldn't budge from her spot beside the window.

"Look, I didn't want to tell you because I thought you'd worry, but I did feel tightness in my chest for the last few weeks."

Popsy felt her body flood with fear.

"I'm not that stupid. I just put it down to the stress of the UK deal. Okay, maybe that was dumb. Looking back now, I can see it was a little more than that. I might have had a small blockage, but the attack and subsequent drugs must have cleared it out." He came over and took her hands. "That's why they can't find anything now. The problem is gone. They've given me every test they can think of: stress tests, blood tests, stand-on-my-head tests, you name it. I've had more needles put in me in the last three days than the Wellesley Botox Clinic uses in a month."

She laughed.

"I'm fine. They can't find anything to upset this ol' heart of mine again." He thumped his chest as if to prove his point. Peter was very convincing, but that was his strength.

"Have the doctors said it's okay for you to go home?"

"That's only so they can justify their massive fees. It's a racket, doll. Look at me. You can see I'm back to my old self, and I'm telling you, I feel great. All the tightness in my chest is gone. Come on, you don't think I'd be leaving if I felt sick. It's all good. Let's get out of here. And anyway, I want to see you behind the wheel of your new birthday present."

Reluctantly, she agreed. "You know business is going to be very stressful for the next few weeks. Are you sure your 'big ol' heart' is up to that?"

He winked at her and picked up the suitcase in one hand while taking her hand in the other. They left the private hospital room.

"You know I love working. It's what I do," he said as they approached the elevator. That's when they were spotted by the head nurse.

"Mr. Power, where are you going?" she called after him.

Peter tightened his hold of Popsy's hand. "Don't look at her. Pretend we didn't hear," he whispered.

"Mr. Power?" the nurse called again, panic rising in her voice. She bore down on them with the affection of a hungry hawk for a spring chicken.

"Come on," Peter said, mischief dancing all over his face. He pulled Popsy by the hand and into the emergency staircase, so she didn't have much choice.

"I don't believe we're doing this," she half-shrieked as she followed him.

"Mr. Power, stop!" the nurse shouted just as the heavy door closed behind them.

Peter laughed. "She was far too bossy for me to live with. Come on, let's blow this joint." He let go of her hand and started down the stairs. Then, to Popsy's amazement, he bounded down them two at a time. It was hard to keep up. Quite unbelievable to think he'd had a heart attack just a few days earlier.

Halfway down, Popsy was out of breath. "I think we can stop for a rest," she called to him. Peter was a full flight ahead of her.

"Come on, it's good for us." He laughed.

"Peter, don't overexert yourself," she shouted, but the truth was she was loving the jailbreak of sorts. She felt like a schoolgirl skipping class with her rogue boyfriend. This was why she still loved Peter.

"I think it would take more than a flight of stairs to take me down. Get it? Take me down?" He laughed, but she could hear that he was out of breath, too. At least she worked out. He usually didn't.

"Peter, I'm serious. Please stop and wait for me."

He did.

"How do you feel? Is there any tightness?" Popsy asked when she caught up with him.

He shook his head and smiled, but she didn't believe him. His color was high. She insisted they take the elevator the rest of the way since they both needed the rest. Peter didn't put up a fight.

By the time they got to the car, they'd both recovered from their stairwell dash, and Peter was more interested in the Ferrari than his hospital stay.

"She really is a beauty," he said enthusiastically and stroked the back of it as he came around to the driver's side.

"Do you want to drive?" she offered.

"I'd love to." He smiled.

Popsy half-expected to be stopped by security at the front door or in the parking lot due to her aiding and abetting the escape of a patient, but nobody seemed concerned. The parking attendant was much more interested in the car than its inhabitants, which suited her fine.

"We have a full tank. Could we take it for a spin on the way home?"

How could she turn him down? The light in his eyes was infectious. He was still the man she'd fallen in love with so many years ago. She didn't care if they were broke or relatively poor. She had Peter, and that was all she needed.

He took the car out onto the Mass Pike, and the traffic became light the farther away they got from Boston. He gunned the accelerator and the beast of an engine sprang to life. It was impossible not to go fast in such a smooth ride. The car cruised up to a hundred miles an hour with ease and clearly still had plenty more under the hood.

"We'll be arrested." Popsy giggled, enjoying the excitement.

"They'd have to catch us first." Peter laughed, but he slowed the car down to a legal speed and took the next exit for home.

Matilda was ecstatic when they got there. "Oh, Mr. Power, it is so good to see you, but it is too soon. Already the hospital has been calling. Rosie, too, she is very anxious."

Peter gave her a reassuring hug. "They're making too much of a fuss. You can see, I'm fine. I'll call Rosie to put her mind at rest. Now, will you make Popsy and me something to eat? Maybe your scrambled eggs on toast? We have some business to see to in the office. Where's my phone?"

Matilda trotted off as Peter dropped his suitcase at the foot of the stairs and headed straight for his study. Once again armed with his cell phone, he was ready for business. Within minutes, he'd pulled up Popsy's bank account details and opened the safe. As promised, there was $20,000 in cash sitting there, just waiting to be spent. He insisted she put $1,000 into her wallet right away. "I don't want you feeling insecure about money. Next, I'm going to take care of that thief at the gas station."

She left to call Rosie from the house phone. She had to assure her daughter that Peter was back to his old self.

"Is he crazy?" Rosie was panicked. "The nurse who called me was not at all happy."

"Why did they call you?"

"Mom, I was with you when you went to the hospital. They had my contact details in case of an emergency from the day Dad went in. Didn't they call you?"

"I've lost my cell just at the moment, but I'll get it back soon. You have to believe me; your father is feeling great. He's promised me he'll slow down. You wouldn't believe what I saw him do in the hospital, Rosie. I'm telling you, the man is a bear."

"Even bears don't last forever, Mom."

"Well, you try to talk sense into him," Popsy snapped, and took the phone into the study so Rosie could talk with her dad, but Peter was gone. She looked out the window and saw him driving away in her new Ferrari.

"I'm afraid you'll have to speak with him later. Looks like he's taken my car out for another spin. You know, I think he really wants it for himself."

"I'm not surprised. Marcus is still talking about it—like a scratched record, in fact. Don't worry. I'll call Dad and give him an earful."

"So much for having lunch with me, and I know Matilda is going to a lot of trouble for his homecoming."

"Aw, Mom, I'm thinking he just went to get you a bunch of flowers or something romantic like that. He'll be back in a few minutes, wait and see. I'll call him now and tell him to hurry home."

Popsy called Sandra next.

"There you are," her friend began. "I called you and some weirdo answered saying you'd stepped out and he didn't know when you would be back. Then got all suggestive. I thought you'd taken up with some boy toy."

"The little shit. He's using my phone." Popsy filled Sandra in on her morning and on Peter's jailbreak. She wasn't impressed.

"Popsy, don't let him go back to work. It's too soon. Peter doesn't have a pause button. He'll give himself another heart attack."

"You know how impossible it is to stop him. The man is a machine, and I have to tell you, he had me convinced. He seems just fine."

"He probably believes that himself, but the doctors know best, and they say he should be in the hospital. Where is he now? Resting, I hope."

"Um, he's gone out."

"What? Where?"

"I don't know."

"You need to protect him from himself. Call him. Scream at him. Get him home and into bed."

For the first time, Popsy felt guilty. Sandra was right, of course. Clearly, Peter was in denial. He'd told her that he didn't believe he'd even had a heart attack. How could she have been so foolish? "I have to go, Sandra. I'll call him. Thanks. Bye."

Chapter 19
Jack & Lil

Jack Hoffman phoned the only person he could think of: his new love, Lily.

"How are things?"

"Crazy," she said, sounding happy to hear from him. "Asian markets are jittery and that means I am, too. Their markets are closed now but the erratic trading is impacting upon my portfolios."

"Never mind about that right now." He sounded distracted. "You're not going to believe who just called me."

"Who?" she asked.

"Peter, and he didn't sound too friendly. He wants me to meet him in Chestnut Hill. Says he wants to talk."

"Dad? What? Isn't he still in the hospital? Have they released him already? That must be a good sign. How did he sound? I hope he's okay."

For some reason this annoyed Jack. She was supposed to be in his corner now.

"You hope he's okay? What about me? What if he has a gun this time?"

"Oh, Jack. This is Dad we're talking about. He's a smart guy. You know he'll come around. Do you want me for company?"

Even this irked Jack. He didn't need his hand held by Lily. Jack was a big boy and capable of handling anything Peter threw at him, as long as it wasn't another punch. He wasn't seriously worried about getting beaten up or shot at. Peter was smarter than that. What really concerned him was that maybe Peter would have another heart attack and everybody would blame him.

The truth was, he really didn't want to meet with Peter, but what choice did he have? They were business partners, or at least they had been up until things went belly-up. How much did Peter even know at this stage? Was he aware the accounts had been frozen? That he and Lily were living together? This was going to be a tough lunch.

He hung up, feeling less satisfied. It would have been easier if he hadn't called her at all. They were barely living together a week and already they were acting like an old married couple. She didn't adore him like she did when they first dated. She wasn't focusing on him when he called her for support. That level of indifference should take at least a few years. Please, Lord, let me not have made the biggest mistake of my life, he thought.

It was still fair to say she had an amazing body. Then again, so did Sandra. But Lily had her youth. He knew he was a fool to be so seduced by young women, but who could blame him? They were exquisite. New, fresh, ripe. Olga had started out like that and so had Sandra, and then they both aged and the magic faded. Not the case with Lily. She was so young and enthusiastic. She wanted sex morning, noon, and night. And it was good sex. They weren't just going through the motions. There was no routine like Olga's Friday-date-night, which he'd come to abhor. It was all too predictable, too humdrum. Lily was unpredictable. She seduced him everywhere and anywhere. She exhausted him and he loved it.

Sure, he knew that he was no youngster himself, but the ladies in his life didn't seem to mind. Lily loved older men. She'd never been attracted to men her age. That was just his good luck, he figured. Down the road—when he hit his seventies and she was still in her forties—would be tough, of course. But he wouldn't let himself worry about that. It was way in the future. Who knew what would happen between now and then?

One thing he did know: financially, he was going to have to start from scratch. Again. It was an ordeal. They'd had so much and lost it all. It was a disaster. He'd been wiped out. From a net value of over $100 million to very deep debt. It was a heartache.

What really annoyed Jack was that deep-down this was Peter's fault. He was always the more ambitious of the two. He always pushed it further, harder, and faster. Jack liked to err on the side of caution, but Peter was very convincing. This last refinancing deal—the one that had drastically overextended their asset base—was so Peter's baby.

Jack had seen the writing on the wall. He'd told Peter it was time to start selling some of their larger assets. Peter had insisted they leverage, using equity in the assets to secure more financing was easy money. They'd continue to grow using their own portfolio as collateral. Well, the collateral was being called in by some very angry banks, and now there was nobody offering money. He'd planned to take the money off the table but never got around to it.

At least he had a condo in Boca Raton he'd paid cash for years ago. He'd also paid off all the mortgages on Olga's house, so she was off his back, except for the alimony. That would be an interesting conversation.

But Sandra was the one he felt guilty about. The penthouse would definitely have to go. She wouldn't even have a roof over her head soon. He had several other properties scattered around Metro West, but he was pretty certain they were all wrapped up in the cross-guarantee bundle. He would go through everything with a fine tooth comb to see what he could salvage. He didn't even have any cash on deposit to give her. Would she go after him in the courts?

He glanced at the clock. He was meeting Peter in Chestnut Hill in half an hour. There was no point arriving late or doing a no-show. This had to be done. First they would address the Lily situation. Jack hoped she was right and her father had cooled off. They were best friends. Wasn't he good enough for her? He would treasure Lily. Protect her and take care of her forever. He would make a new fortune to keep her in the level of comfort to which she was accustomed.

But Jack's conscience needled him. Peter was no fool. He knew Jack's bad track record with women. Peter would also want a younger man for his daughter. Well, tough luck. Life had conspired for Lily and him to fall in love. No father had the power to decide who his daughter ended up with— not these days.

For a moment, his mind turned to his own girls. He had no clue who they were dating or what they were even doing with their lives. It was a sad fact he'd let those relationships slip when he parted with his wife. But doubtless Olga had poisoned their minds, too. She'd made no effort to keep him in their lives. There were never school reports or vacation photos. Just bills. That's all he was now to Olga and his three daughters: the guy who paid the bills.

There was a touch of that between him and Sandra, too. He worked all the hours in the day while she swanned around doing lunches and going to the gym. She had a charmed life—well, up until now. The future wasn't looking quite so bright, but she was still pretty. She'd probably find a new guy fast. And then there was all that baby nonsense. At her age, it was stupid and selfish. He'd said from the get-go, no kids. They'd agreed, but then she tried to change the goal posts. If that didn't qualify for irreconcilable differences, he didn't know what did. Babies? Him? At this stage of life? Totally crazy.

At least he and Lily were in agreement about that. She knew he didn't want babies, and she still loved him. They could have a lovely life together just as soon as he figured out how to recoup his losses. Things had to settle down and Peter would come around. Unfortunate that Popsy and Sandra were so close, but that might start to weaken. Mothers always sided with their daughters. He'd experienced that firsthand. Lily and Popsy would not be separated by Jack's soon-to-be ex-wife. Popsy would come around like she did when Olga moved out and Sandra moved in. It was just a question of time.

He glanced at the clock again. Fifteen minutes. This meeting was not the highlight of his day, for sure. He'd chosen Route 9 as opposed to the Mass Pike because it was closer to his office, but the flipside was that it clogged up faster. As luck would have it, things had jammed up pretty bad. It looked like he was going to be late. Crap. Not the best way to start his meeting.

He decided to phone Peter as a courtesy. As usual, he got voice mail. The guy was practically impossible to reach.

He left a message saying he was going to be late and for Peter to use the back roads if he wasn't already caught up in the jam. Then he hung up and gave more thought as to how he should approach his lifelong business partner.

How could Lily focus knowing what she did? Her two computer monitors churned out the share-price changes from around the globe. The graph looked like a ride on the big dipper, surging up and then crashing down to nothing. Normally this would have had her glued to her seat as she tried to make sense of the changes, but not today. Her beloved laptop blinked out all the information she needed for work but none of the advice she wanted for life. Her mind was on the Capital Grille. It was her favorite restaurant, but not for all the money in the world did she want to be there right now. She paced the white wool carpet that covered the floor of her private office and looked at the clock on the wall. Jack would be with her dad by now.

Should she call her mother? Maybe now was a good time. Her dad was just out of the hospital and obviously back to some sort of normal life, so chances were that she'd be in a good mood. The shock of the heart attack had hit them all hard. Financial ruin was pretty epidemic these days. Loads of high-profile businessmen had gone to the wall and still managed to bounce back, but having a heart attack and bouncing back? That was a little trickier. The problem was she didn't know how serious it was. It couldn't have been that bad if he was back to work after only a few days.

Emily appeared at the glass door. "Still on for tonight? We're going for a drink after work and you're telling me all your deepest, darkest secrets." She grinned.

"Come in and shut the door. Jeez, it's good to see you."

"What's up now?"

"Dad is out of the hospital. He's meeting with Jack for lunch today." Lily looked from the clock to her watch.

"Oh, to be a fly on the wall at that meeting. You're talking about Jack Hoffman, Peter's business partner?"

Lily glanced at Emily and nodded. "My bed partner, too."

Emily let out a long, low whistle and sat in her friend's guest chair. "Hey, that guy really is a player, isn't he?"

"Emily, stop. He's my boyfriend, my long-term partner. Please respect that."

"Sorry," she said and looked at the floor. "Hey, I just realized that as a couple, you guys could call yourselves Jack and Lil." She laughed.

"Except my name's Lily,"

"Poetic license. Don't worry, I'm drawing a blank on the hill part anyway. You know, 'Jack and Lil went up a hill.' "

"Chestnut Hill. That's where Jack's meeting Dad right now." Lily blurted before she had the sense to say nothing.

Emily beamed. "There you go. This is all destiny. It's meant to be. Jack and Lil, it is."

Lily gave her an impatient glare. "Don't go there, Em."

"All right." She gave up and changed the subject. "So, your dad is obviously A-OK, health wise. That's good news, isn't it?"

Lily continued pacing.

"Hey, would you mind sitting down? This room isn't big enough to pace. You're making me dizzy."

Lily obeyed, grateful for some direction. She fell back into her chair.

"Do you want to go out for lunch? We could go to the Intercontinental and get a nice table overlooking the water. Maybe have a glass of wine."

"How can we drink now? Have you been watching Asia?"

Emily nodded. "Why do you think I'm suggesting the wine? Or better yet, let's go to the new fusion bar around the corner and have sushi and *sake*. Perhaps we can boost the markets single-handedly."

Lily relaxed for the first time all morning. "You're the best, Emily. Really."

"Well, there's not a lot we can do about the situation. Are you busy?"

"Busy? Yes. But getting anything done? No. I've been poring over the figures all morning and trying to make sense of which way the markets will go tonight when they start trading again, but it's impossible to call."

"Hey, I thought you always knew. Isn't that why they pay you the big bucks?"

"Ha."

"Is Matt still giving you grief?" Emily asked.

"Nah, we've moved on to the evil-eye stare."

"Charming."

"Honestly, Emily. Do people think I got my promotion because my dad was a big client?"

She looked away. "How would I know what people think, and more important, why would I give a hoot? The world is full of jealousy. Just dance to your own tune. Now, are we dancing down to the new fusion restaurant, or not? Because one thing I do know is, you gotta eat."

Lily was sold. She grabbed her jacket. What Emily said also rang true for her domestic situation. Much better to wait and see what happened with her dad and Jack and then decide how she was going to move forward with her mom. What difference would another couple of hours make?

The Boston streets were full of life and vibrancy. Emily was right. It was a great idea to get out of the office. Too often she went in at four o'clock in the morning to catch the markets before Hong Kong closed for the night and worked right through to the late evening to see how they opened the following day. It was a grueling schedule, but as a single working woman with no kids, she'd been happy the job dominated her life.

Lily had been toying with the idea of slowing down. When she and Jack were a secret, they couldn't spend any time out in public, but things were different now. She was having a few fantasies where they could take long lunches or go to the theater. There were so many things she thought about doing but had never gotten around to, and they had appeal to her now that she was getting older and, more importantly, settled.

Of course, all these daydreams were before the collapse of her dad and Jack's business. Now she was going to have to work harder than ever because it looked like she was the only breadwinner in her house. How ironic. Jack had represented security to her, and now, all of a sudden, it was no longer there.

She pushed the notion out of her head. What did it matter? They were together now and in love. They would just work through this tough patch. That was assuming he survived lunch with her dad today. It made her smile. Lily knew what a force of nature her father was. It would take a brave man to stand up to him, and that's exactly what Jack was doing. That's why she loved him so much. He was just as strong as her father. Maybe even stronger. He was a magnificent man, and he was all hers.

"Have you heard about this restaurant?" Emily asked as they walked along the street.

"Um, no. What's so special about it?"

"The owner is a Japanese guy and he has a full army of Japanese master chefs, but his wife is Chinese and she's brought in her own fleet of Chinese chefs. It's insane. You can get anything from sweet and sour duck to sashimi flounder, but it always has an amazing buzz."

Not surprisingly, Feng Shui was hopping. All the city traders and suits were there. She recognized quite a few from other banks and legal firms in town. It was a small place, but they managed to get seats at the counter where they could watch the various little platters move along on the miniature conveyer belt. It was just the distraction Lily needed. Asian master chefs worked industriously behind the counter, balancing expertly carved pieces of wafer-thin raw fish on neat bundles of white rice. Some were wrapped with little ribbons of seaweed and others garlanded with sliced ginger.

"The knife work would make any plastic surgeon jealous," Emily said. "Where should we start?"

Lily had spent time in China and Japan as part of her Master's in Economics. She scooped up a couple of plates. "Start with this," she said and handed one to Emily. "It's white tuna and it melts in your mouth."

The girls relaxed and chatted about Emily's kids while they worked their way through a few tried-and-tested plates and some wildcard picks.

Lily's ability to speak Mandarin gave them huge credibility with the Chinese staff.

"Trying to get some inside information, is she?" Matt asked as he came up behind Emily.

Lily stopped speaking Mandarin and swung around. "Oh, don't stop on my account," he said, nodding at the chefs.

Then he switched into fluent Japanese for their benefit. Lily could just about make out that he was asking how they were. They nodded back and returned the salutation.

Then the manager came over to them, and it was clear that she knew Matt, too. How annoying, Lily thought.

"Lily, Emily, this is Bao. She's the real boss here." He smiled at the hostess.

"*Ni hao,*" Lily said, showing off her own knowledge of Mandarin.

"*Dzum gwoh hahm seui?*" Bao said and smiled. Then she gave a nod and excused herself, leaving them to decode her sentiments.

"What?" Emily asked.

Much to her annoyance, Lily didn't know. Bao had replied in Cantonese, not Mandarin.

"Mandarin is the international language for commerce in Hong Kong, but Cantonese is a regional language in China." Matt glanced at Lily. "She was asking if we were soaked in salt water."

"What?" Emily said again.

Lily remained silent, annoyed to discover that Matt knew Mandarin, Cantonese, and Japanese, while she only spoke the former.

She turned her attention to her friend. "It means we must have been taught the language in the East. It's a compliment. We're seasoned speakers. 'Pickled in the culture,' if you know what I mean."

"Nice. I think." Emily examined her food and looked a little unsure.

"Where did you learn your Mandarin?" Matt finally asked her.

"In college and Hong Kong. You?"

"I spent a year in Hong Kong, but then I backpacked around China and Japan for a year. Picked up the Cantonese on-the-hoof, so to speak.

"*Manman chi,*" Lily said, gesturing to the small box of takeout he held. Then she leaned into Emily. "That means bon appétit."

"*Zaijian.*" Matt smiled at her and winked at Emily. "That means thanks," he said and left them to their lunch.

"That was so cool, even though I don't know what you said." Emily laughed and helped herself to another little plate as it passed. "Oh. You know, it's a pity you're in love with Jack Hoffman, because you and Matt would have made a really great couple."

"You're the second person who's said that to me in the last few days. My sister Rosie was pushing him on me. He's too young, and then there's the fact that I don't actually like him."

"Well, Lily, I don't know Mandarin, but we have an expression here in the good old US of A that opposites attract. Remember that one?"

"*Bie guan wo*," Lily said, looking exasperated.

"I don't understand you, but I think I get the gist of what you're saying."

Lily laughed. With her mind finally off all her domestic difficulties for the first time in days and the office out of her life for a while, she began to enjoy herself, so it wasn't surprising that was the moment her phone rang. She looked at Emily, wide-eyed. "It's Mom."

"Well answer it, girl."

"Hello, Mom. It's good to hear from you. I've been th—"

"I'm looking for your father. Has he called you?" Popsy asked.

Lily tried to sound calm, but it was hard. If she told her mom, would Jack be mad at her? "What's up?" she asked, playing for time.

"Oh, I let him walk out of the hospital, and now he's disappeared to God knows where. He's not well, Lily. What if something dreadful happens?"

Lily knew she had to come clean. "Don't panic, Mom. It's okay. Jack called me a while ago. He said he was going to meet Dad for lunch. I'm pretty sure it was The Capital Grille in Chestnut Hill." Lily listened intently. "Is there anything I can do?" But her mother had started ranting on the other end.

She felt worse than ever and was close to tears by the time she ended the call. Emily reached over and touched her shoulder.

"What was all that about?" she asked.

Lily filled her in quickly. "Mom is freaking out. She went crazy when I told her about his meeting with Jack and went on about all the damage he's done already and how he was the one who gave Dad the heart attack in the first place. Oh, Emily, Dad is missing in action and everybody is blaming Jack." She felt desperate.

"Call Jack and tell him what you just heard. To be honest, I think you should tell him to skip the meeting. Get your mother to go instead and get your dad back into the hospital. There really is no fool like an old fool."

Lily looked anxiously into Emily's eyes. "This is all my fault."

"Nonsense." Emily shook her head for emphasis. "Let me get the bill and get you out of here. You need to finish up early and get home to Jack and maybe even your mother."

"*Ren wu qian ri hao, hua wu bai ri hong*," Lily whispered.

"Huh?"

It's an old Mandarin expression. It means, 'No person gets a thousand days good luck and no flower can bloom for a hundred days."

"You need to start buying silk flowers, Lily. They'll bloom for a hundred days."

"No, it means that everybody's luck runs out sooner or later. You're not understanding it right."

"And you're not listening to me, girl," Emily said. "Sometimes you have to make your own good luck, and something tells me your time is now, so come on."

Chapter 20

Eggs on Toast

Sandra hit the gym and despite everything, she was sad to see no sign of Sven. She'd half-planned to apologize to him. It was true that he'd been a little forward, but then again, perhaps her response had been too heavy-handed. During their first encounter it was she who was looking for attention. She'd flirted with him and challenged him, so how could she get so nasty when he followed through? Girls led and boys followed. It had been that way for millennia. She pushed herself hard on the treadmill as she thought about it and figured it must have been because she was so hurt and angry with Jack. She just took it out on Sven. That was a little unfair.

She knew that she was a strong woman—perhaps a bit too strong for her own good. Jack had liked her stubborn streak in the early days, but that must have waned. She hadn't spoken to or seen him since he'd walked out of their apartment and her life. She was still so angry and hurt. The only way to keep her friendship with Popsy strong was to absolutely ignore that Lily was Popsy's daughter.

That little skank. How could she? How selfish and shortsighted. Did she not realize that Jack would leave her in the end, too? It was just a question of time. To have one ex-wife was unfortunate, but not too unusual. Two ex-wives, and there was a very definite pattern forming. He liked to trade in the older models for newer ones when the time came.

It was now obvious to her that Jack had the morals of a sewer rat. No—

that was doing a disservice to sewer rats. Jack was even lower. It was easier to be angry with him instead of feeling heartbroken. Sorrow was much worse than anger. If she was being honest with herself, she also had to concede that she'd been thinking of leaving Jack prior to his walking out. Hadn't she said as much to Popsy? The difference was that she probably would have stayed in an unhappy marriage, while he was content to move up and on. Then, of course, there was the other conversation Sandra had had with Popsy. Had she really been considering getting pregnant without telling him? What sort of person did that make her? How underhanded would that have been? What in the world had she been thinking? Maybe he was better off without her.

Was this what Karma was all about? She had been a bad person and now the bad luck had returned onto her. She had nothing—no money, no baby, no husband, and what about Jack? The shit! He had his next recruit—his next victim—ready to go. Little Lily Power. Poor, girl, she had no idea yet how unlucky she was.

What would I do with the rest of my life? she wondered, feeling the panic rising.

Sandra increased the speed on the treadmill. Well, she wasn't going to mope or waste any of her precious time with regrets. She decided there and then that her next ten years were going to be the best of her life and not a moment was to be wasted. She was still young and fit, and she would find another lover, if and when she wanted one. Nothing was stopping her. If she wanted a baby, she could do it on her own now. At least a child might hang around for a couple of decades.

Sandra couldn't maintain the high speed, so she pulled it back a little.

Babies cost a fortune, and along with her husband, she'd lost wealth, too. How could she possibly consider having a baby when she had no means of supporting it? And that was assuming she was even capable of conceiving.

She'd tried to withdraw more cash, but she was told the accounts had been frozen. That's when she realized Jack had been serious about their financial troubles. She was already getting legal advice, but this discovery made her accountant less than optimistic. How could you take a man for everything when he had nothing? Still, that wouldn't stop her from fighting tooth-and-nail for the penthouse, the place in Boca, and all their art and cars. She was going to take whatever was left. Poor Lily, she thought again. At least Sandra got a rich forty-year-old with whom to spend the last fifteen years, while Lily was shacking up with a fifty-five-year-old broke guy. Fool.

How was Popsy going to live with the new situation? Sandra knew her closest friend had big hopes and dreams for her daughter. Of course, she wanted Lily to marry a nice, normal guy her age and give her lots of little babies to play with. Well, that plan was shattered. On top of that, Popsy and Peter had lost all their money.

She brought the treadmill back to a walk. Her blood was pumping, and she was breathing hard. She needed to slow down.

As her pace softened, so did her venom. It was impossible not to regret the end of her marriage. Wasn't it fair to say they'd both been unhappy? Perhaps for different reasons, but still unhappy. He wouldn't give her the only thing she wanted: a baby. And she couldn't give him the one thing he wanted: her eternal youth. Which of them was being the more ridiculous? Jack would someday have to accept that he was getting older and no amount of younger women would change that, and she would have to accept that she wasn't going to be a mom. Not unless she did something about it soon.

As if on cue, Sven walked in. He spotted her and nodded politely. She hopped off the treadmill and went over to him.

"Sven, I'm sorry," she started, hoping that he would be the type of who took apologies easily and moved on. He looked at her with a face clouded in reservation. Guess not.

"Look. I was over-the-top with you the other day. I said a few things. I'm sorry. I wasn't myself." She glanced up and was happy to see that his scowl was gone and he was listening to her. "The truth is, I've been having some personal problems and I lashed out at you, well, because you were there. So, I'm sorry."

He smiled. "Apology accepted."

"Phew. So no hard feelings?"

He shook his head.

"You know, I could give you that tour of Boston if you like, just to make things good between us." This was way beyond where Sandra had planned to go. It just slipped out. She couldn't believe she'd said it, but then again, she couldn't believe she was single again.

Sven looked confused. "But what about your husband?"

Her face fell. "Those were the personal problems I was telling you about. It turns out he doesn't want to be my husband anymore. He's now living with his new girlfriend."

"Oh," he said. "I'm very sorry for you."

The thing Sandra couldn't handle was sympathy. She put up her hand.

"No, no. Looking back now, I have to say it's been coming for a while. I'm sorry it's happened, but maybe it will be for the best in the long run."

"Well, speaking of running . . ." He gestured at the treadmills behind her. Sandra realized she'd embarrassed him with too much personal information. He was anxious to get away from her.

"Oh, yes. Well, I'm glad we cleared that up anyway." She turned to leave.

"Sandra," he said, and she turned around. "You'll need to call me for that sightseeing trip." He pulled his wallet out and quickly found his business cards, then gave her a warm smile. It wasn't flirtatious, nor was it predatory. It was just friendly. "I would still love you to give me a tour of Boston or Wellesley or both if you're up to it. But I know you have a lot on your mind right now." He handed her the business card. "I've been through the same thing. Try to get up and out as much as you can. Focus on having fun, and if I can help you there, it would be an honor." This time he did flirt. She felt a definite frisson of excitement as she took his card.

"Thanks, Sven. How much longer are you here for?"

"I fly out on Sunday. Back to Dublin."

"Well, maybe I'll show you Boston if you show me Dublin sometime?" she said, but didn't mention that she had plans to visit. That would surely scare the guy.

He threw his head back and guffawed, and she could see his full set of upper teeth. At least they were straight and white, and by the looks of things, his own. "Maybe."

Maybe, she thought.

After a quick shower and change, Sandra headed over to Popsy's house. She was determined to give her friend her belated birthday present before another day passed. She'd bought two airplane tickets combined with a hotel package for Ireland. They were changeable, but she really didn't want to start messing with the dates because that was always complicated. February was still a few months away. With this much notice, Popsy would be able to clear her schedule. Perhaps it would all work out.

It was a short drive from her apartment, but it did give Sandra a little time to think. How would they survive if Lily and Jack really did stay together? Would he want to marry Lily? If so, would Popsy and Peter go to the wedding? That would make Peter Jack's father-in-law. It was all so wrong.

Stay strong, she commanded herself as she drove. She turned her stereo on and pumped up the volume to give her strength. Rhianna was belting out one of her older songs,

"Hard." At first Sandra didn't recognize it.

The lyrics thumped on about being strong, and it gave Sandra all the reminding she needed. She was strong. "I am, I can," she chanted. It was something she'd learned from her mother a million years before. "I am, I can," she shouted even louder, feeling a whole lot better.

When she got to Popsy's house, she saw the Ferrari wasn't there, so that meant Peter was still out. Poor Popsy. She would doubtless be a nervous wreck by now. Her best friend was as soft as night cream and just as thick sometimes. Although well-read and pretty academic, Popsy could be ridiculously ditzy at times. She loved her, but Sandra wondered how she could have let her husband escape the hospital. If it was her, she would have pinned him to the bed and had him restrained. Anything to keep him safe. But then again, Sandra didn't have a husband. Not really. Not anymore. Jack was hers in name only. Perhaps she should even go back to her maiden name.

How would she finance her life if Jack really had nothing squirreled away? Was her real estate license even valid anymore? It had been so long since she worked. Breaking up was so messy.

"Oh, Sandra. Thank God you're here. I can't get Peter on his cell." Popsy ushered her into the house and straight into the kitchen where Matilda was busy stirring a pot and praying. It was clear she was caught up in the panic, too.

"Coffee or something stronger?" Popsy asked.

"Oh, a glass of water is good." Sandra smiled. "Look, you need to stop worrying." Popsy and Matilda looked at her as if wanting to be convinced. "You know he's just too busy to answer his phone. If I know him, he's wheeling and dealing to extricate himself from what arose last week. He hasn't had a chance to deal with it."

Popsy and Matilda looked relieved.

Armed with a small cup of what looked like a double espresso for herself and a glass of iced water for her, Popsy walked out of the kitchen and gestured for Sandra to follow. Matilda went back to stirring and praying.

"I spoke to Lily about half an hour ago," she whispered once they were settled in the drawing room."

"Oh," Sandra said and took a sip of water.

"I didn't want to tell you in front of Matilda, but she told me Peter was having lunch with Jack." She looked at Sandra anxiously. "I kept it very short and to the point. I just wanted you to know."

It was a good thing Sandra was sitting down, because she felt her legs go weak. Hearing his name out loud like that—realizing that Jack was still a living, breathing person having lunch with her best friend's husband—was like a heavyweight boxer punching her in the stomach. Jack existing as her nemesis in the hallways of her mind she could just about cope with, but this was new. Other people would continue to be part of his life. Popsy would know things about him that she didn't—like what he was doing and who he was with. That was hell.

"Shit!"

Popsy put her arm around Sandra's shoulders.

"You know, if it's true, Peter has gone to make war with him. We're sick about what he's done. You have to believe that. Jack will ruin Lily's life. He's too old for her, and he's done the dirt on my best friend." Popsy squeezed her shoulders hard. "I love you, and I hate him for hurting you."

"Stop with the sympathy." Sandra jumped to her feet and paced. "Sorry, Popsy, I know you mean well, but I'm still too raw. If you show me any kind of sympathy, I'll crumble. Can we do it like the Brits do and have a stiff upper lip about the whole thing?"

Popsy got to her feet. "Absolutely. Now, will you have some lunch with me? Rosie is on her way over, too. Peter asked Tilly to make him something special, and she's gone to a lot of trouble. Now he's not here to eat it. I'm going to have some very strong words for him about treating Matilda like that, and when I'm finished, you can kill him for taking off without telling me."

"That sounds good." Sandra was relieved to have switched the subject from Jack. "Was that scrambled eggs I saw Matilda making?"

"It sure was, and she makes the best eggs on toast this side of the Atlantic. Did you know she uses half a pound of butter in each batch? Sinful but worth it."

Rosie arrived as soon as she had collected Natasha from pre-school. Like Sandra, she'd offered to come over and keep her mother company until her father returned.

Matilda ended up cooking for Popsy, Sandra, Rosie, and Natasha, and it was a pleasant lunch.

"I almost forgot one of the reasons I came over," Sandra said. "Popsy, it's a little late, but I have your birthday present."

"Oh, Sandra, you shouldn't have. Especially now." She didn't go into the finer points about being broke, not in front of Matilda or Natasha who was learning to listen a little too well these days, but Sandra knew what Popsy was talking about.

"Well, the truth is, I bought this present some time ago. Before, well, everything." She handed Popsy a white envelope with a red ribbon wrapped around it.

"What's this?" Natasha picked up on the excitement. "Can I help you, Grandma?"

Matilda got up to do the dishes.

Natasha lost interest as soon as she saw it was just boring paper, so she handed it back to her grandmother. Popsy studied the contents with a little more care.

"Oh, Sandra, this is fabulous. Too generous, but I love it."

"What is it?" Rosie asked.

"Flights to Ireland and a long weekend in a nice Dublin hotel." She looked at Sandra with enormous gratitude. "You shouldn't have done this."

"Believe me, I need it as much as you. Are you okay with the dates? It's February 7th, I think. I can push it back."

"I could be away for the Friday and Saturday, but these tickets don't have us coming home until Monday, and Rosie and Marcus are flying out on that Sunday." She turned to wink at her granddaughter. "Natasha is coming to visit me for a little vacation when Mommy and Daddy take their break, aren't you?" She used a little girl voice.

"Oh," Rosie said. "Mom, you should go with Sandra. We can reschedule our week away for another time.

"You fly out on Sunday, and we're back in on Monday. It's only one night. I'm sure we can work something out. We could shift our flights back by a day, or maybe Matilda can help me out."

Matilda nodded vigorously from where she stood at the sink. "Natasha and I are best friends. Besides, Grandpa Peter will be here, too."

"What about Peter?" Sandra asked. "I was a little worried if you'd want to leave him on his own."

Popsy shook her head. "He won't let me mind him while I'm here, so I may as well head off with you. Anyway, it's only a weekend, and it's months away. How much trouble can he get into over three nights? And you and I could really do with a little time away." She kissed Sandra on the cheek. "And I love my present. You're very bold, but thank you."

"So we're going to Ireland? I can hardly believe it." Sandra laughed. "Why didn't we do this before? I can't wait to see all those fabulous green fields and experience the famous Irish welcome."

"Oh, I'd say they're going to love you there." Rosie smirked. "You really do look like a million dollars. How do you always look so good?"

"She lives in the gym," Popsy interrupted. "But Rosie, you're looking pretty terrific yourself these days. Have you gone on a diet?"

Rosie laughed. "It's a little soon to see results, but I have started running every day in preparation for my vacation."

"Well, I can see the results. Keep it up. You look amazing," Popsy said.

"Ah, youth." Sandra sighed. "How easy it used to be to carve my body into the shape I wanted. Now I have to work out every day just to maintain what I have."

"What you have is pretty darn good, and don't you forget it. I bet some Irish guy will snatch you up in no time."

Matilda's eggs on toast were sublime and they were at the clearing the table stage when Popsy mentioned Peter again. "Surely he's done by now."

"I left my phone in the car," Sandra suddenly realized. "I'm just going to get it, and I'll check to see if there's any sign of that wayward husband of yours, too."

Despite Peter's absence and the heartache with Jack, Sandra felt better than she had in days as she walked out the front door. Her best friend was thrilled with the present and they were going to Ireland!

Sandra happened to be alone when she opened the front door of Popsy's house. She was alone when she saw Jack and Lily hugging next to their cars. And she was desperately, painfully, and totally alone when Jack glanced over Lily's head and looked at her.

"Sandy," he called, and Lily pushed away. This was the first time she'd seen Jack since he'd told her he was leaving her, and now, so soon, here he was with Lily in his arms. For a moment, Sandra was frozen to the spot. She couldn't run back into the house because they'd seen her. Dammit. Lily's car was parked next to hers. She was incapable of taking a single step forward. To move was to acknowledge them and their love. She never wanted to see Lily again.

Did Popsy know they were coming? Had Peter given them his blessing? Where was Peter? What should she do? In a desperate bid to get away, she made a run for her car. She'd just drive away and explain to Popsy later why she had to flee. But that didn't work. Jack ran toward her, and before she got her door open, he managed to grab her arm.

"Please, Sandy,"

"No!" she screamed. "Get away from me, you bastard!" She tried to pry his fingers loose, but his grip was too strong. Then he managed to get hold of her other arm so he could look her in the face. She pulled hard and then shook to free herself.

"Stop fighting me, Sandra . . ." His voice was urgent, but it had a forced calm about it. When she glanced up for just a second, she could see Lily in the distance. Her eyes were red. She was crying. Good.

"How could you do this? You can't just breeze in here with your new—" Sandra glanced up to be sure Popsy hadn't followed her out. Then she continued a little more quietly, "Your new whore, and you can't just walk in here without any warning."

"Sandra, shut up!"

"Then let me go. If you're here, I'm not. It's that simple." This time she did have the strength to look at him. "You think you can just saunter in here like nothing has changed?" She spat her words at him. "It's not that simple, Jack Boy."

"I have some very bad news. Would you please stop fighting me and brace yourself? You need to be here for Popsy's sake. This is a lot bigger than you or me."

For the first time, Sandra relented. Somehow he'd permeated her shield of hatred. It was bizarre to see him after the last few days. To be so intimate with every minute detail of his face and now to be so disgusted by that same face, felt odd. Standing this close to him was like coming home, and to be in his arms felt normal. But normal was gone, she reminded herself. Jack didn't love her anymore. The new "normal" was standing twenty feet away, crying.

"What's wrong?" She was acutely aware that she was close to tears herself.

"There's no easy way to say this." He took a deep breath. "It's Peter. He's dead."

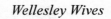

Part 2

Ireland

Chapter 21

Life after Death

"You ladies here for a nice spring break?" the Dublin taxi driver asked Popsy and Sandra. They were both exhausted after their transatlantic flight. It was only seven in the morning Irish time but two a.m. by their body clocks.

Popsy was a changed woman. In the three plus months since Peter's death, she'd lost most of her *joie de vivre* and there'd been no real improvement. Now she was just a shadow of the woman she once was. It was going to take time, quite a lot of it, but for now Sandra would take care of her.

She made the effort to answer because that was their routine now. "Yes, we are. We flew in from Boston. My friend here was born in Ireland, so we're back to see the old homeland, if you know what I mean."

"Oh, I do, o'course," he said. "We've loads of Americans passing through doin' the same thing all the time. Where's home in Ireland?"

Sandra glanced at Popsy, but she was in a daze, looking out the window at the early-morning traffic, so Sandra answered for her. "A place called Rathmichael. Do you know it?"

The driver nodded. "Yeah, it's out the south of the city, just next to the Wicklow border. Does she have any family there now?"

Popsy remained detached. Sandra shook her head. "It's just a sightseeing trip."

Sandra took Popsy's hand and squeezed it as they zoomed along. In the lanes next to them, cars inched forward, bumper-to-bumper, but they were in a designated taxi lane. Dawn was breaking and slowly the city was unveiling itself. Just like Boston, the February nights were still long and the days too short.

"There's any number of ways to get you to Ballsbridge from here, but if I take the tunnel you'll see nothing, so I'll go down O'Connell Street. That's our main thoroughfare—our Fifth Avenue, if you know what I mean," the driver said.

Sandra was about to object when they whizzed past the entrance to the tunnel. It was obvious resistance was futile. Her experience told her to be careful that a €40 ride didn't become a €140 ride. She'd suffered at the hands of swindling taxi drivers before, but this guy seemed to know what she was thinking.

"Don't worry, love. It'll work out much of a muchness on the money front. It's just a chance to see a bit more of the city, like."

"Thanks," she said as she massaged her temples. "But we are a little tired after the trip."

"I'll have ye' at your hotel just as quick, too."

She nodded. Soon, she was happy he'd made the call because she recognized the wide expanse of O'Connell Street from photos of Dublin she'd seen on the web.

"We're really here, Popsy," Sandra said, trying to get her friend involved. Popsy nodded and looked out the window, but she remained in what had become her normal state of detachment.

"This is the River Liffey you're crossing, ladies," the driver said. "It's official, you're on the south of the city now. Much posher." He tapped the side of his nose and laughed. "On your right now, that's the GPO, scene of the 1916 rising, and comin' up on your left is the world-famous Trinity College." Even Popsy seemed to engage a little at this point. They were making good time through the traffic. "Next on your right is our premier shopping district—Grafton Street. I'm thinkin' you ladies might like to spend a few of your very welcome American dollars there. It's where all the nice shops are."

Sandra smiled at him in the rearview mirror. Popsy didn't respond. The truth was, she had no idea what they'd be doing for the next few days. Not sure about Popsy's ability to think straight, Sandra had brought enough money for the two of them. That meant sufficient funds to have a nice time and eat in a few good restaurants, but it sure wouldn't stretch to a good old-fashioned shopping binge like the old days. She and Popsy were capable of blowing $20,000 in one day. Those times were gone now. And Peter's death had thrown a crazy situation into even further chaos.

The life insurance company was refusing to pay out to C&J because it had already filed for Chapter 11, but Sandra's lawyers were watching Jack very carefully to see if he got financial compensation. If he did, some of that was hers. Over three months had passed since she and Jack had split, and also since Peter's death. It was unbelievable how time flew. She was still in The Celtic Crowne, but every day she feared a call or letter would arrive telling her she had to get out. These were not things to worry about this weekend, however. She and Popsy were going to have a good time if it was the last thing they did.

"Coming up on your left now is the Dail. It's our seat of power, where all the ministers hang out, because God knows they certainly aren't workin' in there."

Sandra knew all about Ireland's troubled financial times. She heard they'd had the world's biggest boom, followed by the world's biggest bust in just a matter of years.

Sandra leaned forward and looked out the front window. "But things are getting better now, right?"

He took his right hand off the steering wheel and waved it as if to say "so-so."

"Better is a relative term. We've had a terrible run of it, but yes, I think on balance things are better than a few years back. We need all the tourists we can get, I'll tell you that much. And bring all your money." He turned the car at the top of the street and Sandra winced.

"Sorry, I can't get my head around how you guys drive on the left-hand-side. I keep thinking you're going the wrong way."

He laughed. "That's The Shelbourne Hotel. You might like that place, two fine ladies like yourselves. You'll meet a nice class of gent in there."

Sandra turned to see the beautiful old façade of what was clearly a very grand hotel that was worth investigating, for sure. She sat back again because watching the traffic was making her nervous. Instead, she looked at the beautiful line of red-brick Victorian houses along the sidewalk. As they went from a shopping area to a more residential one, she saw large gracious houses with sash windows coming to life as the city woke up to another day. It was all very pretty.

"What's your friend's family name?" the taxi driver asked after a few moments.

"Heffernan," Sandra offered.

"Well, if that doesn't beat Banagher." He laughed. "I'm a Heffernan! Look." He pointed to his taxi driver I.D. displayed on the glove compartment.

"What's Banagher?" Sandra asked.

"It's a place, love." A place. As if that explained the odd expression. "Howaya, cos?" he asked Popsy. "That's a good one, now. We're family."

Popsy smiled vacantly at him.

"Tell me now, cos. Has anybody ever told you, you look like Goldie Hawn?"

To Sandra's relief, he turned the car off the road and into the safe haven of The Four Seasons Hotel in Dublin's leafy and very up-market area of Ballsbridge. Their arrival cut off the driver just as he was getting into any possible links to Hollywood royalty.

Sandra thought their impromptu tour had been nice, but she knew Popsy wouldn't be capable of small-talk with their particularly sociable driver. She couldn't get the door open fast enough. "Come on, Popsy. I'll get the fare. You head into the warmth of the hotel."

Boston was famous for its cold weather, but they'd exchanged an acceptable, cold New England for a freezing Ireland. The wind combined with the chill cut right through her. It was good to get inside.

Their suite was everything it had promised to be. They each had a separate bedroom with private bathrooms, and in the center was a charming drawing room. It was far too large for two single ladies, but what the heck? It was part of a package and reasonably priced. This Irish recession was good for the U.S. tourist.

As soon as their suitcases were delivered, the ladies took them to their respective rooms. Even though it was just after eight in the morning, they'd agreed to nap for a few hours to catch up from the jetlag.

Once she'd checked out her room Sandra came over and knocked on Popsy's door. She stuck her head around. "How's your room?" she asked, even though she had a pretty good idea that it was the same as hers.

Popsy was sitting on the side of her enormous bed, looking into space. "Yes, it's fine," she said, still with that vacant sound in her voice.

Sandra came in and looked around. "Yep, looks pretty much like mine. I think they're really charming. We have a fabulous view over a large green garden, too. Did you see?" She walked over to the window. "I hear the bath running. Taking a bath before you go to sleep?"

Popsy looked at the carpet and nodded. Baths had become her obsession. She said she was permanently cold and only a bath could warm her. Back in Wellesley, Popsy had been taking up to five baths a day since the funeral. They'd sought medical advice and been told it was a manifestation of the grief and not the worst thing she could do. If it gave her some sort of comfort, let her go for it. It would pass. Sandra hoped the change of routine might help break her of the habit. Popsy needed to come back to reality soon. Naturally, she said none of this out loud.

"I'm going to order some Irish tea and a couple of their world-famous scones dripping in Irish butter. Will you eat with me?"

Popsy shook her head. "I'm not hungry, thanks." Popsy was never hungry now. She'd faded to nothing since Peter's death, but again, Sandra hoped the fresh Irish air might put some appetite back into her.

"Okay, well, I'll just get you a cup of tea, and I won't disturb you if you're still in the bathroom. I'll put it on your bedside table. Enjoy your bath and catnap. I'll organize a wake-up call for one o'clock, and then we can have some lunch together. Our driver is booked for two o'clock."

Popsy nodded. "Thank you," she said.

It wasn't a lot, but coming from Popsy in her current state, it was more than enough for Sandra. She rushed to her friend, sat on the bed, and gave her a hug. "Oh, Popsy, you're so welcome. We all love you so much, and we're going to be okay. You have to trust me on this. We're going to be okay." The passion in her voice had no effect on Popsy. She accepted Sandra's hug, but she didn't hug her back or respond in any significant way. At least she hadn't pushed her away.

"Now," Sandra said as she pulled back, "you and I are going to paint this town red over the next few days. We're going to squeeze in as many sightseeing trips, lunches, dinners, drinks in lovely hotels—anything we can think of—as we can. We only have this weekend to live once, and we're going to make it count. All too soon we'll be on that plane back to our humdrum lives, so let's escape for this weekend and leave all our troubles and pain back in America. Do you hear me, Popsy Power?"

This time Popsy did look at Sandra and managed a small grin and a nod.

"Good. Now go and have a nice bath. I better check out the gym while I'm at it," she said in a matter-of-fact tone as she got up to leave. "Sweet dreams, Popsy. See you in a few hours." Sandra left Popsy alone and went back into their drawing room to call room service.

Within moments, Popsy was slipping into her scalding hot bath. It was too hot and burned her skin. Just the way she liked it. The more pain the better, because then, just for the briefest of moments, she didn't think of Peter and only thought of the pain. It worked now, too. It was so hot she clenched her teeth so she wouldn't scream, and then she was in. When the heat subsided, her mind would be empty again. Empty and able to fill up with thoughts of Peter.

She lay in the piping-hot water and looked around the bathroom. Peter would have liked this. The decor was very modern with walls and floors of coffee-caramel marble and there was an enormous mirror over the bath. He would've wanted to be in the bath with her. Lack of sleep never stopped him. Nothing stopped Peter, and then suddenly, so suddenly, he was stopped. Gone.

She couldn't believe they didn't even get to say goodbye. How could God be so cruel? What had she ever done to deserve this? Why Peter? Why not her? It would have been so much easier if she'd been the one in the car. It was even her car. It should have been her. Of course, it wasn't the crash that had killed him, but the heart attack. Though maybe if she'd been with him, things could have been different.

If she'd just seen him going out the front door, maybe she could have stopped him. Or if he'd had the second heart attack at home, she could have called 911. She sighed. What did any of this matter, anyway?

Popsy knew it was all her fault. She let him out of the hospital. She let him run down those confounded steps. Everybody spent so much time and energy telling her it wasn't her fault, but of course it was. She was the world's worst wife. The most careless woman in the world. What had she been thinking letting him escape the hospital? Now God had punished her. She was meant to mind him, to protect him, to cherish him. And what had she done? Killed him.

If only she'd been in the wretched car with him. If only they could have died together. The girls were old enough to fend for themselves. Death would be so much better than living without Peter.

Popsy didn't care about Ireland. She really didn't want to be here, but the family had insisted. It was only for a few days. She would be home soon, in time for his four-month anniversary at the end of February. The others wouldn't acknowledge it, but she would. How could Peter be nearly four months gone? When she'd first heard that he was dead, she didn't think she would make it to nightfall, but the painful horrible truth was that she did last the day. And then another. And another.

Living without the one you loved was like being the living dead. At least Sandra could hate Jack. He was a bastard. Popsy pointblank refused to speak to him anymore. If Jack hadn't shacked up with Lily, Peter wouldn't have had that first heart attack. He might still be alive today. True, she blamed herself for Peter's ultimate death, but Jack had a part to play in it, too.

For some reason, Lily escaped her wrath. She was still disgusted with her daughter, but she didn't blame her for her father's death. That last day in the hospital, Peter had told her he wasn't mad with Lily, only with Jack, so Popsy did the same. She knew her Lily was still suffering terribly. Rosie was probably doing the best of all of them. Of course she was heartbroken, but Marcus had wide shoulders, and he took care of her so well. They'd very nearly cancelled their vacation plans, but Popsy had insisted that if she was going to Ireland, Rosie was going to the Caribbean to learn to play golf.

Rosie would fly out on Sunday, and Popsy was due to get home on Monday. It was agreed that Matilda would babysit Natasha for one night alone in Popsy's house. They had gotten to know each other when Matilda moved into Rosie's house for a little while to get used to her newest charge.

The busier they all kept Matilda the better, because it was no surprise she was heartbroken, too. Everybody was. There wasn't a person who didn't love Peter, and to have him gone left an enormous hole in all their hearts but most of all, Popsy's. Her life was over. She knew that. There was nothing left for her. Okay, she had the girls and Natasha and, of course, Sandra was an amazing friend, but without Peter, she was nobody. He was her better half, and with him gone, she was just an empty shell.

Popsy put her head under the water and came back up for air. What in the world was she doing in Dublin at a time like this? It was beyond her, but then again, so were most things these days. When the skin on her fingers got wrinkly, she got out of the bath and rummaged through her case for her nightdress and sleeping tablets. Since Peter's death, she hadn't been able to sleep. The drugs were her little friends. So reliable. And they gave her what nobody else could—escape. Blessed escape for a few short hours when she could forget everything.

But then, inevitably she had to wake up to the nightmare that was her new life. Exhausted from the trip and now the bath, Popsy wasn't focusing properly. She couldn't find her tablets anywhere. She'd been sure they were in her toiletries bag, but they weren't. Nor were they in her purse.

When she came out of her bathroom, she saw Sandra's little gift of a cup of tea, and despite promising not to, she had left half a scone beside it. She sat down and took the tea. It was so nice. Still warm and with a richer taste than she was used to. It soothed as it went down. She looked at the fluffy white scone. No, she just wasn't hungry, but the tea was very welcome.

She finished the cup and wondered where in the world those darn tablets had gotten to. In utter exasperation, she decided to lie down and rest. There was no way she would fall asleep, but at least a rest would help. When she went out with Sandra later, she could buy some more of her little friends.

Chapter 22

Life after Love

Sandra had lied to Popsy. She didn't book the wake-up call for one o'clock. She had them phone her at eleven thirty that morning. Popsy needed her sleep, but Sandra was determined to squeeze in a session at the gym before they took off on their sightseeing tour. She knew the food in Ireland was incredible, and she would just have to work it off as she consumed it or else she'd return to the U.S. as heavy cargo. Not an attractive thought.

The scone was her first taste of Irish fare, and it was simply to-die-for. So light and fresh and still warm from the oven. There were raisins throughout, and it wasn't as sweet as she was used to, but she preferred that. Yes, she'd have to work out every day or face the consequences.

Leaving the bed hadn't been easy, either. Sandra was used to luxury, and The Four Seasons was just as good as anything she'd experienced in the U.S. or the Caribbean. It was all quite modern, but the mood was of yesteryear, befitting the old city they were in. The room had a fresh, clean feel while maintaining the same air of opulence that the rest of the hotel had. The curtains, blended with a luxuriously heavy fabric that was a pale shade of caramel, and the tone perfectly matched the floors. At the bottom of her bed was a large plush sofa covered in an oversized flower print fabric, and in front of that was a small table with the leftovers of her scone and the pot of tea. It was all so tasteful—so frightfully European. Sandra loved it.

Okay, enough procrastinating, she thought. Gym time.

She took one of the plastic key cards and tried to put it into the tiny pocket at the back of her sweats. There was something in there already, which was odd because she typically didn't use the back pocket. It was designed to hold an iPod, but Sandra preferred to wear hers on her arm.

She pulled out a business card that had clearly been through the laundry services of The Celtic Crowne several times. It was frayed at the edges, but the small, tight pocket had preserved it well enough to read. It was Sven's business card. She'd forgotten about it. Now she remembered tucking it in there while they were talking in the gym that day. She hadn't even read it at the time.

Sandra tucked the card key in her pocket and headed out, still holding his business card. As she walked, she read: *Sven Richter MD, OB/GYN.*

She laughed out loud. My God. He's an obstetrician and gynecologist. The next line said he was in the fellow of the Reproductive Endocrinology and Infertility Society of the United Kingdom. Well, if anyone could help her get pregnant, it was him.

"Shut the front door," Sandra said, smiling at the same time. She put the card back into the tiny pocket and tapped it for safety. She should call him, she thought, as she jogged down the hall to find the hotel's gym. Was it time for her to move on?

Getting onto a treadmill was second nature to Sandra. It was where she felt her best and also where she did some of her most productive thinking. Incredible to know she was now three thousand miles away from home and all that involved. She worried about Popsy. In all the years she'd known her, Popsy had never been so low.

The day Peter died, everything happened so fast. Seeing Jack and Lily in each other's arms had been hard enough, but when he'd told her Peter was dead, it got so much worse. She heard the words, but couldn't comprehend them. She thought there had to be some mistake. Maybe he'd had another heart attack—but dead? That was too big, too final. It couldn't be the case.

Much as she'd hated seeing her husband with Lily, looking back on it now she was also grateful he was there. Much better to hear it from him than a stranger. What would've happened if Jack hadn't been at the accident? Would the police have called to tell Popsy? The way it happened, she was surrounded by her children and Sandra, but to be alone and told by a cop that your husband, the man you were supposed to grow old with, was gone, and not even having the chance of a good-bye . . . what an appalling thought.

Jack was holding her arms firm in his big, strong hands. "Sandra, you have to focus. We have to do this together. We have to go in and tell Popsy."

"And Rosie."

"Is she here? That's a good thing. Can you phone Marcus? Who else do we need to call?"

Sandra shrugged. She glanced over to Lily who'd been watching them interact, but she seemed disconnected, dazed. Lily was in shock, of course, so Sandra did something she never thought she would ever do, she gently detached herself from Jack and went over to Lily and took her hand.

"Come on, we have to go in to your mother," she said.

Strange what we do in an emergency, she thought now. Of course, she'd done it for Popsy's sake and not Lily's, but still, she was proud of herself.

She remembered going back into the house. Popsy had taken in their ashen faces and sat down.

"What's wrong?" was all she said, but Sandra figured she already knew. Under normal circumstances, whatever they were—she would've ranted and raved about Jack's unexpected arrival, and Popsy hadn't yet made peace with her daughter, but none of that was even mentioned.

Sandra came over and sat beside her.

"It's Peter. He had another heart attack."

"I'll kill him." She shook her head. "Where is he? Have they taken him back to the hospital? I have to go." She pulled away from Sandra and stood. "Where are my keys? Matilda!" She called, but her voice was a little manic. Some sixth sense must have told her that this was a bigger crisis than the last. She looked like she wanted to remove herself from the room.

Rosie said, "Where is he, Jack? He's going to be okay, isn't he?"

Jack shook his head and started to cry. "Peter didn't survive this attack. I'm so sorry."

The wail that came out of Popsy was not of this world. Her legs gave way, but Sandra had her arms around her, holding on for all her might. They slipped to the floor together, a singular unified mass of misery.

"Oh Christ, I'm so sorry, Popsy. I was on my way to meet him for lunch, and when I got there, I came across the accident. His car—that is—your new car—and, well, he had an attack at the wheel and it went off the road just at the restaurant on Route 9. It wasn't a bad crash. I saw him getting loaded into the ambulance. He didn't look hurt. There wasn't even any blood. But then I spoke to the emergency team, told them I was his friend, and asked them to tell me what happened."

Sandra leered at him. Some friend.

"They said he had a heart attack at the wheel. It must have been a big one."

Lily and Rosie hugged their mother, too, and Matilda rushed back in. Everybody was crying. Then the doorbell rang.

"That will be the police," Jack had offered. "They told me I should come tell you, but they would be along soon after."

It had been one of the toughest days in her life. Jack and Lily's affair wasn't as hard on her as Peter's death was. The rest of the day had felt like some sort of dream.

Marcus had arrived pretty fast, and the men took over everything. Popsy's doctor came. Sandra didn't know who'd called him, but it was a great idea. Then the house was full of people. Neighbors, business associates, and friends of Peter's began pouring through the house.

For the next four days, the flow of people and gifts didn't stop. It was an amazing reflection on how well-liked Peter was. Sandra moved into the house to be with Popsy, and for the last few months, she still spent nearly every night there. The girls had come and stayed all day, every day, the week after his death.

The first night Sandra watched Lily walk out with Jack had felt odd, but not painful. Compared to Peter's death, Jack's betrayal didn't seem too bad. She'd made the conscious decision to lock that issue away. She didn't love him anymore. She wouldn't let herself. She and Jack were over. But Popsy and Peter? There should have been years left in that relationship. They weren't done yet.

One of the most difficult times for Popsy was when the car was returned. Nobody had called to say it was coming. A delivery service arrived with it a few days later and they plonked it unceremoniously on the road outside her house. How lucky that Sandra had answered the door and not Popsy. It was she who signed the acceptance forms and got the plastic bag of Peter's belongings. That's when Popsy got her phone back. Up until then, they hadn't known why Peter had run out of the house in such a hurry, but now they did. He'd promised Popsy that he would "send the boys," but he must have gone to the gas station himself. Was that what pushed his heart over the edge?

When the police arrived, they were much gentler than she'd expected. It was a lady cop who sat down with Popsy. Sandra and the girls joined them. The policewoman more-or-less repeated what Jack had told them. All told, it was fortunate it hadn't caused a major catastrophe on the busy road.

Peter's body had been taken by ambulance back to the Newton Wellesley hospital, but Sandra knew this time he wasn't in the safe environs of the ICU. This time, unbelievably, Peter was in the morgue.

With his recent history in the hospital, the autopsy was fast and gave no great surprises. Peter had a massive heart attack. It was quick and chances were that he didn't feel a thing. That was of some small consolation to Popsy.

The funeral was held the following week. It was family only, which meant it was very small, but that's what Popsy had wanted. Too much publicity had hit the press about his death and the company going into Chapter 11 in the days before. She didn't want to be the subject of pity or gossip and wanted the space to grieve in peace. The only time she came out of her almost permanent state of shock was to talk to Sandra about Jack.

"I need to talk to you about the funeral," Popsy had said, sounding almost normal. "Sandra, do you mind if Jack comes?" she'd asked.

"Me? Popsy, that is so up to you. I'll go along with whatever you think is best."

It was the first time they'd actually looked into each other's eyes since Peter's death. It almost broke Sandra's heart to see the pain there. Popsy nodded. "I have no fight left. I feel nothing for Jack, but I think Lily needs him, so if it's all the same to you, I'm just going to let it slide. If Lily wants him, he can come. Okay?"

"Yes."

Sandra had been happy to oblige. She felt the same way. Peter's death seemed to dwarf all other issues.

Thus, at the funeral, there was Popsy being supported by Sandra, and Rosie had Marcus holding her up. Jack kept his arm around Lily, and Matilda carried little Natasha. It was unclear who was taking care of whom.

After a brief service, Peter was cremated. That had always been his wish. A short week after his jailbreak from the hospital, his fun ride in his wife's Ferrari, and his reassurances to her that everything would be all right, Peter was nothing more than a handful of dust in a silver urn in Popsy's arms.

Sandra wondered how a person moves on from something like that as she slowed her run down to a walk. How is it we dismiss so easily the fragility of life, the shortness of it? Things we think are set in stone can turn to dust —literally—in a moment. Poor Peter. Then again, she knew he would be so angry if he could see them now. Sandra looked up to heaven. "I'm sorry, Peter," she whispered. "I'll work harder to get Popsy out of her sadness. I'll get her through this."

"Good-morning, sleepyhead."

"I must have fallen asleep. What time is it?" Popsy said as she woke up looking disoriented.

"That depends on what continent you're on," Sandra said and laughed. "Who cares what time it is in the States? Here it's lunchtime, so up and at 'em, girl. I have a light lunch menu for you to peruse, and then we're meeting up with our driver to explore this place you call home."

Popsy sat up and rubbed her eyes. "Lunchtime? Ah, I remember now. We're in Ireland." She looked at Sandra and actually smiled. Sandra tried not to react, but she was pretty sure it was the first time she'd seen a real smile on Popsy's face since Peter's death. If that was all she got from this weekend, it was enough. She'd been right to bring her here. Ireland would make things a little better. But Sandra didn't say any of this. In fact, she did her best to ignore it.

"Come on, now. No slouching. Time is moving on and we have a lot to squeeze in," she said and left the room to let Popsy get dressed.

From Popsy's perspective, things were better, too. It was the first time in ages she'd woken up without a groggy head. Then she remembered she hadn't taken a sleeping tablet. That was amazing. She hadn't planned on giving them up for ages, if ever. Maybe it was the time change, or perhaps the jetlag, or maybe it was really true: the Irish air had magical qualities. Whatever it was, one thing she knew was that she'd had a terrific sleep without the aid of drugs. That was the first good thing that had happened to her since—since her world ended.

"Thank you, Ireland," she whispered to herself. Then she slipped out of bed and went to get dressed.

Chapter 23

Lily's Lies

Lily pretended to cough. "I know, and I'm sorry, but what can I say?" She coughed again. "I would be contagious."

Jack came in at the end of her telephone conversation and watched her with concern in his eyes.

"Still not going in? Is that a full week you've been out this time?" He sighed. "Lily, you can't keep doing this."

He was annoying her. She already knew she was playing with fire professionally, having skipped at least a week a month for the last few months. She was going to have to shape up soon and was also running out of excuses, but she wouldn't think about that right now.

"What?" she asked, pretending not to understand. "I'm sick."

They were in Lily's apartment, which was now home to both of them, but for the last few weeks it had begun to feel very claustrophobic. Jack had found the smaller size difficult to get used to after the palatial penthouse he'd shared with Sandra for over a decade, and for Lily, it was different having him living with her, week in, week out, as opposed to being an occasional guest. He'd stolen half her closet space and half her bathroom space, but worst of all, he said he needed a study. Of course, she didn't have one, so he was using her second bedroom. There were files and slips of paper, all very important according to him, on every surface. It was really getting on her nerves.

He came over and sat beside her on the sofa. "I know you're still upset and this has been a horrendous couple of months for everybody." He put his arm around her shoulders. "But I don't think you have the flu. Is that what you told them?"

Lily pulled away like a little girl who was angry at a loving but chastising parent.

"I don't feel well. I'm not a child, Jack. I should know if I'm too sick to go to work or not." She was overly hostile, she knew, but he was too darn pedantic. Who did he think he was, her father? Lily felt her eyes tear up again. "You need to go," she said.

Jack stood and raised his hands in defeat. "Okay. Just remember, it would do you good to get out of the house and breathe in some fresh air. Take a walk or something. I could take you out for dinner later, if you like."

Lily didn't respond. She wanted him gone. She needed space, and could think better alone. He said he understood, and within a few minutes he was out the door.

Lily wasn't even sure where he went anymore. With her father's death, C&J was no more, but Jack had explained there was now a huge legal battle. Jack was suing the banks, claiming that they had induced Peter's heart attack. There was an enormous life insurance policy on both men. If either partner died, all mortgages would be paid off instantly, plus there would be a $4,000,000 cash payment for the surviving business partner. But the insurance company claimed that Cap & Jet had ceased trading before Peter's death, and as such, the policy was void and they didn't have to pay out.

At first she was confused, and then she realized the irony. If her father had died when he'd had his first attack, when the company was still trading, the insurance company would have had to pay out millions. But the company had died just a few days before Peter, and that meant the insurance guys were off-the-hook and Jack was stuck with all the bills. How tough was that?

Lily fixed herself another cup of tea. That was all she drank these days. It started the day her father died. She made tea as soon as she was able to move, and she'd been making it ever since. It was good to have something to do, and it was reassuring to hold the warm mug. She didn't always drink it, but making it helped keep her sane. She was having serious difficulty keeping it together these days. The guilt was enormous. Her father's first heart attack was as a direct result of hearing about her and Jack, and she figured that his second was when he was going to meet Jack for lunch. You didn't need to be a rocket scientist, or a cardiologist for that matter, to see the pattern. Peter could handle the rough and tumble of the business world, but when somebody threatened his family, that was too much for him.

Why couldn't her dad have just accepted the situation? He loved Jack like a brother. Why not let her love him, too? But, no. He'd been furious with Jack, and her, too. That's why his stress levels were so high. His death was her fault. Hers and Jack's. How could she ever go back to a normal life knowing that? Shouldn't she be in prison? She'd practically murdered her father, and for what? Jack? Was that a fair swap? Her mother had to lose the love of her life so she could have hers?

But it wasn't a straight swap. Rosie had lost her dad, too. Natasha had lost her grandfather. The price had been very high for Lily to get Jack. If she'd known that claiming him would have meant losing her father, Lily was pretty sure she would have backed away. That was too much pain for too many people. But she couldn't do that now, because the damage was done. There was no going back.

She remembered Jack calling on that awful Wednesday. Halloween. The day her father died. Lily had already been in a pretty grim mood, she remembered. Emily had been so kind. At first she'd been thrilled about the lunch. Her dad had wanted to talk to Jack. Wasn't that progress? Jack had sounded uptight on the phone—the big wuss. Her dad was a good guy, and chances were he was meeting to make peace. Maybe the heart attack at her mom's birthday lunch had brought him to his senses. That's what she thought back then. It had even cheered her up, although it appeared Jack hadn't felt the same way. A few hours later he'd called back. Lily had been giddy with anticipation.

"Well, are you best buddies again? Has he forgiven you for stealing away his little girl?" Lily asked.

"Honey, stop. There's been an accident. It's your father."

"Oh, no. Is he okay?"

"It doesn't look good."

Now she knew he'd been stalling. He already knew her dad was dead, but he didn't want to tell her that over the phone. It would have been too harsh. He was right about that.

"Meet me outside your mom's house as soon as you can," he'd instructed her.

Lily, for once, didn't argue. "Sure, I'm on my way. Are you taking him home? It wasn't another heart attack, was it?"

"He crashed your mom's car just outside the Capital Grille, but the crash wasn't bad. Just meet me at your folk's home as soon as you can but, honey," he said, his tone softening, "drive carefully."

She flew out of the office and told Caryn, her assistant, to hold her calls and cancel her meetings because her father had been in a car accident. Even when Lily got to Cliff Road she didn't think anything was wrong. Jack's face was unreadable. She parked her car next to his and went to hug him.

"Lily," he whispered, his voice was hoarse with emotion.

That's when she got her first inkling.

"Where's Dad? Where's Mom? Does she know yet?"

"Lily, I'm afraid he had another heart attack."

She knew then—in that very instant. It was the solemn look on Jack's face, the sorrow in his eyes, that told her. He wasn't talking urgently as if he had to rush her to a hospital bedside. There was finality in his stance. His body was saying it was already too late.

This she'd analyzed in the weeks after. Back then, she just collapsed into his arms.

"He's gone, isn't he?" she'd asked.

"He is, my love. He's in heaven now." He hugged her for what felt like only a nanosecond when her mother's front door opened. It was Sandra. Back then it didn't even occur to her that it was the first time she'd seen Jack's wife since the news of their affair broke.

Even with the huge emergency that was her father's death, she realized Sandra's reaction had been the ultimate in class and emotional maturity.

She didn't scream or try to hit Lily. Instead, she took her by the hand and brought her into the house. When Lily saw her mother's reaction, that's when she realized her father was gone.

It still felt surreal. She kept thinking he was going to walk into the room and laugh at all of them.

"Gotcha!" he would shout, and they'd all think it was funny.

But that hadn't happened, and slowly she was beginning to accept the incredible magnitude of the situation.

She would never ever see her father again. Jack didn't understand how much that hurt her. She'd always been the apple of her father's eye, and now he was gone, but worst of all, it was very possible that she'd caused his death. How could she ever learn to live with that?

By mid-morning she got up the energy to take a shower. Her hair felt gross, so she stood under the steaming water for a good twenty minutes and cried again. By the time she got out, it was almost lunchtime, but there was still no sign of Jack.

Good, she thought. She really needed a little space from him. His affection was starting to suffocate her, and it wasn't helping to get her out of the doldrums. His advice wasn't much better. How in the heck could she go out for a walk if she'd told the office she was sick? What if she bumped into somebody? Dumb idea.

She'd managed to stay home for the fifth consecutive day, but the price was that she was housebound. That didn't really bother her. February in Boston was a cold time. Snow blizzards were common, and there'd been a big one the night before. Lily knew her mother was due to fly out to Ireland. She wondered if the plane had made it out before the snow came down. It broke her heart that they still weren't talking. Three times she'd called the house since the funeral, and all three times Sandra answered. That had been awkward, but they rose above it.

"I'm sorry, Lily," she'd say each time, "your mom just isn't ready to talk to you."

What could she do? It felt like Sandra had moved in with her mom and taken over. There was no room for Lily. Had she lost her mother, too?

Feeling dejected, she threw on the first thing she found in her closet. It was an old jogging suit in faded gray. She didn't care what she looked like today. Nobody was going to see her except, of course, Jack. And if she looked like hell, he would just have to put up with it. She was letting him stay rent-free, darn it. The only thing that looked more forlorn than her was the inside of the fridge. It was empty of food, which was bad because all her crying had unexpectedly given her an appetite.

She found a family-sized bag of potato chips on top of the fridge. That'll do, she thought, and grabbed the last can of Coke from the fridge. She headed into the living room to watch television. That's when her intercom bell rang.

The last person Lily expected to see at her door was Matt Hamilton. What in the heck was he doing here? Perhaps the company was checking up on her. But they wouldn't do that, would they?

She checked herself in the mirror. She looked terrible. For anybody else from the office and she would have been happy to look like hell in front of them, but Matt? No. She'd stall him. That would be the smart thing to do. After all, she'd said she was probably contagious, so it would be silly to expose him to the germs.

She tried to sound sick as she hit the button on the intercom and said,

"Hello."

"Lily. Hi, it's Matt." He smiled into the camera. "I heard you were feeling bad, and I haven't seen you since—well, in months—so I brought a peace offering." He raised a bouquet of flowers in front of his face so the camera could see them.

"Oh, Matt, that's so sweet. Thanks a million. You really didn't need to. But why are you bringing peace offerings?"

"Ah, come on. I know I annoyed you in the restaurant way back then. I shouldn't have tried to steal you thunder. It's just that I can't stop myself. I'm a competitive guy." He looked awkward.

Lily laughed. "Don't worry about it. I'd forgotten all about that," she said, even though it was a lie. "But, Matt, I really am sick. I don't want to expose you to whatever it is I've got. Maybe it's better if you just leave the flowers there. I'll pick them up later."

He nodded. "I was thinking it just might have been a touch of the Asian flu. Jeez, it's crazy in the office. Have you been watching the markets?"

"Not really. Is it bad?"

"Not for you. Stocks fell through the floor early in the week and a lot of people took a real hammering. But they've rebounded since then. Ironic that being out of the office for so long and leaving your shares alone might mean you're better off than most."

Lily forgot for a moment that she was supposed to be sick. "Hey, that's great! That's this month's bonus."

"Yeah, I guess you're okay." He stopped for a moment as if he was thinking. "Ya know, I'm tougher than I look. I really think I can handle whatever bug you've got, unless it's the plague. Why don't you let me in for just a few minutes? I promise I won't get too close to you."

Lily wavered. He was being really nice, and he'd given her the only bit of good news she'd heard in ages. Maybe it was rude to send him away after he'd gone to so much trouble with the flowers.

"Will you promise not to inhale my nasty germs?" she asked playfully.

"I promise."

She buzzed him in.

Lily didn't need to tell him which apartment was hers, because he'd been there before. He'd driven her home from a work party once. It was over two years ago now, but she was pretty sure he would remember. She dashed to the mirror to check how she looked. How could she spruce up fast but still look sick. She only had a few seconds.

Tearing through her cosmetics, she realized that everything she owned focused on getting her more tanned-looking. She turned in a manic rush to the little locker next to the bath. That's where she kept old stuff she didn't use but didn't want to throw out. There, in the midst of everything, was a container of talcum powder. She put a little into the palm of her hand and ever-so-carefully rubbed a little on each cheek. Then she studied the effect in her bathroom mirror.

Matt knocked on the door. Wow, he was fast.

"Lily?"

"Coming," she yelled, sounding far-too-healthy. She tried to cough as she applied the last little bit of white powder, and then took one last look at herself in the mirror. It really worked. She looked like an extra from a vampire movie. White face and dark eyes—cool. Remembering to cough as she headed to the door, she let Matt in.

"Hey," he said, handing her the flowers. "Wow, you do look pale. Do you have a fever?" He reached out to feel her forehead, but she pulled back before he got the chance.

She coughed again. "Nah, I'll live. Don't worry about it. I'm sure it'll pass in the next day or two." She smelled the flowers. "Matt, these are so pretty. Thank you. You really shouldn't have."

He shrugged. "I thought it would be nice to get lilies for Lily. Is that really predictable?"

"No." She shook her head.

"I heard about your dad. Shit, Lily, I'm really sorry. All that stuff I said about you having friends in high places and getting the promotion because of him, well, I was way out-of-line."

He seemed very sincere. It had been hurtful, and she was relieved to put it behind her.

She nodded. "Thanks for that. I swear I worked my tail off for that promotion. Most girls my age are married with kids. All I do is work. I know I'm as good as any guy, so I should be just as entitled to the promotion."

"You're right. I was just mad you beat me."

"Don't worry about it," she said. "Come and sit down. Can I get you coffee or tea?"

"No, I should be the one getting something for you. You're sick." He smiled as they walked into the little kitchen together. He headed straight to the coffeemaker while she got a vase for the flowers. Matt worked around her and found two mugs without needing to ask where they were.

He sized up her super-deluxe, ultra-modern coffeemaker.

"You know how to work that thing?" she asked. She'd bought it as a gift for Jack who loved super-strong coffee, but she hadn't yet mastered how to work it.

"How hard can it be?" he mumbled as he focused on the appliance. He was obviously a capable guy, confident in himself and undeniably good-looking.

Put it out of your mind, she commanded herself.

He smiled as the coffeemaker kicked into action, hissing and gurgling.

"Oh, well done. I can't even use it." She laughed. "It's Jack's, you see—" then she stopped. Did he know about Jack? "Jack is my boyfriend," she said tentatively.

"Ah, yes." Matt kept his eyes on the machine. If he was hearing something new, he hid it well. "I have to be honest, I've used this machine before. My brother has one," he said, moving the conversation off Jack.

"Oh, I didn't know you had a brother. Is he in Boston?"

"No. Peter lives in Manhattan. Great guy. He's my twin."

"Peter?" Lily's voice cracked. "That was my dad's name."

Matt looked appalled. "Oh, crap, Lily, I'm so sorry. That was so stupid of me. I shouldn't have mentioned it." He put his hands on her shoulders and looked like he wanted to hug her, but Lily shook her head and pulled back.

"No, it's okay," she said while trying to smile. "Really, I'm going to have to get used to this sort of thing." She took a deep breath to compose herself.

"Tell me about your twin. Do you guys get along?"

Matt looked relieved. "Yes, he's my best friend. His wife just had their first baby. A daughter. I'm an uncle."

"Oh, Matt, that's terrific. Congratulations. A little girl?"

The machine stopped, and he was able to pour the first cup. He nodded. "Yep. Anna Hamilton. She's gorgeous."

"I think you'll make a great uncle. You'll spoil her rotten, won't you?"

Matt beamed. "I have every intention. I can't wait to play with her. Of course, she's only a couple of weeks old, but when she's older I want to take her for weekends and teach her all the cool stuff like how to burp and use bad words like 'shit' and 'crap' just to mess with my brother's head."

Lily pretended to look shocked. "You wouldn't." Then she laughed and walked out to the drawing room. The flowers looked pretty when she put them in the center of the table, but all of Jack's stuff was scattered everywhere. She scooped up everything and put it in a neat pile. Matt followed her in.

She turned and took one of the mugs. For a moment, their eyes met.

There was still a spark. Lily pulled away fast.

"Sorry the place is such a mess. Jack only just moved in, and we're still trying to squeeze everything together."

Matt sat down on the other sofa—as far away from her as he could get while still sitting in the same room.

"I have to say, I'm kinda sorry to hear you're settling down, Lily. You see, I was wondering if you wanted to give us—you and me—a chance," he said looking her in the eyes.

"Oh, Matt. Jack and I—" She looked around as if seeing the place would explain her domestic situation. "We've been together for over a year now. I'm very much committed to him," she whispered. "You're a really nice guy, but, well, we nearly got together once and then you seemed to lose interest."

Matt laughed and studied his coffee. "Oh yeah? Is that how you think it went down? Lily, you gave me the cold shoulder so many times I eventually decided to throw in the towel. What can I say?" He shrugged and gave her a sheepish grin. "I guess a tiny part of me hadn't given up completely, but now I think I'm too late."

"Oh, Matt . . ." She hated to let him down. He was being so nice and so honest.

Then he shook his head, still smiling. "Don't sweat it. I just enjoyed our time at Feng Shui. I love that we have so much in common and damn it, you're hot. But if you love this guy, I guess I'll have to accept defeat." He said it without any embarrassment.

She'd never discussed a possible relationship this candidly and calmly before. It was a bit weird but nice at the same time. "You'll find someone perfect for you."

He lifted the cup to his mouth and drained the rest in one gulp. He didn't look like he wanted to hang around now that he'd been given the thumbs-down.

"That's the problem," he said, and wiped his mouth with the back of his hand. "I thought I'd found someone perfect for me." He looked straight at her. Their eyes locked and Lily could feel herself being drawn to him.

The spell was broken by the sound of a key in the door. Jack walked in. He would have had to be unbelievably stupid not to pick up on the vibe in the room. There was an electric current running between Lily and Matt even though they were sitting far apart. Jack came right in and reached to shake Matt's hand. Matt shot to his feet. "Mr. Hoffman! Hey, good to meet you. Lily was just talking about you."

"Oh?" he looked over his shoulder at Lily. "What has she been saying?"

Matt shot her a *yikes* look. "She was just saying how great you've been during this difficult time for her, and for you, too, of course, Mr. Hoffman. I know Mr. Power was your business partner and lifelong friend. Can I offer you my condolences, sir?"

Lily had to stifle a giggle. Matt was playing Jack. Surely he would see straight through it. She interrupted them before it got too comical. "Matt brought us these flowers, darling. Wasn't that nice?" Jack gave the bouquet a quick glance.

"Yes, very thoughtful." Then he took Lily in his arms. "Now, have you given any more thought to where you want to dine tonight, honey?"

"Okay, I think that's my cue to go," Matt said, smiling at Lily. Then he looked at Jack. "Good to meet you, Mr. Hoffman. Get better soon, Lily."

"I'll walk you to the elevator," she offered. Jack didn't stop them.

Outside, Matt took Lily's hand. "I had no idea you were living with *him*," he whispered urgently.

Lily shrugged awkwardly.

"Jesus, Lily, he's old enough to be your—" Then he stopped before he said something really tactless, but it was too late. Lily moved into defense mode.

"We love each other, and we're very committed to making this work."

Matt shrugged. "Whatever turns you on," he said.

"About what you said earlier," Lily started, wanting to clear the air between them, but he put his hands up, then smiled, kissed her cheek, and said, "Hey, you smell like Anna. Is that talcum powder?" He smirked.

She pulled away. "I took a bath just before you came."

"Damn, I guess I really did arrive too late." He laughed. "Look, Lily, forget about what I said. You're obviously off the market." He shrugged. "*Youdeyoushi*," he added just as the elevator door pinged.

You win some, you lose some . . . She knew he was being flippant, and it annoyed her.

When she came back into the apartment, Jack was tearing the place apart.

"Lily, where in the hell have you put all the papers I had on this table?" he barked. "They were very important. You have no idea." He didn't look at her but instead lifted the vase as if they were somehow hidden underneath it.

Silently, she went over to where she'd left the neat pile of paperwork.

He looked at her with annoyance. "You put them away? Lily, you can't just go moving my stuff around."

Lily glared at him.

"Look, just don't touch my stuff. Okay? It's very important that you don't go near any of it."

"This is my home, Jack. You can't speak to me like that."

"Are you sure?" he said, a sharp edge to his tone.

"What do you mean *am I sure*?"

"We talked about this. Have you double-checked you're on the deeds? Is this place in your name or in your father's?"

Lily had forgotten to check. Since her father's death, she hadn't been thinking straight. She thought she might cry again.

"And what the hell have you done to your face? Is that talcum powder? You have a big smudge down your cheek," he said with impatience.

Lily went into her bedroom to look in the mirror. The powder had looked vaguely convincing when she'd patted it on, but some must have rubbed off when she sniffed the flowers. Her cover was so blown with Matt. What a fool she was. Lily wandered back out in hopes of getting solace from Jack, but he was already poring over some documents.

"I think I'll go back to bed."

"It's lunchtime. What are you doing going to bed?"

"I told you I was feeling sick," she snapped.

"And I told you that you were simply faking it and it was time to get up and move on."

Lily didn't want a fight, so she didn't argue. "Okay then," she said. "Whatever you say, Jack." Then she went to bed.

Chapter 24

Rosie Says Good-bye

It was impossible for Rosie to sleep. She woke early on Saturday, and the moment her mind cleared, her first thought was of was her fateful vacation. It was now only a day away. She couldn't believe she was actually going through with it. Marcus was so excited. She was terrified.

Just as she did every morning now, she headed out for her run. She used to have to leave Natasha with Marcus, but he often objected, claiming jetlag or arguing that he was due some downtime, but now she had Matilda.

It had been Sandra's suggestion, and what a wonderful idea it was. Poor Matilda was gutted after her dad's death. Back then she'd spent her days vacillating between hopeful prayers and destitute tears. Occupational therapy played a part, too, because she cleaned more than ever. It was unfortunate that the house she was cleaning was already so spotless. That left Matilda with nothing to do. A couple of days after the funeral, when they were having lunch at her mom's house, Sandra put the suggestion out there.

"If Matilda is going to be taking care of Natasha while we're in Ireland, why doesn't she move into Rosie's house a week or so before, just to get to know the ropes? That way she could bond with the child. It will make the transition all the easier on little Natasha," Sandra had said.

Why hadn't that occurred to Rosie? It was inspired. She was thrilled to have some free time before her vacation. There was so much to do. Matilda was happy to have a child to play with again, and Natasha adored Tilly. The old housekeeper indulged the five-year-old completely. As a result Natasha had regressed back to her childish ways. She was becoming more spoiled by the day with Matilda fawning over her so much. In all honesty, it was driving Rosie crazy, but she was so relieved to have a little time to herself, she chose to ignore it.

In the last few days, Rosie had gotten her hair trimmed and highlighted, and everything else buffed, bleached, or blasted. Between that and the running, she knew she looked every bit as good as she did on her honeymoon—maybe even better. She would give those stupid swingers a run for their money. She still had no intention of actually doing anything with a strange man, but she was going to look the part anyway.

Marcus, meanwhile, had done nothing. Most nights he still drank his ice-cold beer and watched a game. He laughed at her, telling her she worried too much. That it was supposed to be a fun vacation, and she should treat it that way, but she couldn't. Rosie still saw it as a challenge to her marriage. A threat. She was determined to be just as sexy as any woman there. Then maybe when it got to be crunch time, Marcus would see that she was as good as those other women, and he would choose her.

She'd settled into her run and was enjoying the beauty of the fresh snowfall all around her. As usual, the plows had cleared both the roads and the sidewalks, but the gardens were covered in pristine white, untouched layers of fresh snow. It hurt to look at it without sunglasses, but Rosie was armed with hers. Now, with the sun shining, the landscape looked glorious. It should have raised her spirits, but it didn't.

She was too worried about her vacation. Of course, she tried her best to cancel the trip after her father's death, but everybody ganged up against her. Lily said that Dad wouldn't want that. Mom said she would be happy to have Natasha as a distraction. So did Matilda. Marcus said in the strongest possible terms that not going would just make a bad situation worse. Not going wouldn't bring her dad back, and they should go to celebrate that they were very much alive.

As she ran, she thought about her dad.

Can you see me now? If you can, I guess you know what we're up to.

Mentally, she squirmed. Her dad would not approve. He was loyal to her mom all his life. The idea of going on a vacation where the entire plan was to have sex with other peoples' partners would've appalled him. It made her run faster.

Please don't be angry, Dad. I'm doing what Marcus wants. I'm trying to keep him, and looking the other way is the only way I see it happening.

His death had been a crushing blow. Rosie loved her dad to distraction. Everybody always said that she was his double, only in female form, while Lily was Mom's. Rosie liked that. He'd been a good role model. He worked hard and played harder. It was incredibly sad that his business failed just before he died, because he'd worked so very hard all his life.

He didn't deserve to fail, but sometimes that's just what happened. This horrible economic downturn had caught a lot of decent, hardworking businessmen and women by the throat. Luck was so fickle. Things had been so incredibly good for so long. The biggest tragedy in Rosie's mind was that he didn't have much put aside for emergency. Didn't every successful businessman know to take some of the profits away and lodge them in a savings account? The ironic thing is that he'd told her to do it. He'd lectured Rosie about not "betting the farm," as he put it. Why hadn't he taken his own advice? Could it have been Jack's influence?

Screw Jack Hoffman. If only it was he who'd had the heart attack.

Rosie and Lily had reached a kind of truce, but she still had enormous difficulty talking to Jack. She found it revolting to think of him as Lily's boyfriend.

On the day her dad died, when Jack had walked into the kitchen, she'd almost let go of the plate she was holding. Then he dropped the bombshell. It was the last thing Rosie had expected. Sure, her father had a heart attack, but lots of people did, especially men. Even one of Marcus's friends had one a while back. But almost everybody recovered. When she'd heard that her father was missing, her thoughts were about her mom and keeping her calm. It never even crossed her mind to worry about him. She thought he would live forever. He was a force of nature, like a tornado, and not somebody to fall over with a heart attack. How wrong she had been.

Even Natasha took it badly. She'd picked up on how upset her mother, aunt, and grandma were, but when Rosie tried to explain that grandpa had gone to heaven, she'd cried inconsolably. Rosie hadn't been able to cheer her up, but amazingly, Matilda could. She'd sit with Natasha for hours and fold her into her soft, warm embrace, all the time rocking her gently back and forth. She whispered mysterious, lilting Spanish words, none of which Natasha could translate, but she got the message loud and clear: Tilly loved her.

Matilda was so good for her little girl. Natasha had fallen for her new nanny and Rosie got to keep up with her running. The situation was a win-win. She wondered what the chances were of keeping Matilda forever. She sure had the space, and she needed the help. Matilda was a consummate professional when it came to cleaning, but even better, she was an amazing nanny. Her mom wouldn't want to lose Matilda, but now that Rosie was used to her around the house, she really wanted her to stay. She resolved to discuss it with her mother first, and then with Matilda, but all of that could wait until she returned from the Caribbean.

Her mind turned to her husband. When her father had died, Marcus was, as usual, a tower of strength. He let her cry and rage against the injustice of it all. He'd held her when she woke in the middle of the night, suddenly remembering that he was gone. They'd even managed to make love the night he died. He'd been so tender with her, so gentle. He really did love her, and she him. It's just that he seemed to need a little extramarital fun, so she would just have to accept that.

Now that the vacation was actually happening, she had a certain fatalistic approach. Whether she liked it or not, it was going to happen, so she may as well get happy about it. Besides, sex wasn't everything. There would be exquisite white, sandy beaches, scrumptious cocktails, and wonderful shopping. This was her first real break since Natasha was born, and she was determined to enjoy it, no matter what the sleeping arrangements were.

When she got home, she had a nice lunch with her daughter and Matilda. Marcus was away with work. He was flying in that evening, and they would fly out very early together the next day. She had agreed with her mom and Matilda that they'd move Natasha to Cliff Road today because Sunday would be too hectic. Her mom was due back from Ireland on Monday afternoon, so it would actually be two nights alone for Matilda and Natasha. Matilda was comfortable with that, and Natasha was ecstatic to be going on "a vacation" to grandma's house.

"Can I bring all my dolls?" she asked as they threw a few things in the suitcase that afternoon.

"Of course."

"And my duck coat and boots?"

"Yes. You might need your winter coat, too. It's February and it's very cold."

"Tilly says I can stay up late and we'll have a party tonight, just her and me."

Rosie listened to her darling little daughter ramble on about her big plans for her time alone with Matilda. She was very happy with the situation. And she wondered again why she hadn't done this before. Her mother and Matilda were a terrific support. She toyed with the idea of getting a summer vacation break with Marcus, maybe to Europe. How cool would that be?

Her mom had phoned from Dublin the previous night, and it was the first time Rosie had heard her sound happy since before the funeral. She wasn't laugh-out-loud-happy, but she was able to hold a normal conversation. It was only their first day, and they'd spent the afternoon sightseeing. Her mom was genuinely engaged when she told Rosie all about the old roads and buildings she recognized. Sandra had been so wise to take her away. A change of air and scenery did the soul good.

Rosie drove Matilda and Natasha to her mother's house. It had already been agreed that Nat would take over Rosie's old room, and Matilda would sleep in the guestroom next door. She usually lived in the guesthouse out by the pool so she could have her own space, but that wouldn't work if she was looking after Natasha.

They entered the house and there was a beeping noise. "Matilda, what's the alarm code? I don't remember it ever being on before."

Matilda bustled ahead and tapped the numbers into the keypad.

"Times change, Rosita," she said, using Rosie's old pet name. "Usually there's always somebody here, so we have no need."

Tiger, the cat, arrived to welcome them.

"Tiger," Rosie and Natasha chorused together. Rosie scooped her up into her arms. "Were you locked in here all this time?"

"Your mother only left yesterday. She's fine for just one night alone. She has litter box in the bathroom."

The idea of kitty litter was enough to make Rosie put the cat down again.

They unloaded the car and then Rosie headed up to her old room with her daughter. She put all the little dresses in the closet and filled the chest of drawers with everything else.

It was only then, as she settled Natasha in, that she felt her first real rush of anguish about leaving her precious little angel.

Rosie had been so focused on the resort that she hadn't given any thought to the suddenness of leaving her daughter. Before Matilda entered their lives, it was perhaps true that Rosie spent too much time with Natasha, but suddenly to go cold turkey? How would she cope? It was one thing to head out for a run or a manicure, but to get on a plane and fly to another country? That was different. They weren't even leaving until the next day. Whose crazy idea was it to leave them at Cliff Road—alone? She could stay. True, their flight was early in the morning, but Rosie was okay with early starts, being married to a pilot. They got up at all hours.

She was sitting on the bed with all of these last-minute panicky thoughts running through her head when Matilda walked in and sat down on the bed next to her. She put her arm around Rosie's waist.

"Oy, you are running too much, *chica*. You have become too thin."

"Oh, Tilly, I think I don't want to go. How can I leave my baby?" she whispered, because she didn't want to upset Natasha. Fortunately, her daughter was far too busy deciding where each doll should go.

"I know. I can see it in your eyes." Matilda sighed. "I had this very same conversation with your mother about twenty-five years ago, maybe more."

"More," Rosie added. "I was twenty-nine last month."

"That's just the point, *chica*. The time goes by so fast. You must enjoy yourself, and you owe it to your husband. Someday, sooner than you think, Nat will be gone off with her man, so you must put your husband first and the child next."

Rosie didn't answer. She watched Natasha playing.

"I took care of you when your parents went away, and we had a great time. This will be the same, I promise."

This much Rosie knew was the truth. Matilda was a terrific nanny. She was more than capable of anticipating Natasha's needs.

"I'm sorry. I've never actually left her before. We've been together since the day she was born, and I didn't realize it was going to be so hard."

"No," Matilda argued vehemently. "Don't make it hard, Rosita. It is fine and normal. Mamas need time out, too. No crying now. You know she is in good hands, so go and have some fun." Rosie was glad Matilda was still capable of being bossy when she needed to be. Rosie went over to her daughter.

"Okay, Nat. Mommy's going to say good-bye now. You'll be just great with Tilly. I know you've been looking forward to your vacation here."

Natasha beamed from ear-to-ear. "We're having a party as soon as you go, so you gotta go now, Mommy."

Rosie thought her heart would break. "I'll call you guys, and remember grandma will be home the day after tomorrow."

"We're gonna have another party then." Natasha giggled in anticipation.

How could she worry about her daughter? It was obvious she was delighted with the change of scenery. Rosie forced herself to be stronger than she felt. She didn't make any more fuss about being gone seven whole days. She just kissed Matilda and Natasha and got out of the house before she started to cry.

Back in her car, though, she let the tears fall. Nobody ever told her it would be this hard. Lots of her friends had gone on vacations and left their children behind. She'd never heard about them falling to pieces. Was it just her? Was she unhinged or perhaps too dependent on Natasha already? She felt panicky. Was she one of those clingy moms who didn't know how to let go? Poor Natasha. That would be awful.

Maybe her mom was right and what she needed was another baby. She wondered how Marcus would feel about that. They hadn't discussed it because learning to take care of Natasha had really been a full-time job. Rosie had been taking birth control pills since she stopped breastfeeding. The doctor had already told her she would have to stop by the time she was thirty and consider other forms. She wouldn't think about it until after she got back, of course. The knock on her car window startled her.

"Lily, what are you doing here?" she asked as she rolled down the window.

"Hi, Rosie. I told Mom I would pop in to see if Matilda needed anything since she doesn't have a car. What about you?" She leaned in. "Hey, are you crying?"

"Oh, it's nothing. I was just saying good-bye to Natasha. I didn't realize how tough it would be."

"I can only imagine. But you know the week will fly by, and you'll be back refreshed and rested before Natasha even notices you're gone."

"I know. I really do. My head gets it, but my heart is breaking."

Lily squeezed Rosie's shoulder. "Look, I'm here. You know I would do anything for my niece. I give you my solemn word of honor that if anything goes wrong, I'll step in. If she needs any help, money, medical care, you name it, I'm on it. I've got your back, Sis."

Rosie looked at Lily. Really looked at her. They seemed to have so little in common. Not looking alike was only the tip of the iceberg. Their sense of values were at odds, just as their tastes in men, and their ambition levels. Everything, really. But here was some common ground—Natasha. She patted Lily's hand. "Thanks, Lily. I know we've had our differences, but I do appreciate your support with Natasha."

"Go. Have a ball. I can always call you on your cell, and you've left your contact details with Matilda and Mom, right?"

"Uh, no. I told them we'd be reachable by cell, and I'll call them."

"Oh, so you're still going to that place. I don't know why I'd assumed you'd changed your plans with everything that's happened." She pulled her hand back. "Okay," she said, but the warmth was gone. "Well, you can call us and don't worry; I'll look out for Natasha."

Rosie suddenly felt the need to leave. She started her car and nodded.

"Thanks for everything. I'll talk to you soon, okay?"
"Yeah."

Lily watched Rosie go. What kind of a fool was her sister? She had it all. A guy she loved and who loved her. Most important, everybody approved of the match. Marcus was handsome, a good provider, and a doting father. It was nauseating. Then, as if that wasn't enough, Rosie had an adorable little girl. Natasha was so cute and smart, and everybody loved her. Now Rosie was going to risk all that for a quick thrill? Was the girl absolutely stark-raving mad? Her sister's red BMW turned a corner and was out of sight, so Lily headed toward the house.

The truth was that Lily was sorry not to have Natasha for the week now. It would have been a great distraction and a perfect excuse to stay away from work. She would much rather have played with the little girl for a week than pretend she was sick. Maybe she'd ask her mom if she could "borrow" her niece for a night. That would be so much fun. Lily had a double bed in her second bedroom. Right now it was covered in Jack's files, but he could move them for one night, and the three of them could pretend to be a little family.

Chapter 25

Failte

Popsy sighed when their car pulled up outside the hotel. "Peter would have loved this." It was Saturday evening, and they were bidding farewell to their driver of the last day and a half.

"Thank you, Gerald. We had a fantastic time with you. Again, a million thanks," Sandra enthused for the umpteenth time.

He'd whisked them everywhere they wanted to go. They knew it was going to be good from the moment they got into his lovely, comfortable Mercedes Benz on Friday. He wore a gray chauffeur's uniform and cap and was the perfect gentleman from start to finish, but he also had that incredible Irish charm and the sparkle in his eyes that Irish men were famous for. His charm had sure worked on Popsy and Sandra.

"*Failte go Baile Atha Cliath.* Welcome to Dublin." Those were his opening words.

"Aw shucks, I bet you say that to all the girls," Sandra said and right away they were on the best of terms. They were in the back of the car, so most of their communication was either with the back of his head or the rearview mirror.

"I understand you want to head to the south of Dublin first, is that correct?"

Sandra leaned forward to talk with him, but then Popsy said, "It is. Can you aim for Ferndale Road in Rathmichael? I'll direct you from there. Well,

I hope I'll be able to if things haven't changed too much," she said and smiled.

Sandra was silently thrilled. Popsy had all but given up communicating with strangers since Peter's death, and she'd become accustomed to speaking for both of them, but it looked like Popsy had found her voice again. A good first.

He took them straight out to Rathmichael, where Popsy had grown up. She said the biggest surprise for her was how much had changed.

"Do you still have any family out here, madam?" Gerald asked.

"I'm afraid the only family I have in these parts are in Shanganagh Cemetery. That will be our next stop."

He gave a sympathetic nod. "I wonder if any of the old neighbors are still here."

"I very much doubt it. When I lived here it was all fields around us. We didn't have any neighbors for miles. Things have changed drastically," she said, looking out the window. "Where I remember old country roads, now you have motorways. Where we had big rolling hills to explore, somebody has put up thumping big housing estates." She didn't sound too thrilled but Sandra was just happy to hear her talking again.

"Oh, Popsy, look at that little church. Was that there when you lived here?" she asked.

"Honey, that church was there when St. Patrick was here," Popsy said, which made Sandra laugh. "You think I'm joking? I'm not. I remember doing a school project on it when I was seven or eight. Let's see . . . The church you're looking at is a rebuild. It's only about two hundred years old. I think it was built in the early 1800s, but they have records of a church being on these grounds going back as far as Norman times, so that's around 1170, the time of Saint Patrick. They even believe the founder of the church may have been a religious man called Bishop Mac Toil. His death is recorded in the records at 550AD, so I guess he built it before that. It's pretty safe to assume this church was first built in the late 500s." Popsy stopped and laughed at herself. "Funny, the things you remember," she said and looked from Sandra to Gerald. Sandra was stunned into silence and was staring at Popsy in open-mouthed wonder. Even the driver had gone quiet.

"Now that beats Banagher. I've been out here millions of times and I never knew that," he said. "Late 500s, you say? I'll remember that."

Sandra snapped out of her shocked silence. "There's that saying again. What's Banagher? And why do you want to beat it? I don't get it."

Gerald laughed. "Sure, how would you know? 'That beats Banagher' is another way of saying 'isn't that amazing.' Banagher is a place. In fact, I think there are two of them. The one I know is in Offaly, in the middle of Ireland, but I think there's another in Northern Ireland, too. Very nice town by all accounts, but I have no idea how the expression came about."

"Stop," Popsy almost shouted, and Gerald hit the brakes.

Popsy leaned forward and reached over Sandra to push her electric window down. She stared at the large, white house nestled in a web of enormous old oaks standing back about a hundred yards from the road.

"Is that it?" Sandra whispered.

Popsy nodded. "Yep, that was home."

"Lovely home, madam."

"It does still look majestic," Sandra said. "But is that a car park out front?"

"Looks like it's being used as an office building now," Gerald ventured. "There are too many cars for it to be a private residence. Would you like to go in? I could ask for you, if you like."

Popsy cowered back into the seat and shook her head. Sandra took her hand.

"It's okay. They wouldn't mind, especially if it's not even a private home anymore."

"No, let's go. I have wonderful memories of the big old kitchen with its jet black Aga—that's a range to you, Sandra. Also, the bright morning room filled with sunlight and flowers. No, I don't want to go in there now to see people sitting at desks, staring into computers in what used to be my childhood playroom. My memories are better than that."

Sandra had written off her years with Jack because of their breakup. Yes, their last year together had been acrimonious, but the times before had been good. She would do well to take Popsy's example and choose to remember the good times. Lock them away and keep them precious. They were hers and they were real and they were good. It made her feel a little better.

"Gerald, would you take us to Shanganagh Cemetery now, please?" Popsy asked.

Sandra had been a little nervous about Popsy visiting the grave of her parents so soon after Peter's death, but her worries were unfounded. Her parents were long-deceased, and she was calm when she found the gravesite they shared. It had been a few decades since her last visit, and she looked happy to be back. Sandra watched her friend like a hawk for any sign of anxiety, but her fears were unfounded. If anything, she seemed at peace.

Popsy looked around. "It's nice here," she said.

"I guess—as graveyards go. I'm not in any hurry to move into one, if that's what you're suggesting." Sandra kept it light, and Popsy smiled.

"It's just, I was thinking about how Peter chose cremation over burial. I think I'd prefer to be buried so my people could come visit me well into the future, like I'm doing now."

Sandra just nodded. It was the first time Popsy had spoken about Peter so freely. Was she beginning to accept that he was gone? She'd been worried about dragging Popsy to Ireland while she still seemed so depressed and disconnected but it was looking like her fears were unfounded.

Usually, when Sandra had a problem, she would ask Popsy, or in the past, Jack. Those options were gone, so she'd had to get more resourceful. She took all the advice she could get from the fount of all wisdom—the internet —and it hadn't led her astray. The experts insisted it was good to "move on" after a death and a change of scenery was a great idea. It also went through issues like talking about the dead and using the past tense, which Popsy was doing. This was all good. It seemed Popsy was recovering.

"Would you like me to leave you alone with your parents?" Sandra asked.

Popsy shook her head. "There's no need. They're not here anymore. It's only their tired, old bodies. I know their spirits are with me no matter where I am, just like Peter's." Popsy touched her parents' headstone and bid them goodbye. Then she took Sandra by the arm, and they walked out of the cemetery together.

On Friday night, they'd stayed in the hotel to dine. Even with the morning nap they were still pretty exhausted and happy to take it easy. The restaurant in The Four Seasons was excellent. It was perhaps a little quieter than Sandra would have liked but Popsy seemed pleased. They agreed that Saturday would be spent wandering around South County Dublin, going to all the places that Popsy had gone to when she was young.

Gerald had told them the really good shopping was in a place called the Dundrum Shopping Center, but that hadn't existed when Popsy was young, so she had no real interest in seeing it. She'd wanted to revisit places like the adorable little villages of Monkstown, Dalkey, Killiney, and the town of Dunleary, as well as Blackrock, because that was where she'd hung out with her friends when she was a teenager. The pier in Dunleary was also part of her special memories, and she was determined to walk it.

"Why is it so important?" Sandra had asked.

"It's where I had my first kiss," Popsy said with a shy smile.

"Hey, cool." Sandra laughed "But the real question is, with whom?"

Popsy smiled whimsically. "Mark Butler. I wonder where he is now. And before you ask, I have no desire, and I mean *no* desire, to find out. Do you hear me?"

"It would have really spiced up the weekend. I mean, it's all well and good visiting old houses and cemeteries, but looking up an old boyfriend? Now that could be fun."

Popsy put her hand up. "Sandra, give me time. Peter is still my man. I still love him. I do not want to look up any old boyfriends."

Sandra realized she'd gone way too far. "I'm sorry, Popsy. I'm such an insensitive idiot. Please forgive me."

Popsy shook her head and drank a little wine. "There's nothing to forgive. Today was really nice, and I can't wait to show you all the places I used to go."

They woke early on Saturday, and Sandra did her session in the gym while Popsy took her first bath of the day. Gerald arrived promptly and whisked them away to another day of adventures, starting in Blackrock. Popsy told them that, unlike Rathmichael, she was happy to report that not much seemed to have changed. Of course the names on the shops had, but the basic layout of the main street and its two little shopping centers were as she remembered.

One of the highlights was finding a great book shop in Blackrock. Unlike the super-sized bookstores in the States, this store was small with little alcoves. It was intimate, and they thoroughly enjoyed wandering around and finding a good book. They stopped for a coffee, too, because Sandra couldn't get enough of those Irish fruit scones with real Irish butter.

"I'm going to have to up my gym sessions," she said with a moan when she polished off yet another and looked hungrily at the half that Popsy had left untouched. "Are you going to eat that?" she asked.

Popsy laughed and pushed it across the table. On the upside, she did eat half, Sandra thought. At least she was back to eating.

Monkstown was just as nice as Blackrock. It was a good deal smaller, but the little crescent of shops was charming. A large church towered over the small seaside town. Then it was on to Dunleary.

"What the heck does that sign say? 'Dun Laoighre?' I can't even pronounce it," Sandra complained as they arrived in the port town.

"That's how the Irish spell what you know as 'Dunleary.' You know, there's a fully functioning and very much alive language in this country. Ireland has Irish," Popsy explained. "Everybody learns it in school."

"But there's a *G* in the middle. Whose idea was that? It's physically impossible to pronounce."

"Irish sounds a lot like Arabic. It's quite guttural. You have to use the back of your throat."

Sandra tried but sounded more like she was choking. Popsy laughed and shook her head.

Part of the town had become pedestrianized, so they were able to wander around all the little shops.

There were families on the promenade out for some fresh air and a good walk. Young lovers held hands and stared into each other's eyes, oblivious to where they were. There was the occasional runner and powerwalker, but most people seemed to be walking their dogs.

"Is it the law to own a dog here?" Sandra asked.

"We're a people of the land. We love our animals."

"Oh puh-lease." Sandra laughed. "When was the last time you cleaned up after Tiger?" she asked as a woman got out a bag to clear away her pooch's creation.

Popsy winced. "Yeah, I think I've lost touch with my Celtic Karma."

"I always thought the Irish were most famous for their hospitality. Will we go out tonight and find a livelier place to have dinner? I mean, The Four Seasons was great. But it was a little quiet, don't you think?" She knew Popsy couldn't be pushed too much, but she was dammed if she was going to return to Boston without at least finding some mischief.

"What did you have in mind?" Popsy asked.

"That hotel our taxi driver showed us when we were coming in from the airport—I think it was called 'The Shelbourne'—that looked pretty neat."

"I knew it well, a long time ago. Best place in Dublin for afternoon tea."

"I wasn't thinking of afternoon tea, Popsy. I was thinking more of cosmos than coffee."

"Sounds like a good plan."

"But speaking of food, I'm getting hungry. How about some lunch?"

Popsy laughed. "I don't know where you put it, but you'll have to wait. We have to walk to the end of the pier and back. That's what everybody does. Come on, take it up a notch," Popsy said and walked faster.

"I've already killed myself in the gym this morning. I thought we were taking mellow little strolls around dainty local shops. I didn't realize you wanted a full-body workout."

Popsy ignored Sandra and inhaled deeply. "This feels great. Breathe in, Sandra. Can you smell that fresh sea air?" Seagulls cawed loudly overhead and Popsy looked up. "Funny. I'd forgotten what they sounded like. There aren't any seagulls in Wellesley."

"They can't afford the rent," Sandra joked and Popsy laughed. She actually laughed.

"I like the sound of them. They make me feel like I'm home." Popsy looked happy, so Sandra parked her cynicism. Seagulls didn't do it for her, she decided, as the huge birds swooped too close for comfort. They weren't pretty at all and she knew anything that big must produce a significant-sized bird poo. If she was alone she would have gotten out of there, but this wasn't about her. It was all about Popsy.

"It's good to be home, Sandra. I love the salt air on my lips and filling my lungs. It invigorates me."

Sandra forgot about her dislike of the seagulls. She was getting Popsy back. Ireland could build her up again like nowhere else, but she didn't say it out loud. Even though she was thrilled to hear her friend say it, Sandra didn't dare comment because she didn't want to break the vacation-spell that Popsy was under.

"My mother walked this very pier every day of her pregnancy with me. Isn't that awesome?"

"Wow, that is cool."

"It is. I just remembered that now. After I was born, she walked me in a stroller. She told me that when I was a little older, I would fight to get down and then try to run back toward Dunleary. Gosh, I'd forgotten how much this place is a part of me." Popsy stopped and looked at her. "Sandra, thank you for bringing me back here. Thank you so much."

The depth of gratitude and love on Popsy's face almost overwhelmed her, and she thought she might cry. Instead she gave her oldest and dearest friend a great big bear hug before resuming their walk.

As they reached the end of the pier Sandra asked, "Is there a pillar you have to walk around or a part of the wall you touch to acknowledge doing the length of the pier before you head back?"

Popsy shrugged. "No, not really. We usually just turn around and head back, but hang on a second, I want to go in here first." She pointed to an opening in the wall that led to the other side.

When they walked through, they found a few people sightseeing. Popsy walked over to a flat piece of rock that had no apparent use other than for people to stand on. "This is where it happened," she said.

"What?"

"My first kiss," Popsy mouthed so she wouldn't be overheard.

"Oh, yeah? Terrific." Sandra laughed and gave the area a little more attention. "It's a great place," she offered. "I mean, at least it's somewhere you can come back to when you want to, unlike me."

"Why's that?" Popsy asked as they headed back into town.

"My first kiss was in Tony Lopez's bedroom. I think whoever lives there now might find it odd if I asked them if I could take a trip down memory lane in one of their bedrooms."

Popsy laughed. "You have a point there."

"Now, can we please head back and find somewhere nice for lunch?" Sandra demanded. Gerald directed them to an amazing little Italian restaurant, and then he took them out to the village of Dalkey. After that they drove on to Killiney. Sandra adored the big houses out here. "It feels like Wellesley," she said.

Popsy laughed. "Yes, if Wellesley was by the sea, which it isn't, and I haven't seen a single clapboard house since we got here. But apart from that . . ."

"I don't know. It's just the feeling."

"Money," Popsy said.

"What?"

"Money. That's what they have in common. Killiney is full of billionaires, and so is Wellesley. That's what you sense."

Sandra laughed. "Not everybody in Wellesley has money anymore."

"I'm sure it's the same here," Popsy said. "Speaking of money, Sandra, there's something I need to discuss with you."

"Not this weekend," Sandra said. "This was my birthday present to you, and I don't want you spending even a penny."

Popsy shook her head. "It's not that. So much has changed since you bought me this amazing birthday present. Back then we were both Wellesley Wives. Then we were both rich."

Sandra sighed. "Those were the days. Now neither of us are Wellesley Wives, but for different reasons. You're a Wellesley widow." She squeezed Popsy's arm. "And I'm a Wellesley divorcee. Doesn't have a very nice ring to it, does it?"

Popsy stopped. "Sandra, my accountant called last week. It appears my life insurance came through. That is to say, Peter's life insurance."

"I thought it was all caught up in the Chapter 11 proceedings."

"That's his work insurance. He had a personal policy on both his life and mine, so what I'm trying to tell you is even if I lose the house, which I think is a given at this stage, I'll still have money. You're like a sister to me. I want to give you half of it. We've been through so much together,"

Sandra raised her hands, but Popsy ignored her. "If the situation were reversed, I know you would do the same. Please let me do this."

Sandra was embarrassed and confused. She was used to being the one who took care of Popsy, but she knew she was going to need help financially if Jack really had no funds. She started to cry.

Now it was Popsy's turn to comfort her.

"Come on, it's not that bad. It would have been worse if I was looking to borrow money from you," she said.

Sandra laughed through her tears. "True. Then we'd really be in trouble."

"Put it out of your mind for now, but I just wanted to tell you that we're going to be okay, moneywise. I don't mean that we're going to be fabulously rich like we were, but we'll have enough to buy a place and live a modest life if that's what you want."

"My lawyers are still trying to get alimony out of Jack," Sandra said, but a shadow crossed Popsy's face. Then she realized anything she got from Jack, she would be taking from Lily, too. This was all too complicated.

"We can talk about it more when we get back to Boston, but I just didn't want you to worry, that's all."

"Now I'm the one who's thanking you." Sandra smiled.

"Isn't that what friendship is all about?"

They hugged again and headed back to the car.

****

It had been a fabulous couple of days. They were both thrilled they'd seen so much of Dublin and revisited most of Popsy's past, but by Saturday night when Gerald dropped them back at the hotel, they were exhausted

In the lobby, Sandra said, "I don't know why you didn't get me here before now, Popsy Power. Dublin is an amazing city. The people are so nice, the food is ridiculously good, and the scenery is just breathtaking. We didn't even do any shopping, and I still had a ball. I didn't realize that was possible."

"I'd forgotten how nice it is. I guess you get settled in a place and time just ticks by."

"Well, don't you dare get settled now. I know we are exhausted, but this is our last night here. Go upstairs and put on your best party dress. I'm going to check with reception to see if there are any messages and get them to make a dinner reservation for us at The Shelbourne and order us a taxi. Is that okay?"

Popsy nodded. "You're certainly keeping us busy." She smiled. "But I just want to go for a quick bath first."

Chapter 26

Late-Night Ladies

Stepping into The Shelbourne was a little like stepping into an Agatha Christie movie. The grand façade let them know they were somewhere special. Their beloved American flag hung proudly beside the Irish green, white, and gold over the front door, along with other European flags. Just outside stood the ever-smiling doorman, resplendent in his tails and top hat.

"I feel like I'm in a Dickens movie." Sandra giggled.

"Oh, no. Dickens is too dark and the stories always involve poverty. I'm thinking more like *The Great Gatsby,*" Popsy suggested.

"Much better idea." Sandra took her by the hand, and they walked into the hotel lobby where bellboys in pillbox hats hovered. A blazing fire welcomed new guests to sit and relax on two enormous sofas that flanked the marble fireplace. Overhead, a gigantic chandelier twinkled a million hellos with bright droplets of light.

"We are so staying here the next time we come to town," Sandra announced. They walked over to the smiling receptionist.

"Hi, I'm looking for the bar," Sandra said.

"Would that be the Oyster Bar or the Horseshoe Bar?"

Meanwhile, Popsy took a moment to enjoy her surroundings. The last time she'd been in The Shelbourne was with her late mother. She wandered into the room on the right. It was pretty much as she remembered it: a collection of smaller tables with Queen Anne chairs against the walls, along with the occasional chaise. It was sublime, elegant, and perfect.

During the day, this is where they served their renowned afternoon tea, but tonight it was full of party people enjoying themselves. The room overlooked busy Dublin traffic and just across the street was the famous St. Stephen's Green. Popsy wondered if she'd have time to walk through the park the next day. Sunday had been set aside for her to show Sandra around Trinity College and Grafton Street, but she might be able to fit that in, too.

She tried to remember where she'd sat with her mother. It was in a window seat, that much she recalled. It was where she'd first told her mom about an American boy named Peter. That was so long ago. They were all gone now—her mother, her father, Peter. She was alone.

"There you are! Come on, I know where we're going." Sandra hauled Popsy out of her daydream.

The Horseshoe bar was packed, and there was an intoxicating atmosphere of good cheer. It took her ten minutes to get served but during that time, Popsy managed to find seats at a small table. They had to share it with two men who were deep in conversation, but they nodded and smiled as if to say that using the same table was no problem. There were four or six people at all the other tables, crammed in like sardines. They got settled with their drinks.

"What do you think? Crazy, isn't it? It's so busy," Sandra said as she looked around.

"Maybe there was a game on in town today or a conference in the hotel. There must be a reason it's so busy."

The man sitting next to her said, "Ah, there's a reason all right. It's Saturday."

Popsy laughed. "Is it always like this?" she asked, sipping her dangerously strong mojito.

"Nah, it will really get going in about an hour or so." He grinned. Was he suggesting it was going to get even more crowded? How would that be possible? If nothing else, it would cause a fire hazard for sure.

"So, I'm guessing you girls aren't local."

"I'm the tourist, but Popsy here is a real Irish girl," Sandra said.

"You're Irish?" he asked, looking at Popsy. "You could've fooled me."

"I've been gone a long time," Popsy said. "Living in the States for the last thirty years."

He gave her a slight up and down, but she saw it. My God, he's checking me out, she thought in horror. No way.

"We shouldn't have let you get away." His tone was serious, as if the country had parted with her by accident. Then he took a sip from his pint of Guinness.

Popsy looked at Sandra with panic on her face, willing her friend to intervene. It worked.

"I'm Sandra and this is my friend Popsy," she said and reached across the small round table to shake hands. It was a formal gesture, and somehow cleared the air of anything other than a completely civil conversation.

"Jeff." The man said, smiling. "Jeff Fitzpatrick. And this is my partner, Simon."

"Nice to meet you." Popsy kicked herself for not picking up on the fact that they were together. Boston had a huge gay population. She should have been more empathetic. Looking at him now, she noticed he was wearing a navy cashmere sweater. His short dark brown hair was perfectly trimmed. His general finish was polished and well-tended. He looked good. Why couldn't straight men be more gay? She said nothing and took a few large sips of her mojito.

Jeff nodded, smiling. "So, tell me, what are you girls doing in Ireland? Sightseeing? Checking out the old home town?"

"You got it." Sandra went to sip her drink, and looked into her empty glass in surprise.

"They go down easy, don't they?" Simon asked, speaking for the first time.

He was well-dressed, too, in a pale blue cashmere sweater and dark denim jeans. His hair was longer and light blond.

"If I were you, I'd order two glasses each this round. One for now and the next will be good to go when you're ready for it. The queues are so long at the bar."

"That's illegal in Boston," Popsy said.

"What?"

"You can only have a single drink in front of you at any given time."

"There would be a civil war if they tried to introduce that rule over here. It's considered a national pastime to *line them up*."

"Is that what you call it? Lining them up? Literally lining up your next few drinks?" Sandra asked, enthralled.

"Yep. What can I say? We have a very relaxed attitude about drinking. But you must never drink and drive," Jeff warned. They both nodded earnestly. "Because it will spill all over your lap."

They all burst out laughing, and Popsy realized that she'd downed her drink pretty fast, too. "I'll get us another."

"Get two each or you'll be up and down all night," Simon reminded her.

"Can I get you anything?" Popsy asked, which in itself was amazing. She had never bought a guy—gay or straight—a drink before. Peter was always there to get them. The memory didn't hurt her. It was too fleeting, and she was preoccupied trying not to get squashed by the sheer volume of people. Simon shook his head and pointed to the couple of pints they already had lined up. The idea really had merit.

Just like it had with Sandra, it took her a good ten minutes to work through the crowds. When she got the barman's attention, she didn't need to think about it. "Four mojitos," she said.

Sandra was well settled with her two new companions when Popsy got back. She was laughing and tasting Jeff's Guinness. "It's so heavy and bitter. I had no idea it would be so, so—"

"Good?" Jeff suggested.

Sandra hesitated. "Well, I'm guessing it's an acquired taste."

"Whatever it is, you've acquired a white mustache," Popsy said and laughed at Sandra's expense. "Don't wipe it away. Please let me take a photo of you."

"I think I'll stick with my mojito," Sandra said after Popsy had captured the moment.

"What's in them anyway? They taste fantastic," Popsy said.

Simon laughed. "Seriously? You ordered drinks without knowing what's in them?"

Popsy, who was feeling better than she had in ages, pouted like a teenager. "I liked the idea of drinking a mojito, and they look pretty."

"Well, they consist of mint, rum, sugar, lime, and club soda."

"Wow, you know your drinks," Sandra said.

"I worked as a bartender in Miami one summer."

"The States? Miami can sure be a party town, but you still came home?" Maybe he and Jeff had been together a long time.

Simon burst her romantic bubble. "I only had a summer student visa, but it was a blast."

They compared summer jobs and favorite places to visit when suddenly Sandra began acting very odd. She tried to hide behind Popsy, but it didn't work because a man was standing right behind Popsy's barstool. Then she dropped her head and looked like she was studying her lap. The guys glanced at Popsy.

"Sandra, what in the world are you doing?" she asked, but Sandra was busy covering her head with her hands.

"Quick, hide me," she said in a panic.

Sandra hadn't managed to hide herself at all. If anything, she was attracting attention with her arm-flapping and body-diving. Popsy had a buzz from almost two mojitos and found it all a bit funny.

"Why?" she asked stroking the back of Sandra's head.

"It's Sven. I wondered if I would bump into him, but I never thought we would. Damn it, Dublin is a big city. "

"Sven who?" Simon looked around as if that would help.

"Sven Richter. He's this guy I met in Boston, and I knew he lived here, but that's not why we came," she whispered loudly, still staring at her lap.

Popsy thought it was hilarious. "Sandra," she giggled, "we came because we're revisiting my home country. It's not a problem if you bump into him. It's just a coincidence."

"Ya think?" She glanced up and looked across to the bar door again. He wasn't there.

"He caused quite a reaction in you, though," Jeff teased. "I'm guessing this guy was more than a friend?"

Sandra sat up straight again. "No, we only talked a few times. It's just that he seemed like a nice guy."

"A nice guy," Jeff and Simon chorused together and nodded knowingly at each other.

"Ah," Sandra squealed. "There he is—no wait . . . Oh." She looked guilty and smiled. "Sorry. False alarm." She took another large gulp of her mojito.

"So that's not him?" Popsy laughed. "Looks like you have Sven on the brain. You're seeing him when he's not even there."

"No," Sandra said. "It really did look like him."

"We believe you." Simon smiled, obviously meaning the exact opposite.

"The only reason he's on my mind is because I found his business card in the pocket of my sweats yesterday. I was supposed to call him months ago and a few things happened, so I guess I forgot. He lives in Dublin, even though he's German."

"All very international and high-flying," Jeff offered as he moved on to his second pint. "What does this Sven do?"

"He's a doctor," Sandra said and then looked at Popsy. "Specializing in reproduction and gynecology."

Even through the haze of two mojitos, Popsy realized what a coincidence this was. Did her friend still want to have a baby? Could Sven help her? She grasped Sandra's arm. "Ohmygod, you should call him," Popsy said excitedly.

Sandra didn't look so sure.

"I'm serious, Sandra. What is it you're always telling me? 'Life is not a dress rehearsal.' We have to chase our dreams and just go for the things we want. We both know how short life is and how fast time flies. What are you waiting for? He even told you to call. You're not being pushy."

"She's right, you know," Simon said. "You should phone him."

Sandra looked from Simon to Jeff. Even he was nodding. "Go for it," Jeff said.

"This weekend isn't about me hooking up with new guys. It's about Popsy finding herself again. It's about girl-time and us getting to have some fun together. There'll be plenty of time for men."

"I'll drink to that." Simon smiled as he finished his second pint.

The girls were well into their third mojitos and Popsy was a good deal more under the influence than she was used to. That's when she saw a floor waitress for the first time.

"Now where the heck has she been all night?" Popsy asked, and called her over to order more drinks for the four of them. The men tried to protest.

"I insist," Sandra said, clearly a little tipsy. "You guys are the best. You're better than a therapist. Maybe that's what I need—a therapist."

"You seem very together to me," Jeff argued. "Why do you think you would need a shrink?"

Sandra shrugged.

"We've had a tough couple of months," Popsy said. "Sandra and her husband of fifteen years just broke up."

The boys looked sympathetic.

"We didn't break up. He walked out on me for a younger woman."

Simon hissed. "The bitch."

Popsy and Sandra glanced at each other. "Well, that other woman is my daughter," Popsy admitted with a good deal of embarrassment.

Even Simon, who seemed fairly unshakable, looked shocked. He pointed to Sandra. "Your husband has shacked up with her daughter?" he pointed at Popsy. They both nodded and then the strangest thing happened. All four of them laughed at the ridiculousness of it all.

"He was my husband's business partner, too," Popsy said, and they laughed even more. It wasn't that funny. But it released the pressure.

"And I thought the gay circuit was bitchy. You guys win," Jeff said, raising his glass in a toast.

Soon the waitress arrived with their drinks, and Jeff pushed one over to Sandra. "Here, have some more. It will make you feel better."

"Yeah, a mojito for my mojo! Hey, that's neat because I lost my mojo and here I am." She hiccupped and grinned. "I've found my mojo in a mojito in a Dublin pub."

"Who'd a thunk it?" Jeff grinned.

"Thunk it?" Popsy had never heard the expression before, and that, combined with her three full mojitos, was enough to make her laugh uncontrollably and infectiously. They laughed until they produced tears of happiness. It was so good for them to decompress. The boys looked on in mildly inebriated amusement.

When it subsided, Popsy was feeling better than she had, not only in the last few months, but in years. She hadn't felt this light and silly in as long as she could remember. Mojitos were going to become her new drink of choice. She would have to learn how to make them.

"Now, tell me about you guys. How long have you been together?"

Jeff and Simon looked at each other and then back to Popsy.

"About two weeks," Simon offered.

"No, it's two weeks to be exact," Jeff said.

"Oh hey, so this is all pretty new," Sandra said and raised her glass to them. "Well, go you guys. I really hope it works out for you. Really I do. Everybody deserves to fall in love."

Again the men glanced at each other, and then Simon turned to Popsy. "What about you, then?" he asked. "Are you in love?"

She knew Sandra wanted to answer for her. She always rushed to Popsy's aid these days, but the drink gave her the courage to speak up for herself.

"My husband died in October of last year. It was a massive heart attack."

Jeff took hold of Popsy's hands. "Oh, God bless you. How can you be so brave?"

Popsy shook her head. Sympathy would reduce her to tears in seconds. "Well, we came over to Ireland to have a change of scenery and a little break from everything. It's good to get away."

"Here, here," Simon added. Then his expression changed. "You know what you ladies really need?"

"I smell trouble. What do you have in mind?" Sandra asked.

Simon nudged Jeff. "Let's take these girls dancing. We'll stay out all night and party like there's no tomorrow."

They didn't need to be asked twice. Popsy had had her fair share of all-nighters when she was a student in Dublin. It was a lifetime ago, but the mojitos kept her going, and the music in the nightclub was infectious. The boys seemed to know everybody, and there was a huge age range, so she and Sandra didn't feel like the grannies of the night. They completely forgot about their dinner reservations and ended up eating hot dogs and fries from a street vendor with their new friends at around two a.m., and then again somewhere around five a.m. Then they went back to dance some more.

Toward the end of their fun, Sandra was dancing with Simon to the classic Gloria Gaynor song, "I Will Survive." Popsy was standing with Jeff watching everything. Sandra caught her eye across the dance floor and gave her the thumbs up. Then she mouthed, "Are you okay?"

Popsy smiled and nodded. She really was okay, she realized. This was fun. This was moving on with her life.

Popsy groaned when she woke up on Sunday. "I'm never going out, again —ever."

There was a groan from beside her—not what she was expecting. She opened her eyes and slowly turned her head.

"Sandra, what are you doing in my bed?"

"Harrrrummmmmpppphhhh!"

She tried to sit up, but her head was pounding like a bass drum. Then she tried to stand, but she was shaky, very shaky. "What time did you come in?" she asked but still got no reply.

By the time the nightclub had closed around six in the morning, Popsy was ready to come home and Jeff had had enough, too, but Simon and Sandra wanted to keep going. In the end, it was agreed that Popsy and Jeff would head out while Simon introduced Sandra to the wonderful world of early houses. Popsy had never heard of them, even from her wilder days in college.

Early houses, it turned out, were pubs that opened in the small hours of the morning and served drinks until regular pubs opened. Jeff said he thought it had something to do with sailors coming into port very early in the morning and wanting a drink. Whatever it was, Popsy hadn't had any interest in going.

What she really needed now was some strong coffee and maybe one of those famous "full-Irish" fries. She took her morning bath and left Sandra in bed. The chances of moving her were pretty slight anyway. She was out cold.

While Popsy ran her bath, she brushed her teeth and took off her makeup from the night before. That's when she found her sleeping tablets at the bottom of her toiletries bag. She'd gone another night without needing them. Okay, a sleeping tablet was a better option than—what was it by the end of the night? Five mojitos? But even so, it meant that she'd managed to fall asleep twice in Dublin without them. Wasn't that progress?

As she soaked, she recalled the night before. She'd spoken about Peter's death. She'd told strangers she was a widow. Another first. Peter would have been proud of her. She'd gone out and had a good time. She'd even partied. He would laugh if he knew. Popsy understood it was never going to be the same again, and she desperately missed him, but Sandra had been right to get her out of Boston for a few days. It helped her remember there was a great big world out there, and it was her job to live a full life until a time when she and Peter would be reunited.

She tucked into an enormous fry for breakfast. She was starving. Probably from all the dancing from the night before. She thought about waking Sandra when she saw that the restaurant was wrapping up their breakfast service but decided against it. She needed sleep more than she needed food.

It looked like their plans for the day were shattered. There was no way Sandra would be in any fit state to tour Trinity or appreciate *The Book of Kells*. Maybe better to let her recover for as long as she needed and just go for a walk later. Their visit to Dublin was supposed to be escapism and fun. Well, they'd sure done that the night before.

Popsy thought about her family. Rosie was off on her romantic escape today. How wonderful for her and Marcus to get away together. That's what a good marriage needed to survive—time spent invested in each other.

That meant little Natasha would be at Cliff Road with Matilda. Popsy wasn't worried. Matilda was very capable. She didn't have a car, but if there was an emergency she'd catch a taxi. That was unlikely anyway and Popsy would be home in a day.

Then she thought about Lily. Her younger daughter had tried so hard to make peace with her, but it was all so mixed up. It was hard at first to focus on forgiving Lily when she'd just heard her husband was dead. She put a lot of the blame at Jack's feet, and Lily was literally in bed with him. She'd tried to excuse her daughter, but she just couldn't. The closest she came was when Lily asked if she could check on Matilda and Natasha. She'd nodded and managed to say, "Thanks," but that was it. That was as civil as they'd got.

"Damn them all," she grumbled, and a passing waitress came over to her.

"Is everything to your liking, madam? Can I get you anything, some more toast perhaps or some more coffee?"

She forced Lily out of her mind and smiled.

"No, thank you. Everything is absolutely wonderful." The waitress nodded and left her in peace.

About twenty feet in front of her, a sliding door was ajar, causing the snow-white net curtain to billow open just a little. The sky was a deep February blue with no clouds that she could see. Winter would be over soon, and the days would get longer and warmer.

Popsy decided to count her blessings. She had an incredible friend who was sound asleep upstairs, and they'd enjoyed an amazing night of fun and dancing. She knew she was lucky to be sitting there with wonderful food and exquisite surroundings. If she could just live in this moment and not think about America, she realized that what she had told the waitress was true. Everything *really was* absolutely wonderful

Chapter 27

The Reluctant Swinger

"Clothing or no clothing?" The young and fully-clad girl asked as she processed Marcus and Rosie's check-in.

Rosie almost choked "Excuse me?"

"I said, smoking or non-smoking?"

"Oh, sorry, I didn't hear you correctly. Non-smoking."

Rosie wasn't sure what she'd been expecting. Gargoyles and little devils at the reception desk? Another possibility was Playboy-bunny-type airheads doing suggestive things with their pens. But no, it had all been pretty normal. The check-in area was small and decorated in bright Caribbean colors, and as they were being processed, they were offered a cocktail. Rosie would've liked it if the drink was stronger, but she was grateful for anything right now. Her nerves were in ribbons, she was so anxious.

Marcus picked up a load of pamphlets on things to do along the coast, while Rosie clung to the counter. She heard some raucous laughter somewhere in the distance, perhaps in a pool or bar area, but she hadn't seen anything crazy, and nobody had made a pass at her or Marcus in the first three minutes—phew!

"Isn't this wonderful?" Marcus enthused when they were at last alone in their room. He held Rosie's hand, and they stood on the balcony of their fabulous suite overlooking the Caribbean Sea. To be fair, it really was exquisite. Snow-white sand sloped gently down to a breathtaking turquoise expanse. Their suite was in a building that was almost on the beach. The complex was made up of a series of smaller units nestled into lush tropical gardens. Only two buildings had the incredible sea views. Marcus had chosen the best the complex had to offer.

"Yes, darling, this really is amazing," she replied honestly.

"Now that we're here, it's not so scary, is it?"

She nodded, but inside she was terrified. Rosie had always been the wildest in her group of friends. Somehow, over the years, she'd lost herself. Well, she decided, it really was time to find herself again.

"A drink?" she suggested thinking that a little Dutch courage might help her nerves.

"We just had one. Let's get into our swimsuits and go exploring instead." He was so excited, and Rosie knew she couldn't delay it any longer. She shrugged and agreed.

The only advantage of this stupid vacation was that she'd never in her life been so motivated to get into good shape. When she walked out of the bathroom in a navy string bikini, Marcus did a double-take and let out a low, soft whistle of appreciation. "Hey, baby, you look amazing," he said.

"You like?" She did a twirl for him. Maybe, just maybe, she could seduce him and keep him all to herself. If he really had a good time, Rosie figured, perhaps he wouldn't feel the need to wander. And so it was that their first sexual encounter was with each other.

She was thrilled. She loved him and would have happily spent the week having sex with him and reading beach novels to fill her days. Combine that with some good food and a few sightseeing trips, and that would be the vacation from heaven as far as she was concerned.

Marcus seemed pretty happy, too. "That was amazing, babe. You're so gorgeous, you know that?" he said after their lovemaking.

She nodded. "I love you," she whispered.

"I love you, too." He kissed her on the nose. "And what a bod. What have you been doing for the last few months? I mean, you weren't in bad shape, but a six pack?" He ran his fingers down her hard stomach.

She looked down at her now ultra-flat tummy. "I know. That only appeared a few weeks ago. I was pretty amazed myself. I think I've just been running so hard and then when I ramped up the weights sessions, well, this happened."

"You know, you're going to be very popular at the pool parties."

Her mood plummeted. "And that doesn't bother you?" She was genuinely amazed at the way he handled the jealousy.

He shook his head. "Nah, I know you love me. This is just sex. It's not about love; it's about trying new things."

That was the part Rosie didn't get. "But what if you have sex with a woman and you fall in love with her?"

Marcus slapped his forehead. "I thought we'd been through this. You know love and sex have no connection in a guy's mind. Sex is sex, and love is something altogether different. Sex is a little like—oh, I don't know—well, it's like kissing. You can just do it and then move on. Women are brainwashed into believing it's something more, but it's not. It's just a physical act like eating or sleeping. A bodily function. You like to have lunches with different groups of women, right?"

She nodded as she lay beside him on the king-size bed. "Well, it's like that. Lunch."

"Just seems to me that some men have bigger appetites than others," she said.

He took it as a joke and laughed. "Yes, and some women, too. Now come on and put your amazing bikini back on. I have to find my swimming trunks.

Rosie loved the navy bikini. It was her first time in a string one since she was eighteen. She also bought a navy and white robe to go over it, and she had a broad navy straw hat, too. Even her flip-flops were white with little navy dots to match. If she was the biggest prude around the pool, at least she would be the best-dressed.

Finally, armed with her oversized sunglasses and the new hardback bestseller, which could also be used as a weapon, she was ready for this— whatever "this" was. Marcus wore his swimming shorts and his Ray-Bans. It was obvious he'd given no thought to what he wore and yet, annoyingly, he still managed to look great. They walked around the pool together. It was so beautiful. There were two couples in the water getting quite friendly. Whether they were married to each other or not, she wasn't sure, but they didn't pay her any attention, and for that she was grateful. Between the pool and the beach was an outdoor bar. Caribbean music pulsed out of speakers that masqueraded as rocks nestled in among the flowers.

"Let's get a drink?" Rosie tried again. She knew she sounded like an alcoholic, but this was no ordinary situation. Three couples were at a table in the bar and another two couples sat at a different spot. They were all around Rosie's age, and they looked pretty normal. No crazy swinging going on here, she thought, beginning to get a little more comfortable but still clinging to her husband.

He ordered her a large piña colada. It was gorgeous. It was in a humongous frosted glass, full to the brim with a bright-yellow liquid that looked and tasted like a smoothie. Slotted onto the top of the glass was a slice of fresh pineapple and a little pink paper umbrella to remind her that she was on vacation. Marcus had chosen a bloody Mary.

"Cheers, babe." He clinked her glass, and they took a seat together.

The six sitting right next to them glanced over and said hello. Marcus nodded back as Rosie studiously ignored them. She knew she was being rude, but she was scared of sending out any kind of inviting message. She finished her piña colada too fast. "Let's check out the beach. I wouldn't mind a swim."

"Watch out for the sharks," a female voice said from behind her. She swung around to see who'd spoken. It was one of the women sitting at the table of four. She smiled at Rosie but turned her attention to Marcus. Then she winked at him. She winked at Rosie's husband right *in front of Rosie*.

"I think most of the sharks around here are on dry land," Rosie snapped back a little too fast.

The other three sitting with the table "oohed."

"Touché," one of the men said, while the other made a "meow," kind of sound, suggesting a catfight was possible. It looked like Rosie had managed to put her would-be competitor back in her place, for now.

"That was a little harsh," Marcus whispered as they walked to the beach.

"She winked at you, Marcus. She actually winked at you right in front of me. Bitch."

"Honey, this is a swingers' resort. We're supposed to be doing a lot more than winking."

"We just got here. Isn't there some sort of settling-in time? You know, an introduction night or something?"

"More like an induction night."

They had reached the sand by now and Rosie took off her flip-flops. "What's an induction night?"

"I read about it at the front desk notice board. Most guests arrive on Saturday and Sunday, so they have a special induction session where some of the couples who've been here for the last week meet and greet us over cocktails."

"You sure that isn't *meet and eat?*" Rosie asked. "That was one tough cookie at the bar. You're not going near her, do you hear me?"

Marcus laughed. "The whole idea is there are no rules, and you're making them already."

Rosie sighed. He was right, but this was all so crazy.

"Want to go swimming?" she asked, not really feeling like it.

"What about the sharks?" Marcus laughed.

"They have nets." She looked out on the shimmering aquamarine water. "Pity they don't have them up here on the beach, too."

After the swim and a little mellow time catching the last of the day's sun, they headed back up to their suite to get dressed for dinner. Rosie had decided to go pretty conservative for her evening wear. She didn't want to send out any overly friendly messages. Then, when Marcus was in the bathroom, she called home.

Natasha was having a great time, and so was Matilda. True to her word, Lily had checked in to make sure everything was all right, which clearly it was. Now would have been a really good time for Matilda to need her tonsils out, or her appendix—Rosie wasn't fussy. She just needed an excuse to get Marcus home, but no such luck. The housekeeper was in perfect health and Natasha even better. She wasn't missing her parents at all.

The meet-and-greet session was held in the main dining hall. Tables flanked the edges of the room, and in the center was a dance floor. The building was designed to look like a giant beach hut. Instead of walls, it had thin white tree trunks crisscrossed in an X-shape to hold up the thatched roof. Sliding doors for bad weather were well concealed behind bamboo screens. Air conditioning blasted from hidden vents in the straw roofing, and the gentle music serenaded them from more speakers disguised as rocks. For later, there was a bandstand set up and ready to go, and beside that a podium with a microphone. Was that for karaoke later? If it was, she would sing "Jolene" by Dolly Parton and see if the women in the room got the message. Swinging aside, though, it had a nice ambience.

The center of the dance floor was where everybody stood now, holding a drink and trying to mingle. To her relief, they were all fully dressed. She wore cream-colored silk pants and a gold-colored string top. Over this she had a light brown cotton jacket. She'd succeeded in keeping her body covered, and she still looked like a million dollars. Funny how just a few months could make such a difference. Her mother told her it wasn't the weight loss but the tightening up of everything that made her look so good. Tonight, for the first time in her life, she was worried about looking too good. She shouldn't have worried, though. There was every kind of person here. Some were very glamorous and beautiful and others were normal, next-door-neighbor types.

Marcus got them both a gin and tonic then took her by the arm to "mingle."

Pretty soon they were talking to a British couple who'd also just arrived.

"Is this your first time at Broader Horizons?" the lady asked them.

"Yes, it is," Marcus said. "We have a five-year-old at home, so I guess you could say we've been 'otherwise engaged' up until now."

"Oh, congratulations," the woman said. "A boy or a girl?"

"A little girl—Natasha. Rosie's mother is taking care of her."

"You're Rosie? Hello, I'm Fiona, and this is my husband, John." Rosie liked the look of Fiona. She seemed very normal. A little older but nice. She had a slight build with very fair skin covered in freckles, blue eyes, a smiling face, and her hair was trimmed into a sensible bob. She didn't look like a wild child—quite the opposite, in fact. She looked more like a sensible fourth-grade-teacher type.

"I'm Marcus," her husband said. Rosie managed a smile and a nod. It was the best she could do.

"We've been doing this for years, haven't we, darling?" She turned to John and stroked his cheek.

He gave a thin smile. "Of course, our children are much older than yours. In their teens and one in college."

Then you should have more sense than this, Rosie thought mutinously. After a few minutes, another couple joined their conversation. They were about the same age as Rosie and Marcus and seemed very giddy. Both hot to trot, she decided and best avoided.

About twenty minutes into the evening, a very beautiful woman stepped up to the podium. A man came up and stood beside her. She switched on the microphone and called for everybody's attention.

"Can you all hear me?" she asked in a chirpy, cheerleader voice.

On instinct, Rosie disliked her. Of course everybody could hear her. The area wasn't that big and she had the microphone at full volume. She introduced herself as Mandy and her male companion as Brad and went on about how happy she was that everybody had chosen Broader Horizons. She went over all the facilities they had to offer like the various pools, the private beach, snorkeling classes, the playroom, blah blah blah. Finally she got to the rules that Rosie had read on the website about a million times. Then she reminded everybody that their vacation was primarily about having fun and exploring various options within the confines of a healthy, happy environment.

"And the last thing, but it's very important. I'd like to remind you all one more time that 'no means no,' " she said with another chipper smile.

Then Brad made his little presentation. He talked about the water skiing classes and the necessity for wetsuits. Ditto the scuba diving. Something to do with rushing water and chafing. She didn't want to know the finer points.

"So, Fiona tells me this is your first time?" whispered a soft voice in her ear.

She almost jumped out of her skin. It was the English woman's husband, John or something.

"What? Oh, yes. We're . . . new to all of this."

He put his hand on the small of her back and said, "Well, if you'd like an old hand to show you the ropes, as it were, I'd be happy to take you into the playroom. We could have a little fun." He smiled at her encouragingly and one of his eyebrows disappeared up into his choppy bangs. The man wasn't unattractive. He had a slim build, with hair that had once been black but was now more gray. She tried to guess his age. Fifty? More? Wasn't there supposed to be an age limit in this place? she thought. His hair and eyebrows were thick, giving him the look of an American bald eagle. Or was that just the way he was looking at her? Like she was lunch? Rosie backed away from his clammy hand. He was smiling now, but the smile didn't reach his eyes. So this is how the field mouse felt when the eagles were swooping.

She pulled away from his moist hand. "Oh no. I mean, that's a no." Then she pasted on what must have been more of a manic smile than a friendly one. "And we all know that no means no," she said in a voice that was a little too high-pitched while backing away from the wolf in Ralph Lauren clothing.

He nodded. "No problem. Perhaps later in the week," he said as she retreated, standing on her toes and backing into other people.

The crowd had swelled, and the music was getting louder. The caterers had started bringing platters out to the buffet bar. With any luck, dinner was going to start soon. Where the heck was Marcus? He'd been right beside her all evening, but now he'd disappeared.

She scouted around the gardens, looking for him. Pretty little lollipop-style street lamps lit her way around the pools and flower beds, and she ended up in areas of the complex that she hadn't seen earlier. She found the infamous "clothing optional" Jacuzzi.

Then she thought she heard something. She walked a little farther, and saw a couple having open-air sex on one of the lounge chairs. Rosie couldn't believe it. She'd never even seen another couple "doing it" before.

The woman opened her eyes and smiled at Rosie. It was shark woman. Rosie couldn't get away fast enough. She was pretty sure that she could hear the woman laughing, which only made her run faster.

"Hey, babe, there you are. What are you doing out here?" Marcus asked when she ran into him.

"I—I couldn't find you, so I went to look and I found a couple—oh, Marcus they were having sex by the Jacuzzi. It was that woman who winked at you earlier. She, she—"

He took her shivering body in his arms. "There, there," he said. "She was a bit overwhelming. Relax, Rosie. Don't let her get to you. This place is really cool and most of the people I've spoken to are very nice and normal. Stay with me, and you'll be fine. They're serving dinner, and it looks really good."

How could he possibly think about food with all this debauchery going on around him?

"I thought you might have found your way to the playroom already. You look so hot tonight." He gave her butt a possessive squeeze. "Rosie, I'm fine with you going a little wild here, but just remember you're coming home with me," he added as he took her by the hand. She liked the sound of that and headed back to the restaurant with him.

"I got us a table with that couple from earlier, Fiona and John. They seemed nice enough."

Rosie stopped in her tracks. "Oh, Marcus, I'm not sure. I mean—well, if we're going to be totally honest with each other, I may as well tell you he already propositioned me."

Marcus laughed. "Good for him for trying. Are you going to go for it?"

Rosie looked at him incredulously. Was she hearing him right? Did he really not care? "No, I'm not. Did you see him? He's a dirty old man. He could be my father." She got teary. Now was not a good time to think about her dad.

On top of all this nonsense, she knew that she was still reeling from her father's death. The problem was that his heart attack had only motivated Marcus even more to do the whole "exploration within marriage" thing.

Back then, Marcus had tried to convince her that her father would have rather gone quickly than survive as an invalid, but Rosie wasn't just crying about that. That was part of it, but she was also crying about the death of their marriage vows. This she hadn't shared with him. He just needed to be with other women. She had to get herself together and get with the vacation, or what was the point in coming in the first place?

"I'm okay." She pulled away. "Really, I am. It's just getting used to the new rules."

"But that's the beauty part of it." He wiped away a tear. "There are no rules. Now let's play."

Dinner with Fiona and John was uneventful. They behaved as if it were a regular dinner, and John didn't make any moves on her. There were no lascivious looks or wandering hands. The band had started playing calypso music. The atmosphere was perfect. Rosie was also happy to see there was no shortage of white wine.

After the food, people danced. Rosie was aware of couples disappearing together and then reappearing, but it was all very discreet. That's what this place was for, she reminded herself. A DJ took over after a few hours, and the music went more mainstream. Lady Gaga's "Bad Romance" took on a whole new meaning, as did every other song, but she was happy to dance with Marcus. The Spice Girls sang "If You Wanna Be My Lover," and Enrique Iglesias went on about his "Dirty, Dirty Dancer." But when Katy Perry sang "I Kissed a Girl," Rosie asked to sit down again.

With any luck, the night's festivities were almost over. Maybe she and Marcus could get to bed and their first night would soon be over. Okay, so she'd been propositioned once and seen another couple *in flagrante delicto*, but she'd survived to tell the story, and truth be told, she felt a little more worldly for the experiences. The food, drink, and music were terrific. Marcus was being very attentive. She decided this wasn't the worst night of her life.

Her husband, it appeared had picked up on her good mood. He leaned in to her.

"You're having fun, aren't you, angel?"

She smiled and nodded.

"Would you like to take it up a notch?"

Panic hit her stomach. "What?" she asked, playing for time.

"Fiona tells me there's a gang heading over to the Jacuzzi. We could go, too, if you like."

Oh God, oh God, oh God. What could she say? No amount of wine could prepare her for this.

"Uh, Marcus, I don't think I'm feeling quite that brave just yet."

He looked unhappy.

"But you go on if you want to."

His face lit up. "Really? That's okay with you? It's just that Fiona wanted to take me into the playroom earlier, and I said no because of the situation with John. But I mean, this is what we're here for. You won't mind if I go? You could join us as soon as you feel up to it. Or . . . would you like me to wait with you?"

She knew that that would be even worse. She'd have an insufferable time sitting there watching everybody else going off to some kind of screw fest. That was all Marcus really wanted. If she really loved him, she had to let him go. Isn't that what all the songs said? It was time to set Marcus free.

"Go." She smiled. "I think I'll take a walk. Who knows, I might even end up in the Jacuzzi with you," she said, lying smoothly.

Marcus stood. "Only if you're sure."

"I'm sure." And she was. She was sure there was no way she was going to end up in that Jacuzzi—not ever.

Chapter 28

No Smoke Without Fire

"Come on, sleepyhead. It's Monday, and we go back to Boston today," Popsy said as she woke Sandra with a cup of strong coffee and her favorite Irish fruit scones. "Our driver will be here in an hour, and you still have to pack."

Sandra groaned and rolled over in her super-comfortable bed. She had turned in early, but she was still in bad shape. All day Sunday she'd been in a haze and only now—a full day and night after her drinking binge with her new buddy, Simon—was she starting to feel half-human. She pulled herself up into a sitting position.

"Thanks, Popsy," she said, but she'd already gone to pack. In reality, it wasn't two nights of sleep, because she didn't get in until about eight on Sunday morning. In her party state of mind, she'd insisted that Simon come back to the hotel with her, and he'd crashed out in her room. That's how she'd ended up in Popsy's bed.

Popsy was furious when she found out, and it became clear pretty quickly that Sandra wasn't in any state to wander around Trinity. Popsy didn't say anything, but she was pretty frosty when Sandra did surface around mid-afternoon on Sunday.

Simon had headed back to what would doubtless be just as chilly a reception from Jeff, but neither he nor Sandra minded. They'd had a lot of fun. She'd laughed all night, and as for the early house, that was a blast. It was full of late-night revelers who didn't want to go home, either. Three guys had made passes at her—three. And that wasn't counting Simon who spent the night and morning telling her she was gorgeous and what a fool Jack Hoffman had been.

It was just the medicine Sandra needed to feel loved and admired. Popsy was a good friend, but she hadn't been in a position to support her that much over the last few months. In all honesty, Sandra had put the big, ugly crises that was her life in a box and locked it away while she focused on Popsy. That's what Simon said anyway, and it made a lot of sense. Still, she felt bad about not getting to Trinity or the famous Bewleys's on Grafton Street. She'd been looking forward to that. Rumor had it that they had the best scones anywhere.

Popsy came back in.

"Hi there," she said, but Sandra could hear the edge.

"Look, I'm sorry I missed most of yesterday. I didn't mean for it to happen, but I guess I just needed to let off a little steam."

Popsy nodded, but her lips were set in a thin line of disapproval. Then she went back out. This annoyed Sandra. She'd apologized. What more did the woman need? Sandra followed her.

"Hey, you can't still be annoyed with me, can you? I mean, over tea last night you gave me a tough time. I apologized then and now again this morning. What more can I do?"

Popsy looked at her. "We only had three days. Three. I'm not saying don't go out to party, but did you have to write off one third of our vacation because you had to go at it so hard?"

"Popsy, I didn't realize it would go on so late, but I have to say in the calm light of day, it was amazing. It was great to let my hair down, and Simon was just the guy to do it with because I was perfectly safe with him. I don't mean to take away from what you've been through, but have you forgotten that I've lost my husband, too? Okay, he might not have passed, but at the risk of sounding unsympathetic, that might have been easier?"

Popsy gave her a dirty look. "You think that? Seriously?"

Sandra knew she'd gone too far and that Popsy's pain was still intense. "Oh God, Popsy, I'm sorry. Nothing can be as hard as losing your husband." She rushed to hug her, but Popsy backed away and flopped onto one of the sofas. Sandra sat on the edge of the other. "That was so cruel of me. I know you're going through hell, adjusting to life without Peter. I'm so sorry."

Popsy raised her hands. "No, Sandra, you're right. I am being selfish.

Your life has been appalling, too, and you were brave to say it. I haven't been any support to you, and I just let you take care of me. That's wrong, and I'm sorry," she said and came over to Sandra. Now it was her turn to cry.

"I didn't mean to ruin your last day in Ireland. I would never have done that on purpose. But that night just reminded me that I was still alive. Oh, Popsy, life is such a mess. Look at the two of us. Just a few months ago, we were at the top of the pack—Wellesley Wives. Everybody wanted us at their parties and charity events. Now, what will we do?"

Popsy hugged her. "We have each other, and you know the darkest hour is just before dawn. We'll be fine." Sandra didn't reply, but she was calmer now. Popsy pulled back and smiled. "I have an idea. Why don't we try to get a job?"

"I assume you're talking about when we get back home—like you don't want to do this today or anything." Sandra laughed.

"Oh, I hadn't thought it through that much. I'm not sure we could work here without a visa, so I guess we would have to do it at home, but it could be fun. Or . . . we could work here illegally."

"What? Are we outlaws now? What did you have in mind?"

Popsy sat back. "I have no idea, but you know I love flowers, so I was thinking I could open a little flower shop," she said and smiled.

"And I still have my real estate license. I was just thinking about it recently. I know real estate is in the toilet right now, but I think I could take a refresher exam and renew it if it's outdated. But you do know the fastest way to get rich?"

"Marry money," they both said.

Their spat was over.

Sandra hugged Popsy. "We're too close to let anything come between us."

"I agree," Popsy said. "But you have to get going on your packing. I'll head down to reception to check out."

"You can't do that. This was my treat, so I need to sign off."

Popsy's voice was soft when she said, "Sandra, you've been so kind. You flew me over and paid for the hotel, but you have limited funds, and you know I want to give you some of Peter's life insurance money. "

"We can argue about that when we get back to Boston," Sandra said. She hadn't yet agreed to accept the amazing gift.

"We have to support each other financially and emotionally from now on," Popsy said. "We're like the *Golden Girls*, only much younger."

Sandra laughed. "You're a tonic, Popsy, and you're right. We'll muddle through."

"Muddle? I don't think so. We'll sail on through—like swans—graceful on top and paddling like hell underneath," she said, then headed out.

Sandra didn't move. She was too comfortable, sitting on the big, white sofa. It was impossible to stay depressed with Popsy around. That was the magical component of their relationship. It always seemed that when one was down, the other rallied. For the last few months, Popsy had been in a bad place and Sandra was there for her. But as soon as Sandra showed any sign of weakness, Popsy rose to the challenge and became the support. As she stood and headed to her room, she realized it was better than a marriage.

If Jack came home in a bad mood, she would never pander to him but would be cool and aloof. Likewise, if he saw she was sad or tearful, he would look to heaven, make some derogatory comment about women, and go off to his study. Perhaps her marriage had been on the road to ruin even without Lily Power. Still, it would have been better if Jack had had the decency to break up with her before he found her replacement. Even nicer if he found a replacement outside their social circle and within their generation. She was still too angry to think about it.

What a relief to hear that Popsy had money, though. Sandra had been worrying how long she would last on her $100,000. Sure, it was a lot of money but not when you were looking at the rest of your life. Naturally, she would fight Jack for more, but if he didn't have it, what could she do? She'd already returned all her jewelry to her personal jeweler in Wellesley. They'd been friends for over a decade. He was very discreet and a terrific salesman. She left her pieces with him and he said he would sell them on her behalf through the shop, piece by precious piece. He'd told her if she was in a desperate rush, he could sell them fast at the diamond exchange, but she would get a lot less. Worse yet, if it was what he called a "fire sale," he could buy them from her at a quarter of what they were insured for. Sandra told him she could wait and get the best price. There had to be around $400,000 worth of jewelry in her collection. She'd been thinking she could use that money to buy a small house, but now Popsy was talking about them sharing a place. It was a nice idea.

Popsy was being very generous with the insurance money, but Sandra had been careful not to accept just yet. There was so much to consider. Yes, Popsy was her best friend, and they were just about as close as two straight women could be, closer than sisters even, but there was the whole Lily/Jack thing to think about, too.

If Sandra stayed, she would have to see Jack regularly, and she didn't know if she was that strong. What if Lily got pregnant? It wasn't unthinkable. Everybody knew that Jack was finished with having babies, but if Lily just had a little "accident," what then?

Sandra knew she shouldn't dwell on things like that. It really had nothing to do with her. The reality was she should try to put as much distance as possible between herself and Jack, now that it looked like their break was permanent.

Being in Ireland had given her more objectivity. It was good to get away because she could step back and look at her life from a more candid perspective. Meeting Simon had been terrific. The fact that he was gay was an added bonus. Had he been straight, Sandra was pretty sure she would have tried to seduce him. She already had a creeping suspicion that she might have tried to "convert" him at one point that night.

Before he left, they'd swapped contact details and swore to stay in touch. He'd been very strong on the moving-up-and-on advice and even told her to leave Wellesley. He thought she should move to New York, to LA, or even Miami to have some fun and find a new love. That was easy for him to say. He was just getting settled into a new relationship in the party capital of Europe. Who did she know in any of those other cities? Still, it was something she should at least consider. Staying in Wellesley would not be easy. Not if Jack and Lily were going to live in the same town.

She was pretty sure Jack was living with Lily in her Boston apartment, but it was only a matter of time before Popsy forgave Lily. What then? She would start visiting Popsy, and wouldn't she occasionally bring Jack? That would become the norm and where would that leave Sandra? Hiding out in a bedroom, avoiding the man who'd dumped her for a younger model? Olga had moved with her girls. That was the smart thing to do.

Sandra pulled out her suitcase but then spotted her cooling coffee and the perfect Four Seasons scone. The packing could wait another few minutes. Savoring what might be her last scone in Ireland, she toyed with the idea of staying there. Was it really so crazy? Boston was three thousand miles from Dublin and the same distance from California. She'd always assumed that Ireland was farther away, but it was only a five-hour flight—a mere hop and a skip. She sure liked the way they partied, and she loved the food. The climate didn't seem too bad. It was cold, but not as harsh as the Boston winters.

Popsy had said something about visas. Maybe she wouldn't be allowed to stay. She would need to investigate that. It could be tricky. Then she thought of Sven. He managed to live here even though he was German. It really was a shame they hadn't met. He was so cute. But what did it matter? She was going home to her old, crappy life in a few hours. That was the horrible reality.

Popsy came tearing into her room just as Sandra was finishing her scone.

"Sandra, you won't believe what they told me downstairs! Dublin airport is closed. There's some big volcanic eruption in Iceland and no planes can fly over it. All of Scandinavia is closed down, and there's no air travel at all between North America and Europe." Her eyes were huge with panic and disbelief.

"What about our flight?" Sandra asked.

"That's what I'm trying to tell you. We can't get home."

"Because of the smoke?"

"It's not just smoke. It's clouds of ash and that means tiny particles of stone. They would jam up a plane engine. It's very dangerous, in fact."

"No smoke without fire."

"What does that mean?"

For a moment Sandra was quiet and then smiled broadly. "I'll tell you what it means. We're stranded. We can't get home, and that means we're still on vacation."

"No, Sandra, this isn't good. I was supposed to be home to take over for Matilda today. She's terrific, but she can't drive. She can't fill the house with food. I need to get back."

"Popsy, sit down and stop panicking. Have you re-booked this suite for another few days?"

"Oh, I never thought of that. I was focusing on getting home. Could we catch a boat, do you think?"

"That would take weeks. Switch on the television and find out what you can about the volcano, and I'll book us in for another few nights. Don't worry, Popsy. Things will be back to normal soon enough. We'll call Matilda and everything is going to be fine, you'll see," she said before leaving the room.

As she walked through the lobby, she bumped into Gerald, their driver. She'd really liked him.

"How are my favorite American ladies?" he asked.

"We're great, but I don't think we're going to be able to catch our flight today. The airports are closed."

"Well, if that doesn't beat Banagher," he said, using his favorite expression again. "I was to drive a couple of guests to the airport earlier this morning and they're cancelled, just the same. It's causing pandemonium."

Sandra loved his musical voice. The five syllables of pan-de-mon-i-um sounded like a children's nursery rhyme, but what he said was worrying. "What do you mean?

"Well, the hotel is full. It's always full, and now the clients that were due to check out have nowhere to stay. Hotels are filling up by the minute. Better get yourself sorted quick, love."

This hadn't occurred to her. She said good-bye to Gerald and headed for the already-crowded reception desk.

"You were right," she said to Popsy a little sheepishly half an hour later. Popsy was still glued to the flatscreen in her bedroom. Even in a crisis, Sandra marveled over how immaculate the room was. Popsy's case was packed and zipped up, sitting by the door and ready for departure.

Sandra's room, on the other hand, looked like a bomb had hit it. Clothes and shoes covered the floor, and handbags, scarves and an alarming amount of bras were scattered all over, all creating a general flea market feel. Her suitcase lay open and empty on top of her rumpled bed. Yet, somehow, the chaos worked for her.

"What's wrong?" Popsy asked.

"Well, it's the biggest eruption ever recorded from this volcano. It's belting out like a billion tons of ash per second or something like that. They're pretty stressed out downstairs. They say they're fully booked tonight, so we can't keep the room, but there are a lot of their new arrivals that were due to fly in today who won't make it, so there's a good chance that by mid-afternoon they'll have quite a few cancellations. If we hang around, we should get a room, but we do have to get out now. What a drag."

"But, what about Natasha?"

"We'll get home in a day or two. Matilda can manage that long. Didn't you say Lily offered to help? I don't think they're going to starve. And anyway, doesn't Roche Brothers deliver to you every week?"

Popsy looked back at the television. "They're saying the airports could be closed for up to a week. We could be stuck here for much longer. Nobody knows."

"Wow." Sandra sat down next to Popsy at the foot of the bed. "Well, I guess we could take a boat to the UK, then a train down to Europe, and catch a plane over to South America. Then we could fly up to Boston that way."

Popsy looked at her with a shocked expression. "That sounds a little excessive."

"Well, you're the one freaking out about Natasha. She's fine, Popsy. Phone Lily and tell her to get over there, and I'll finish packing."

"Finish? You haven't even started yet. I saw the state of your room."

It looked like she was beginning to accept that there was absolutely nothing she could do about the situation. Good, Sandra thought.

She took a shower and threw her jeans on along with the sweater she'd brought for her day at Trinity College and thought about suggesting that Popsy take her to *The Book of Kells* now that they had more time. But she wasn't really that enthusiastic about it. She squeezed everything into her suitcase and sat on top of it to get it closed.

Popsy came in just as she was finishing up. "Well, I woke poor Matilda up. It's only seven o'clock in the morning at home. She sounded a little upset, but it was because she thought we were in danger. We're not in danger, are we?"

Sandra smiled and shook her head. "It's a couple of thousand miles away. The only thing I'm in danger of is not fitting into my jeans if I eat any more of those scones. Popsy if we're going to spend a few more days here, can you keep the scones away from me, please?"

Popsy said, "I spoke to Lily, too." She hadn't woken Lily. At seven a.m., her younger daughter was already at work. "She went straight into panic mode—a bit like me, actually," she said and laughed. "She said she would get out of work early and head straight over to make sure they were okay."

"That's nice of her." It killed Sandra to say something polite about her husband's new mistress, but she wanted Popsy to calm down. "Do you think you should phone Rosie?"

"It's probably a good idea. Would you believe I don't actually have the name of the hotel she's at, but, naturally, I have the number of her cell. Silly of her to go away and not give me all her contact details, but I suppose that's the way the world works now. It's all mobile phones. Anyway, I'll phone her later. It's too early to call her while she's on holiday. To be honest, I think she'll be fine if Lily and Matilda are with Natasha. I feel so bad, though. I shouldn't have gone away."

Sandra pulled her oversized case off the bed. "Don't go there, Popsy. Who would have thought a one million-year-old volcano would block our path? That's so random. It's not your fault."

"Hey, you don't suppose its fate, do you?"

"What do you mean?"

Popsy looked like she was working her imagination hard. "Maybe it's destiny that we can't go home yet. The girls are learning to stand on their own two feet without me."

"Rosie's in the Caribbean with her husband for a romantic vacation. The last place her feet should be is on the ground."

"Sandra! That's my daughter you're talking about. Please."

"Well, if you really do think it's destiny, why am I here, too?"

After a moment, Popsy said, "You're meant to call Sven!"

"Come on, you can't be serious. What about the thousands of other people that are stranded all over because of this silly volcano?" She shook her head to say she didn't believe any destiny notion.

There was a knock on the door. Then a girl's voice came from the other side. "Housekeeping," she called.

Sandra headed to the door while Popsy went to get her suitcase. "Sorry, I was so crude about Rosie. Whether it's fate or just good old-fashioned Irish luck, we're stuck here for a while so we may as well make the best of it. Right?"

"Right," Popsy as they left their beautiful suite together.

"So, if we're going to make the most of it, I have a proposition to put to you."

"What are you talking about?"

"Let's go to Banagher," Sandra said, her eyes lit up with excitement.

"What? Where?"

"Banagher. Let's go to Banagher. You talk about fate. I'd never heard about this place before this weekend, and everybody we've met since we came here talks about it. Do you remember Gerald using the expression *that beats Banagher*?"

Popsy wasn't convinced. "Yes, and the driver before him—the taxi guy who brought us in from the airport. But, Sandra, that's just two times—two guys. Random incidents. That was just a coincidence."

They got into the elevator and headed for the ground floor. "Well, you're the one who was talking about fate. Maybe this is fate, too. We have a few days to kill, and we don't have a room for tonight. Now, we could look at this as being a scary thing, or we could do a *Thelma and Louise* and go where fate takes us. I say Banagher."

"Do you even know where it is?"

"No, but we'll have to rent a car and I'm sure it'll have a GPS."

"What if the volcano clears? I do really want to get home as soon as we can."

"They'll have TVs there, Popsy. This is Ireland. It's only the size of the state of Massachusetts. We could be up and down to Banagher in a day if we wanted, but it would be fun to stay there for a few days and just live in a small Irish country town."

The elevator doors opened and they walked out into the luxurious lobby of The Four Seasons. Sandra kept talking. "All of this has been really amazing, but part of me feels like it's just another five-star experience. Let's go to Banagher and stay in a B&B."

"A what?"

"A bed and breakfast. We can go for long country walks in the real Irish countryside. We'll meet real Irish people. The folks we've met in Dublin have been very nice, like Simon, but he's almost like a Bostonian. All city people are similar. Let's get out of town now that we have these extra few days."

"You're too funny, Sandra. You should hear yourself—so enthusiastic. I guess we've done Dublin. Maybe you're right. I haven't been outside Dublin for years and Banagher is as good a place as any. Where is it again?"

"I think it's in county Offaly. That's in the midlands. So we can do it?" Sandra asked.

"Heck yeah, why not?" Popsy laughed. "But wait, you know they drive on the wrong side of the road here, and the cars are stick shifts."

"We'll figure it out," Sandra said and threw her arm around Popsy's shoulder.

"I think you mean *you'll* figure it out. If we do this, you're driving. Deal?" Popsy said.

"Deal."

Chapter 29

Supermoms: Fact or Fiction

"You can't be serious," Caryn, Lily's assistant, said. "It's only three o'clock. You've been missing in action so much around here, that last week somebody asked if you'd left. I know it's been tough with your dad, and then your health problems, but reports are piling up on my desk. I need about two-hundred signatures before end of business today, and you have a conference call with the Hong Kong office in two hours. They won't be happy if you skip that."

The threat hung in the air. Caryn was telling Lily what she knew already —that she was neglecting her job. Ironic that this was the first time she really needed to hold onto it, what with Jack being broke and her trust fund vaporizing, but that only seemed to bother her.

She covered her ears. "It's my niece. My mother was supposed to take care of her and she's stranded in Europe, thanks to a volcanic eruption. Her babysitter left a message on my voice mail saying she has a problem. There's nobody else. I have to go."

"That won't be the only eruption if Jones hears you left early again," Caryn grumbled.

"You don't have to tell him. In fact, if I pick up Natasha fast and get her settled with some game or DVD she likes, I bet I can swing the conference call, too. What do you think?"

"I think you're crazy. I have twin nieces. They're seventeen now, but I remember when they were five, like your niece. It was as if they were telepathic. They were always at their worst just when I wanted to watch something on TV, and when you're on the phone? That's when they go really crazy. Trying to take a conference call with a five-year-old around is just insane."

Lily wasn't convinced. Natasha was easy to bargain with. She would do anything for candy. If she made the bribe big enough, Natasha would give her peace for a five-minute call. She decided it was worth the risk. Better than doing a no-show and Mr. Jones getting wind of it.

"Just put the call through to my cell phone. It's scheduled for five, right?"

"Right," Caryn agreed reluctantly.

Lily didn't wait for her approval. This was too serious. It was her chance to redeem herself. She swept out of the office.

The last few months had been hell for Lily. She'd enraged her mother the day of her dad's first heart attack, and they'd been at loggerheads ever since. It was eating her up inside. Lily loved her mother, but her problem was simple: she loved Jack more. No woman should ever have to choose between the love of her life and her family. It was just wrong. The only other person she could think of who'd been faced with this kind of decision was Juliet of *Romeo and Juliet* fame, and that hadn't turned out too well for any of them. Lily shuddered. Was she a Montague or a Capulet?

Jack had tried to convince her that her father's death wasn't her fault. He'd been working too hard and had put his body under too much stress. It was just "one of those things." If Jack was right, why was she still harboring so much guilt? Maybe if she saw a psychologist for a few sessions, it might help.

As she got into her car, Lily felt paranoid as she looked at all the security cameras. There was no way her early departure would go unnoticed, but there was a chance that Mr. Jones wouldn't hear—a small chance.

An advantage of quitting work early was that she missed rush-hour and got to enjoy some daylight. The evenings would get longer soon, thank goodness, and the snows would disappear. Everything felt better with the arrival of spring, she decided as she pressed harder on the accelerator. Lily rarely drove too fast, but she had a strong need to get to Natasha. With Rosie and her mom away, she was the child's closest living relative in Boston. She drove faster.

"Auntie Lily!" Natasha squealed and rushed at her legs to hug them. Lily winced as her pure silk magenta skirt got pawed by chocolate hands and a face covered in white sugar icing. "Tilly and I are baking. Do you want to taste our cake? We were making it for Grandma, but her plane is late." She said it so matter-of-factly, like it didn't matter at all.

What a relief, Lily thought. She'd been nervous that Natasha might have been upset by the change in plans but it appeared not. The two of them went back into the kitchen where Matilda was sitting down and wiping her forehead with a dish towel. Lily could see she was in pain.

"Tilly, are you okay? You don't look too good."

Matilda looked at her. "Oh, Lilita, I am getting too old for this." She sighed.

Lily laughed. "Has she exhausted you? You're not sick or anything, right?"

"It's my back." Matilda rubbed it and looked pained. "I think I pulled it last night lifting Natasha. I'm taking a strong anti-inflammatory, but it is still so bad. I have to lie down. You have to help me with the child."

"Oh God." Lily went over to Matilda and hugged her. "Do you want me to call a doctor or get you to the hospital?"

Matilda waved her hand. "No, no nothing like that, but I have to lie down. I really can't walk around. It hurts too much. Natasha wants me to run and play catch. Usually is no problem, but not today with my sore back."

This was not what Lily wanted to hear. She'd only really seen herself as backup, but with Matilda out of action, the entire twenty-four hour caring for Natasha would fall to her. What would she do about work? She glanced at her watch. Still over an hour before her conference call. She was okay there.

"First things first." She turned her attention back to Matilda. "Have you taken something for the pain?"

Matilda nodded. "My things are in the guest bedroom upstairs, but I cannot climb up steps. If you get them and bring them to the guesthouse, I will be okay. It's all one level. I will manage there, but you have to take Natasha with you."

Lily couldn't believe her bad luck, but what choice did she have? Then she remembered pre-school. "Natasha goes to some sort of pre-K in the mornings, doesn't she?" Lily asked hopefully, but Matilda shook her head. "It's February vacation."

Lily was beaten. She had no choice but to step up.

They got Matilda settled back into the guesthouse and Lily turned on the television for her. Natasha went back to the main house to get her a large slice of chocolate cake while Lily made her a cup of strong tea, just the way Matilda liked it.

"Will you be okay if I take Natasha back to my house with me?" Lily asked, worried that she might have to look after two people, but Matilda allayed her fears.

"Oh yes, Lilita. I know my back. If I rest all evening and overnight, I'll be able to get around tomorrow. After a few days I'll be fine again. It was just an accident. But you? Can you do this and work also?"

Lily forced a laugh. "Yeah, no problem."

"I think you are some sort of supermom," Matilda said proudly.

She almost laughed. How hard could it be to balance work and a child? Millions of women do it. "We can come by tomorrow to see how you are," Lily said, wondering how exactly she could be in the office while taking care of a five-year-old and visiting Matilda. If only there was three of her.

Natasha came back in to the house. "I got the cake," she announced, holding up a plate with a large wedge. It looked like half the cake.

"So I see." Lily laughed. "You did a great job. Leave it here on the table next to Tilly's tea. I think we'd better clean up the kitchen a little now. What do you think, Natasha?"

"Aw, I don't want to clean. Let's play chasing instead."

It was a reminder to Lily just how much work a child was. Time to start bargaining. "Tell you what. If you help me clean the kitchen, we'll have a big slice of cake afterward, and I might even find some ice cream to put on top of it. What do you think?"

It was all the incentive the little girl needed, and she ran toward the main house. It made Lily laugh. "I see what you mean about needing a lot of energy to keep up with her." She got down and kissed Matilda on the cheek. "You stay here and rest, and I'll check in on you before we leave. Then we'll come back in the morning. Okay?"

Matilda nodded. "Thank you for taking her. This is a big help."

"No problem," she said. "It's the least I can do."

"Lily, you are a very good girl. You remember that, and don't ever believe anything else." She pointed at Lily as if to make her point stronger. "You are a very good girl."

The years washed away and Lily felt like she had when she was small and Matilda told her how good she was. Somehow, she'd forgotten. No matter how hard she worked now, she never felt like a good girl. To hear Matilda say so almost made her cry. How could Tilly think she was good? She'd invoked the unrestrained wrath of her mother, had probably caused her father's death, and her sister hated her. No. The last thing Lily was, was good.

"Back soon," she mumbled. Then she got to her feet and out of the little house as soon as she could.

The kitchen was all the distraction she needed. There was chocolate everywhere. The situation was so dire, it made Lily laugh. Natasha was already on a kitchen chair over the sink full of bubbles. The water was freezing cold, but Lily figured it was better than burning herself with scalding water.

She "helped" Natasha wash all the dishes and made the place look good again. The little girl was quick to remind her about the ice cream deal, and Lily intended to follow through on her promise. If she didn't, Natasha would be slow to cooperate next time. Then they sat down to a plate of delicious chocolate cake and ice cream.

"So, Nat, you know the way Matilda has a sore back?" Lily asked gently.

"Mmhm." Natasha nodded, mouth too full to speak.

"Well, I was wondering if you'd like to come to my house, just for a few nights, and stay with me and Uncle Jack. My back is great, and we could play all kinds of games. When grandma gets home, you can come back here and have the vacation you were going to have with her. What do you think?"

Natasha looked a little uncertain. "What about Tilly? If her back is sore, we should take care of her."

"That's a very good point. We're coming back here tomorrow morning and maybe we can bring her a get-well present. What do you think?"

Natasha nodded enthusiastically and shoveled in more cake. When her mouth was full, she asked, "Is Uncle Jack living in your house?"

Lily nodded and smiled encouragingly as if to imply that this was an added bonus, but Natasha looked sullen and said, "Maybe we could stay here with Tilly."

"What does Uncle Jack have to do with it? He'll be at work most of the time. You won't see him much, and you know he loves you," she said.

Natasha shook her head. "I don't think he does."

Lily dropped her spoon onto her plate. "Whatever makes you say that? Jack loves you. Everybody loves you."

"Not Uncle Jack. He's always mad."

This floored Lily. How could one so young come out with this stuff? Was it true? She was sure she remembered Jack making a fuss over Rosie when Natasha was born, but that was a long time ago, but she couldn't recall a single time during family gatherings when Jack had held, or even spoken with, Natasha. Well, that was about to change. She was Lily's niece and he would damn well bond with her whether he liked it or not.

"Let's bring him some of your chocolate cake. Then he'll go crazy for you. He'll want you to live with us forever and ever!"

It worked. Natasha burst out laughing. "I can't stay forever. Mommy and Daddy will be home soon. I have to go home to my house."

"Oh, okay. You and I can play and maybe, if Jack is very nice to you, we'll let him play, too."

Natasha gave her aunt a thousand-kilowatt smile and said, "I'll have to get my Moo first."

"Good thinking. You go up to your room and get everything you'll need, and I'll follow you up as soon as I finish up here. Deal?"

Natasha nodded and was up and out in a flash.

Just as Lily finished up, the phone rang and she answered it.

"Lily, thank God you're there. I just got Mom's message. She's stuck in Ireland?" Rosie said sounding like she was in serious panic mode.

"Hi, Sis. I know, but don't worry. Everything is fine. Natasha is coming to my place tonight, and Matilda is resting." Lily thought it wise not to mention the bad back situation. Her sister would only panic more. "Your daughter's doing great. She really is a pleasure to be with, so full of fun. I can keep her for a few days—or however long it takes—and I have Tilly for backup. How are you? Having a good time?"

"Uh, yeah. The place is fabulous. The sea is the most incredible color of turquoise, and the beaches are so white you can't believe it, but what about you? Will you be okay with Natasha? Should I talk to her?"

"I'm sure she would love to speak with you," Lily said and then called up the stairs. Natasha came bounding down. "It's your mom." Lily handed Natasha the phone and the child squealed with glee.

"Mommy, Mommy," she said. "We made chocolate cake and I even had ice cream with it. I love Auntie Lily." Pause. "Yeah, silly plane." Another pause. "It's okay. Aunt Lily is taking care of me and I have my Moo." She clutched Moo, a soft toy that was well-worn with love.

Lily remembered how it had started life as a brown cow with a black nose and big eyes. Now the eyes were gone, and it had lost its form almost completely, but for Natasha its value was incalculable. It would be a dark day when Moo disappeared.

"Here, Aunt Lily," Natasha said and handed the phone back to her.

"Lily, I can't thank you enough. Do you want me to come home? I'm sure

I could get a flight out."

"No way. You just relax and enjoy your vacation. Mom will be home in a day or two and really I'm fine with Matilda here."

"Oh, I forgot to tell Mommy that Tilly's back is sore, and I'm sleeping in your house," Natasha suddenly remembered, but Lily distracted her by pointing to an extra toy she'd left on the kitchen counter.

"Well, okay," Rosie said, sounding only half-convinced. "Just call if you need me to come home. If anything is wrong, anything at all, just phone me, okay?"

"Okay." There was no way she was going to let Rosie know if anything went wrong. She was determined to care for her niece for as long as was necessary. This was her chance to redeem herself in both her mother's eyes, and her big sister's. It was too good an opportunity to miss, and anyway, she loved Natasha. It would be fun to pretend to be a mom for a few days.

When Natasha was packed up and they'd said good-bye to Matilda, they headed off together. "You don't have a booster seat," Natasha said when they got to Lily's car.

"Oh, does grandma have one we can borrow?" Lily asked as she headed to the garage. Her mom's Mercedes wasn't there. It was at the airport. Her new Ferrari was, though. The car her father had died in. It made Lily stop in her tracks.

Parked next to it was her dad's older Ferrari. It was black and a little more understated, but not much. She doubted anybody had driven it since he died. The reminders were harsh and unexpected, and she felt a sudden jab of raw, real pain, like a knife going through her. Dad was gone, and it was her fault.

"Her car isn't here," Natasha interrupted her anguish. "You're going to have to buy one," the five-year-old announced.

"Where do you buy a booster seat?" Lily asked.

"At Toys"R"Us." Natasha climbed into Lily's car. "You don't even have a back seat. Where will I sit?"

"It's going to have to be the front," Lily said. She hadn't even left Cliff Road and already she was feeling overwhelmed. Lily GPS'd the closest Toys"R"Us and headed for it. Then she checked the time again. This was getting too close. The conference call was in fifteen minutes.

How would she manage Natasha and take the call? she wondered as she pulled into the parking lot and they entered the store.

"So tell me, do you like Toys"R"Us, Nat? I mean, I know they have so much stuff. There must be loads of good games and dolls here."

Natasha clapped her hands. "They have every single toy in the world."

"Well, I have a deal to make with you, kid," Lily said. "You're a smart chicken. I think you'll like this. Auntie Lily has a business call she has to take. If you stay quiet, I'll let you choose a reward. What do you think?"

"What kind?"

"You can pick out any toy you want, as a present, if you let me talk on the phone without interrupting me. Do we have a deal?"

"Yeah." Natasha clapped again and ran off in the direction of the dolls. It was obvious that she knew the Natick store well. "She's gorgeous. Is she yours?" a woman asked her.

"Yes." Lily didn't mean to lie. It just came out. Silly, really, but it just felt so right. She probably was, for all intents and purposes, Natasha's mom for the next few days. Why not take the credit? A little naughty but no harm done. And anyway, it felt nice to be a mommy. She followed Natasha around the various aisles and glanced at her watch again. The call would come in at any minute.

"Now, Nat, you do remember our deal, right?"

"It might not be a doll," Natasha said, looking panicky.

"That's no problem. It can be whatever you like."

As if by magic, Lily's phone rang and she was transported to the world of Hong Kong derivatives, stocks, and shares.

She managed to focus on her call while shadowing her niece. She even managed to make a few constructive suggestions when asked, but what she didn't manage to do was keep up with Natasha when she suddenly bolted toward the back of the store. Lily panicked. She was still pretending to listen while she half-walked, half-ran in the direction Natasha had gone. There was no sign of her. She risked putting her phone on mute for a nanosecond.

"Natasha," she yelled.

"What do you think, Lily?"

She took the phone off mute. "Oh, yes. Maybe can we see this in writing first before we make a decision?"

"It's just a follow-up call. Can't you commit to that?"

Damn. "Uh . . . yes, that's fine," she said, still looking for Natasha. No sign of her. "Look I have to go. That's fine." She hung up even though she could hear they were impatient with her half-attentive attitude. She would deal with that later.

"Na-ta-sha!" she yelled, now in a serious panic. She'd almost lapped the store and she still couldn't find the little girl. How was that possible?

She felt a hand on her arm, gentle but firm. "Ma'am, have you lost a child?" It was a young male employee wearing a Toys"R"Us red T-shirt. His voice was calm, which kept her calm. In fact, she felt a little crazy. Natasha was almost certainly around a corner somewhere.

"Yes. It's silly, really. She was beside me one minute, and then she just took off. I don't know where she went."

He took her to the front desk. "I'll keep looking," she offered.

"No, no," he said and smiled. "We'd prefer you stay here. Now, tell me, was it a boy or a girl? How old? What were they wearing?"

The man mouthed something to another staff member, and then the metal shutters came down on the store windows and doors. Lily felt real-time slowing down as she tried to take in what was happening around her. She wanted to keep looking.

"Her name's Natasha," she said breathlessly as the intercom kicked into action.

"Ladies and Gentlemen, please bear with us. We have a code Adam. Repeat. A code Adam. This is not a drill. Our shutters will stay down until the situation has been resolved."

Lily couldn't believe what she was seeing. The man got her to focus. "We don't want to give out her name, but it's a little girl, right?"

"Yes."

"Age?"

"She's five with long blond hair and dark-brown eyes. Her daddy's eyes." It was good they didn't give out Natasha's name, she realized. If someone had taken her, they didn't want to give the kidnapper the information. "Oh dear God," Lily cried. "Where is she?"

A crackle came from a walkie-talkie.

"Restroom's clear," a voice said.

They were systematically searching the premises. This was all really happening. It wasn't a movie. She had lost her niece over—over what? A stupid business call.

"What is she wearing?"

The intercom crackled again. "We're looking for a five-year-old girl. She has long blond hair and dark brown eyes."

What was she wearing? What was she wearing? Lily asked herself. She couldn't remember and tried to think. When they'd walked in they were laughing, and she was tickling her.

"Chocolate! There's chocolate all over her white T-shirt. She's wearing blue jeans and a pink, puffy jacket."

The words "blue jeans" and "pink puffy jacket" came over the intercom, but her blood was pumping so hard through her brain, that she was having difficulty standing or focusing.

Then she saw them. A lady in a Toys"R"Us T-shirt was carrying Natasha and walking toward Lily.

Lily didn't wait. She ran and took her from the wonderful lady who'd found her irreplaceable niece. "Natasha, where did you go? I was so scared." She was crying. This made Natasha cry, too. "Shhh, baby, shhh. Everything's all right now. I have you and I won't let you go."

"Thank you. Thank you so much," she blurted, squeezing Natasha tightly.

How could she have put Natasha's life in danger? How could she have been that stupid? The store's metal shutters glided up again.

Chapter 30

The No Club

It was evening in Mexico, too. The first day of Rosie's vacation had been surprisingly good. She'd hit the pool early that morning. In fact, before the restaurant staff had come on duty. That meant she got to have a good look around. She gave a lot of thought as to where they would spend the day and had finally settled on the two lounge chairs closest to the bar. Her reasoning was that it was public, and with any luck, she wouldn't be propositioned if she sat there. So far, her plan had worked.

Her husband had turned up sometime around mid-morning looking and sounding a little rough after his late night. She knew that he'd most likely had sex with another woman, or even several other women, the night before. But they couldn't really talk about that now—not in public. He bent over and kissed her on the forehead just like he did at home.

"Hi, honey," he mumbled, his voice deeper than usual from lack of sleep and too many cocktails.

"Everything okay?" Her voice had sounded higher-pitched than usual.

"Yeah." He laughed. "I think so. What a night." He'd plonked down on the lounge chair beside her. "You should have come; you would have loved it."

Her husband was so casual about the whole thing. He wore his sunglasses and his swimming suit, and he'd obviously just taken a shower because his hair was wet and slicked back, but he still looked worn out.

"You want a coffee?" she asked, rather than discussing the night before.

Marcus looked around. The place had gotten a little busier by then. A few other bedraggled spirits had gathered around the pool but most were reading or snoozing in the sun. The entire decor was white, but the lounge chairs had deep turquoise-colored cushions for comfort, and the pool boy handed out beach towels in a paler shade of aqua. It was so luxurious, and the weather was perfect. "Coffee sounds great. You want?"

Rosie nodded. She was ready for a break.

He took off for the bar and soon came back with her large black coffee and his small double espresso, along with a few enormous Danish pastries.

"Think I'll skip that." Rosie was thinking, as always, about the calories.

"All the more for me," he said and laughed. "I need the sugar hit."

After his coffee and the pastries, which he polished off effortlessly, Marcus went for a swim. He was the only swimmer in the pool, and Rosie checked if anybody was watching him. There was. Two different women heard the small splash of his near-perfect dive and looked to see who would surface. Rosie didn't know whether to feel proud of her man or threatened by the onlookers. Usually, she could sit back and smile, safe in the knowledge that they could look all they wanted, but he was hers. Here, all bets were off. This was all too weird.

"Be an ostrich," Rosie reminded herself. "Just let all of this flow over you," she'd whispered, and then she pretended to read.

Marcus seemed oblivious to it all when he came back to her and splashed her with his wet hair. She squealed and complained, but he laughed it off. Then she risked another glance at Marcus's earlier admirers. One looked away when she caught Rosie's eye, and the other had already gone back to her book. For that moment, Marcus was hers. But just for that moment. She'd been nervous about how they would be around each other after his late-night fun, but it appeared that they were just the same as ever.

He asked her about her book, and Rosie raved about it. Then he fell asleep. She always thought that sleep was the sign of a clear conscience, but how could that possibly be the case? She'd sat there with her nerves in ribbons, terrified she might be propositioned while he—the philanderer—just slept. It was infuriating.

"Be an ostrich," she'd repeated. "Just don't look up."

And that's how they spent the first morning of their vacation together at Broader Horizons.

The problem was that by lunchtime Rosie was hungry. She also needed the restroom. She could call a waiter over to get her a menu. There was a little flag at the top of her lounge chair. She'd seen them before. All she had to do was raise it and somebody would come to take her order soon enough. But whether she liked it or not, she was going to have to get to a bathroom. Nobody could do that for her.

Waking Marcus was futile. He would laugh at her. By then the area around the pool was fairly busy. Most of the lounge chairs were full, and some party people had already started on the cocktails. She saw glasses of Buck's fizz heading to a table and two bloody mary cocktails to another. If things had been quiet and hung over in the morning, they were definitely getting the buzz going by early afternoon. She had to stop psyching herself out and get up the nerve to walk to the restrooms.

After taking a last reassuring look at her sleeping husband, she got up. She was wearing a nice pink bikini, but she had it covered with a little cotton pool dress because she didn't want to give anyone the idea she was looking for attention, or worse still—action. Just as she'd planned, she kept on her wide-brim hat and enormous dark sunglasses. Her plan was to look good, but aloof. Most of the women were in tiny bikinis or even topless, so she was pretty confident the message she was sending was loud and clear: don't come near me. Nobody did.

Rosie made it to the restroom without being asked for sex. When she came out, still armed with her hat and sunglasses, she was feeling a little braver and wandered around the lobby. It was broad daylight and not too threatening. She couldn't see anybody doing anything too outrageous. In fact, outside of the swinging, it looked like any regular vacation resort on an exquisite beach with aquamarine water. Pity to miss all that out of fear.

Rosie wondered if she would be brave enough to go down to the water's edge. At night, things definitely got a little wilder, so now was the time to explore. At least she could scream if someone came at her and just like the night before, if she was approached, she could always say no. "Because no means no," she said to herself.

"It sure does." Her range of vision was impaired by the wide-brimmed hat, and she'd had no idea there was a person standing anywhere near her. She swung around to see who it was.

A man with sandy blond hair and a broad smile, stood there looking at her. She guessed he was about forty years old.

"Excuse me. I didn't mean to startle you. I just heard you say, 'no means no,' so I'm guessing you're in the 'no' club," he said, his smile never faltering.

"The what?"

"Let me guess. This is your first time at one of these 'booty camps.' You don't really want to be here, but your husband, who you clearly adore, does, and you're scared to death." Then he stopped and looked at her. "Am I right?"

She smiled and nodded. "You got all that just from, 'no means no'?"

He laughed. "Believe me, it's not hard to guess. All you're missing is a big book to use as a weapon if the need arises."

Rosie looked sheepish. "It's back at my lounge chair."

He put out his hand. "My name is Sam. Sam Sinnott. I'm not making a move on you. I'm just saying hello."

Rosie was relieved to meet a "normal" person. "Hi." She shook his hand. "I'm Rosie Kelly. My husband is out there sound asleep, and thank you for not making a move on me."

"You'd be amazed how many of us are here. 'No people,' I mean."

"What did you call it? The No Club?"

"Oh yes." He nodded. We're an exclusive club, a bit like the resistance in World War II. We're very secret, but basically we're the visitors at Broader Horizons who would rather say no."

"Do you meet in secret to have clandestine chats?" She laughed.

"Well, I don't know. We'll have to wait and see."

It was reassuring that she wasn't alone.

They walked out toward the pool together. "This is my fifth time at this game. My wife's a little younger than me and she's, shall we say, broad-minded. She's my second wife, and she doesn't want kids. She just likes to party. Anyway, she told me early into our relationship that she wanted an open marriage, so we come to Broader Horizons once a year."

"Wow. But you don't seem to like it."

Sam shook his head. "I really did try to get into it the first time, but I don't know. What can I say? I couldn't get my head around it. I'm Jewish. I had a strong mother, and I just can't go around with a load of women and then head home like it's all normal. I let Cindy do what she likes, and now I just look the other way."

Rosie laughed. "I don't think it has anything to do with being Jewish. I started out Roman Catholic, so we're pretty big on guilt, too. But I do agree with you about not being able to come to terms with it."

They walked out into the super-bright midday sun and stopped. "Look," he said, "I'm really not making a pass at you, but my wife is . . . otherwise engaged. Would you like to join me for lunch at the beach hut restaurant?" He looked so serious and sincere that Rosie didn't feel in any way threatened by him. She looked over to where her man was still out cold. He obviously hadn't had any sleep the night before.

"Sounds great. I'm starving and that's my husband over there." She pointed to a sleeping Marcus. "So I'd love the company."

They headed away from the boardwalk and onto the white sand of the beach. Just to the right was a smaller building with the same thatched roof as the main restaurant. Rosie hadn't even seen the beach hut restaurant before. There were seven square tables, so it wouldn't sit any more than thirty at once. Perfect, she thought. They were right on the beach, so they had an unobstructed view of the beautiful crystal clear water. The waves were small today, and white sails glided by in the distance.

"This place is so beautiful," she said, as they took their seats and were given menus.

"Isn't it? I've been to the Broader Horizons in St. Lucia and in Italy, but this has the nicest view."

"Even better than St. Lucia?" Rosie removed her "suit of armor"—the hat and sunglasses.

"That was a nicer complex, but look at that sea. It just doesn't get better than this."

Now that they were sitting opposite each other, Rosie noticed Sam did look a little older than she'd first thought, perhaps in his late forties. But he was still a nice-looking man. His pale-blue eyes sparkled, and his tan was deep mahogany. He wore a white linen shirt and pants. If she had to guess, she would have assumed he was into multiple partners. Looks could be deceiving.

"So," she said, "do you think there are many people here in The No Club, or are we a rare breed?"

Sam shook his head. "I think there are a great many of us. In fact, I would go so far as to say almost half would start out saying no." Then he shrugged. "Of course, I think once they're here, quite a few might be convinced to give it a go. I guess that was the case with me a few years back, but now I'm certain I'm a 'no' kinda guy."

"Half the guests? That can't be."

His face took on an air of seriousness again. "Do you mind if I order a bottle of wine?

The day was looking up. "What a wonderful idea."

"Red or white?" he asked. "Although I should tell you all they serve in this restaurant is fish and things from the sea."

"White wine is perfect, please," she said.

After ordering their wine, Sam said, "The way I see it is that couples end up here because one person in the relationship is into it. Sometimes there's two, but one is usually the pusher and the other follower. That's what I've come to notice over the years. For example, your husband pushed you into this vacation, and you caved in the end."

Rosie blushed, but the sun was so bright she hoped it wasn't too obvious. "There was a time I was as outgoing and adventurous but not anymore."

"You sure you're not Jewish?" He smiled, and she laughed.

"Don't worry. You really don't have to do anything you don't want to here. For what it's worth, from my experience, Cindy goes wild while we're away, and then it's everything back to the usual when we get home. Our marriage is sound and loving. It's just that she has to let off steam once or twice a year, and then she's back to normal."

"Normal?"

"Does that sound strange? What I mean is, we have a normal, monogamous marriage outside of these crazy vacations."

The wine waiter arrived and poured some into Sam's glass for him to test. He smiled a thank you, swirled, sniffed, and sipped the wine just like her father used to. He had a certain appeal, and he was funny, too. Maybe this vacation wasn't going to be totally horrendous if she could just keep Sam company while their respective partners "let off steam," as he put it.

Sam nodded and the waiter poured.

"So, tell me about you, Rosie Kelly." Sam smiled at her and took a sip of cool white wine. "Where are you from?"

"I live in a town called Weston, just outside Boston. Marcus is a pilot, and we have a little girl. Her name is Natasha. She's five."

"You have a child?" He looked surprised. "Forgive me, but for some reason I assumed you were too young or too thin or something. I don't know why, I just got the idea that you hadn't started a family yet."

She was flattered but tried to ignore his compliments. "Probably because we're here. It's not a family resort."

"I have two daughters with my first wife, and they're in their teens now. That's why I'm fine with Cindy not wanting kids. Children are very expensive. I have college tuition coming down the track soon." He took a large gulp of wine as if he needed fortifying just thinking of the school fees.

"What about you? Where do you live?" she asked.

"I'm a Miami man now, although I was born and raised in the U.K." He shrugged. "What can I say? I love the Florida sun."

"That explains the deep tan."

"Yep." He laughed. "I don't know how you can live in the snow. Do you have family there?"

"My dad passed away a few months ago."

"Oh, I'm sorry."

Now it was her turn to gulp the wine. "Thank you. I tried to use it as an excuse not to come here, but Marcus said it would be a great escape."

Sam nodded sympathetically. "How long are you here for?"

"We only got here yesterday. We're here until next Sunday."

Sam smiled again. He had a bright smile. His teeth might have been a little too white, but maybe that was just the deep tan making them look whiter than they were. Either way, she liked his constant smile.

"We're also here until next Sunday, so you and I can keep each other company if you like, while the others get up to . . . whatever. What do you think?" He raised his glass. "Cheers, Rosie."

Rosie was delighted to have an ally in this hazardous terrain. She raised her glass, too. "Cheers."

Lunch turned out to be fantastic. Her swordfish steak was impossibly fresh, and he said his lobster was delicious, too. The Caribbean green salads were crisp and light with all sorts of bonuses like strawberries and blueberries. Rosie loved it. She didn't really want to part company with him after their lunch and what turned out to be two bottles of wine, but she thought she'd better head back to see if her husband was looking for her. Sam said he understood and gave her his phone number so she could call him any time. Other than that, he said he'd see her around the pool and teased her that she would be impossible to miss with her hat and glasses. The thing she liked most about him was his sense of humor. He made her laugh, and she didn't feel threatened. It would be easy to have a friend like him to hang around with for the week while Marcus partied.

When she got back, Marcus was gone and with two bottles of wine in her system, Rosie was happy to nod off in the sun for a little while. When he came back later in the day, he stroked her hair and said, "Hey, babe. When did you get back?"

"Oh, hey." She yawned and stretched.

"Are you wearing sunscreen? You're looking a little red."

This was enough to wake her up. "Oh, I completely forgot," she said. "I just came back and you weren't here, so I decided to take a nap. What time is it?"

"It's vacation time," Marcus said, dismissing her concerns. "We don't wear watches here."

She giggled.

"Hey, have you been drinking?" He raised an eyebrow as he ran his hand down her arm. "Are you starting to have some fun?"

"Well, actually I met this nice man—" she started, but he put up his hand.

"Shhh, no details. I'm so happy you've gotten into the swing of things. I was beginning to worry you weren't going to let go. It's terrific, isn't it? Crazy, but terrific."

Rosie stopped short. Marcus thought she'd had sex with Sam. Worse than that, he was *happy* about it. Should she clear up the misunderstanding? He didn't seem to want to know the truth. Was that how this thing worked? He would do what he did, and she would do something elsewhere, but they wouldn't compare notes? Regular romance was so much more straightforward.

"Just tell me you had a good time."

"I had a good time."

"That's the best news I've heard all day, angel. This vacation is so amazing. I love you so much, you know that?" he whispered, and kissed her. Pretty quick, Rosie knew that he wanted to do more. She kissed him back softly, but her mind raced. Where had his lips just been? Who had he kissed last? How had he kissed her? How did she compare? As her panic rose, her libido fell, and Marcus sensed her tension.

"Honey?" he asked her, their faces only inches apart.

"Oh, Marcus it's those other girls, I can't stop thinking about it. What you've been up to, *who* you've been up to."

He stroked her cheek in an almost paternal gesture and rubbed her lips with his thumb.

"Shhh, baby. You think too much. Don't give them a second thought. You know you're my queen. You're better and sexier," he said and kissed her again, "than any of them."

She didn't want to think about the other women, but they kept floating in her mind's eye. Was he with Sam's wife, Cindy? Had he been with Fiona yet? Marcus pulled back and looked at her a little more seriously.

"Do you want to do this, or should I leave you alone?"

There was an edge to his voice that scared her. She worried that if she didn't sleep with him right now, he would simply find somebody else. She jumped to her feet and pasted a smile on her face. Nobody was taking her man from right under her nose. Nobody.

"Come with me," she said with an inviting smile and took his hand.

"Lead the way, baby." The edge was gone and happy, flirty Marcus was back. They went up to their room together and she put all other thoughts out of her head and they had a great time in the oversized Jacuzzi bath in their suite. Rosie wondered if perhaps it was designed for four but didn't suggest it in case Marcus thought it was a great idea.

When they were cuddling in bed together later, it felt good. Rosie decided her new friend, Sam, was right. Okay, he didn't call it the Ostrich Plan, but it amounted to the same thing. He just ignored what his wife did on vacation. Rosie would do the same.

"Come on," Marcus said, getting out of bed a little while later. "Want to go hang out by the pool again—maybe have a cocktail while watching the sun go down?"

"Sure, you go. I forgot to bring my cell phone down to the pool, and I see I missed a call from Mom. I'll just listen to that because she'll be on the plane now, but I want to call home and make sure Natasha's okay."

When she got the message from her mother about the volcano, the panic started. She tried and failed to call her back, so she called Cliff Road. That's when Lily confirmed the volcano, her mom's delayed return, and how she was stepping in to help. Lily assured her that she had everything under control. Naturally Rosie was distressed but had to accept the new situation and get on with her vacation. Lily convinced her that their Mom was in absolutely no danger, would be back soon and under no circumstances was Rosie to cut her holiday short.

She headed down to the pool to fill Marcus in on the home news. Then she lay back on the thickly padded lounger and looked around. Things were calm and serene because a lot of people had gone to get changed for dinner, or perhaps they were doing what she and her husband had been doing earlier. The heat had gone out of the day. There was no wind, so the air was very still. It was quiet, and she could hear the birds chirping. Maybe they'd been singing all day, but she hadn't heard them over all the noise. The birdsong was nicer than all that ambient music. They sounded like they were in the palm trees and thick mango groves.

The pool boy gathered up the towels, and she glanced over at her husband. His eyes were closed.

Rosie let her eyes close, too, and enjoyed the feeling of the late sun on her face. She thought about her life. Lily had Natasha. Her daughter was safe and happy. Her husband was content, and she'd found Sam.

With him to keep her company, a week in the resort would be a lot easier —maybe even fun. She was very lucky to have found him and to have discovered "The No Club." The more she thought about it, the more she decided she couldn't possibly tell Marcus. If he wanted a no questions, no lies situation, that suited her just fine. Sam would be her little secret. She wasn't breaking any laws.

Chapter 31

A Near Miss

"Isn't that breaking the law?" Popsy asked.

"Making an illegal U-turn?" Sandra asked.

"That's what she said," Popsy agreed. "We must have come the wrong way."

"Make an illegal U-turn," the GPS commanded again in her robotic voice.

"Oh look, there's one now." Popsy pointed to the U-turn sign with a line through it.

Sandra heaved a sigh and glanced in her rearview mirror. "If you say so." She swung into the right-hand lane. Then she pulled a sharp U-turn around the center island. There was a loud screeching of brakes followed by a honking horn.

"Where did he come from?" Sandra squealed when she saw the other car.

"Very rude man."

At least the GPS was happy again. "Continue straight ahead," it commanded, but the whine of a police siren told them otherwise. Instinctively, Sandra hit the brakes and pulled over.

"He's right behind us," Sandra said in surprise.

Popsy turned around. "I think he's flashing his lights. Why does he want us to stop?"

"What? Oh great. That's all we need," Sandra moaned as the police car pulled to a stop behind her. She fumbled before she managed to find the correct button to get the window down.

"Hello there," the police officer said when he got to her car.

"Hello, sir," Sandra said, on her best behavior.

"Can I see your driver's license, please?"

Shoot, I should have had that ready, Sandra thought. "Popsy, do you know where my purse is?"

"Back seat. I can't reach it."

"Can I get it?" Sandra asked, feeling a little nervous.

He nodded and stepped back.

"You're not local?" he asked.

"Uh, no, we're American. Well, I am. My friend was born over here, but she's lived in America for a long time."

The policeman looked into the car and over to Popsy, who smiled back and gave him a little wave. Sandra felt guilty just because she was talking to a cop. The car was a two-door, so she had to figure out how to get her seat to move forward.

"Tell me now, do they not have the same traffic signs in America?" he asked.

"Excuse me?"

"The illegal U-turn sign. Is it the same in the States as it is here?"

Now Sandra understood. "Well, I know this sounds nuts, sir, but the GPS told me to make the U-turn. I don't know why."

"The GPS?"

"Yes."

He laughed. "You're telling me the GPS told you to break the law?"

"No. It wasn't like that. It said to make an illegal U-turn and then we saw one, so we did it. It's taking us to Banagher."

"It'll take you to jail faster if you pull that stunt again," he said. Then he laughed. "I'm sure it told you to make a legal one, not an illegal one."

"Oh." Sandra thought for a moment. "Now that you mention it, that would make more sense. But I swear it sounded like it said illegal."

"And tell me, if the GPS tells you to rob a bank in the next town, are you going to do that, too?"

"Sorry. I'm just beginning to realize how dumb that was."

He looked over at Popsy. "You should have more sense if you're Irish." Then he turned back to Sandra. "I'll tell you what. I'll let you off this time because you're tourists, and God knows we need them, but no more stunts like that, right?"

"Right."

He nodded. "Wait till they hear about this one back at the barracks. Those GPS things are great, but don't follow them blind. Remember to engage your brain at the same time. Yes?"

"Yes, sir. I'm sorry, I won't do it again."

"Right so. Drive safely now and enjoy the rest of your holiday," he said, and headed back to his car. He was still shaking his head in disbelief as he drove off.

Popsy and Sandra burst out laughing and Sandra said, "I can't believe I did that. I let a machine tell me to do an illegal U-turn."

"Vacation brain," Popsy said.

"What?"

"Vacation brain. That's what Peter used to call it. When we went on holidays sometimes we just kind of tuned out and did dumb things. I think we have a touch of holiday brain."

"Well, on the plus side, that means we're really in the vacation frame of mind," Sandra said, and then started the car up again.

"No, Sandra, the plus side is that we didn't get thrown in jail for dangerous driving. That really was a close one. We got lucky."

"Lucky is good." Sandra smiled. "I like 'lucky.' Let's stay that way."

"You're on," Popsy said and smiled back.

Earlier, they'd left The Four Seasons as arranged, and when they got to the airport, they spoke to the airline about when they could realistically fly home. The attendant said she was sorry, but she couldn't give them an exact timeframe and advised them to keep watching the news. As soon as it was safe, air travel would recommence.

Then they'd picked up a little car for the next part of their adventure. It was much smaller than Sandra was used to, but the price difference was enormous. She'd wanted to get a high-performance car for their road trip, but it would have cost several hundred Euros a day more, and Popsy wouldn't let her. She'd reminded Sandra they were poor, to which Sandra replied she kept forgetting and it was nicer to be rich.

A little while later, they loaded up their own suitcases into the tiny trunk of their little silver two-door Toyota Aygo. It was a tight squeeze, but they'd managed. The only confusion was when she'd had gotten into the passenger seat and Popsy had to remind her where it was.

Sandra had said they'd be fine once they hit the open road, and they were —right up until they got pulled over.

Popsy said, "Thanks, Sandra."

"What for?"

"Coming up with this *Thelma and Louise* plan. For getting us out of the city and into the real Ireland. It's so good to be here and it was all your idea —coming to Ireland in the first place, and then coming to Banagher once the plane was delayed. I probably would have parked in The Four Seasons and worried myself silly until the airport opened again. Even if that's tomorrow, it would have been such a waste of a day. This is much better, so thank you."

Sandra smiled. "I couldn't have done it without you, Popsy."

It was mid-afternoon by the time they got to Banagher, and they were thrilled with the town.

"I had no idea it was on the water," Sandra said admiring the town's marina.

"Or how pretty it is," Popsy said when they drove over the enormous bridge that spanned the river.

"I wonder what river this is."

"It's got to be the Shannon," Popsy said as she looked out over the blue shimmering water. "If I still have any of my school geography. It's Ireland's longest river."

"Even I've heard of the Shannon. What about the Liffey? Isn't that the one Dublin is on?"

"Go you." Popsy punched Sandra's arm. "You know your Irish geography."

"Oh, look! There's a B&B sign. Let's see if we can get a room."

The lady who opened the door to them was very nice, but she couldn't help.

"I'm sorry," she said. "It's just the season is usually quiet around now, and I thought it was a good time to get some work done." As if on cue, a husky builder came out of the house and walked past them with a bucket of cement powder.

"You could try Mrs. Miller at The Boathouse. It's a pub, to be honest, but they have a few guestrooms, too, so she calls herself a B&B. It's usually pretty busy, but being a Monday, you might be lucky. Of course, there's also the hotel in town, The Brosna."

They got the directions for both, but once they were back in the car, they agreed that since they were on a budget, they'd make for the B&B. What they hadn't anticipated was how fortunate they were to find The Boathouse.

There was no way they would have come across it without the directions.

They soon realized why. The Boathouse was difficult to find by road but easy to reach by water. From the front, the house looked fairly unassuming. A small hanging sign announced The Boathouse was established in 1967. The woman who ran the place must have been a fantastic gardener, because early flowering tulips and waves of daffodils bloomed along the little pathway up to the front door. The grass was cut short and a little gnome held a placard that said WELCOME.

There was lots of room in the driveway, so Sandra left the car there and they headed in together. First, they walked through a small porch with two armchairs. As Sandra looked back over her shoulder, she wondered why anyone would bother to sit there. The garden was pretty enough, but beyond that the view was of the small country road and then a big field. It wasn't exactly jaw-dropping scenery. The front door of the house was inside the porch, but it was ajar so they went inside without ringing the doorbell. The room they entered was a bar.

Small tables furnished the place and each had four little barstools. They'd been recently wiped down with a cloth because there were still damp streaks visible. The corner table was larger than the rest, and it had built-in benches. Along the back wall was a bar counter made of deep mahogany.

"This is like one of those imitation country Irish pubs you get in Boston, only I guess this is the real thing," Popsy whispered.

"Yeah, I wonder where everybody is." Sandra craned her neck and looked around. "Excuse me," she called, "Anybody here?"

"I am."

The voice came from the doorframe at the far end of the bar. Sandra figured it went to a kitchen or stock room. A woman walked over to greet them.

"Hello, ladies, I'm Mrs. Miller." She wiped her hands on a dish towel. "Welcome to The Boathouse. Is it a late lunch or an early tea you were thinking of?" They had great difficulty understanding what they came to find out was her Kerry accent. Mrs. Miller was from Killarney in Kerry County, and had only lived in Banagher for forty years. Apparently that still made her a relatively new person in the town, but from what Mrs. Miller said, her Kerry accent was still as strong as it was the day she'd met and married her husband.

"Um, we heard that you had rooms to let. We were hoping we could book one for a night," Popsy said.

"No, a few nights." Sandra looked at her friend. "We don't know how long we'll need to stay."

Mrs. Miller put down the towel. "Well, I only have five rooms and four are gone, so you would have to share my small room. It does have two beds, but it's tight. I usually let it out to students in the summer, or the boat hands."

Sandra thought about this for a moment. It was a change from The Four Seasons for sure. Maybe they should check out the hotel in town.

Put Popsy made up her mind for her. "We'll take it. We're tougher than we look. Tell me, though, I thought it was off-season. Why is the place so busy?"

"The lads are in town to work on the boats. Being winter, they're all out of the water and now's the time to get 'em fixed up for next summer. It's mayhem here." Mrs. Miller smiled. She obviously liked mayhem. "And yourselves? What brings you girls to Banagher?"

Popsy glanced at her watch. "We should have been touching down in Logan Airport around now, but that volcano has grounded all planes across Europe. That's why we don't know how long we'll be here."

"Well, America's loss is our gain," she said in a matter-of-fact tone and gestured for Sandra and Popsy to follow her. "Come with me now, and I'll take your details and give you the room key."

Mrs. Miller told them they could unpack at their leisure and "wander about the place to find their feet." She let them know she could make them toasted or normal sandwiches anytime, but dinner would be served in the bar between six and eight p.m. Breakfast was whenever they woke.

Sandra didn't bother asking if there was a gym in the town of Banagher. She would run on the country roads instead, though she preferred the gym because the treadmill was easier on her joints.

Another reason she liked the treadmills was it meant that she could measure the exact miles she'd run, along with the rate and the time she took. But their driver, Gerald, had told her that an Irish mile was not the same as a U.S. one. It seemed crazy to Sandra, but how could she measure her runs if they used different miles? Everything else was different, too, so it was hardly surprising. She would just go out and run for what felt like a good stretch, and that would have to do. She was a little neurotic about her running stats, but she had no choice. Popsy, on the other hand, had slipped back into the Irish system with ease.

"I love this place," Popsy said when they were unpacking the car. "Can you smell that air? I swear it feels fresher than back home."

"Vacation brain," Sandra said. "The air in Boston is just as clean. They do quality checks all the time."

"Can you not feel a stillness in the air here that just doesn't exist at home? Maybe it's the river, or the fact that we're in the midlands of Ireland, but it feels like time is standing still."

Sandra laughed. "The truth is I get it, too. It really feels like time is moving slower. Have you noticed that there are no car horns beeping, no landscapers tearing up the peace with their lawn mowers—nothing." She stopped for a minute and listened to the silence. "It's perfectly still. Cool, right? Now come on and let's get these suitcases to our room and go for a walk."

"It's not quite The Four Seasons, is it?" Popsy laughed as she held up the old-fashioned metal key. There was no chance of getting a plastic card key here, but then, there were no check in or check out times, either. This was an altogether more relaxed environment and one Popsy favored over the five-star-luxury kind.

A few minutes later they'd unloaded their car and hauled their oversized cases up the narrow stairs and into the tiny room that was called "number five."

"Oh my gawd!" Popsy moaned when she saw the room. It was unbelievably small and cramped. By the time they'd hauled their luggage in and situated themselves, there was barely room to move. The single beds were pushed up against the walls and between them was a space of a few feet. That was now where Sandra, Popsy, and their enormous cases were crammed.

She laughed now. "Beginning to regret Banagher?" she asked.

"This room is smaller than my bathroom at the hotel in Dublin. This isn't a bedroom. It's a closet."

Popsy sat down on her bed to make more room and decided to make the best of the situation. "Oh, so what? We won't be here too long, and it's all part of our great Irish adventure."

Sandra said, "I guess you're right. I've gotten too soft—too used to the good life. This is fine. A bit tight but fine."

"Should we even bother to unpack?" Popsy asked as she looked around for somewhere to hang her clothes.

"There's no closet." Sandra laughed.

"No drawers, either."

"Ohmygod, there's no en suite," Sandra gasped.

There was a knock on the door. "You girls settling in okay?" Mrs. Miller asked. "I have towels for you, here."

Popsy crawled to the bottom of her bed to avoid knocking anything over, and went to open the door.

"Oh my, those are big suitcases. There'll be no room for you with those things," Mrs. Miller said. "We could maybe put them in the storeroom after you've unpacked."

"We're fine, thank you. Really," Popsy said. She didn't want to highlight that there was nowhere to actually hang their clothes. "Now, can you tell me where our bathroom is?"

"Ah, everybody shares here," she said proudly. Then she pointed back down the stairs. "You'll have passed them when you came through the hall from the pub."

They'd walked past doors marked "ladies" and "gents," but Popsy had assumed they were for the visitors to the pub and not for people overnighting. She would have to walk through public halls in the morning before she got the chance to brush her teeth or shower—Oh, God.

"We'll laugh about this when we're back in Wellesley," Sandra said when Mrs. Miller had left them alone again.

"Are you sure?"

"I think I need to go for a run. Are you okay to wander around here by yourself for an hour?"

"I'll be fine. You run and I'll go for a walk by the river."

Left to her own devices, Popsy found her way to the back of The Boathouse. What it lacked in bedroom finesse it made up for in outside décor. It was simply heavenly. Popsy soon realized the front of the house didn't get much attention because all of the love, effort, and serious gardening went into the back where it overlooked the River Shannon.

Metal benches stood on either side of the back door. Both were nestled into beds of lavender. The shrubs had been cut back for the winter, but Popsy could see the first signs of new growth. It made her long to sit on those benches in high summer when the lilac buds would be full and open and smelling like heaven.

A gravel path led from the back door down toward the river where four wooden picnic tables stood. On either end of each picnic table were large wooden barrels crammed with spring flowering grape hyacinths.

To the sides of the garden, Popsy could see wide and much-loved flower borders just beginning to wake up.

What a lovely place to visit, she thought, and began walking down the gravel path to the river.

She would tell Rosie and Marcus about this place. They should bring Natasha here. Standing by the water's edge, Popsy looked back at the house to see how it would appear to boaters. Now it looked even prettier. There were window boxes under every window and like the old wooden barrels, they were crammed with spring bulbs—miniature ruby tulips and glowing yellow daffodils. It was already picture-postcard beautiful.

Popsy could see why it would be so attractive to American tourists. It would be attractive to anybody. But it was famous for being a pub and not a boarding house. That was pretty obvious after having seen the rooms. She wondered why the pub was so popular. Guess, I'll find out tonight, she thought as she looked out over the water.

There was a small jetty. It must be where the boats docked when they were visiting.

Now, though, the river was quiet. According to Mrs. Miller, boats were out of the water and being fixed up over the winter. Popsy figured that's what was happening down in the marina, and so with nothing better to do, she decided to wander along the riverbank, hoping it would lead her there.

She glanced at her watch. It was only four thirty. Time really did seem to move more slowly in Banagher. What a nice thought.

It was easier to get to the town by foot than it had been by car. With just a short fifteen-minute walk, Popsy found herself in the center of the marina. It was also quiet. Being a Monday, she figured most boat owners were at work, paying for their boats. But the crane down at the water's edge was busy and she heard voices, so she decided to investigate.

She watched in fascination as the men worked to harness a massive boat that was resting on a trailer next to them. It seemed to take an age as they checked and double-checked all the pulleys and tow ropes. The man that seemed to be in charge signaled to the crane operator to "take up the slack." The machine's great metal arm went to work and hoisted the boat up until all the straps and ropes were as tense as the guy in charge clearly was.

"Hey," he yelled, but the crane operator seemed to think the boss meant "stop." The boat was barely suspended off the trailer, but still he wanted to triple-check all the connections.

She was beginning to lose interest when the crane got the nod to hoist again, and this time the enormous boat rose up and away from its trailer. The noise of groaning metal scared her. She didn't know if it was the crane or the boat that seemed to suffer from the strain, but slowly it was maneuvered up and over onto a dry dock stand. At this point, another five men moved in to help as they pushed and pulled to ensure the boat landed with a gentle thud onto its new position. It was remarkable to see the river cruisers out of the water. They appeared so graceful and balanced on the river, but out in dry dock they looked oversized and cumbersome.

A fish out of water, she thought, and walked closer to have a better look.

She'd had the good sense to stay well back when the heavy lifting was being done, but now she didn't think she'd be in anybody's way. She was smart. She would keep her eyes open and not become a nuisance.

One didn't manage to raise two girls and get them to adulthood without having eyes in the back of your head, she told herself.

"Would you stand back, hey you—lady!" It took Popsy a moment to realize that the man was actually shouting at her. He ran over, grabbed her by the waist, and pulled them both to the ground. It all happened so fast, Popsy didn't know what was going on. But as they rolled through the dust, she got a glance skyward and saw a large metal object glide right over their heads.

It didn't make sense. She'd been watching the crane's metal arm. It had been on the far side of the driver's cubical.

The man dragged her by the arms along the rough cement back about fifteen feet to safety.

"Of all dumbass things to do," he mumbled. His accent was from the north of Ireland.

"What just happened?" Popsy asked as she rubbed her arms.

"You nearly got yourself killed, that's what," he said. "Jesus, woman, have you no sense?"

"Sorry. I thought I was out of the way." She saw that the crane had stopped. Its second arm was only a few yards from where they stood.

"I didn't even see that," she said, shocked.

"Hmm, I figured as much." He was rubbing his elbow that had obviously taken the brunt of their fall.

Then Popsy got annoyed. She wasn't a fool. She wasn't in the habit of walking into harm's way. "Well, it should have been cordoned off with a hi-viz ribbon around it saying to keep out."

"Like that hi-viz ribbon back there?" He pointed.

There it was, about twenty feet behind her. How had she missed it?

"I'm really sorry."

"Yeah," he said, which she took to mean she was forgiven.

"I'm Popsy. As you may have guessed, I'm a tourist here."

"Well, hello, Popsy." He grinned. "And yes, I had kind of assumed you weren't from these parts."

"Well, I don't think you are either with that strong northern twang."

He stood and offered her his hand. "You know an Ulster accent from a midland? Most Americans wouldn't."

"I'm not American. I'm Irish. I've just lived there for a long time."

"And I've lived here for a long time, too. Just never lost the Strabane accent."

"The man from Strabane."

"That I am." He nodded. "Now, do I need to escort you back behind the tape or can you manage that yourself?"

"Oh, I think I can do that." She sniffed defensively.

"Good." He gave a slight bow. "If you'll excuse me, I need to get this boat locked down. We don't want any more near misses tonight." He walked off to bark orders at the men who'd been awaiting his instruction.

A near miss? So that's what I am.

She felt embarrassed and cross with herself. How stupid had she been to walk into harm's way like that? she thought as she headed back to the safe side of the high-visibility ribbon.

"Stupid, stupid, stupid," she chastised herself, and then realized she didn't even know the name of the man who'd saved her life.

Chapter 32

Matt's Move

"Stupid, stupid, stupid! What did you think you were doing?" Jack thundered. Lily had never seen him so angry.

"Can you at least keep your voice down?" she whispered and glanced to the sofa where Natasha was sitting and watching television. "I don't want her to hear you. And anyway, what should I have done? My mom and Sandra are stranded in Ireland. Rosie is on her first vacation since forever, and Matilda's back is out. Natasha is my niece, and I'm the only family she has in town."

"You can't just go around adopting any little waifs you see."

Jack wouldn't listen to reason. "She's not a waif. She's my only sister's only child. In fact, now that I think of it, she's your goddaughter's daughter. I figured you might have shown a little more understanding." Lily felt her blood begin to boil. "And another thing, I can do whatever I like. This is my house. I have a spare room, which by the way, I see you have totally taken over with your files and Lord knows what else. Well, you can darn well clear them out now or I will, because I want it for my niece."

"You know what, Lily? If it means that much to you, do what you like." He sighed.

Lily thought the fight was over, and she'd won. He'd caved to her wishes. So she went into the second bedroom to prepare it for their little houseguest. Natasha was watching *Sponge Bob*, apparently oblivious to the adults' disagreement. She was piling up Jack's files in a neat stack on the bedside table when she heard the front door bang shut.

"Natasha," she called in a panicked voice and rushed back out to the living room. She hadn't told anybody about her Toys"R"Us experience, but she was a lot more nervous now. Had she wandered off again? But no, Natasha was still glued to the sofa. Lily knew she'd heard the front door.

"He's gone," Natasha said.

"What? Jack's gone out?"

"I told you he didn't like me," Natasha said, not taking her eyes off *Sponge Bob*, but what she said broke Lily's heart. She rushed over to cuddle her niece. "Oh, it's not you, kiddo. It's Uncle Jack. He's just a grumpy old man."

"Yeah, and he doesn't like kids," Natasha added.

How could one so young understand so much? Lily wondered.

It was Tuesday morning and Lily was hopeful he'd come home less angry. She'd tried to call him, but it went right to voice mail. She'd even left messages begging him to come home and swearing she would make it worth his while. But he didn't return her calls, and he didn't come back to the apartment.

Needless to say, she hadn't slept a wink. Why was he being so unreasonable? Did he really hate kids that much? She knew that Jack and Sandra didn't have children, but she'd let herself believe it had to do with Sandra not wanting them. Of course, Jack had grumbled that he was "done with having kids," but she hadn't really believed that. Surely she would be able to convince him to have them with her. She knew she could play him like a fiddle, and this was just another tune. She wanted kids, and when she fell in love with Jack, she'd assumed that he would give her what she wanted. Seeing how he'd reacted to Natasha worried her, but Lily had stupidly assumed she would get her way.

She couldn't believe that he'd stayed away all night. Where had he gone? To a hotel? How sad was that? And wrong. They were together now, and they had to work through their difficulties, not run away from them.

She tried his cell again. No answer. It was almost seven a.m. when Natasha awoke. She didn't seem too traumatized after witnessing Jack's storming out. Last night they'd made s'mores and eaten them in front of the TV watching *Toy Story*. They'd had a great night. "What are we going to do today?" she demanded while Lily was making her toast.

With all the commotion of the evening before, Lily hadn't really thought through her work life too much. The Toys"R"Us experience was such a big jolt. She knew now there was no way she could juggle taking care of her niece and going to work. How did Rosie make it look so easy? She'd had no idea how much pressure taking care of a little person was.

She decided that she would tell Rosie about the Toys"R"Us incident when she got home and apologize from the bottom of her heart, but she had to keep Natasha safe until then. Work and her niece just could not mix. Something had to give, and it wouldn't be Natasha. She really had no choice. She would have to phone the office.

"Jones already knows about you disappearing early yesterday, and he's on the warpath about your conference call last night. You have to come in," Caryn said.

"Well, I can't. It's a family emergency."

"Another one? You sure have a lot of emergencies for one family," came the curt reply.

Lily knew she was playing with fire, but what choice did she have? She put work out of her head and focused on her niece. They had pancakes for breakfast and played coloring games on Lily's iPad because she didn't have any coloring books in the house. Then they got ready to visit Matilda.

"We need to bring her donuts. They're her favorite," Natasha said. Then the buzzer rang.

"Thank God." Lily breathed a sigh of relief. "Jack's back."

Using the doorbell was a little melodramatic, she thought, but whatever works for him. They had to talk it out, and it was better to do it as soon as possible.

"Hello?" she said through the intercom, going along with his game.

"Lily, hi, it's me, Matt. I heard from Caryn you had a family emergency."

Despite her being upset it wasn't Jack, Lily was grateful for a friendly voice. "Oh, Matt, hi. Yes. Come on up."

Matt was a natural. Within minutes he and Natasha were best friends. It was obvious he loved kids, and they loved him. She filled him in on how she came to be sitting for Natasha.

"Can we take Matt to Matilda's?"

"I'm sure Matt has to get back to work." Then she looked at him shyly. "Sorry."

Matt, had been on his knees on the floor with Natasha, and now he stood.

"I'd like that. I was in the office most of the night, so I have a few hours off coming to me." He smiled.

She knew she shouldn't have accepted, but it was just so nice to have somebody helping her out. With her mother and Rosie away and barely speaking to her and Jack now angry at her, Lily had nobody. Emily was a true friend, but Matt was here and he was being so kind. He had a nice smile and Natasha liked him a lot. How could she possibly turn him down?

"We'd love your company if you wouldn't be too bored with us. We're going to visit my old nanny—the lady who'd been taking care of Natasha—and after that, well I don't know. We'll find something fun to do in town, I guess."

~*~

Matilda was happy to see them. She was particularly happy to see the donuts, too.

"Oh, Lilita, you remembered," she said, and Lily winked at Natasha who already had the innate maturity to say nothing. What an amazing kid.

"What news from your mother?" Matilda asked.

"Oh, I didn't check."

"I've got it." Matt pulled out his phone. "All flights are still grounded. I'm afraid she's going to be in Ireland for a wee while yet." He tried to say it with an Irish accent, and it made Lily laugh.

Matt amused Matilda and Natasha with his ability to make Tiger flick her ears, and then he played chase with Natasha around the garden.

"He is a perfect gentleman," Matilda said when they were sitting at the kitchen window watching Matt and Natasha outside.

"Yes, he is," Lily agreed.

"Is he married?" She was pushing, but Lily just laughed. She nudged Matilda gently, shoulder-to-shoulder, but not too hard because of her back.

"No, Tilly, he's not married, but he's too young for me and I am happy. That is to say—well, I'm with Jack." She looked away and tried not to tear up.

"Is everything okay, Lilita?"

"We had a huge fight, and he stormed out. I don't even know where he slept last night. He won't return my calls."

Matilda shook her head and wrapped her arm around Lily's waist. "He is not the man for you, Lilita. *Lo siento.* I am sorry but he's not. He's not a good man. But that one," she said and gestured toward the garden, "he's a good man and I know he likes you, too."

"How do you know that?"

Matilda laughed. "He plays with your niece like she is his own daughter. Believe me, he likes you."

It was stupid, of course. Lily knew that. She was with Jack, and that wasn't going to change. She'd already paid too high a price for the relationship, and so had a lot of other people: Sandra, her mom, her dad. She wasn't going to back out now—not ever. If she had to spend the rest of her life paying for the damage she'd done, she would. Even if it meant no babies, she would give in to him. She had to stay with Jack or else breaking Sandra's heart would have been for nothing. It was nice to think that Matt liked her, he'd more-or-less told her so, but what did it matter? She was off the market. She was committed and would honor that commitment.

By the end of their visit, Matilda was showing signs of fatigue, and Lily knew it was time to go.

"Remember what I say, Lilita. He is a good man," she whispered.

Driving back into Boston a little while later, Matt said with his best Columbian accent, "So, Lilita, I'm a good man?"

At first she was embarrassed, but then she saw the humor in it and punched his arm gently. "You be nice about my Tilly. Just because she thinks you're a good man doesn't mean you are."

Matt gave her an exaggerated hurt look. "You still don't think I'm a good man?"

"Oh, Matt, I think you're great. You know that." She tried to sound flippant.

"How about the Pru?"

"What?"

"When was the last time you were at the top of The Prudential building?" He was referring to one of Boston's tallest buildings. "Natasha would love to run around the viewing gallery up there. We can show her the airport with all the planes coming and going, and we can point out Fenway Park. After that, I'll treat you gals to lunch in The Hub on the top floor. What do you say?"

Lily turned around to look at Natasha. "What do you think, honey? Want to go for an adventure in town and then Matt can take us to a fancy restaurant for lunch?"

"Do they have fries?"

Matt laughed. "Yes, Natasha. They have fries, and I'm pretty sure they have ice cream, too."

"Yeah, let's go." She clapped with enthusiasm.

Lily smiled. Matt really was terrific with kids. He was vibrant, full of energy. What a great shame Jack wasn't like that. There was definitely a price to pay for falling in love with an older man.

The three of them really enjoyed the viewing gallery. Lily had forgotten how pretty the city was from a height. It was obvious that Matt was a regular because he knew the city inside out. He was able to point out all the landmarks, which was no easy thing, because the snow cover was still pretty thick.

Natasha got a thrill out of looking through the binoculars, so Matt kept pumping the machine with quarters so she could see everything. He also had to lift her up because she was too small to reach the eye pieces without him. Lily was so grateful for his help. She didn't know what she would've done if he wasn't there and told him so as they left the viewing gallery.

"Matt, thanks for all your help today. You really are a natural with kids. I can see I have a lot to learn."

He smiled. "I love them. I told you about my new niece."

She nodded. "Yep."

"Lily—"

"Matt—" she started at just the same time, and they both laughed.

They got into the elevator for the rooftop restaurant and of course Natasha insisted on pressing the buttons, so she focused on her instead of Matt. It was easier.

When they arrived at the restaurant, it was clear Matt was a regular here, too, because he shook hands with the head waiter and Matt's "reserved" table appeared.

Not surprisingly, it was the corner table, so it had one of the best views of the entire city. The enormous walls of glass were crystal clear, and they could see the cars below scoot by like Matchbox toys.

"I love this place," Natasha said, gleeful.

"How did you make a reservation?" Matt hadn't used his phone since suggesting they go there.

"I didn't. It pays to have friends in high places," he whispered.

"I'll say. Do you come here often?" she asked, feeling a little jealous. Obviously he had a higher client entertainment budget than she did.

Matt laughed. "What? No, I'm friends with the head waiter. We worked together years ago in the North End when we were younger. We're still buddies." He clapped his hands together. "Now, what are we going to eat? I highly recommend the grilled sea bass." He winked at Lily.

"And for you, little miss, may I suggest a huge plate of Hub fries with a kiddies' burger?"

"Yeah!"

"Once a waiter, always a waiter," he whispered to Lily.

"It's more than that," she said with a laugh.

Matt pretended to look hurt. "What do you mean?"

"It's just good old-fashioned sales talk. Whether you're convincing a five-year-old to eat her lunch, or you're making a pitch to the CEO of some Asian bank to buy from your portfolio, it all amounts to the same thing: you're a silver-tongued salesman, and a good one at that."

"Well, thank you, I think."

"Can I have a Coke?" Natasha asked.

"How about a Shirley Temple?" Matt suggested.

"I don't know what that is." She looked confused, but she also looked incredibly cute pushing out her bottom lip and scowling.

"Trust me, Nat. In fact, why don't I choose the drinks for all of us?"

Ten minutes later, Natasha had a favorite new drink, and Lily was equally happy with her glass of Veuve Clicquot champagne.

"What a way to spend a Tuesday," she said as she relaxed into the surroundings and enjoyed her champagne.

"It is kinda cool," Matt agreed. "Lily, what is it you wanted to say to me earlier?"

She knew what she was going to say. She'd wanted to tell him that she really liked him as a friend, and she really appreciated his help with Natasha, but she was in a relationship—one she couldn't, and wouldn't, get out of—and he had to understand that. But now she couldn't say it. This day had been too perfect. He was being so kind. It would be cruel. "I have no idea," she said, lying. "It wasn't important. But what about you? I think you were going to say something, too."

"Uh, yes, I was, actually." Matt looked at Natasha for a moment but then he turned to Lily. "I'm moving to the Hong Kong office."

"What?"

"I'm moving to Hong Kong. In fact, that's why I was working all night. I'm kind of operating on Hong Kong time now. I love Boston and it will always be home, but it's a serious promotion and you know I want to move up the corporate ladder." He smiled at her and looked almost bashful

"Wow," she said. "It sure will be quiet around the office without you. We'll really miss you, Matt."

"You're going away?" Natasha looked panicked.

Matt squeezed her little hand. "I have a new job, Nat. A bigger one in a city called Hong Kong. It's pretty far from here, but we can Skype if you'd like. We don't have to stop being friends."

"I Skype Daddy when he's away on his airplane. I can Skype you, too." Then she turned her attention back to the enormous plate of fries that had just arrived.

Lily was still digesting the information. "Matt, I really am happy for you." Then a thought hit her. "A couple of weeks?"

"I'm wrapping things up here now."

"Wow, that's fast."

"Yep. I just wanted to tell you rather than have you hear it around the office. And while we're on the subject, I wanted to apologize for ragging on you about your promotion and your dad and all that. It was really cruel."

She gave him a tiny nod. It was difficult to talk about because deep-down she wondered if perhaps there was some truth to it. In the back of her mind, the idea had been festering ever since Matt's outburst.

"I don't want to argue with you, but do you really believe I got my promotions because of my dad?"

He shrugged. "Who knows how the minds of management work? Either way, I should never have said what I did. It was really unprofessional, not to mention idiotic. I'm sorry."

"I thought you'd already apologized for that. The lilies, remember?"

"Ah, yes, but I kind of felt that Jack Hoffman got in the middle of us that time."

"Okay, already," Natasha said. "Can I have another Shirley Temple?"

Lily was relieved that her niece was there. It kept the mood light and stopped them from saying too much. Matt seemed relieved, too. He laughed and raised his hand to get the waiter's attention. That's when Lily saw him stifle a yawn.

"Oh, Matt, I just realized you've been up all night and now we're keeping you up all day. You have to sleep some time."

He waved her concerns away. "What, and miss ice cream?" He smiled at Natasha.

The little girl looked at him and grinned, and when her multicolored sundae arrived, she looked like she'd won the lottery.

"Matt," she said digging into the mountain of dessert, "will you marry my auntie?"

Lily almost choked on her cappuccino, and even Matt was speechless for a moment. Then he burst out laughing.

"What can I say—kids."

"Yeah—kids." Lily said, but her voice came out as a squeak, and she wished the floor would open.

Then Matt leaned over the table and whispered to Natasha, "I can't even get a date with your Auntie Lily, Nat, and now I think she's in love with somebody else."

Natasha shook her head. "I know all about Uncle Jack, but I like you better," she said without taking her eyes off the ice cream.

"Maybe, but I'm moving to Hong Kong, too, so it's really not possible, honey. Now, can I have a taste of your ice cream?"

Lily just sat there, dumbfounded. How did a five-year-old come up with this stuff? What a kid. Was she really going to forfeit having babies because Jack already had his? They were going to have to have a very serious talk about children.

It was mid-afternoon by the time Matt drove them home. Lily could see how exhausted he was, having been up for over thirty hours by then.

"I would love to ask you up, but you need your sleep. Are you going back in to the office tonight?"

He nodded. "I'll work by night and sleep by day for the next few weeks, just to ramp up to the move."

"Very impressive," she mumbled.

"I could help you again tomorrow if you like."

"Yay!" Natasha bounced up and down. "Maybe we can go to the zoo or on a big boat."

Lily laughed. How could she fight her niece? "Are you sure you want to?"

"Heck yeah, it's a blast. I love kids, and it's good to clear the head after a night of number crunching."

"When will you sleep?"

"On the flight to Hong Kong."

"Go home, and go to bed right now, Matt Hamilton. If you feel like it, swing by in the morning or call me if that works better for you."

"Sounds like a plan."

Lily kissed him on the cheek and Natasha gave him a big bear hug and kiss good-bye. Then they headed into Lily's apartment.

Jack was home already. She smelled his aftershave before she saw him, and felt relieved. He must have come home to shower and clean up after a night in a hotel.

"Jack?" she called.

He met her in the living room, but he took one look at Natasha and his marble-faced stare returned. So the fight wasn't over.

"Natasha, I want you to go brush your teeth. You had a lot of ice cream this afternoon."

"I love Matt. He plays with me."

If Lily didn't know better, she would say Natasha was telling Jack about Matt on purpose. Then she pranced off. Even at five, she could see the adults were going to argue.

"Matt?" Jack asked. "The guy I met here last week?"

Lily nodded. "He's moving to Hong Kong. We had some business to discuss, so he took Nat and me out for lunch." Lily wondered why the heck she had to lie. She wasn't ashamed of going out with Matt. Nothing untoward happened.

"When is he moving?"

"A couple of weeks."

Jack nodded. He seemed to accept that there was no threat—which of course there wasn't.

"Look, Jack, we have to talk. Where did you go last night?"

He ignored her question and asked, "How long is she staying?" while jabbing his finger aggressively toward the bedroom door.

"For as long as it takes. Listen, can you and I have a civil conversation about this without it deteriorating into a fight?"

"There's nothing to discuss. You knew how I felt about children and within a few months of me moving in, you pull this stunt."

She couldn't believe what she was hearing. Was this the same man she'd fallen in love with over the last year? Her Jack was a soft, caring man with incredible warmth and charm. He was strong, too, but not bitter or selfish. What had changed?

"Jack, I didn't pull any stunt. My sister needed me and I'm helping her. I'm the same person I've always been. What I don't understand is what's come over you. I knew you didn't want kids with Sandra, but I didn't realize that meant you didn't want them with me, too. Is that what you're saying? Because I really do see children in my future, and I want you to be their father." She said it softly and tried to move toward him, but Jack backed away.

"What is it with women and babies?" he growled at her. "Lily, you know I've done the baby thing. My kids are grown. I also happen to be broke and will have to support two ex-wives very soon. Where in the hell do you think I could get the time, energy, or funds to support another baby? I can't even believe we're having this conversation. I will have another baby when hell freezes over."

She looked at him in bewildered amazement. How could their love have disintegrated so fast? Lily felt herself getting dizzy. She had to get to a chair. This was absolute madness. It just wasn't happening.

"I had no idea you felt so strongly about this," she mumbled and sat down on the sofa in the living room. "Natasha and I—we'll move back to Mom's until she and Sandra get back. We'll stay out of your hair."

"There's no need. Sandra is away and I've moved back into The Celtic Crowne until we sort this out."

"You've moved back into Sandra's?"

Jack looked impatient. "It's not Sandra's. It's mine, too, you know. And I would hardly be staying there if she was. It seems like the perfect solution. I'll move back in here when the child is gone."

"The child has a name, Jack. It's Natasha. She's my niece, and I love her. I'd thought if you loved me, you would accept her into your life willingly."

Jack didn't flinch. "Yes, well, you thought wrong."

That's when she realized what was happening. He really was moving out. This wasn't just a fight. The love of her life was moving out because of Natasha. Or was there more?

"Am I missing something here?" she asked. "Is this all about Natasha, or do you want to go back to Sandra?"

He shook his head. "Did you not hear a word I said? Of course I'm not moving back in with Sandra. She's in Ireland. I'm moving out because you're putting a child between us. You're the one who's changed the goal posts here, not me. Don't try to make me the monster. You have a simple decision to make: which do you want more? Me or kids? Because you can't have both. It's decision time, Lily."

Chapter 33

Working Girls

"It's decision time, Popsy," Sandra said in exasperation.

"It's just a karaoke night, not the Oscars."

Popsy was choosing between her black wraparound wool dress and her regular jeans. She put the jeans on again.

"I swear these are getting tight on me. I've been eating twice what I do at home. Mrs. Miller's cooking is just too good. That french onion soup at tea tonight was amazing, and as for the homemade broccoli quiche we had at lunch . . . well, I'm just eating too much."

Sandra had witnessed her friend's appetite returning and was delighted with that development. Banagher was definitely working its magic on Popsy. Actually, Sandra wasn't sure if it was Banagher or Mrs. Miller. Their landlady was a very interesting woman once you got to know her.

Popsy's near miss with the crane had seemed to unlock something inside her. When Sandra had come back to the pub after her run that afternoon, Popsy was sitting alone at the bar working on her second gin and tonic. Mrs. Miller was polishing glasses and checking on the kegs.

There were two very odd things about this scene: Popsy never drank alone, and she never touched gin. She only drank wine or champagne and now, of course there were mojitos to add to the list. Was Popsy increasing her drinking? Sandra would have been scared if Mrs. Miller hadn't given her a sort of a half-nod and a sideways glance. She had the situation in hand. With a nod back, Sandra went off to have her post-run shower.

It took her twenty minutes to get the cantankerous hot water system in the downstairs shower to work, but with a little luck she got to it just before the men came in from the marina. There was no doubt they would use up all the hot water. When she finished, she headed back up to her bedroom wrapped only in Mrs. Miller's old bath towel. That's when she met a very attractive man coming down the stairs. All he wore was a towel wrapped around his waist. He had a cute accent like Liam Neeson—Irish definitely. When she got up to her tiny bedroom, she was surprised and happy to find a hair dryer in the bedside cabinet. Before she'd finished drying her hair, Popsy arrived and flopped down on her bed.

She told Sandra how she'd almost cracked her skull open with some stupid crane down in the little port and how a nice man had saved her. But she also beat herself up about how stupid she'd been. She was angry because she knew it had been idiotic to put her own life, and the life of that nice man, in danger. Popsy had cried on Sandra's shoulder and her just blow-dried hair. What turned out to be four gin and tonics were way beyond Popsy's limit, and her perspective was understandably altered.

Popsy had told Sandra that she thought maybe it was Peter giving her a helping hand. Perhaps he was trying to get her to heaven with him. It's possible he'd spoken with The Man Upstairs, who'd given him the nod that Popsy could join Peter in heaven, and now this do-gooder had gotten in the way, and she'd missed her chance to be with him.

Sandra was nervous. There was no mention of this on the self-help websites she'd looked at. Popsy cried and wailed that it was her fault Peter was dead, and it should be her in heaven right now. She said that while she was very grateful for everything Sandra was doing, it was like putting a Band-Aid on a broken leg. It couldn't fix things. Her pain, her guilt, her shame for letting Peter die would never go away. She said it would've been better if she'd just died.

Then Popsy collapsed. Sandra thought maybe she'd gotten her wish and suffered a heart attack. She tore down the stairs to find Mrs. Miller.

"I think my friend has had a heart attack," she yelled.

The landlady followed her up the stairs but with less urgency. Sandra managed to balance the suitcases on top of each other at the bottom of her bed, so Mrs. Miller was able to walk straight in and sit next to Popsy, who was out cold. She felt for a pulse and opened Popsy's eyelids.

"You're all right, love." She turned to Sandra. "I used to be a nurse, so I can tell you I know what I'm talking about. Your friend will live. Popsy, is it?"

"No, Sandra."

"Her, I meant." Mrs. Miller pointed to Popsy. "Not you," She rolled her eyes.

"Oh, sorry. She's Popsy. I'm Sandra."

"Well, Sandra, I can tell you that your friend is not going to die. Nobody ever died of a broken heart, and that's the truth. Maybe more's the pity, but nonetheless, it's the truth. She'll be fine after a good night's sleep." Mrs. Miller got up as if to say the matter was settled.

"So she hasn't had some sort of attack?"

"No. Sure, I've had a broken heart myself. The only thing that's wrong with her outside of that is the poor child is drunk as a skunk. She'll sleep it off if you'll leave her alone now and not be at her." She turned to leave but then she spotted the sleeping pills next to Popsy's bed. "Are these hers?" she asked.

"Yes, she's used them occasionally since her husband died."

"And he's gone how long?"

"Almost four months now.

Mrs. Miller looked grave. "There's a time to use these things and a time to stop. Now is a good time to stop. Put them out of her sight, and if she asks for them, tell her you have no idea where they've gone, but tell me, too, mind. I'll get her busy enough that she sleeps—no problem."

Mrs. Miller handed the pills to Sandra.

On that Monday night, their first night in Banagher, Sandra was forced to go down to have tea by herself, because Popsy was out cold. Mrs. Miller enlisted her to "help out a bit," in the kitchen.

"The lads are always starving after a day down with the boats. I could do with a spare set of hands," she said. "You help me here now and I'll give you tea on the house."

Sandra was thrilled with the distraction. She didn't like sitting alone in a bar. In fact, she'd never done it, and she didn't want to start now. There wasn't a television in her room—not that she could have watched anyway with Popsy sound asleep, and she doubted that room service was included in their package.

Within an hour, Mrs. Miller had Sandra serving up mushroom soup and roast chicken to the guests she referred to as "the lads," in rooms one through four.

"And which of you lads is the hero that saved her nibs above asleep earlier this afternoon?" Mrs. Miller enquired when she and Sandra were clearing away the soup dishes and putting out the heaping plates of roast chicken and baked potatoes. Two of the younger men pointed to the hunky guy she'd met on the stairs earlier.

"Yeah, Shane Maloney, and why doesn't that surprise me?" Mrs. Miller asked. "You, Shane, I'd swear you have eyes at the back of your head." She patted him maternally. "Good boy. You did well. She needs lookin' after for a while. That's what Sandra here is up to. You lads be nice to my lady guests, now. No funny business. You be proper gentlemen, you hear?"

They all mumbled a promise of sorts, except Shane Maloney, who maintained a stoic silence.

Later, when Sandra was helping to wash the dishes, she said, "The guy that saved Popsy—Shane, is it?"

Mrs. Miller looked at Sandra with suspicion. "What of him?"

"Well, he just seemed a little quiet."

"That's our Shane. He's not a big talker."

"But he is big." Sandra laughed.

"And a fine-looking man he is, too. He's widowed, you know. Like your friend." Sandra got the point. She thought Shane and Popsy would be a good match.

"I'm single, too."

"Widowed?"

"No, my husband walked out on me a few months ago."

Mrs. Miller nodded sympathetically but Sandra got the feeling she felt widowhood trumped deserted wife. Then she remembered Mrs. Miller herself was a widow. Sandra chose to ignore her obvious preference for bereaved over busted up. "So, does Shane have a girlfriend?"

Sandra had made a promise to herself that if the opportunity presented itself in Ireland, she would find a little "distraction." Not a new love or anything that complicated, just plain sex. The sooner she had sex with another man, the sooner she could start rebuilding her life after Jack. Seeing Shane on the stairs sure made her remember she was a red-blooded woman. But was he on the market?

"Shane? You're barking up the wrong tree there, girl. Any of the other lads and they'd love to spend some time with you, I daresay, but Shane? I've never seen him with a woman in the fifteen years I've known him. He never got over the death of his wife, and I think he's pretty set in his ways now."

"Fifteen years? I thought he was a guest like us."

Mrs. Miller shrugged. "Some guests stay longer than others," she said.

"He is a guest, but he moved in fifteen years ago and never moved out. It was his first summer in Banagher. I think he liked working with the boats. By the end of the season he reckoned he had nothing to go back to, so he stayed here to do any work that needed doing on the boats over the winter. That was a long time ago. He runs the whole show up there now."

"Does he own the business?" Sandra asked, her hope rising. He would be even more attractive if he was rich, but Mrs. Miller shook her head.

"Lord, no. He just works on the boats off-season, but he's like a son to me now. I give him the room and he does what I need about the house. There's a lot of man's work to do around here, and my John is gone twenty-three years now. Shane helps me out all the time. He's a good boy."

"I'm sorry you lost your husband." Sandra noted that there seemed to be a lot of death in these parts.

Mrs. Miller nodded. "John's long-gone now, but I still miss him sometimes. Your friend, she has a way to go. It's a hard road, and if you don't mind me saying, I think what she really needs is to stay busy."

"What do you mean?"

"Well, she would have walked herself into an early grave if it weren't for Shane being there. She was obviously in some sort of a daydream or maybe even a living nightmare—God bless her. You should get her working; keep her mind moving. Then she won't have time to think about her loss."

"That's why I brought her to Ireland. To get away from it all for a few days."

Mrs. Miller seemed to think about this for a while. "That's all well and good, escaping for a bit, but she still has nothing to fill her mind. She needs her brain to be occupied. Like I said, you both need to work. Leave me with that. I'll have a think about it."

Sandra was grateful to have somebody to confide in. "You know, when she came up to me this evening she had this crazy idea that maybe she was supposed to die. That her husband had made is so she'd hit by the crane so she could join him."

Mrs. Miller didn't seem to think this was crazy at all. "Well, if he did, a higher force put Shane in her path and brought her back to earth with a thud. She's meant to be here, and so are you. It's all part of His plan." Mrs. Miller glanced up at the ceiling respectfully.

Sandra was not a big believer in "master plans," but her companion seemed so convinced, she didn't dare argue.

"Come on, so," Mrs. Miller said. "Those boys will be ready for apple pie by now."

The next day, Tuesday, Popsy suffered with her worst hangover in years but other than that the day seemed to fly by. They started the day by checking up on the volcano. Their cell phones didn't work at all, but Popsy used a pay phone and managed to talk to Lily who assured her that all was well in Boston and promised she'd talk to Rosie.

With the day stretching in front of them, they took a long country walk, and by the time they got back, Mrs. Miller had a list of chores for them to do. She told them if they helped out enough, she would halve their boarding fee, which was kind of funny because they didn't know what they were paying anyway but figured it couldn't be that much.

Even though it was work, something neither woman was used to, they still enjoyed themselves. Sandra seemed to have an affinity for the bar. She quickly learned how to change a keg and run the glass washer. It was odd that Mrs. Miller had one of those and not a regular dishwasher. She learned how to work the till, but still had difficulty figuring out the euro coins.

It was all too funny because there was nobody actually in the pub. Life in The Boathouse was quiet and had a rhythm. The men went off in the morning and the ladies puttered about the house. Mrs. Miller tried to pique Sandra's interest in cooking, too, but that hadn't worked out so well. Her attention span just didn't stretch that far, and Tuesday's red pepper quiche wasn't as good as usual.

Meanwhile, Mrs. Miller got Popsy into the garden. "You've come to me at a great time, *a gra*," she said. Popsy remembered that *a gra* was Irish for 'love.' It was a term of endearment and often a maternal sort of pet name. She liked Mrs. Miller using it with her. "I'm behind on the work, truth be told. I got all the spring bulbs down in plenty of time last autumn, but I've done nothing about the seeds that should be in the soil these last three weeks. There's spring cuttings to be taken, too,"

Popsy didn't quite understand what she was supposed to do, nor could she make out all of Mrs. Miller's words because the Kerry accent was so strong, but she was happy to watch the woman at work and copy what she did.

They started in the potting shed. Popsy thought the room was like a scene from a Harry Potter movie. It was small and musty but quite beautiful. A potting table stood under the small window that overlooked the river. The panes of glass were green around the corners. Terracotta pots of varying sizes were perched on dusty shelves in no particular order. In the corner stood a stack of different gardening tools—shovels, hoes, rakes and others she didn't recognize. It was organized chaos and lovely to Popsy.

Mrs. Miller showed her how to mix the correct ratio of soil and vermiculite into clean trays and then dampen it down. Then she gave her an envelope of seeds. "I collected these from the penstemon last year. They're mighty flowers. They love it here. Spread them thin over the soil, girl."

Mrs. Miller dropped a few seeds onto the soil to show Popsy how it was done and then she took over. She'd never tried to sow seeds before. It was incredibly satisfying and all-absorbing. When she was happy the tiny seeds were settled and well spaced out, Mrs. Miller showed her how to cover the tray in plastic wrap to make it airtight.

"They need to fight for life. It's hard work cracking out of that little seed you know," she said. "Life is hard for all of us, but it's worth it, and that's the truth." Mrs. Miller didn't look up so Popsy wasn't sure whether she was talking to the seedlings or herself, or to Popsy. It didn't really matter.

When the seedlings were all settled, Mrs. Miller gave her a small jar of hormone rooting powder. "This helps the plant to make new roots," she explained. "Mind it well, because it works on humans, too." She winked.

Popsy was intrigued. What was Mrs. Miller saying? That she should put down new roots? Why was she telling her to do that?

Out came a set of terracotta pots that Mrs. Miller filled with a mixture of soils. "This is a different mix to what the seedlings want, mind you," she said. "Seeds need a light, feathery soil for their tiny roots. Cuttings like something with a bit more substance, more grit."

"Oh, okay," Popsy said, a little surprised.

"Well, a baby takes a different bed to a full-grown person, don't they?" she said as she examined one of the pots. "It's the same with plants." When she said it like that, it made perfect sense.

As soon as their pots were good to go, Mrs. Miller took her out into the garden, both of them armed with sharp scissors and garden gloves. She showed Popsy how to take a cutting from the lavender. Then she brought her over to the hydrangeas and dogwoods. With each plant, Mrs. Miller showed her how to take the cutting from the mother plant, dip it in rooting powder, and then punch a hole in the soil with her little finger to settle the tiny new plant into its new home.

"And these will grow into big new plants?" Popsy asked, enthralled.

"Only if we give them the right care. As of now, they're very vulnerable.

They've lost their support system. It will take time for them to become self-sufficient, but they will and what's more, they'll bloom beautifully, much like humans." This time Popsy was pretty sure Mrs. Miller was referring to her, even though she hadn't looked at her directly.

After the cuttings were settled, she learned how to wrap the little pots in airtight plastic bags to encourage the new growth, and then they put them in the heated glasshouse to keep them warm and get as much light as possible. The afternoon flew by.

Later on, Popsy and Sandra helped her serve up food for "the lads," and then the three women ate together.

"So, I have you for as long as that volcano blows?" Mrs. Miller asked.

Popsy nodded. "Then it will be time to go home."

"Well, doesn't God work in mysterious ways?"

Popsy wasn't so sure. She glanced over to where Shane sat with the men. They hadn't spoken since he'd saved her life except for one time when she felt the need to thank him again. He seemed embarrassed and abruptly distant. She didn't want to make him uncomfortable, and now she avoided him. Deep-down, she still didn't know whether she was grateful he'd saved her life or if she hated him for it.

Popsy and Sandra were happy to fall into bed early on Tuesday night after all the fresh air, and Mrs. Miller had warned them that Wednesday night would be "late." She said, "They come from all around for the Wednesday Karaoke Night." It sounded like fun.

The following morning, Mrs. Miller said she'd already checked the news and all the airports were still closed, so Popsy phoned Lily again. She reassured them, again, that all was well, and she would stay in touch with Rosie.

Then she and Sandra went for their morning walk and afterward Sandra decided to go into town for a little exploration. Popsy was more than happy to stay in the garden with Mrs. Miller. Wednesday's lesson was all about seed sorting. She learned all there was to know about how to harvest the seeds from the big daisy heads of the rudbeckia and black-eyed Susans. She got firsthand tutoring on the differences between annual and perennial sunflowers and the lovely lupines that threw up mighty spires of color in the early spring. Mrs. Miller was a great believer in seed soaking. Popsy learned a lot and loved it.

Later in the afternoon, she came to Popsy with a small bundle of envelopes labeled with the different seeds.

"Take these home with you when you go, *a gra*," she said. "These flowers, when they bloom, will remind you of your time with us." Popsy was so grateful she almost cried. Her days in the garden were the only time she felt relief from the pain of losing Peter. The seeds offered hope for the future—something she was lacking. She treasured the gift and promised to plant them with care when she got home.

For all of her time in Ireland, she'd managed to avoid thinking about her home. It wouldn't be hers for much longer. The lawyers were talking to the banks. She had enough money, thanks to Peter, but the property portfolio was all going to go into the vortex of debt. Where would she go? Where would she live?

"Are you all right, *a gra*? Do you not like the seeds?"

"No. Yes. No, I love the seeds. I just don't know where home is anymore," she said honestly.

Mrs. Miller nodded with sympathy.

"Don't think about that now, *a gra*. Go and get ready for the karaoke night. It's a real bit of fun, now. Put something pretty on. It will give you a good laugh to see all of us doing our thing. It's the highlight of my week. You'll see."

"So, you think I should wear the jeans?" Popsy asked.

"No, I think you should wear the dress. It's so pretty."

"Oh darn. Okay." Popsy groaned.

Sandra was just about to ask why Popsy was so worried about what she was going to wear, when she realized that Popsy cared. She actually cared. Was she starting to live again? Had a few days with Mrs. Miller put her back on the road to recovery? Maybe the old Popsy was coming back.

"Wear the dress," she said with even more enthusiasm now. "We're going to have a terrific night and that's an order! Karaoke, here we come. What're you gonna sing anyway?"

Popsy swung around. "I'm not singing," she said, with a horrified look on her face. "I'll just watch everybody else."

"Now, Popsy, what if everybody said that?" Sandra argued, picking up her hairbrush and pretending to use at as a microphone. "You have to join in, too, you know. You can't just be a spectator."

Chapter 34

Rosie Swims With the Big Fish

"You can't spend the week just being a spectator. You're gonna have to jump in some time, honey." He was unhappy with her reluctance to try out the playroom.

He'd told her on Tuesday afternoon when he first tried it that it was pretty wild because you could see what everyone else was doing. "You wouldn't want to have a case of performance anxiety," he'd said and laughed nervously.

Rosie was happy to stand her ground. She didn't make a big deal about it, but now that she knew she wasn't alone, it gave her a boost of confidence. "If that does it for you, go ahead, but personally I would like any and all of my encounters to be discreet." Sam agreed it was a good idea to let Marcus believe she'd been with other men. He'd managed to navigate his way through this crazy situation already, so she figured the best thing to do was to follow his lead.

Tuesday passed much as Monday had. Rosie enjoyed the sun all day. Once or twice she saw men give her an appreciative stare, but she shook her head and they took the hint. Other than that, she read and enjoyed the glorious Caribbean sun. She was turning a nice nutmeg brown, and she loved getting through a book a day.

Marcus was up and down like a rabbit, and that's not all he was doing like a rabbit. Strange as it was, it didn't seem to bother her anymore. As the days progressed, Rosie came to understand she no longer cared what her husband was doing. What had bothered her prior to the vacation was the idea she might have to do the same thing. For Marcus, it really did seem to be just a physical act. He wanted to have sex with other women. Maybe it was a caveman thing. Airline pilots were notorious for cheating. Marcus, at least, had the decency to communicate his needs. As long as she wasn't expected to get involved, she was happy.

Early Tuesday evening, they again retired to their room together after a few cocktails, and Marcus had slept with her. He consistently reminded her there were condoms everywhere and there was no chance of either of them catching anything if they were careful. She thought it was funny that he was trying to reassure her. How could he ever reassure her about anything while he was openly sleeping around? She slept with him willingly because she hoped it would bring him back to her. The more he was with her, the less he could be with others.

Tonight was toga night. Twice during the day she'd seen Sam, once at lunchtime and another in the middle of the afternoon. On both occasions, Marcus had been with her, so Sam didn't make any indication that he knew her.

It was kind of amusing that she was the one having the clandestine affair. She was friends with a man she was actively *not* having sex with. Marcus would be scandalized.

The music had turned to a slow set and Marcus had gone to the bathroom, so Rosie left the restaurant, not wanting to get asked to dance by some other lecherous husband. She decided to go admire the sea view by night and sat down at the water's edge. Just like the daytime, there were pleasure boats out on the water, but now it was pitch-black. All she could see were the lights on the boats as the calypso music skirted along the water's surface.

"They look inviting, don't they?" Sam said as he came up behind her.

Rosie swung around. "Oh, I didn't hear you. Hi, Sam, it really is beautiful here, isn't it?"

He sat down beside her. Like everyone else, Sam was wearing a white bed sheet wrapped around his body to look like a roman emperor. He'd also managed to get a crown of laurel leaves, which gave him the edge.

"How did you find a Roman crown?" she asked.

Sam felt the headpiece. "There's been a toga party on every Broader Horizons vacation I've ever been on. At this stage, Cindy packs them as a matter of course."

"I think I saw your wife tonight. Is she the one dressed as a Roman slave?"

Sam looked a little embarrassed. "That's her. She brought her own costume."

It was without doubt the most suggestive costume at the party. Cindy Sinnott had what could best be described as three very small bits of leather bound together by thin strips of leather and a few laces. She also wore thin, flat gladiator sandals, the straps of which wrapped up her legs as far as her knees, and she had a dog collar around her neck. There was no way she was going home alone.

"Does it bother you?" Rosie asked.

Sam looked resigned. "Hey, if it makes her happy, who am I to get in the way?"

Despite what he said, she could tell it bothered him.

"Rosie, I was thinking of heading out on the water tomorrow. I hear Playa del Carmen is a great spot. Loads to do. I was just going to go on one of those catamaran group rentals. I'm okay to do it alone, but would you like to get out of Broader Horizons for the day?"

Rosie didn't need to think about it. "I'd love to. What time are you leaving?"

"Say we meet at the front door around ten a.m.?"

"Oh, Sam, that really sounds fantastic. Count me in. I'll be there. Thanks."

The first thing Rosie did when she woke on Wednesday was call her sister. They got all the news stations on the TV in her room, so she knew Europe was still trapped in a plume of volcanic ash, but Lily insisted she and Natasha were still fine. It was only when Rosie spoke to her daughter that she heard all about Matt. The big question for Rosie was: where was Jack? Didn't he mind? Then again, who was she to talk? She was heading out on a catamaran with a man who wasn't her husband, while Marcus got up to Lord knows what.

She didn't need to make her excuses to Marcus before she left their hotel room, because he wasn't there.

Rosie had chosen her navy bikini and a navy pair of cotton shorts for her sailing day, along with a blue-and-white striped T-shirt and her large dark sunglasses. She remembered a beach towel but decided against her wide-brimmed hat.

When she got to the lobby, Sam saw her and smiled.

"Wow, I'm a lucky guy," he said. Then, as if it was the most natural thing in the world, she kissed him on the cheek. It just felt right. She really liked him—not in a physical way, but as a good friend. They caught a taxi into town, which was already buzzing with activity.

"Marcus didn't even come home last night."

"Neither did Cindy. I wouldn't worry about it, though. They probably just fell asleep in some room or another," he said. Rosie took strength from this and decided to put the whole thing out of her mind.

Be an ostrich, she reminded herself.

~*~

It was a glorious day. She was going out on the water with a new friend. Life was good.

"Playa del Carmen is a lot bigger than I thought it would be," she said as she watched the buildings whizz by.

"Yes, I read up on it. I think it has around one hundred fifty thousand people, and that's without the tourists, but it's the water that blows my mind. People know about the Caribbean islands, but this is just as beautiful. It's still the Caribbean Sea."

Rosie was embarrassed. They were down at the port and Sam paid the taxi driver. "I thought that was the Gulf of Mexico," she said and pointed to the ocean.

Sam didn't laugh. "You would be right if we were farther north. Most of the east coast of Mexico overlooks the Gulf of Mexico but from Cancun, where we flew into, looks out over the Caribbean Sea."

"Well, what do you know? Who would have thought geography could be so much fun?" She laughed. "Now, which way do we go?"

Sam and Rosie walked along the port like any other couple on vacation. Some of the shops were only starting to open. For the most part, they sold souvenirs, "I love Mexico" T-shirts, or postcards. There were a lot of tequila glasses for sale and, of course, sombreros. Rosie knew they were in a big tourist spot, but it was just so good to get out of Broader Horizons.

"I have to admit, I'm so happy to be away from that place for a few hours," she said.

"Is it still really upsetting you?"

"Well, yes. I mean, my guard is always up. I'm scared somebody is going to hit on me at every turn, and I'm just trying not to think about what Marcus is doing. I'll just bury it deep inside me and never deal with it," she said as they walked onto the next shop display.

Sam said nothing but looked at her intently. It was clear that he was listening to her and taking her seriously. She liked that.

"We have this thing we do." She picked up a set of maracas that were on display. "It sounds crazy. Marcus and I pretend to be like an ostrich. When there's something we don't want to deal with, we just bury our heads and let it pass over us."

Sam raised an eyebrow and nodded.

"You think I'm nuts?" She shook the maracas, but they were very loud so she dropped them back onto the display table.

He smiled. "No, not at all. Some problems are worth ignoring and they simply pass, but others, you really need to talk about. I guess time will tell which category this falls into. The ostrich, you say? I like it. Maybe that's what I'm doing about Cindy's wild ways," he added with a smile.

They walked some more and then he spotted the boat rental sign. "Here we are. I saw the pamphlet for it in the hotel lobby and decided to investigate," he said.

Then he put his arm around the small of her back as if to usher her in a gentle fashion. To Rosie, it was just a friendly gesture, but to any onlooker, they looked like the perfect couple.

She'd brought her money and had every intention of paying for her ticket, but Sam insisted on treating her. "It's not a date. It's just one friend taking another friend out."

Rosie thought he was very gallant, and in the end, she accepted.

Carlos, who skippered the catamaran, took the money, gave Sam the tickets, and told them to come back at noon. They would be driven to the boat which was docked in Puerto Aventuras.

Since they had a little time to spare, Rosie suggested breakfast in a waterfront cafe. They were soon sitting down with strong coffees and a couple of pastries.

"So, I'm guessing your mother is back from Ireland."

Rosie had forgotten how much she'd shared with him at their last lunch together. It was nice that he remembered.

"No, there's a big volcano that's stopped all air traffic in Ireland and most of northern Europe. Mom and her friend are stuck. My sister has taken over babysitting my little girl."

"She's five, right?"

Again, that nice feeling of being with someone who listened to her. "Yes. Her name's Natasha. This is the first time I've been away from her in five years, and my mom is supposed to be babysitting along with a nanny, and she goes and gets stranded in Ireland. What are the chances of that, I ask you?"

Sam bit into the apple-filled pastry and crumbs fell everywhere. Rosie found him endearing.

"But you're okay with your sister taking care of her?"

She bit into her strawberry-filled Danish and nodded.

"It's great to have a sibling you can trust. I only have one brother and all he's ever done is take from me. He's borrowed thousands of dollars over the years, which I know I'll never see again. He even made a pass at my first wife. He really is a waste of space."

"Oh, I'm sorry to hear that. Do you see him much?"

Sam shook his head. "As little as possible. But your sister seems to have your back. That's how it should be. You're lucky."

Rosie thought about all the fights she and Lily had of late. "To be honest, we haven't been getting along that well. I really disapprove of some of her life choices, and she went crazy when I told her about my coming here."

"You told her?"

Rosie nodded guiltily. "Mistake?"

He gave her a sideways glance. "I'd say so. It's not the sort of thing you tell folks. They would think you're, well, crazy. And on top of that, they might believe you'd try to try to steal their partner."

Rosie's face fell. "Small chance of that in my sister's case. She's living with my godfather."

"As in living with—romantically?"

"Yes. We're not related to him by blood. He was Dad's best friend and business partner, so it's all kind of messy at home. He's also about a hundred years older than she is, but for some reason, she loves him. He walked out on his wife, who happens to be Mom's best friend. That's who Mom is in Ireland with right now. We're all so damn incestuous."

Sam wiped his mouth with a napkin. "I'll say. Sounds like you guys need to get some space between you. Why do you all live in each other's pockets?"

Rosie shrugged. "I don't know. Boston is a great town. Where we live, it's really beautiful. None of us wanted to move. Lily moved away for college, but when the job came up near home, she was back like a shot."

"I know Boston's good. A lot of my neighbors are snowbirds. They come down to Florida during the New England winter, and then head back up north for your summers."

"That's what Mom and Dad used to do. I'm not sure what she'll do now. I'm afraid Dad's business went into Chapter 11 just before he died. I'm not sure what sort of financial position my mom will be in when the dust settles."

"I'm sorry to hear that," he said.

"Oh, I don't think she'll go hungry—well, I hope not. I mean, I'd take her in before I'd see that happen, but she knows her house will have to go, and that will be hard. They also have a place in Palm Beach. I'm pretty sure that won't last, either." Suddenly Rosie was a million miles away as she thought about her poor mom's situation and her dad—gone too soon.

Sam squeezed her hand. "Rosie, it will get better."

She snapped back to reality when she felt his hand. It was nothing, of course—just one friend reassuring another, but still. She pulled her hand back. He seemed to understand.

"I'm sorry," he said.

"No, I'm sorry. You're being so kind to me, and I'm acting like a spoiled brat." The truth was, she was terrified of giving him mixed messages. She didn't want to have sex with him. She just wanted a friend.

He seemed to sense where she was coming from. "You're not a spoiled brat." He smiled. "You're a magnificent woman. A strong woman with your own sense of values, which, for the record, I think are right on. You sound like a pretty terrific daughter and mother, too, so cut yourself a little slack if you and your sister aren't on the best of terms right now. Maybe your ostrich thing has some merit." He smiled again. "Just do the ostrich with your sister until it blows over. If I was a betting man, I'd say she and this older guy thing will run its course and she'll come to her senses. Just you wait and see."

"Thanks for saying that."

"No problem. Now, let's go and find our boat."

A little while later, Rosie and Sam were among a group of about twenty tourists on an incredible sixty-five foot deluxe Catamaran. It was her first time, and she was amazed how much room there was on board. Almost immediately, the engines started up and the boat made its way out of the marina of Puerto Aventuras.

There were so many pleasure boats of varying sizes around them. Everybody was on vacation, and the atmosphere was terrific. It was hard to remember that it was a chilly mid-February back in Boston while the sun was beating down on them in the Caribbean Sea. As soon as they were clear of the harbor, they let the sails up and out. It was exciting watching the enormous wall of white unfurl and billow as it filled up with wind. Then the momentum changed as the engines were cut and the sails took over. Everything seemed to go quiet.

"Enjoying this?" Sam asked.

"Yes, it's amazing. Funny, Boston is on the coast, but we're not boating people. We have friends that have a power boat and they've taken us out a few times into Boston Harbor, but sailing is a whole different experience."

Sam said, "I'm big into sailing. I have a boat in Miami, but I still like this." He walked across the deck and then looked back to her. "Come and sit on the netting."

At the front of the boat, instead of having a normal boat deck, there were two large sheets of thick netting through which you could see the water. If you were to drop something, it would be lost forever into the sea, she realized, and double-checked that her wedding ring was snugly on her hand.

Rosie was a little nervous at first, but after watching the others do it, she felt reassured. People put their towels out and lay on them. Rosie and Sam followed. It was very refreshing, too. Almost as refreshing as the cocktails they served as soon as they were clear of the port. The music was cranked up, and the atmosphere was festive.

About forty-five minutes later, they arrived at what the skipper told them were the most magnificent coral reefs along the Mayan Riviera: the Xpu-Ha Reef.

"Wanna snorkel?" Sam asked.

"What? With tanks? I don't know how."

He shook his head. "You worry too much. It's just with foot fins, a snorkel, and a face mask."

"It's not the sort of face mask I'm used to," Rosie said, thinking about her regular facials back at the spa in Boston.

"I have a PADI cert. I'll take care of you."

"A what?"

"It's the Professional Association of Diving Instructors. It just means I know how to dive with tanks, so we should be okay with just a little snorkel. No tanks, I promise. At least not today."

One of the crew came up to them. "You gonna snorkel?" he asked with a bright smile and a broad Caribbean accent.

Rosie only had to think about it for a moment. "We are," she said, and then looked anxiously at Sam. "But you won't leave my side, will you?"

He shook his head. "Not for a second."

The boat stopped at a point where the water was so clear, the seafloor was visible.

"He tells me the water is only six to twenty-feet deep here. If we stay where it's shallow, it'll be no different than being in the swimming pool back at the hotel."

Sam was trying to reassure her, but she was okay.

"No, this is fine. It's just so beautiful," she said, looking into the water.

Without even getting wet, they could appreciate the teeming sea life. It seemed like thousands of tiny fish were swimming around the boat in perfect synchronicity.

They got fixed up with fins and snorkels, and then Sam headed down the steps at the back of the boat. Once in the water, he gestured for Rosie to follow. She was a little clumsy with her fins, but soon she was swimming over to him with her mask on and her snorkel in her mouth. He gave her the okay sign which he'd already explained was an international diving sign for letting the other person know everything was fine. She nodded and tried to talk, but it was impossible with the snorkel in her mouth. That's when Sam took her by the hand and swam away from the boat. He put his face in the water, and she copied him. She'd played around with snorkels when she was a kid, but it had been a long time ago. Not unlike riding a bike, it came back pretty fast, and she was soon distracted and forgot to be nervous.

The fish were impressive when she'd seen them from up on the catamaran, but they were even more stunning when she was actually in the water with them. There were large canary-yellow fish the size of dinner plates. From the side they looked huge, but when they turned to swim away, Rosie saw how tall and skinny they were. There was also a bizarre-shaped, spiky fish that was black and white like a zebra.

All the while, she held Sam's reassuring hand and followed his lead. At one point he tugged her hand to get her attention, and she looked up. He was pointing far away, and even though the water was crystal clear, at a distance of fifty feet the sheer volume of water meant she couldn't see well. She shook her head, but he was insistent. He kept stabbing his index finger to get her to keep watching, and that's when she saw something big— perhaps as big as she was—swimming toward them. Rosie's first instinct was to panic. Was it a shark? She squeezed Sam's hand hard, but his expression gave her the security she needed.

He shook his head and gave her the scuba "okay" sign again. The fish came closer, and that's when Rosie understood it wasn't a fish at all. It was a beautiful, graceful, and totally free dolphin. She squealed in delight through her snorkel. The creature whizzed by them with unbelievable speed and circled some other tourists, too. Maybe the dolphins were used to tourists, and they came to visit the catamaran on a regular basis, but for Rosie, it was the highlight of her vacation.

Before they were even back on the boat, she was saying, "Ohmygod, Ohmygod, Sam that was just the most amazing thing I've ever seen in my life. Wasn't she beautiful? Did you see how fast she was? I had no idea they could move so fast." She clambered up the steps as she babbled with excitement.

"What a truly un-be-lieve-able experience! Thank you, Sam. Thank you for taking me out here today. So much better than sitting in the complex and reading."

He laughed. "If you liked that, you might like to try the tanks sometime."

"You know, I really think I'd like to investigate that possibility," she said brightly.

After their dive, the crew presented them with more cocktails and a perfect lunch of steak or fresh fish. Rosie didn't have the heart to eat fish, having just met some face-to-face, so she stuck to the side salad, but Sam had no such qualms. He dug into an enormous plate of fresh lobster as they sailed along the beautiful coast of the Mayan Riviera.

By the time they got back to their hotel, they were both tired but very happy.

"I really can't thank you enough, Sam," Rosie said for the umpteenth time.

~*~

When she met Marcus later that afternoon, he commented on her mood and even deeper tan.

"Hey, babe, you look really great. Seems like the Mexican air suits you. I'm guessing you had a good day?'

"The best." She had every intention of telling him what she did. She just wasn't going to mention Sam. It would be easy to say that she went into town to explore a little but got sidetracked and ended up on a catamaran. That was all pretty close to the truth, but Marcus didn't give her the opportunity.

"Shhh." He kissed her on the mouth. "No details. It's enough for me to know you're 'getting into the swing of things,' as they say around here." He smiled. "I just want to know when you're going to try out the playroom," he said, teasing her again. "That's where all the sharks are."

"Ah," she said with a twinkle in her eye. "But, you see, I think I'm more of a dolphin girl myself."

"Okay," he said, and let the matter drop.

Chapter 35

Lily's Lunch

"No, I will not let this matter drop." Emily refilled her and Lily's wine glasses. They were supposed to go out together for a girls' night, but Lily explained that she'd acquired a live-in-niece, and the farthest she was going was to her kitchen.

Now that Natasha had finally gone to bed, Emily wanted to hear everything.

"So, he moved out of here and back into his old apartment that he shared with his wife?" she asked.

"Yep, that's it in a nutshell. Sandra's not there and I think she'd be furious if she knew, but I'm not telling her, and I doubt he has, either. I don't think they're talking much." Lily was miserable. "I don't know who he's talking to these days. He seems to be angry with everybody and everything."

"Watching Cap & Jet fail couldn't have been easy. Did you see the article on it in *The Sunday Globe* a few weeks back?" Emily asked tentatively.

"No. He never mentioned it. Was it bad?"

"Pretty much. It said the business was more like 'Cap in Hand,' as in begging for money. Sorry."

Lily shrugged. "There's not much any of us can do about it now."

"Where did the name 'Cap & Jet' come from anyway? I always assumed it had something to do with the aviation industry."

Lily laughed. "They liked that idea in the beginning. They passed themselves off as big shots even when they were only starting out. I've heard the story loads of times. When they were going into business together, they couldn't come up with a name. It was going to be something simple like 'Peter and Jack Industries' or 'Jack and Peter Industries.' But they were so darn competitive, they couldn't even agree on whose name should come first, so they came up with the idea of an anagram."

"What?"

Lily got a pen and paper and began writing. "Take the first three letters from each of their names P,E,T, J,A,C and then add the A,N,D into the mix, and you come up with Cap & Jet."

"How clever." Emily laughed.

"Mmhm, and their logo was a cartoon of a little smiling airplane with a flat cap on its head. I still remember it well. Of course, they let go of the old logo when it became outdated and the company grew. Then they came up with something more abstract and abbreviated it to C&J. But that's how the name came about."

"I doubt many people know that."

"I doubt many people know most things. God, I miss Dad," Lily said. She put her wine down on the floor and curled up in a ball on the sofa.

"You have a lot to deal with, Lily." Emily stroked her hair. "I know it's hard, what with running after Nat all day, but have you had a chance to think about your, uh, discussion with Jack?"

"Discussion? Is that what you'd call it?"

"Okay then, argument."

"I think 'full-scale war' might be closer to the mark," Lily said. "I mean, he's moved out and told me to make up my mind. That it's him or kids." She picked up her glass again.

"Well, that's the part I was subtly trying to get to. Have you thought about that?"

Lily shrugged. "I guess that's all I'm thinking about. We really should have discussed this months ago, at the early stage of our relationship. I knew he and Sandra didn't have kids, but I assumed it was her choice. I mean, she's kind of a gym bunny and, of course, she's old."

"How old is she?"

"Same as Mom, I think. Maybe a bit younger, so heading toward fifty. I mean, come on, of course she's not going to have kids, but what about me? If I want kids, it's going to be in the next six or seven years. I was kind of thinking I'd like two."

Emily continued stroking Lily's hair. "So, you do want kids?"

Lily pulled her head away, but she really wanted to pull away from the question. "Oh gawd, Em. What do I know? We only moved in together a few months ago. There was bound to be a few adjustments. I mean, there always is, isn't there?" She needed advice, but Emily was looking blankly at her. "All relationships go through ups and downs. What about you and Richard? You went through it. We're supposed to work through these things together, maybe get counseling."

Emily slapped her forehead. "Counseling? That's for couples who are together a long time and need to get things straightened out. But you? You should still be in the blissful honeymoon phase. You just started living together. In fact, you're not even living together anymore. He's moved out, remember?"

"What are you saying?" Lily was nervous.

Emily put her glass down and stood. Then she put her hands on her hips and stared at Lily. "I'm saying, *run*. Run as fast as you can. You've never been the best judge of men, but you really excelled this time. Jack Hoffman is so *not* the man for you. He is a bitter, selfish, twisted old man, and he will always try to dominate you and boss you around."

Lily started to cry and Emily sat down and wrapped her arms around her. "I'm sorry I was so harsh, Lil, but you're not thinking straight. I don't know what you see in this guy, but you have to trust me. He's not the one for you.'

"You don't understand. I can't pull out now. Dad is dead, Sandra is heartbroken, and I've committed to Jack. I can't go back. If I do, Dad will have died for nothing. I will have destroyed Sandra's marriage for nothing. And as for Jack? I know you don't think so, but he loves me. Really, he does. He just doesn't want kids."

"I guess we all make mistakes as we plod along through life, but the point is, when we realize we've screwed up, or we just come to the conclusion that something isn't working, the plan should be to fix it. You didn't kill your dad. He had a heart problem."

"I darn well didn't help."

"And what about the collapse of his business? And his lifestyle? No, you have to let that go. Your dad was the captain of his own ship. But here's the thing. You're the captain of yours, not Jack. You have to do a lot of soul-searching and decide if you want kids or not. If you do, you have to get out."

"Maybe I could live without children," Lily said without conviction.

"Yeah, and maybe I could live without wine. But I don't want to. I love wine and for the record, even with all my complaining, I love my kids, too. They make sense of life. Don't sell yourself short."

"Don't talk to me about selling short." Lily groaned. She'd gotten into serious trouble at work after her very unprofessional conduct. The HR department had phoned her about her high level of absenteeism, and even Mr. Jones had called her. He expressed his "concern" about her apparent lack of focus. Lily had tried to assure him that she was going through some particularly extraneous circumstances, but he didn't sound convinced. He even went so far as to suggest that a less stressful role in the company might be attractive to her if things other than work were occupying her time. Matt's warning rang in her ears. Was a job offer in the Antarctic in the cards? She knew she was going to get a demotion if she didn't step up to her responsibilities, but she just couldn't find the motivation.

Emily got to her feet again, but this time she pulled Lily by the hand. "Stand up."

"What are you doing?" Lily laughed and got up with reluctance.

Emily looked around the room. "Where is there a mirror in this place?"

"What do you want a mirror for?"

"Just tell me where we can find a full-length mirror."

"In the bedroom. Why?"

"Come on, I want to show you something." She pulled Lily along as she might do with her own kids, until they got to the promised full-length mirror. Then Emily made Lily stand in front of it. "Now, tell me what you see."

Lily dropped her gaze to the floor and pulled her sweater sleeves down over her hands. She tried to turn away. "Oh, Emily, can't we just sit down and talk?"

But Emily held Lily's shoulders firmly and made her square up to the mirror. "Humor me. Just tell me what you see."

Lily took in an enormous lungful of air for support. There was no way she was going to get away from Emily, so she may as well go through with this crazy game.

"I see a woman with bullfrog-bloated eyes and hair that needs a good wash. You know, I am kind of mess, now that I look at myself."

"Look deeper. I'm serious, Lily. What do you see?"

Lily studied her reflection a bit more seriously this time.

"Look deeper," Emily said again.

Lily tried to. She ignored the puffy eyes and the straggly hair and looked at herself from the top of her head down to the chipped nail polish on her toes. Her pedicure needed redoing. She was not taking very good care of herself. Slowly she looked back up her body again until she was staring into her own eyes. They looked back at her.

"Empty," she whispered.

Emily softened her grip on Lily's shoulders but kept her looking at the mirror. "Good girl." She spoke softly. "That's good. Now, tell me, what else do you see?"

"Lost, hurt, stupid, stupid, stupid." She started to cry again.

Emily turned Lily around and hugged her. "There, there, it's okay, Lily. This is all going to pass. I know you don't believe me, but things will improve, I promise."

"How can you say that? How do you know?"

"I just know." She took Lily by the hand and brought her back out to the sofa where she picked up her wine glass. "You did really well. I'm proud of you."

"What was that?"

"I saw Dr. Phil do it one time. Evidently it makes you face yourself or something like that, but here's the thing: you said you were empty and lost."

"And stupid."

"Yeah, well, I'm going to ignore that part because we both know you're not stupid. A little misguided, maybe, but not stupid. So my question to you is, if Jack is the right guy, why are you feeling lost and empty?"

The question hung in the air as they sat in silence for a moment. Then Emily said, "A good relationship with anybody, not just your lover, should make you feel good about yourself. You should feel secure. Take you and me, for example. Okay, we're not lovers, but as friends we build each other up. We support each other and care for each other. You should have that times ten with the love in your life. I don't think Jack builds you up, I think he undermines you, and to be honest, over the last twelve months, I think he's eaten away at your self-confidence to the extent that you're now lost and empty. Your words, not mine."

Lily sat back, deep into the cushions with her knees up to her chest and her arms clasped around them, while Emily sat on the edge.

"You know what I see? I see a beautiful, young, intelligent woman with her whole life ahead of her. I see a woman who *should* have children with a man who wants them, too. I see a woman who's being exploited and destroyed by the man she loves. He's toxic. You have to break free. I'll help you, but you have to cut loose from Jack."

"Seriously? After all the damage I've done, you think I should just throw in the towel and give up?'

"You're not giving up. You're fixing."

"What about Sandra?"

"Stop thinking about everyone else. Focus on you."

"And Dad?"

"Hello. We've been over this. Just tell me you'll think about what I've said. Okay?"

"Okay."

"Tell me about today." She sat back.

For the first time all night, Lily smiled.

"It really was wonderful. Matt's a good friend."

"Isn't he?"

"That's all he is, you know. We're just good friends."

"Lily Power, did you just use that line? Are you for real?"

"But it's true. Did you know he's going to Hong Kong?"

"Yeah, and I know you think he's too young for you. Too bad. Anyway, tell me about your day."

Lily had slept in because she'd cried herself to sleep after her fight with Jack. He didn't take all of his stuff, but it felt a lot like a breakup. He'd insisted it wasn't. He was just giving her space to decide whether she wanted to move forward or not.

Her phone woke her after eight, and it was Matt.

"Have you guys made plans yet?" he'd asked, full of enthusiasm.

"Morning, Matt," was all she managed. "Us guys?"

"You and Natasha. Because I have an idea. Can you meet me down at the marina in about two hours?"

"What are you talking about?" She wasn't fully awake yet, and nothing he said was making sense.

"Guess you really were asleep. The marina in the harbor you can see from your apartment."

"Oh, that marina. Why? Do you have a boat down there?" Everybody knew the price to dock in Boston's downtown marina was sky-high, and she'd never heard Matt mention a boat before.

"I'm not telling you anything yet. Just get yourself and Natasha down to the clubhouse at, shall we say, ten-thirty?"

She and Natasha gulped down a quick breakfast and then went back to

Cliff Road to check on Matilda and get word from Ireland. There was still no sign Popsy and Sandra would be home any time soon. Finally, they took a quick detour out to Weston to get Natasha some warmer clothes. By the time they reached Matt, they were already half an hour behind schedule.

"I'm so sorry we're late. We had to go out to Weston, among other things —"

Matt put his hand up. "Hey, no problem. I had stuff to do here anyway."

He was so laid-back. Lily had never seen him riled.

"Are we going out on the water, Matt?" Natasha asked, full of excitement. She ran at him and hugged his thigh.

"We are, doll," He laughed and tried to hug her back.

Lily froze in her tracks.

"Everything okay?" he asked. "You look like you just saw a ghost."

She nodded. "It's just that Dad used to call Mom doll. It's silly, really. I just hadn't heard anybody else use that expression since, well, Dad."

He touched her arm. "Sorry, Lily. I didn't mean anything by it. It's just that Natasha looks like a doll. She's such a cutie."

Lily tried to pull herself together. "No, I'm the one who's sorry. I'm still a little shaky about it."

"Of course you are," he said. "It's gonna take time. I lost my dad a decade ago, and I still miss him."

"Do you?"

Matt shrugged again and turned his attention to Natasha, who was still hanging on to his leg like it was a tree trunk. Natasha squealed with laughter as he used his "big bad bear" voice to thrill her even more. Lily watched them play together and felt bad it wasn't Jack. She felt guilty, too, that she didn't know about Matt's father. There was a lot about him she didn't know, and she wasn't going to discover much more now that he was leaving.

Within half an hour, Matt had them out in the middle of Boston Harbor. It was busy, even though it was pretty cold. Lily and Natasha had come prepared with plenty of layers on, so they didn't feel the chill. And besides, the sun was glorious. Natasha was scared at first, but then she got into it. She got to sit next to Matt as he steered.

Matt explained that the boat belonged to his brother who'd just had the baby, and he'd told Matt he could use it on the condition he was careful.

There was a room downstairs with a kitchen, a little bathroom, and even a second bedroom beyond that. It could sleep five or six people in a pinch. The girls went out onto the bow of the boat with Lily keeping a firm hold on Natasha. They didn't stay there long, though, because it was too cold. And besides, it was better to stay in and admire the incredible cityscape of Boston Harbor.

Matt took them across the water, and they were able to dock at a restaurant in the Seaport district.

Lily wasn't surprised when Matt walked into Legal Sea Foods and mentioned he had a reservation. He really was an amazing guy and left nothing to chance. What she hadn't known was that Legal Sea Foods had three floors: the first floor was casual, and the second was fine dining. But Matt took them to the third floor where they had a table overlooking the water and their boat, and he told them about the retractable glass roof and walls.

"All of this pulls back, so in the summer it's an outdoor restaurant, but for our New England cooler months, we can still enjoy the view from under the comfort of thick glass," he said.

"I'd love to see it all retracting," Lily said.

"Well, I guess we'll have to come back in the summer for that." He smiled. She caught his eye and felt that spark again. Was he flirting with her? Not possible. He was going to Hong Kong, and she had a boyfriend.

After lunch, they took the boat back to the marina. It had been a wonderful adventure, but it was a lot of excitement for little Natasha. She had fallen asleep with her head on Lily's lap before they'd even berthed. When the boat was safely docked, Matt scooped her up, and she didn't wake when he moved her and placed her tousled blond head on his wide shoulder.

Together, they brought Natasha to Lily's car in companionable silence. Then Lily adjusted the booster seat to the recline position and Matt slipped her in and strapped her in without disturbing her.

"Well done," Lily said.

"You'll never be able to carry her into your apartment. I should tail you in my car and help."

Lily shook her head.

Without Natasha's loud banter, there would just be her and Matt. The truth was, Lily was nervous. What if something happened between them? She could feel the chemistry growing and was doing her best to ignore it. Distance was what she needed. There was also the chance Jack had decided to come back. What would he think if Matt was there again? She knew she was spending too much time with him, considering she was committed to another man, but he was just so easy to be around—as a friend, of course.

"I'll manage," she said. "And, Matt, thanks a million. You really are a great friend." She put her hand to his face and stroked his cheek, but he took hold of it and turned his head to kiss her palm. It left no doubt that Matt wanted her.

To her shame, Lily didn't pull back. She liked him, more than ever now. Why did she turn him down when he was chasing her before?

"Are you sure I can't tail you?" he asked again.

She didn't trust herself to speak, so she pressed her lips tight and nodded. Then, with reluctance, she pulled her hand back. "I'd better go."

She looked into his eyes, and he looked right back at her with intent. If she didn't get away soon, something was definitely going to happen. She walked around to her car door, but what she wanted to do was something she shouldn't be thinking about.

Focus, she commanded herself. "I . . . I . . ." She couldn't think of anything more to say. "Thanks." What the heck was wrong with her? "I had a great time, Matt. You're terrific. Thank you." Her voice was artificially bright and buoyant.

"You're pretty darn terrific, yourself," he said.

"So, he took you and your niece to Legal Sea Foods, where it's practically impossible to get a reservation, and you're still trying to tell me there's nothing going on between the two of you?"

Emily brought her back to reality with a thud.

Lily laughed. "I'm telling you. He's amazing with kids. He was a real help with Natasha. But he's just a friend, a good friend."

"Yeah," Emily said as she glanced at her watch and downed the last of her wine. "And I'm the Harbor Master."

Chapter 36

Karaoke Night

The entire pub had joined in with the singer, and Popsy had to shout at Sandra to be heard. "Another five pints, two double gin and tonics, and one white wine," she yelled over a classic Black Eyed Peas song.

Mrs. Miller had warned them it would be a "brisk night," but nothing had prepared them for the boisterous crowd that now filled the place. Monday and Tuesday had been so calm with just them, "the lads," and a few passersby, but tonight there must have been about eighty or ninety people in a room that comfortably accommodated fifty.

Nearly everybody had a song prepared, and Popsy had met a lot of Mrs. Miller's neighbors. They were a very friendly bunch, but boy could they drink. There seemed to be no limit to the amount of pints Sandra was serving up, and the wine flowed like water. Mrs. Miller banned half-pints on Wednesday nights because the place was just too busy, but nobody seemed to have a problem with that.

"Can you believe this noise?" Popsy shouted, still smiling.

"At least it stopped Betty from doing her Celine Dion numbers," Sandra yelled back.

There was no way Betty could have heard the insult with the noise, but Popsy did and she laughed. Betty had been the first to arrive. She was one of Mrs. Miller's good friends and completely tone deaf, but that didn't stop her from trying and strangling, "My Heart Will Go On."

Popsy cleared the tables of glasses as fast as Sandra could refill them. Mrs. Miller had suggested this arrangement when they'd come down earlier, and they agreed happily. They were enjoying the work because they felt it really got them into the community, much more so than if they were just the American tourists sitting on the sidelines. Sandra had teased Mrs. Miller about any chance of getting paid, and the landlady had surprised them by saying she would.

Athlone, in Westmeath County, was one of the larger towns near Banagher, and it had a college full of party-loving students, so hoards of them had turned up around eight and in the space of ten minutes, the place was full. Mrs. Miller's karaoke night had garnered a reputation in the locality, and Sandra had been told by some of the students that even the local police force gave it a wide berth. It was good for the town and the local community.

Wednesday was, of course, the beginning of the weekend to any self-respecting student, and the Irish loved to sing. But what started as a student thing had quickly snowballed. Within a matter of weeks, the whole town was turning up for the fun. Then the party had taken on a momentum of its own and now, several years later, the Wednesday Karaoke Night was ingrained into the web of Banagher life. The college in Athlone had even included a reference to it in its college prospectus. When they'd found their lodging, Sandra and Popsy hadn't had any idea what an amazing little discovery they'd made.

It was pretty clear from the start that many of the students had a regular act. The audience would either applaud or jeer, depending on the standard, but for the most part they were a forgiving, supportive bunch.

It was four young guys who'd gotten up on the tiny home-built stage to take on the Black Eyed Peas song, but the hit was so well-loved that everybody joined in. Then a group of four girls got up and tried their version of Katy Perry's "California Girls." Again, the pub exploded into song. But there were the few who'd drunk a little too much and their choice of song could have been better. Or indeed—no song.

A couple of girls tried to sing the B-52s' "Love Shack," and after that when they annihilated Bob Marley's, "No Woman No Cry," they were eventually told to sit down. Popsy settled them with another glass of white wine and a complimentary bowl of nuts, so they didn't take it too hard. She noticed Shane heading out the door around then, too. It wasn't much of a surprise. She didn't see him being the karaoke type.

The door closed behind him, but it swung right open again and to her delight and great surprise, in walked Jeff and Simon, their friends from The Shelbourne Hotel. Popsy tried to catch Sandra's eye, but it was impossible. She was focused on settling pints of Guinness, so Popsy weaved in and out between the overcrowded tables and got to them herself. She threw her arms around Simon who was closest to her, and then reached over to give Jeff a kiss.

"Guys, it's so good to see you," she shouted. "What brings you to dear old Banagher?"

"You do!" Jeff laughed as he took in the madness around them.

Then Simon said, "I phoned Sandra this morning to see how you ladies were getting on. I was wondering if you made it home all right because of the volcano. She told me you got waylaid, but this is wild." He looked around the pub with amusement.

"Isn't it? And look at us, we're working." She laughed. "Still, it's so good of you guys to visit. You're lucky you got her on the phone. The reception is very erratic around here. Oh no, do you have somewhere to stay tonight? I'm afraid this place is full."

"We booked into the hotel in town before we left Dublin. We've already checked in. It's fine. But hey, how in the world did you find this and . . ." Jeff asked, as he looked at Popsy from head to toe, taking in the cloth in her hand and the small white apron over her black wraparound dress, "how did you end up working?"

"I know, crazy right? But I have to tell you guys, we're having a blast." She turned and pointed to Sandra. "Look who's pulling the pints."

By now Sandra had spotted them and was waving frantically, so the boys made their way through the heaving room of people. Popsy was so happy to see their drinking buddies from the weekend before. She'd been quite frosty with Simon when they'd last met because he'd crashed out in Sandra's bed while they were at The Four Seasons. But that was all in the past now, and she was just ecstatic to see a familiar face. Sandra introduced them to Mrs. Miller, who was happy to meet them. Soon, Jeff and Simon were squished in with a table of technology students, and it didn't take long for them to get into the swing of things.

Early in the evening, before things got too manic, Sandra had said she could almost tell what somebody was going to sound like just by looking at them. Popsy tested the theory, and despite a few exceptions, it really seemed like Sandra had a point. The big, boisterous guys sang the big, loud songs, the pretty little girls sang the cutesy numbers, and the old women went for the ballads.

It seemed the evening had peaked. Everybody who needed to sing had sung, and now a few groups were getting up for their second attempt. Jeff got up on stage. He was thin and stood at about five-foot-five. As usual, he was dressed with impeccable taste. Tonight he wore dark denim jeans and a white GANT shirt. Jeff smiled at Simon who gave an ever-so-slight-nod. He must have known what was coming, but Popsy was anxious for him. She'd seen the crowd boo down a bad act. If Jeff's performance was weak, they would be merciless. But she needn't have worried.

Since Simon was the one who'd partied with Sandra, Popsy assumed he was the more extroverted of the two, but it turned out she was wrong. As Jeff moved into Elvis Presley's "Fools Rush In," she realized his voice was unbelievably powerful considering the size of his ribcage. Popsy stopped clearing the table and watched him. He was singing in perfect tune with the volume and strength of a professional baritone twice his size. The audience was quick to realize how good he was because a bit of a hush fell over the pub. Even Mrs. Miller, who never stopped moving, took a break.

As soon as she figured out what he was singing, a girl in the front row tried to sing along, but she was shushed by her friends. This was something special. Jeff actually sounded like The King, even though there was no physical similarity, and he didn't try to pout like Elvis. He stretched his hand out to the women in the front row. One of them took it. Jeff looked to Sandra behind the counter and then turned and very deliberately looked at Simon. They locked into each other's stare.

The pub erupted into applause as Jeff wrapped up the song. People were on their feet and stamping the floor. Popsy had never experienced such an electric atmosphere. At last, she was beginning to understand what the world meant about the Irish being party people. It was like some kind of group therapy, with a lot of alcohol to get the thing in motion.

Jeff was being slapped on the back by fellow revelers as he made his way back to his chair. Then the karaoke machine started up again.

The girl next to Popsy slapped her forehead. She must have recognized the tune before even the lyrics had begun. "Here we go again." She groaned.

Popsy had started back to work, but she turned to see who had mounted the little stage. Mrs. Miller was singing. Her eyes were closed and she was wrapped up in her ballad about her heart being low. Popsy had never witnessed anything like it. The song was a new one to her, but it sounded fundamentally Irish, even though the words were in English. It had a sad but haunting quality to it—like it was from the Ireland of the famine days.

Of course, Mrs. Miller's strong Kerry accent could have had a lot to do with that, but the sorrow in the song was so overwhelming that it touched Popsy. She stopped working again and when a girl got up to go to the restroom, for the first time that night, Popsy sat down. She wanted to watch Mrs. Miller sing.

The words about surviving alone pierced her heart. Mrs. Miller was singing the song of Popsy's life. The pain she felt—that which she was so incapable of explaining to her friends or family—was exactly what Mrs. Miller was singing about. Popsy felt the tears began to flow down her face as all the ladies in the pub joined in again, singing about their hearts being low.

It was so true, Popsy thought. Men just didn't understand how deeply women could love and how much it hurt when a love like hers and Peter's ended. That's when she realized with a start that it was another anniversary. Peter had been gone fifteen weeks today. The time was going by so fast, and she'd almost missed her Wednesday anniversary.

Mrs. Miller was finishing up and she got a sizable round of applause. From what the girl had said earlier, Popsy assumed they'd heard her sing the song before, but for Popsy, it was a first—a revealing, touching, wonderful song that so completely encapsulated her life right now. Of course, the younger girls wouldn't get it. They hadn't been hurt by life yet. Their time will come soon enough, Popsy thought wearily.

She had to get out of the pub. There was no air in the room. It was too hot, too crowded, too everything. She ran out the door and went into the restroom to splash her face. It was the same bathroom she and Sandra took their shower in every morning. On Monday night she'd been too drunk to notice there was no bathtub, and on Tuesday after her long walk and her afternoon in the garden, she was okay without one. But now she really needed her therapeutic bath. She had to get into the water and submerge her head in scalding water to get away from the world—a world without Peter. She needed her bath, but where could she go?

"The river," she said to her reflection. "It'll be freezing, which will be just as good as scorching."

Sandra had also been blown away by Mrs. Miller's performance. She thought it was every bit as good as Jeff's, who could so win *America's Got Talent*. Sandra wondered if they had *Ireland's Got Talent*. The landlady's song was incredibly touching, but it was also downright sad. If it was supposed to move you, it sure had succeeded because Sandra went right up to that Karaoke machine to see if they had the song she was thinking of, and when she saw it did, she hit the buttons and grabbed the mic before she could talk herself out of it.

Even as the music intro started up, some of the girls clapped enthusiastically.

"Mrs. Miller, that song you just sang—that was epic. Really awesome. But you know, while we all suffer from broken hearts, I have to say, there are many ways of dealing with them." She kicked into Beyonce's "All the Single Ladies" and just as they did with Mrs. Miller, the girls in the pub joined in. Sandra changed the words a little to suit her life. It made her feel great.

Even Mrs. Miller, who'd taken over behind the bar, smiled.

Afterward, Sandra headed back to the bar to resume her pint-pulling duties and revelers applauded her, tapped her on the back, and told her what a great job she'd done, but there was one voice she hadn't expected to hear.

"Now that was impressive," someone said in a warm German accent.

Sandra swung around. "Sven! How in the world did you end up here?"

He smiled. "I heard about your singing on the local news."

"Huh?"

He shook his head and laughed. "Joke." He looked a little lost.

Then Sandra realized he was nervous. Sven, Mr. Gorgeous Hunky Single Doctor, was nervous. It made him even more attractive. "Seriously?" she asked.

"Your friend, Popsy. She called me this afternoon and told me you'd found my business card but you were too shy to call me, so she did it for you. Now, here I am." He held out his hands as if offering himself up to her.

Sandra looked around the pub to see where Popsy was. "I'll kill her," she said, but she didn't mean it. She was actually thrilled to see Sven again, even in this crazy atmosphere of young students who were now singing George Michael's "Faith."

Her old gym buddy looked even more attractive. While most of the students were dressed in jeans and hoodies or T-shirts, Sven was in a pair of cream chinos, a white shirt, and a navy jacket. He oozed class and maturity, and he was easily the most attractive man in the place. She squeezed his hand.

"I'm really glad you came." Then she looked around the pub again. "Where is Popsy?" Simon and Jeff were watching her and Sven with great interest. Popsy had obviously managed to fill them in on her surprise. They smiled, but when she mouthed the word "Popsy," and raised her shoulders as if to say "where is she?" they shrugged.

Popsy wasn't thinking straight. She walked through the garden and down to the water's edge. She wasn't afraid of the cold. She didn't care. She just needed to be under the water where there was no sound and no reminders of Peter. It had worked in her home in Wellesley and in that hotel in Dublin. It would wipe away the pain here, too. She took off her shoes and stood next to them on the grass verge. It was a clean bank, straight into deep water. But even from where she stood, she could see the current moving the water along. It didn't matter if she climbed out a little farther down the river, she just had to submerge. She jumped.

The shock was startling. The water was colder than she'd expected. It was totally dark, too. Already she'd moved a few yards down from where she jumped in. Her head popped up, so she dove to get under the surface again. The water stung her face. It was freezing. She tried to turn so she could swim against the flow, but it was too strong, it pulled her along and down.

My God, she thought, I'm actually stuck in this current. It started to pull her down deeper. She swam against it but couldn't break to the surface. She needed a new lungful of air, fast, but it was useless. She wasn't strong enough to fight the current.

Popsy didn't mean to, but her body took over. She took a gasp for air and water flooded into her lungs. Again her muscles involuntarily heaved and tried to choke the water out, but more came in.

I'm drowning, she realized. I'm drowning. I'm going to die. I don't want to die. I don't want to leave Sandra or the girls.

She kicked again with all her might, but she was getting dizzy. She'd run out of oxygen, and when she reached out, she wasn't sure if she felt fresh air or just a jet of cold water. It was all happening too fast. She didn't have enough time.

Her last thought before she blacked out was, "This is not what I want."

Shane had jumped in after Popsy. Her hand came out one last time, and he grabbed it. The miracle was that he saw it at all—a complete miracle. Once he got hold of her, he kicked hard and pulled with all his might to get her head up and out. It took all of his strength to pull her with him as he fought to swim out of the swirling black currents, but God had made him a strong swimmer.

This mighty river will either take both of us or neither of us, he thought and I'm not going to die tonight.

He'd known it was bordering on suicidal to jump in after her, but he could hardly watch her jump to her death and not at least attempt to save her. There had been no time to call out. He'd assumed she was just going to the water's edge to look at the view. That's what most people did. It was when she'd taken her shoes off that he became alarmed. And then without fuss, she'd jumped. It was surreal. He'd already watched his beloved wife die in front of him, and he wouldn't have a second woman's death on his conscience.

He dragged her limp body up onto the grassy river bank a good three-hundred yards downriver. The currents were notoriously strong on the Shannon, and they could drown a weak swimmer with no problem.

Shane smacked her face. "Popsy, can you hear me?" No answer.

Next he laid her to the side so she could spit up the water in her lungs, but her body was limp. "Don't give up, girl, come on now," he shouted and then looked around. "Help!" he screamed.

He needed to try mouth-to-mouth, so he turned her back over and pinched her nose. Then he sent up a silent prayer that his lifeguard training wasn't too rusty, took a deep breath, and brought his mouth down onto hers. Her chest rose and dropped, so he did it again.

"Come on, girl. You have to fight for life. Come back to us." He looked around. "Anybody?" he yelled again.

Silence, as well as darkness, cloaked him. He breathed air into her lungs a third time and thankfully, this time she coughed and spluttered. "Good, girl," he encouraged her as she spit up the water that would have killed her. "Good, girl. You'll be okay now," he whispered, then picked her up.

As Shane approached the bar, he saw two Athlone students and yelled, "Get me Mrs. Miller!"

They ran inside. In a moment Mrs. Miller was ushering Shane up the stairs and showing him to Popsy's bedroom. She blessed herself and went to fetch more blankets for Popsy, who was now semi-conscious but weak.

Popsy managed a limp smile for Shane when he laid her on her bed. "Did you save me again?" she asked.

He nodded. "We're making a bit of a habit of this."

She stroked his face. "Thanks. That was stupid. Stupid. I didn't mean to . . ." She ran out of energy and closed her eyes.

"Right now, that's enough," Mrs. Miller said. "I have to get that wet dress off her. Shane, you'll have to help me."

Sandra came bursting into the room. "Popsy!" She fell to her knees next to where Shane was kneeling beside the bed. Popsy opened her eyes. "So sorry, Sandra . . . wanted a bath—dumb. Sorry." She closed her eyes again.

Sandra laughed over her panicky tears. "Of all the dumbass things to do. I swear I'll kill you once you're better." She kissed Popsy on the cheek.

Mrs. Miller said, "Shane, you need to call a doctor. Sandra can help me here."

"There's a doctor downstairs," Sandra said. "His name's Sven. You can't miss him. He's a big, blond German man in his forties and he's wearing a cream shirt, I think. To be honest he's a gynecologist, but he's still a doctor."

Mrs. Miller nodded. "Good. Go and get him. Use the microphone if you need to."

Shane left and arrived back with Sven just as Sandra and Mrs. Miller were getting Popsy wrapped up in warm blankets.

"Let me know how she is," Shane said.

Sandra walked out with him.

"You're soaking wet, too. You need to change." She put a hand on his shoulder. "You're freezing. That was a heck of a brave thing you did."

He shrugged as if to say it was no big deal. "I was just in the right place at the right time."

"Again," Sandra said and smiled. "Popsy's a lucky lady."

Mrs. Miller came out. "Shane, you have to get out of those wet clothes. Sandra, you come downstairs with me and keep the bar going. God knows what state it's in down there."

But everything was fine in the bar. Jeff and Simon offered to help out, and Sandra convinced Mrs. Miller to give them a try. Pretty soon the whole place was drinking Miami-style cocktails.

Shane changed and went back to check on Popsy. When he got there, Mrs. Miller said, "The doctor says she's going to be okay, but what she needs now is rest. Please stay with her for a bit."

There was nowhere for him to sit so he plonked himself down on Sandra's bed and watched Popsy while she slept.

"Rest now," he whispered, looking at her properly for the first time. She was beautiful. Delicate, and maybe a little too skinny for his liking, but she was beautiful. She seemed to be in a deep sleep. At least she was breathing again. It had been a close call.

"You gave me a hell of a scare, girl." Popsy laid there, eyes closed, unresponsive. "You can't quit life. None of us can. We have to keep going, and that's the truth," he said.

"You might not believe me, but I don't want to die," Popsy whispered without opening her eyes. Her voice was croaky from all the water.

"You're awake."

"I am," she said. She didn't move a muscle. "And alive, thanks to you, Shane Maloney. When I have the energy, I'm going to give you a great big hug to say thank you for saving my life—again."

A little while later, there was a knock on the door and Mrs. Miller popped her head in. "That's enough for tonight," she said. "You both need your rest. Out you come, Shane."

Downstairs in the pub, word had spread of the events at the river, but Mrs. Miller told them it was just an accident and everyone was fine. Shane listened from the door but didn't go in. Instead, he went down to the water's edge. He stood at the spot where Popsy had jumped and then picked up her shoes—the only evidence that it was no accident.

Chapter 37
Time to Say Good-bye

It had been amazing luck that Sven was there when Popsy fell in the river, but he'd said he was more concerned about her mental state than the physical and that Popsy really needed a psychological evaluation if it had been a suicide attempt. Over Thursday and Friday, Popsy worked hard to convince everybody that it wasn't. She said she was heartbroken, but she didn't want to die.

In the end, Sandra believed her. She knew her friend well and that while losing Peter was the biggest heartache of her life, she didn't have a death wish.

Jeff and Simon had backed Popsy and said she wasn't the suicidal type. They returned to Dublin on Thursday morning and promised to visit Boston very soon. The friendship was sealed. They promised Mrs. Miller they would be back for her famous Wednesday Karaoke Night, and she told them Jeff was the best Elvis impersonator she'd heard in decades. There was even talk of them having a cocktail night once a month.

Unlike Jeff and Simon, who'd only come down to Banagher for a night and stayed in the local hotel, Sven had booked a room in a local Hidden Ireland House. He told Sandra it was a magnificent old mansion built in the eighteen hundreds, and it had been lovingly restored. His room had an enormous four-poster bed, and he tried hard to convince her to come back with him to "talk," but she refused to leave Popsy's bedside.

The next morning when Popsy woke, Sandra reminded her that Sven was in town. "You have to go. You have to go now. What are you doing here?"

"I couldn't leave you, not after your fall."

Popsy waved her hands. "Go to Sven. I'm absolutely fine."

So Sandra went.

~*~

The Hidden Ireland House was easily found, but when she saw it, she got a little inhibited. It was a palatial looking thing with humongous granite gates up to the front door.

Sandra bit her lip and drove the little rental car up the long and winding lane to the old house. She figured Sven must be interested if he came all this way, and she owed it to herself, and to him, to see where this thing was going. The house was quiet and she wondered if anyone was even awake yet as she mounted the steps to the huge, oak front door. It opened before she got a chance to ring the bell.

"I heard the car. It's good to see you," he said and smiled.

"And you." She felt awkward, but when he took her in his arms and kissed her, and she kissed him right back, she knew instinctively this wasn't some knee-jerk reaction to "get back in the game." It was more than that. He stopped kissing her and looked into her eyes. "I have wanted to do that from the first moment I saw you working out in the gym in Wellesley."

"All the way from Boston to Banagher. I guess we never know what life has in store for us." She smiled at him and tightened her arms around his waist. "I'm so glad you came down to Banagher to find me."

"Here's to finding each other," he whispered. Then he kissed her on the lips again and took her up to his room and his four-poster bed to kiss her everywhere else.

The next morning, Popsy found Shane down at the marina, but she was very careful to avoid the boat crane. As she approached, he gave "the lads" a five-minute break and came over to where she was hovering.

"Mornin'," he said.

"I've come to say thank you—again," she said. "And I promise I'll be more careful with my life from now on."

He nodded. "You can't swim in the river. The currents are too strong."

"I know, but I love baths and there weren't any in The Boathouse. I just really needed one. A bit crazy, I know."

"You said it, not me."

"I'm not usually this careless with my life. It was just those two times," she said, looking at the crane and then out at the water.

"Life is precious, Popsy. Don't throw it away."

"I'm not. I mean, I wasn't. It was a mistake—honest." He shrugged as if to say, "whatever," but that annoyed her. "Look, I've been through a hell of a lot, and the last thing I need is some guy thinking I'm a whacko. Just because you jumped into the Shannon and pulled me out, that doesn't give you have the right to judge me."

Shane laughed.

"What is it?" she asked.

"I thought you were coming down here to thank me, and now you're giving me a tongue lashin'."

"A what?"

"You're giving out to me, woman. What did I do to deserve that?"

Popsy stopped. "Oh, yes, I'm so sorry. That wasn't meant to happen. So, Shane . . ."

He looked up when she used his name, and it was the first time she got a good look at his eyes. They were lovely, a pale blue, like the midsummer sky.

"Can I buy you lunch? You know, to say thanks?"

He shrugged again. He did that a lot.

"Do you have a lunch hour or something?"

He looked awkward and reluctant when he agreed that he could get away for an hour at one o'clock. Popsy was beginning to wonder if she'd made a mistake, but it was already done. She had no idea where she could take him because Sandra was gone with the car, so she asked Mrs. Miller for advice.

"The weather is unusually warm. Why don't you make him a picnic lunch and have it down by the river? Not too near the water, mind you."

"Is it dry enough?" Popsy looked out the window of The Boathouse.

"Sure. Besides, if it gets wet, you can find shelter quickly."

Mrs. Miller was right, as usual, so Popsy fixed up a fine picnic with her help. Then she headed back out to the marina with her basketful of goodies and the big old quilt Mrs. Miller had given her.

Shane seemed delighted with the idea of a picnic. They chose a spot not far from The Boathouse and shook out the blanket. Popsy laid out the food, and he opened the bottle of white wine that Mrs. Miller had slipped in without her knowledge.

"This is very nice," he said and handed her a glass.

"It was Mrs. Miller's idea," Popsy confessed taking the glass from him. She was glad to see that Shane seemed a lot more relaxed. Sitting down on the blanket, they were eye-to-eye, and he didn't look down so much. "Ah, that one is full of great ideas—some better than others."

"What do you mean?"

"You don't know?"

Popsy shook her head.

"She has my heart scalded about you since the day you arrived. She's trying to fix us up."

Popsy's silence said it all.

Shane laughed. "You really had no idea?"

"None." Then she was embarrassed. "Ohmygod—this picnic, you don't think that I did all this just to . . . you know."

Again, he laughed. "What? Seduce me? No, Popsy, relax. Mrs. Miller may not be able to see, but I understand that your heart belongs to another. You're not exactly on the lookout for a new man, not like that friend of yours, Sandra. She's a right firecracker, that one."

"You like her?"

"Me? No, not in that way. She wouldn't be my type, but I think she looked quite happy to see that doctor last night. They might do well together." Shane took a ham and cheese sandwich.

"Tell me now," he said as he chewed, "Popsy is an unusual name. Is it short for something?"

She smiled. "I was christened 'Poppy,' but my nickname was always Popsy, which is just as well because then I started to date Peter, that's my late husband . . ." It was still hard to talk about him in the past tense. "Well, if I'd stayed Poppy, I would have ended up being 'Poppy Power.' That would have sounded dreadful, so I stuck with my nickname all these years. I called my girls Rose and Lily so we would all have that in common—names that are flowers. But my eldest calls herself Rosie. She hated Rose." Popsy shook her head.

"Did you know from the first time you met him that he was the one—Peter, you say?"

She nodded. It was good to talk about him. "Yep, I knew straight away."

"He must have been something."

"What about you?" Popsy asked, comfortable in the knowledge he knew she wasn't looking for a man. "Tell me about your wife."

Shane gave her a sideways glance. "Mary was small and blonde, a bit like you," he mumbled as he examined the various sandwiches.

Popsy was out of practice talking to men about such things, and there was the added complication that Shane kind of spoke in riddles, with him being Irish. American men were much easier to read. But she thought he was saying that she was his type. She had to make sure he understood where she was coming from.

"I lost my husband just four months ago, Shane. It's going to take some time to get used to that."

This time he looked straight into her eyes. "I understand. I lost my Mary seventeen years ago, two years before I found this place. Lord, I can't believe it's been that long, but I have to tell you, there are days I still believe she'll walk in the door. I think there's a part of you that never gets over it. But one thing you should know is that it does get easier to live with."

"Does it? Because the pain in my heart . . ." Popsy began to cry, and Shane leaned over and hugged her. There was no awkwardness in it. He was like a big brother. He understood her pain because he'd been through the same thing.

"I know, girl. I know. Let it out. It does you good."

And that was the beginning of their friendship. Popsy's tears didn't last too long and afterward, they enjoyed the rest of their lunch. She sat with him and the other lads at tea that night, too, because Sandra was with Sven, and Popsy was happy she'd found a new "friend."

On Friday, she made another picnic lunch and spent it with Shane. She heard all about Mary and how she'd lost her battle with cancer. He spoke freely about getting over the death, how he'd never found another woman to replace her, and that he'd never really wanted to.

But he was also very firm with Popsy about the need to live and enjoy life. If he'd learned anything, it was that the years went by so fast and she needed to focus on the good things. Popsy swore she would. She also told him about the loss of most of her money. Her house would be repossessed soon, and she had no idea where she would live. There was enough money left to start over, but she had no idea where she would go or what she would do.

"Well, I daresay there would always be a bed for you here if you're willing to muck out in the bar or do a spot of gardening."

Popsy smiled. If somebody had told her even a month ago that she would be grateful for a job in a little country pub deep in the heart of Ireland, she would have laughed at them, and yet, so much changed that the idea had appeal.

It was at tea time on Friday night when Mrs. Miller was able to confirm the volcano had, at last, gone back to sleep. News services were saying the ash was clearing fast and planes would be back in the air the next day. Sven went online and got them reservations to fly out on Saturday evening. Sandra cried, saying she didn't want to leave him, and he didn't want her to go.

Popsy was sorry to say good-bye to Shane, too. He was the first person she'd met since Peter's death who really understood what she was going through.

"You've become a good friend, Shane. Can I call you?" she asked, when they were leaving on Saturday morning.

"Anytime." He smiled and hugged her. It was remarkable the change she'd witnessed in him since he'd saved her life—twice. He'd been distant and avoided eye contact when they first met, but now he was warm and so very friendly. Shane admitted he didn't do well meeting new people, but she wasn't new anymore. She was part of The Boathouse family. Popsy liked the idea, but she also had a family back in Boston. Her two daughters needed her, and she had to figure out her future. She had to head back home.

Mrs. Miller was obviously very sad to see them go. "The place won't be the same without you. Come back soon, please."

Popsy and Sandra packed up their enormous cases and wedged them into their tiny car, then headed out of Banagher with heavy hearts. Sandra said she had made Sven leave an hour before they did. Long good-byes were terrible. Mrs. Miller and Shane were there to see them off, and that was hard enough. They were emotional as they hugged their new friends good-bye.

"I'll phone you when I get home," Popsy said to Shane.

"And remember, life is for the living; keep smiling," he said.

"I will, and I'll be sure not to get into any more dangerous situations because I won't have you around to save me." She meant it as a joke, but when she said it, she realized just how sad she'd be not to have Shane nearby.

"You were a fool to let her get away," Mrs. Miller said as they waved the car off.

"Her husband has only just died. She's not ready. I'll grant you, she is an amazing woman, but she needs more time," Shane said, still waving at the back of their car.

"Fine. Give her time but not too much. She's the one, I'm telling you."

He finally stopped waving when the car turned around a bend and was out of sight. "You know something, Mrs. Miller? You may be right, but tell me now, is it just me or do you think she looks a little like Goldie Hawn?"

~*~

"Out of all the Broader Horizons vacations I've been on, this has been the best," Sam said on Saturday morning when they met in the lobby. Rosie was standing next to the suitcases while Marcus took care of the final bill. It was remarkable how fast the time had flown by. After all her worries and panic, she'd managed to get through the week sane and she also had a wonderful time with Sam.

The catamaran would be something she'd never forget. His friendship was a gift, too. They'd joked about going on future swinging vacations together so their partners could do what they wanted, while Rosie and Sam explored. They'd even swapped numbers, but Rosie doubted they'd ever use them. Whatever they had, needed to stop here. It was unspoken but understood between them.

"Thank you for everything, Sam. You've been a true friend. I loved our time together, especially all those liquid lunches and the snorkeling."

"I never did manage to get you deep-sea diving." He smiled.

"Some other time," she suggested, knowing it would never happen.

"Some other time." He took her hand and squeezed it. They looked at each other honestly and openly. If it had been another time or place, they would have kissed, but they were both married and came from a school of thought that marriage meant loyalty to that partner. Sam was the first to laugh.

"Funny, we could have done anything we wanted to all week, and now that it's time to go, I'm really beginning to regret that."

"I know what you mean," she whispered but pulled her hand back at the same time. Marcus was near.

"Babe, all done. Ready to go?" He came up to her and eyed Sam up and down. He must have sensed something. "Everything okay?"

Rosie swung around. "Everything's fine. Shall we head out?" she asked a little too brightly. Marcus looked even more suspicious.

"Yeah, let's go." He glared at Sam as he took Rosie's suitcase.

"Who was that guy?" Marcus asked when they were alone in the taxi.

"Oh, just a guy I met."

"Does he have a name?"

"I thought we agreed—no names."

When they were checking in at the airport, Rosie went to the restroom while Marcus waited with their luggage. He was still in a dark mood, convinced there was something going on between that man and Rosie. Usually, he would have ignored it when her phone beeped to announce a new message, but because of the paranoia, he had a look.

UR HUSBAND DIDN'T LOOK HAPPY
TO SEE ME.
HOPE U DIDN'T GET GRIEF. IF YES,
REMEMBER TO MAKE LIKE AN
OSTRICH! XX SAM

Marcus couldn't believe what he was seeing. There was definitely something going on.

"So who is Sam?" he asked when Rosie got back.

Guilt washed over her face.

"Who?"

"Sam? Your little friend back at Broader Horizons."

"How do you know his name? What happened to 'ask no questions, tell no lies?' "

He held up her phone.

"Are you going through my text messages now?"

"It beeped. I thought it could have been from Lily about Natasha."

"Now you're worried about Nat? When we're going home? All week you haven't given her two thoughts because you were so busy getting it on, and now you care about your daughter? "

"I care about Natasha just as much as you. I heard the phone beep, and I wanted to make sure everything was okay. But it was your *friend*, Sam. And he knows about our ostrich plan. Rosie, what the hell is going on? You and this guy, are you more than friends?"

"Well, I'll tell you something. We weren't lovers. We didn't screw. We didn't want to."

"Ha!"

"This may come as a shock to you, but I didn't want to have sex with a club full of strangers. I just wanted to get away and have some time with my husband. It was you who wanted to do this, you who pushed it through. I just went along with it to keep you happy, to give you what you wanted. You knew that I didn't want this kind of vacation. Don't deny it. So don't you dare try to lay some sort of guilt trip on me!"

By now they were getting an audience.

"No woman I was with knew my real name. They never knew anything private about me. I certainly didn't give them my phone number. He has your real name, your real number, and you even told him intimate details of our life—like the ostrich thing."

"Nobody knows you? Well, good for you. So you just screwed them and left them. Are you trying to say that's better? What planet are you living on? I gave you a hall pass to do whatever the heck you wanted while I did nothing, and yet somehow I'm the one who's being accused here. What more do you want?"

"Honesty. I was completely honest. You knew what I was doing, and you knew it meant nothing. You, on the other hand, did something much more dangerous than have sex. You became intimate with this guy. You became friends."

"Friends? Is that a crime now? I don't believe this!"

Airport Security approached them at this point. "Excuse me, ma'am, sir. You'll have to calm down."

"Calm down?" Rosie said. "Calm down? He's been shagging half of Mexico, and what did I do? One little boat ride. One day on a catamaran, and I'm the crook."

"You went on the catamaran with him?" Marcus couldn't believe what he was hearing. "You've been *boating* together?"

"Yes, boating—not boinking—boating!" Rosie screeched. "You know what, Marcus? Screw you. I deserve better and so does our daughter. I've had it! Do what you want. Go where you want, because I'm done with this bullshit. Catch another flight. I'm not flying home with you."

"Ah, finally something we agree on!" he roared and marched away.

~*~

Lily and Natasha spent Saturday morning at the Boston Aquarium. They got to see sharks and some incredible-looking tropical fish up-close. Lily was determined to enjoy the last full day with her niece as much as possible. She hadn't spoken to Jack on Thursday or Friday. She really thought he would call, or perhaps even come over with flowers to apologize, but she'd heard nothing. Today was decision time. Sandra was coming home. It meant that Jack would have to move back in with her. She was sure that Sandra would be livid when she discovered he'd lived in her apartment while she was in Ireland. Lily even thought about calling her mom to tell her, but she figured she should stay away from that particular situation.

Natasha was so exhausted by the time they got back from the aquarium that she fell asleep in front of the television. Lily's heart warmed to see her with her beautiful eyes closed. She looked even more adorable when she was asleep.

How can I live without having babies? she wondered.

Gently, Lily carried Natasha into the spare bedroom and laid her on the bed. She would sleep better there, and it also meant that she'd be well-rested for her parents when they got home later.

Jack let himself into the apartment at lunchtime, which for some reason caught her off guard. Of course, she should have been expecting him. He would want to move out of Sandra's place well before she arrived home.

"Hi," he said.

"Hello, Jack."

"Is the child still here?"

"She is, and her name is still Natasha. She's napping in the spare bedroom."

"I thought she might be gone by now," he mumbled.

"No," Lily said, keeping it cool. He was being very difficult about this. There should be some sort of compromise in a relationship, but Jack wasn't willing to give an inch. Still, she'd done a huge amount of soul-searching during their time apart, particularly since her talk with Emily, and she'd reached her decision.

She would stay with Jack.

She was in too deep, and she couldn't back out now, even if it meant she couldn't have children. That was the price she'd pay. True, she hadn't realized it at the time, but she was a big girl and had to stand by her responsibilities.

"Jack, I think we have to talk."

"Yes, I agree," he said.

"Look, I'm sorry I've caused you so much grief about the baby thing. I didn't know how strongly you felt about it."

"Yes." He sounded angry.

"Well, the thing is, you can forget it. I'll let it go. I won't have children if it really means this much to you."

"It does. I don't want any more kids. I'm too old and too poor."

It broke her heart to hear it, but that was that. Her future was mapped out. Maybe she could focus on her job. It sure needed some attention. She'd received a written warning for non-performance and was on shaky ground. It appeared the same went for her relationship.

"The thing is, I might be too old to have kids, but you're not, so . . ." He looked uncomfortable. "I've given this a lot of thought, and I think we need to break up."

"What?"

"You and me." He looked at her with a concerned expression "You're a great girl, but we're wrong together. I see that now. You need a man your own age. You need to live your life and have a few kids."

"I don't believe I'm hearing this. We've done so much damage already."

He put his hands up. "Don't remind me. I know it's all a mess, but maybe we can stop it from being an even bigger disaster. Go and find yourself a younger man, like that Matt guy who's always hanging around. He obviously likes you."

"But what about you?"

"I'm done here. I'm going down to Boca Raton. If I'm going to be broke, I may as well be broke where the weather is nice."

Lily didn't know what to say. She felt numb, but a tiny part of her was relieved, too. He'd taken the decision out of her hands. She was no longer honor-bound to him.

"I do have some good news for you," he said.

"What?"

"This place is in your name. There's no mortgage on it, so your dad really did right by you. The deeds are in the lawyer's office. He's going to have them delivered to you on Monday, so keep them somewhere secure, like your own attorney's safe."

She nodded, but she wasn't really taking in what he was saying. She couldn't get over that he was leaving for Boca Raton.

"Aunt Lily . . ." Natasha was standing in the door of the guestroom.

"Did we wake you, sweetie? Do you have your Moo?" Lily rushed over. Natasha looked nervously at Jack.

He smiled. "Hi, there." It was the first time he'd been nice to her. Then he came over and kissed them each on the forehead the same way a father might kiss his two beloved daughters. "Goodbye, Lily. You're a wonderful lady, and you'll make somebody a terrific wife and mother," he whispered. "It just won't be with me."

Then he walked out.

Chapter 38

Coming Home

"We're home," Popsy called when she opened the door.

On the plane, Popsy had convinced Sandra to move in with her permanently. She'd already stayed there almost every night since Peter's passing and she admitted that she wasn't keen to return to the penthouse with all its bad memories.

The first out to greet them was little Natasha. "Mommy's home, too," she said. "But Daddy isn't."

Popsy wrapped her granddaughter in a big hug. "Did he have to go back to work already? How unfortunate. Don't worry, pet. I'm sure he'll be back in a few days."

Then Lily and Rosie came out.

"How was your vacation?" Rosie asked.

"Oh my, where do we start?" Popsy looked to Sandra for support.

They all settled around the kitchen table where Matilda joined them. Popsy was all too aware that Sandra had her own issues going on and would find it difficult to be with Lily. There was so much treachery there. Sandra did have Sven in her life now, and she hoped that would make it a bit easier. She'd always said the best way to get over a man was to be with a different one. Popsy nudged Sandra and winked. Sandra smiled back.

Then she turned her attention to her daughter. "Lily, I'm so sorry we got held up with the volcano. Did you get by okay with Natasha?"

"Natasha and I had a ball, didn't we, kiddo?" she said.

Natasha clapped her hands and said, "We went on a boat with Matt and we went to the aquarium and the restaurant at the top of the Prudential, and Matt got me fries and a Shriley Temple."

"That's a lot of Matt." Rosie gave Lily a sideways glance.

"Jack is gone," Natasha said.

Everybody listened.

"What?"

"He wants her to have babies with somebody else, like Matt."

Even Lily looked stunned. "What makes you say that? You weren't even there when he was talking about Matt."

Natasha shook her head. "I heard him."

"Lily?" Popsy reached out and touched Lily's cheek. Sandra said nothing.

"It's true. He moved out a week ago, but he came home today and said we were over. He's moving to Boca," she said, and then started to cry.

"I think I need some wine," Sandra said and walked over to the fridge.

"I'm sorry, Sandra. I broke up your marriage and for what? He's moved on again. He doesn't want to be with me, either."

Sandra sloshed the wine into five glasses and handed them out. Then she came over to Lily.

"Can I have a word with you outside, please?" she asked politely and put her wine glass down on the table. Lily jumped to her feet like an obedient child.

Popsy protested. "Sandra, what are you—"

"Alone," she said with authority. "We'd like to be left alone." Then she turned on her heel and walked out of the kitchen with Lily following meekly behind. Lily cast a nervous glance back at the women at the table, and Matilda pushed her chair out like she was going to follow, but Popsy put her hand out to stop her. "Let them go. They need to sort this out—just the two of them."

Matilda settled back down, blessed herself, and then reached for her wine.

Lily was terrified but a huge part of her needed to do this. Whatever it was Sandra was going to say, she wanted to hear it so they could put it behind them. She followed Sandra out to the front driveway.

Finally, Sandra stopped walking and turned to face Lily.

"This is where you were standing, that first day I saw you with my husband."

Lily said nothing. "Do you remember?"

Lily didn't move.

"Answer me, do you remember?" Sandra shouted.

This time she jumped and nodded. "Yes. It's the day Daddy died."

"That's right. Emotionally, I parked everything that day because of Peter's death, but I would like to deal with it right now. Okay?"

Lily studied the ground and nodded meekly.

"Answer me!" Sandra shouted again.

Lily's head snapped up and she said, "Yes."

That's when it came—a smack so hard and fast, it knocked Lily clean off her feet. "That's for screwing my husband. I've been waiting to give you that since the day Jack walked out on me. You little manipulative, calculating bitch! Just because I love your mom doesn't mean I have to like you. You screwed my husband and now you say you're sorry to me?" She sounded incredulous. "Across the kitchen table?" Even more incredulous. "Are you for real? Do you have any idea what you did?"

Lily got to her feet again, but she wouldn't let herself cry. If there was another slap coming, she would take it. She deserved it. "I don't think I did."

"Huh?"

"I said, I don't think I actually did realize what I was doing. I'm not excusing it. I'm just saying I think I was stupid beyond words. I fell for him and didn't think it through. Unbelievably stupid—I know. But, Sandra, I really am so sorry. Can I do anything to make it up to you? Anything?" She risked looking at her attacker.

"I can see the outline of my hand on your face," Sandra said, looking uneasy. "I'm sorry, Lily, but that slap has been brewing up in me."

Lily shook her head vehemently. "Don't apologize. I deserve that, and more." She took a deep breath. "I have to tell you something else, because I don't want any more secrets. Jack lived in your penthouse when he moved out of my place. I don't know where he is now, but I'm telling you so you know." She looked at Sandra, half expecting another smack.

"Relax, I'm not going to hit you again. You're not worth it. But him? Just wait till I'm through with him. That bastard."

Lily's shoulders dropped in relief.

"Don't get me wrong. I'm still angry about what you did. It will take a long time for me to get over that betrayal, but just so you know, I'm not sorry about losing Jack Boy. We weren't good together. But if you ever touch a man of mine again, I swear I won't be held responsible."

"I swear," Lily said. "I was such a stupid, selfish idiot. I swear I'll never go near another man again, and I'll be indebted to you forever if you forgive me."

"I'm not saying to not ever go near a man again, just not one that's already spoken for."

Lily put her hand on her heart. "On my mother's life. I swear."

"Okay, less swearing on your mother's life. She's my best friend you know, and that has a lot to do with why I'm going easy on you. That and the fact that Jack is an ass." She started back into the house. "Wait till my lawyer gets through with him."

Lily fell back into silence and followed a step behind. It looked like Jack was now the focus of Sandra's anger, so it was better to stay quiet.

"So tell us more about this man of yours, Sandra," Rosie said when they walked back into the kitchen. If anybody other than Rosie noticed Lily's face looking a little red or her hands shaking as she quietly opened another bottle of wine, they didn't say anything.

Sandra lifted the mood considerably when she talked about karaoke and Sven. She told them about Jeff, Simon, and her initiation into an early house. Popsy showed them a photo of Sandra sporting a frothy white Guinness mustache. Sandra regaled them with stories about Gerald, their wonderful chauffeur from The Four Seasons, and how he'd brought them to the house where their mom had grown up. She got animated when she told them about the wonderful Boathouse and the amazing Mrs. Miller who kept everything and everyone running. They all laughed with disbelief when they heard that both Sandra and Popsy ended up with jobs, and there was even a brief reference to her mom's friend, Shane.

It was getting late and Popsy yawned and said she had to go to bed. "I'm still on European time. My body thinks it's four in the morning." She stood to go.

"Mom, I was wondering if Natasha and I could stay here tonight in my old room. It's just that, well, Marcus and I had a big fight, and I don't want to go home."

"Everything okay, love?" Popsy asked.

Rosie shrugged and didn't say anymore but went to her mother's arms like she used to when she was small. Popsy wrapped her up and squeezed her maternally.

"I've got you, love," she whispered. "Stay here tonight." The two women stayed locked in each other's arms for a few moments until Rosie broke away. She sat down on one of the kitchen chairs and Popsy sat next to her. "Marcus and I . . ." she faltered seeming to look for the right words. "Well, he and I, we seem to want different things out of our marriage."

Popsy stroked her daughter's hair. "Is there a middle ground? Some way you can reach a compromise?"

"That's what I thought we'd done, but it appears Marcus wasn't happy with that."

Rosie folded her arms on the table and collapsed her head onto them to let herself cry. These were the tears she'd been holding back for months. These were the tears she'd wanted to cry when Marcus suggested the stupid swinging thing in the first place.

This is exactly what she'd feared could happen. Once the intimacy was gone, so was the trust and the sacred bond they'd shared. Surely their marriage was going to unravel now. She should have said no when he first came up with the idea. She should've shot him down right away. That's what any sane woman would have done. Then he would have had to put up or shut up. But no, she had let herself believe his rantings. When they were surfing the net to find out about swingers, she had chosen to think that she could do this crazy vacation and then put it away in a little box like it was one of the suitcases. She really had convinced herself that everything could go back to normal but now she knew that was crazy. Now she was just as morally bankrupt as he was. She couldn't tell her mom about any of this. It was enough just to be with her and let her emotions out.

"I knew something was up. I sensed it before you went away. Even back at my birthday when you came to visit, I thought there was something on your mind, but Rosie, you weren't ready to let me help. Tell me now. What can I do?"

Rosie looked up. "Oh, don't beat yourself up, Mom. I don't think there's anything anybody can do. He's just a little wild, and I've become a fuddy-duddy."

"You? A fuddy-duddy? Are you crazy? You're an amazing mom, wife, and daughter. You keep yourself in remarkable shape. To be honest, I don't think I've ever seen you look so fit and toned, and with your new tan, you look like a million dollars. And as for being a fuddy-duddy, tell me, what car do you drive again? Ah yes, you're the daughter with the fire-engine-red BMW. You're also the girl with the passionate personality. You're the diva, the firecracker, the party girl. Where did you get the idea that you were a fuddy-duddy?"

Rosie laughed. "I used to be all those things, but not anymore."

"You should have seen yourself when you spilt the red cabbage here the day of my birthday lunch. It was like a national disaster. All hell broke loose. Trust me, Rosie, once a diva, always a diva." A strand of Rosie's bangs had fallen down onto her cheek and the tears made it stick there. Her mom lifted it away. "You're just like your father, you know? You're a powerhouse of energy, you're intoxicating. You're so loving and you're the only part of him I have left," she said. "I love you and please don't change—ever." They hugged for a long time.

When they pulled back, Rosie asked, "How are you, Mom? How are you holding up?"

She shrugged. "Some days are better than others." But then she smiled. "It was great to get away. Funny how things work out. I didn't actually want to go, but it was the best medicine. It just reminded me there's a whole world out there, so I shouldn't get too caught up in mine."

"I hear you."

"What are you going to do about Marcus?

Rosie winced. "I don't know. Maybe a trip to Ireland would be a good idea?"

Her mom laughed. "You can't run away. He's your husband, and you have Natasha to think about. You'll have to work it out. You know, your dad and I had our arguments, too. We tried to keep them hidden from you, but every marriage has friction. If it didn't, it would be a very dull marriage."

"But there's a difference between friction and World War III," Rosie said.

"I guess the more passion there is in the good times, the more passion there will be in the bad times."

"Lucky us," Rosie said.

"What do you make of Lily?"

"Wow, that was a hell of a bombshell. I certainly didn't see it coming—ditched by an oldie."

Her mom laughed. "Hey, watch what you say about oldies."

"Natasha did very well."

"What do you mean?"

"Did you see the necklace she was wearing? I assumed it was a piece of costume jewelry, but then I had a closer look. Lily gave her a platinum and diamond-encrusted Tiffany's key on an beautiful diamond-studded chain."

"What?"

"Nat said Lily told her she was finished with it. Needless to say, I traded it for a chocolate chip cookie."

"Rosie!" Popsy looked appalled.

"What? I couldn't let her keep it. She would lose it. I talked to Lily, and evidently it was a present from Jack she no longer wanted. I told her I would keep it safe and she could give it to Natasha when she's around sixteen."

"Good thinking. Poor Lily." Popsy sighed.

"Other than the wealth, I don't know what she saw in him in the first place, but I'm guessing her self-esteem will be at an all-time low after this."

Her mom looked pensive. "Unless . . ."

"Unless what?"

"Unless Jack did the first decent thing he's ever done in his life. Natasha said that Jack wanted Lily to have babies. Maybe he let her go because he loved her and wanted her to have a full life."

Rosie slapped her forehead. "Mom, you're too much of a romantic. I don't think Jack is that benevolent."

"Maybe not," her mom said with a shrug. "So you see, you're not the only one with problems in your life." Then she stood and put her hands on her hips. "Now, up to bed you go. We'll both have a good night's rest and tomorrow we can have a proper think about how to get Marcus to calm down and get you guys back together. Okay?"

Rosie stood and wrapped her arms around her mother who was a good two inches shorter than she. "Okay, Mom. You're the best. Thanks." She started to walk away but then turned around. "Oh, by the way, I was wondering. Have you given any thought to your future with Matilda?"

Popsy shook her head. "I really don't know. The truth is, I don't need her that much now that there's only me and Sandra to look after, but we don't even know where we'll be living soon enough. Then there's the cost of keeping her, which I really can't afford anymore."

Rosie put her hand on her mom's wrist.

"Mom, I would love it if Matilda came to live with us. She's an incredible help with Natasha, and they love each other. I wouldn't have asked if you'd said you wanted to keep her."

"Are you kidding? It would be the perfect solution," her mom said and hugged her. "You see? Things have a way of working themselves out."

Sunday morning should have been a late start, but Popsy and Sandra were up with the dawn because their bodies were still on European time.

"I'm going for a run," Sandra said. "I think I gained a few pounds in Ireland." She groaned.

"Knock yourself out." Popsy laughed. "I'm going to have all-American pancakes. They really don't know how to do them over there. Not even at The Four Seasons."

"Oh, good idea. And I want some burned toast smothered in coarse-cut marmalade." Sandra looked at Popsy and smiled. "I think you're glad to be home."

"I am. My girls need me, and I love this old house." She looked around her kitchen and stroked her beloved pine table. "That said, I know things are about to change. We'll have to make some plans now that we're home."

"Let me go on my run. You cook up your all-American breakfast, and after that we'll go through your mail and talk about our options. We're in this together, kiddo, don't forget that."

It wasn't long before Natasha turned up, pulling her mother by the hand. Rosie was just awake. Her hair was messy and she was rubbing her eyes. It looked like she'd slept in a baggy, creased T-shirt.

"I smell pancakes!" the little girl squealed with delight. "Aunt Lily makes great pancakes, too."

"Oh, Rosie, I'm sorry you didn't get to sleep in. Would you like coffee?" Popsy asked as her daughter flopped into a kitchen chair.

Sandra poked her head around the door. "Morning, Rosie."

"Oh, I thought you were gone," Popsy said.

"I was heading out, but I found this guy hovering around outside looking like a lovesick puppy." She pulled Marcus into the kitchen by his sleeve.

"Daddy!" Natasha ran toward her father at full-force. Marcus lifted her up into his arms and kissed her all over her face. "Oh, baby, it's so good to see you."

Popsy glanced at Rosie who was manically pressing her hair down and sitting up a little straighter. It was obvious she still loved Marcus. That was a good place to start.

"Will you have a coffee, Marcus?" Popsy asked as if his arrival was the most normal thing in the world.

He looked nervous. "Uh, yeah, that would be great. Thanks, Popsy." Then he looked at Rosie. "Can we talk?"

"Natasha, I need your help to make the pancakes as well as Aunt Lily does them. Will you show me how she does it?" Popsy asked. Nat seemed excited to move on to higher callings like Pancake Cook.

Marcus and Rosie walked into the drawing room where they could talk in private.

"I'm sorry," he said, looking at her with desperation on his face. "I had no right to fly off the handle like that. I was totally in the wrong, and everything you said was right. This vacation was my idea. I pushed it on you, and I'm sorry I got so jealous."

Rosie sat on her mother's sofa and let him talk.

"I see some of the guys at work having affairs, and I didn't want to do that, but I was curious about what they had, what I was missing. This was the only way I could figure out how we could explore it, and yet stay open and honest. Rosie, I don't know how you feel about other guys, but you're by far the best woman I've ever been with. What I mean is, it's different with you. It's real. It's us."

"You think that now?" she asked calmly. "Funny. That's not what you've been saying for the last week in Mexico. Down there it was all 'great' and 'wild.' " Rosie rolled her eyes. "In Mexico I was the one who was being dull and conservative. What is it you said? I should live a little and loosen up? Stuff like that."

Marcus began to pace the floor. "I admit it, in Mexico I did try, but it's only when I got back here—alone last night—that I was able to think clearly. Empty sex is crap sex."

"Ha," she interrupted him. "Ha and double ha. Jesus, you couldn't get enough of it last week, Marcus. Anytime, anyplace, anywhere. You were at it like a jackrabbit. And me? I made a friend. That was my big sin. I found a nice guy to talk to. How in the hell do you think talking with someone could be as bad as what you were doing?"

Marcus stopped pacing. "Look, Rosie, I came over here to say I'm sorry. Really, I am. I love you and Natasha. Can we please go home?"

She looked at her husband—the man she'd loved so much for so long—and for the first time in her life, she wasn't so sure. "You made me do that, Marcus. You railroaded me into a horrendous situation, a situation you knew I didn't want to be in, and now that we've done it, you're sorry. Well, I have to tell you, I don't think that's enough."

"What?"

Rosie was surprising even herself. "I know that maybe Natasha might have come into our lives a little while before we planned it, but you proposed of your own free will. I never pushed you into that."

"I never said you did." He combed his hands through his hair.

"No, but I think a big part of me was seeking forgiveness for getting pregnant before we were married." She shook her head. "But I don't feel that way anymore. I'm very comfortable with the person I am. I have a daughter and family I adore. You, on the other hand? I really don't know if I even know this reckless, marauding asshole you've turned into."

"Asshole?"

"Yes, Marcus, an asshole! What would you call a guy who forced his wife into a swingers' resort?"

He looked confused. "I didn't force you, I might have convinced you, but I didn't force you."

She needed to think about this. She heard Natasha squealing with pancake-making-delight in the kitchen. There was her daughter to think about, too.

"So that man . . . Sam?" Marcus asked sheepishly and sat on the sofa, but with at least two feet between them.

"Like I said, he was just a guy in the same boat as I was—literally."

"Yeah, he took you out on a boat." He looked hurt. "But you didn't have sex?"

She shook her head. "His wife is into all that swinging stuff. I think you even met her." She used air quotes when she said the word *met*. "But Sam and me? We just talked. And the day we went into town, we went on a commercial tour boat. It was a public cruise. Nothing odd or intimate about it. He was a great guy, and I was happy for his company, because it saved me from all the other lechers."

Marcus looked wounded. "Like me."

"Look, Marcus, I did it your way. We tried that stupid swinging thing. But I'm telling you, if that's what you want, you're on your own. I'm not into that, and I know I'm not the young, wild thing you married. I've changed, but I'm glad I've changed. Now I'm a wife and a mother, and for what it's worth, I'm proud to carry those new labels—or at least I was. Now I'm not so sure about being your wife. For me and Natasha, I think life is about moving on together and evolving to fit our new circumstances. What you're grasping at, what you want me to be, that's gone. It sounds a little like Jack Hoffman where you're constantly looking for a newer, younger model."

Marcus jumped up. "No, that's not me. That's what I'm trying to say." He paced the floor again. "I was so stupid. I don't want those women. I want you. You're magnificent and beautiful and so much smarter to get all this stuff already. I'd be lost without you, Rosie. You're the best thing that ever happened to me." He stopped. "I love you. You're my rock. I need you.

Will you please forgive me for putting you through that swingers stuff?"

Rosie stood. "Shhh," she said. "Somebody will hear you."

"I don't care if they hear me shout that I love you and you're the best thing in my life."

She was so torn. She loved him, really she did, but he'd put her in an awful position. Yes, a family would be better for Natasha, but what sort of mother would forgive and forget such crazy carrying-on in her marriage?

She looked at the man she once loved so much, but now loved less, and shook her head slowly. "I'm sorry, Marcus but I don't think I can go back to where we were. You've blown that bridge away. I can't come back to you, into that marriage. I think I would make a pretty crappy role model for Natasha if I did."

"What are you saying?" He looked crazy-panicked. "I'll do anything, Rosie." His eyes welled up with tears. "Don't leave me. I'll do counseling, I'll go to therapy. I'll do whatever you want, just don't give up on us!"

She looked at his face with the tears flowing down as freely as her five-year-old. Who was she kidding? She still adored him.

"Okay, okay, we can try." She was crying now. "But Marcus you risked our marriage and our family just to try and recapture your stupid youth. We really need counseling—both of us. We need to work through this, whatever the hell it was, because it damn near broke us."

"Yes, yes," he cried and risked taking a step towards her. "Can I, can I hold you?" he whispered. She had never seen him weep like this. Cautiously she walked back into his arms. "Dear God, in heaven, I love you," he said as he kissed the top of her head. "I'll never ever do anything to jeopardize us again, I swear it, Rosie," he vowed with a trembling voice.

"And you're going to a doctor to get checked out after all that, that—oh, Jesus . . ."

"Yes, of course. I love you so much. I'm sorry, baby. So, so sorry."

Their reconciliation was just in time because Natasha had finally run out of patience. She came crashing in through the door. "Here you are! Pancakes are ready." She looked at her father and tilted her head in concern. "Don't cry, Daddy, we have plenty of pancakes." Natasha didn't spot that her mother was crying, too. She took Rosie and Marcus by the hands and pulled them back into the kitchen.

"Have you got a moment?" Lily asked her big sister.

Rosie nodded. "What's up?" she asked as Lily walked her into the drawing room.

Lily sat down on her parents' oversized sofa, put her hands on her lap, and studied her knees. "I'm sorry," she said. "It seems to be all I'm saying these days. But I really mean it, Rosie. I'm sorry for being so mad at you and judging you the way I did. I see now that I'm the idiot in this family."

Rosie sat down next to Lily and enveloped her in her arms just like she used to when they were small.

"Shhh, you don't have to apologize to me. I need to apologize to you."

But Lily's eyes had filled with guilty tears. She looked at her sister and argued, "No, everything is my fault. I was so hard on you that day we had lunch. You had the courage to tell me everything, and now I get it. You were just trying to keep your marriage going." She squeezed Rosie's knee. "I think we all know at this point that I'm completely clueless when it comes to love."

"You know more than you think," Rosie sighed, releasing her sister from her hug but keeping an arm around her shoulders. "You were so right about that swinging vacation. We shouldn't have gone. I should have stood up to Marcus back when you told me to, but I wasn't brave enough. Why didn't I listen to you?"

Lily looked up at Rosie as her tears made their way down her cheeks, but she made no attempt to wipe them away. "Seriously? You think you should have listened to me? The biggest fool in the world?"

Rosie wiped her tears away.

"Believe me, Lily, you're not the only one who's learning as you go."

"Are you and Marcus okay?"

Rosie pulled her arm back and hugged herself. "I really don't know. We came real close to breaking up, but we're going to give it another go—with help. We're going to do counseling." Then she looked at Lily. "You know, I wasn't with anyone else in Mexico. I couldn't do it. I want you to know that. I need to know you still have faith in me and know that I'm not a tramp." She couldn't hold back the tears then.

"Hey." Lily put her finger on Rosie's lips. "I hear you and I respect you no matter what. You're so strong, Rosie. I've always admired you. I'm pathetic. Look at my catastrophic life choices."

"Don't beat yourself up so much. You're the one who called me in here for this talk. That was very brave of you, and it was the right thing to do. And about your love life—you weren't alone. Jack can be very persuasive, and it does take two to tango."

"You think?"

"And you're young."

"I'm not that much younger than you. Oh, Rosie, how do you keep it all together?"

"Uh, hello?" She pointed to herself. "You call this 'together?' I nearly lost my marriage in the last week."

"Speaking of losing things, I have another confession to make. I nearly lost your daughter. I'm such a klutz. She was with me one minute and gone the next. We were in Toys"R"Us and she just disappeared, but I have to admit, I was on a stupid conference call at the time. The metal doors even came down. It was a full-scale emergency." She was terrified as she retold the story but Rosie just held her hands.

"Lily, it's okay. Natasha is here and she's fine. She's done that to me, too, when I was texting a friend. She's a little hellion in that place. If I'd known you were going there, I would have warned you. Whose suggestion was it to go to Toys"R"Us?"

"Hers," Lily said. "She told me we could get a booster seat there."

"She played you!" Rosie laughed.

"I'm sorry."

"Lily, you have nothing to apologize for. I have every faith in you. I always have, even when we argued. Do you think I would have left Natasha with you if I had any doubts? You're an amazing person and some day you will make a terrific wife and mother."

Lily cried harder and hugged Rosie.

"Thank you, I think I was just jealous of everything you have."

Rosie pulled back and laughed through her tears. "Me? You're the pretty, skinny sister with the high-flying job." Then she wiped at Lily's face. "Well, normally you're the pretty one. With all that mascara running down your face, you're not at your best right now," she said and winked.

Lily found a Kleenex in her pocket. She wiped her face and blew her nose. Then she looked from the well-used tissue to her sister. "Guess I should have offered it to you first, huh?"

Rosie gave her a gentle shoulder shove. "Give it to me. We're made from the same DNA anyway."

"Rosie you have that big house and your gorgeous husband, and don't get me started on Natasha. I could steal her, I love her so much. I've always been envious of you!"

Rosie kissed Lily's nose. "We're quite a pair. I love you, Lily."

"I love you, too."

By mid-morning Rosie was giving Matilda a ride to see some friends, while Natasha traveled home in her dad's car. When she brought up the offer to move in with them permanently, Matilda had cried, and it took a few moments for Rosie to figure out they were tears of relief and joy.

"I knew Popsy would have to leave Cliff Road, and I was so worried that I would have no work. I am too old to go to a new family. But you, Rosie, I know you so well. Natasha is a very good girl, but you must have another baby soon." Rosie laughed. If Matilda only knew how they'd almost become a single-parent family.

"One day at a time, Tilly. One day at a time."

"You know you can stay here as long as you like," Popsy said to convince Lily, but she shook her head.

"I need to get home. I want to blitz the house; really clean it."

"Are you trying to exorcise Jack?" Popsy asked.

Lily laughed. "A little of that, but you wouldn't believe how sticky the place gets with a little kid into everything."

"Are you okay, Lily?"

"Oh, Mom, I feel so guilty. I've just been such a selfish little idiot."

"You know, your father was never angry with you about Jack."

"What? How can you say that? You know he was furious."

"Oh, he was furious, but not with you. He told me that day in the hospital . . . the day he died. I was so angry with you, but he was very adamant that Jack was the grown-up and you were just a kid. Those were his words. He forecasted that you would break up. He was very wise, your dad."

Popsy came over and held Lily's shoulders firmly. Then she looked her in the eyes.

"I see Sandra had the full showdown with you yesterday, too." She stroked her daughter's cheek and red eye.

"Nothing I didn't deserve," Lily said.

"Okay, enough," Popsy said with considerable force as she gripped Lily's shoulders. "Are you going to spend the rest of your life feeling sorry for yourself, or are you going to get up and on with your life? These years are going to be your most exciting and dynamic. You can't go around acting all maudlin. I want you to shape up and ship out. Chin high, chest out, tummy in, and get back in the game."

"Uh, okay." She laughed. "Wow, what got into you?"

Popsy released her grip. "Ireland."

"It really helped you, didn't it? Getting away, I mean."

"Yes, I would highly recommend traveling. It gives you a better perspective." This she said with great assertiveness, but then she got a little playful and said, "You also get to meet new people."

Lily said, "Mom, is there something you need to tell me? Somebody in particular back in Ireland?"

"Don't worry. It's nothing scandalous, but there was this one guy." She stopped and tried to find the right words.

"Tell me," Lily insisted, linking her arm through Popsy's.

"He's just a friend, but he's the first person I've met—well, this is going to sound stupid, but he's the first friend I've made since your dad died, so he's just mine."

"I get that."

"He's a widower, too, so he knows what I'm going through, and that means a lot to me. It's not romantic or anything, but it's nice to have a friend who gets me."

"Is he cute?"

"Lily, I just said it's not romantic. He's just a friend."

"It's not romantic *yet*, but maybe some time in the future . . ."

"He's three thousand miles away, so it's totally impractical, but we can e-mail each other, and he phones."

"Has he called you since you got home? You just landed."

Popsy looked guilty. "Eh, yes. He wanted to be sure that I got home okay, after the volcano, you see."

"Of course." Lily laughed. "He would have to check that you were all right after the volcano. This guy's sharp," she teased. "Did you have a nice talk?"

"I missed his call. The point is, I loved your father more than anything in the world, but he's gone, and I have to continue living. So do you, pet. No guilt, no looking back. Do you hear me?"

Lily kissed her on the cheek. "I hear you, really I do. In fact, listening to you talk about getting up and on has convinced me to make a call when I get home."

"To Jack?"

"No! Matt. Now, don't get excited. Like you said, he's just a friend."

Chapter 39

Skydiving in Spring

"You're leaving me, aren't you?" Popsy asked one morning when she and Sandra were opening the mail together. It had become a daily custom. Sandra and Popsy were at the big old pine table with two strong espressos and an Oreo each.

Sandra smiled. "Sven wants me to come back. He's getting impatient, and I really like him."

"We've been back home what? Two months? And you're missing him more each day. You have to go, Sandra," Popsy said. "I mean it. You have to. You owe it to yourself." She squeezed Sandra's hand.

"On our last night in Banagher, he took me out to that little porch at the front of The Boathouse. I remember thinking when we first arrived that it wasn't very pretty because it had no view to speak of, but that night it was so beautiful with the sun slipping behind the dark-brown fields. He told me he was already sure that he wanted to be with me and now I think—no, I know—I really want to be with him, too. I need to go back there, Popsy. I can't stop thinking about him."

Popsy smiled. "I know. I see it on your face when you're on the phone together." Then she sat back. "Sandra Richter. It has an interesting ring to it. Hey, wait a minute, is that Richter as in Richter scale, what they use to measure earthquakes?"

"Yep, and boy, did the earth move."

"Sandra, you are shameless!"

"I asked him about it. Richter is the German word for judge."

"Well, he's certainly a terrific judge of characters if he's fallen for you. You're my best friend."

"And you're mine. Will we be okay so far apart? Will you be all right living alone?"

"You know I will. I knew you'd be flying the coop soon. I even said to Lily that it might be just me moving into her apartment in two weeks."

Sandra looked anxious. "I worry about you, especially with Lily going to Hong Kong."

"Don't. She's as unsure about working with Matt as you are about living with Sven. If it doesn't work out for her, she'll be back in Boston in a heartbeat, and she and I can live together. If she does stay out there with Matt, I'll still have Rosie and her family nearby. They seem to be getting through whatever it is that hit them."

"That's a relief. I think they're a lovely couple," Sandra said.

"And Marcus is my biggest fan since I gave him Peter's old Ferrari."

"That was very generous of you and it makes no sense to leave it in the garage getting rusty," Sandra agreed.

"Same goes for me. I'll be very busy while you're gone. I'm thrilled about taking up that job offer from Karen at The Flower Pot. I've discovered I like to work, and you know I love flowers. If I ever get the nerve, I'm going to open my own shop and call it 'Poppy Power.'"

Sandra looked around Popsy's kitchen. "You have a lifetime's collection of things here. What will you do with all of this stuff?"

"Everything will be sold or given to charity except the items the girls might want. I don't need any of it anymore. I have everything I need in here." She tapped her heart. "The only thing I really care about is this table and Rosie has asked for it, so I can visit it at her house in Weston. It's not going too far."

Popsy opened her first envelope.

"As soon as I've moved into Lily's place, I'll hand the keys of this dear old house over to the attorneys. After what we've been through, I think it will be a relief to part with it."

Sandra nodded and opened an envelope. "You know, I found it easier after I left the penthouse. I felt like the ax that had been hanging over me was suddenly gone, and don't get me started on Jack moving in when we were in Ireland. If I never see that jerk again, it will be too soon." She pulled something out of an envelope and held it up. "Oh, look! DSW is having a fifty-percent-off shoe sale today. We could go there when we finish."

Popsy smiled and nodded. Legal-looking deeds were in her envelope. She read the cover page. "This is from Jack," she said. "These deeds were in the safe in the office." She kept reading. "My God, it's the deeds to Natasha's apartment in town. Peter must have bought it for cash."

"Hey, you could live there for the next fifteen years. She won't need it for a while yet. Have you seen it? What's it like?"

"Yes, I picked it out myself about five years ago. It's lovely. I remember all three of us going to look at them just as they were being revamped. It's not far from Lily's apartment either, which is kind of nice. I think it's being rented out now and the income is going into a trust fund for Natasha." She pulled out more papers. "Sandra, there's a second set of deeds here. Jack bought one for cash, too, and he's signed it over to you. Looks like you're getting something from the old dog after all."

Sandra snatched the letter and read. "About time," she whispered. "You know, I've been so busy trying not to think about what I was going to do, that I never imagined he would pull a rabbit out of the hat like this."

Popsy squeezed Sandra's hand. "You must rent it out and still go to Ireland. Are there tenants in it?"

Sandra went back to scanning the letter. "Yes, he's depositing the proceeds into my personal account. You're right. Looks like Jack is going to support me after all," Sandra said. "This is amazing, Popsy. It means I'll be able to pay you back the life insurance money you gave me."

Popsy ignored that and opened another letter. "This is the account I requested from the Ferrari dealership. Looks like I don't owe them a thing. The repair work from Peter's bump was paid for with the car's insurance, and Peter really had paid for it in full on my birthday. Today is a good post day, Sandra."

"It sure is," Sandra said, and took another envelope and opened it. "We're invited to the opening of a new hair place downtown."

"Shred it." Popsy laughed. "Have you ever tried those home hair dye kits?"

"No, but there's a first time for everything."

Popsy opened her third letter. "Hey, this is a twenty-dollar coupon for DSW. We're so going to buy shoes this afternoon."

Sandra's phone beeped, indicating a new text, and she jumped on it fast to see who it was. The smile was a thousand kilowatts bright.

"Anybody interesting?" Popsy teased. She already knew.

Sandra smiled coyly. "Maybe."

"Go for it—tell him."

Sandra looked concerned. "Am I moving too fast? What if I'm making a stupid mistake?"

"If it's a mistake, you can come back and live with me in Lily's flat, or Natasha's, or even your own. But what if he's right for you? You've already told me he'd broken up with his wife because she was a career doctor and kept putting off having children because of her work. Sven is determined to give this a go, and he wants a baby as much as you do. You owe it to both of you to move on this one."

"But what if we fizzle out in a few years?"

"What if you don't?" Popsy argued.

"Well, what about you and Shane?"

"What about us?"

"Are you going to go for it?"

"It's too soon. I'm not ready." Popsy stood, uncomfortable with the turn in the conversation.

"Jeez, Popsy. He calls you every day now, and I see how happy you are when he does. He's already long-distance-courting you and you're the only person who hasn't realized it."

Popsy sat back down. "You think?"

Sandra smiled. "If I'm willing to give love a second chance, you should be, too."

"Who said anything about love? It's not even a year since Peter died."

"Who said anything about having to wait a year? We're not as young as we used to be, woman. At our age we need to get on with our lives. What are you waiting for?"

"Do you think I could ask him to visit me here?"

"Yes, oh yes, I think that would be an amazing idea. He would love to come, and if you're living in Lily's place, there are two bedrooms if you're not ready to take that next step."

"I'm nowhere near taking that step. I just wondered if he'd like to come over as a friend, but Lily's apartment would work well, because it's right beside the harbor and Shane loves boats." Then she looked at Sandra. "I've been having embarrassingly vivid dreams that, um, well, about Shane."

"Oh?"

"It's nothing."

"It's something. Invite him over next time he calls. Okay?" Sandra asked.

"Okay, okay, already. Jeez, he'll probably say no anyway." She opened the last letter. "Oh look, it's another DSW coupon. Do you think this is a sign?"

"For sure." Sandra laughed. "Let's go shoe shopping."

An hour later they were dressed and looked like a million dollars. "Which car do you want to take?" Sandra asked. "Mine, your Merc, or the Ferrari?"

Popsy faltered. "I haven't been in it since Peter's crash," she mumbled.

"Let's skip it, then."

Popsy gave her a thank-you nod. "You know, I think I'm happier in my old car. I was never really a Ferrari kind of girl."

"I know what you mean. You're classier than that."

"But you like it, don't you?"

"What can I say? I'm louder than you. I like flash."

"Well, that's that, then. Happy Birthday." Popsy beamed.

Sandra's jaw dropped. "I can't take that car. It's yours. It cost a fortune. If you don't want it, sell it. You've already given me a ridiculous amount of your life insurance money—which I will pay back—but really, Popsy this has to stop. I can't take any more from you."

"You? Take from me? Ha!" Popsy said. "You've done nothing but give to me since Peter died. Give, give, give." She took Sandra's hands and looked earnestly at her. "You gave me the birthday present of a lifetime. That trip to Ireland saved my sanity. You know I don't want the car, and we both know you like it. Play with it for a few weeks, and then sell it. Use the money to get yourself set up with Sven. This is Karma. Please take the car, Sandra. I would love you to have it."

"We'll talk about it later."

They got into the Mercedes and put on their sunglasses. Popsy cranked up the stereo and Lady Gaga poured through the stereo speakers from somewhere under her seat.

"Let's go and shop till we drop—with our coupons. Then you need to phone Sven and tell him you're on your way. After that, we'll go for a nice lunch somewhere and maybe even have a few cocktails. What do you think?"

"Cocktails at noon? It's like I always said, Popsy, you can take the girl out of Wellesley . . ."

And they said together, ". . . but you can't take Wellesley out of the girl!"

"So tell me the truth, you really haven't thought about skydiving with Shane?" Sandra said.

"Skydiving?" Popsy was lost.

"Doesn't that ring any bells with you?" Sandra asked. "It was the night Peter and Jack had the European investors over, and we were talking about sex. You were worried somebody might overhear, so you referred to it as skydiving."

"Had I been drinking?"

"Maybe just a little."

Popsy laughed. "I wonder if Shane would ever be interested in skydiving with me," she said, then pressed the button so her car roof glided back and Gaga's music filled the air around them. The music was so loud, Popsy didn't hear her phone when it rang, and that gave Sandra the chance to grab it and answer it first.

"Hi, Shane, it's Sandra. Popsy wants to know if you'll come and visit her; only she's too shy to ask."

Popsy killed the music and stared at her friend in disbelief.

"Don't look so horrified. That's what you did to me back in Banagher with Sven." She handed the phone over. "He said yes, by the way."

Popsy rolled her eyes.

"Hi, Shane, sorry about that." He was laughing down the phone line. "Um, I was going to ask you—if Sandra hadn't butted in, if you'd like to come visit Boston?"

"Popsy, there's nothing I'd like more," he said. She could tell by his tone that he was smiling.

"You'll come? Really? That's great news." She gave the thumbs-up sign to Sandra.

"When do you want me?" he asked.

"What?"

"When should I come over to Boston?"

"Oh, as soon as you like, I guess."

"What about next week?" he asked, his Strabane accent cascading up and down.

"Next week?" Popsy suppressed the urge to panic. "Gosh, yes, that would be absolutely fine. You'll be able to help me move."

"You? You're moving house? Jesus, don't risk your life again—at least not until I'm there."

She listened and laughed. This felt right. "No, I won't do anything life threatening, Shane."

Sandra checked her reflection in the side mirror and adjusted her sunglasses. "You've come so far, Popsy," she whispered. "Now ask him what he thinks about skydiving."

(It's never) The End

Dear Book Club friends,

I really hope you enjoy **Wellesley Wives**. When I was writing it, I was conscious of the possible discussions and debate it could spark, so, for your entertainment (and to stir it up a little!) I have included ten book club questions. I want this to add to your enjoyment of the book and give you some food for thought. Naturally there are no right or wrong answers because every point of view is valid in its own right. For this reason I have given my own personal answers to these questions on my website, www.Suzyduffybooks.com. It might be interesting to check out my site and see if we have the same points of view about the various characters or if we are diametrically opposed. Either way, it's just for fun.

Happy reading,
Love Suzy

Questions

1. What was the theme/essence of **Wellesley Wives** and what was its purpose?

2. Was the setting of particular importance? Having read about New England and Ireland, what strikes you as the biggest differences? Which do you think would the nicer place to live and why? Does age have an impact on your opinion?

3. Do the characters seem real and believable? Can you relate to their predicaments? Have you or anyone you know gone through some of these situations? Which ones? How did they deal with it?

4. Do they remind you of someone you know? How and why?

5. In what way do the events in the story reveal more about the author?

6. Is it a satisfactory ending? What would you like to have seen done differently?

7. Which woman do you relate to most—Popsy, Sandra, Rosie or Lily? Do their ages have any bearing on how they dealt with their situations?

Or do you think their personalities are so set that they would have been similar, had for example, Lily been forty when she went through what she did with Jack? Would Popsy have bounced back at the same rate ten years older or ten years younger?

8. Which man do you dislike most?

9. Is there any hope for Jack?

10. What are your feelings on swinging?

CPSIA information can be obtained at www.ICGtesting.com
Printed in the USA
LVOW080226191012

303558LV00001B/91/P